CRASH

About the Author

Toby Vintcent served as an officer in the British Army with the 16th/5th The Queen's Royal Lancers during the Cold War as part of NATO's Rapid Deployment Force. He then had a successful career at Merrill Lynch, and has been Director of International Affairs at the British Equestrian Federation. Toby Vintcent's lifelong passion for Formula One resulted in his first book, *Driven* (2014). He lives in Oxfordshire, the heart of F1 country, with his wife and son.

Praise for *Crash*

'Reading this book will cause you sleeplessness, irregular heartbeat and spikes in your blood pressure. I read it just before and during the journey to Russia for the recent Grand Prix, and while I was out there, but the plot resonated so much that even on the nights I told myself I really had to sleep, I could never get more than four hours because I literally didn't want to put it down'
David Tremayne, *GrandPrix+*

'A great read!'
Joe Saward, F1 journalist and F1 Business Commentator

'Like the sport it describes, *Crash* is fast-paced and thrilling, deftly capturing how sport can be manipulated by politics. Whether you're a fan of F1 or not, you'll keep reading'
Jonathan Legard, F1 TV and BBC Sports Commentator

'What a fantastic book! I started reading it on the train and it was literally unputdownable. The fact that someone like me – who hates all cars, but particularly fast ones – can get so quickly hooked says a lot about Toby's skill as an author. He is a consummate professional who knows how to make a reader turn the pages – and he has made me aware of and respectful of the human drama in F1 … The tension leading up to the crash is superbly managed – a master class in leaving the reader breathless'
Edward Wilson, Author of *A Very British Ending*

'*Crash* blends Jason Bourne, Formula 1 and *Law & Order* in one high-octane fast-paced drama'
Jake Sanson, *Downforce Radio*

Praise for *Driven*

'A great read … a great plot … I couldn't put it down'
Murray Walker

'*Driven* – it howls along like Lewis Hamilton
round the streets of Monaco!'
Boris Johnson

'A fast-paced read for any speed demon'
David Williams, *London Evening Standard*

'Author Toby Vintcent takes inspiration from F1's
on-track action and off-track paddock politics in
weaving together a page-turning conspiracy thriller. His
attention to detail captures the spirit of current F1'
***F1 Racing* Magazine**

'It's a page turner, for sure, and I thoroughly enjoyed it as
I read it in two days when I should have been working on
stuff prior to the Austrian Grand Prix. That says it all'
David Tremayne, *GrandPrix+*

'I read many books about motorsport, and so know that enjoyable
fiction in Formula 1 is rare. *Driven* is a superb thriller which
I thoroughly enjoyed from the first to the final lap – a page-
turning story with a cast of engaging characters in a highly
authentic and believable depiction of F1. This is a brand-new
way for us all to enjoy motorsport from Toby Vintcent'
Chris Aylett, CEO, Motorsport Industry Association

'A thrilling read that captures the essence of the
Formula 1 battle both on and off track'
Patrick Allen, MD, Silverstone

CRASH

TOBY VINTCENT

A

Arcadia Books Ltd
139 Highlever Road
London W10 6PH

www.arcadiabooks.co.uk

First published in the United Kingdom by Arcadia Books 2016
Copyright © Toby Vintcent 2016

ISBN 978-1-910050-79-8

Typeset in Garamond by MacGuru Ltd
Printed and bound by TJ International, Padstow PL28 8RW

ARCADIA BOOKS DISTRIBUTORS ARE AS FOLLOWS:

in the UK and elsewhere in Europe:
BookSource
50 Cambuslang Road
Cambuslang
Glasgow G32 8NB

in the USA and Canada:
Dufour Editions
PO Box 7
Chester Springs
PA, 19425

in Australia/New Zealand:
NewSouth Books
University of New South Wales
Sydney NSW 2052

For Anne-Marie and Sammy.

Dedicated to my parents.

About the Formula

The Formula referred to in this story is a fictional composite. While it includes authentic elements used by the FIA over the last few years, no similarity with any given year's Formula should be looked for or expected.

PART ONE

Катастрофа

"Katastrofa"

CATASTROPHE

ONE

They were screaming along the Île Notre-Dame, bathed in unbroken Montreal sun as they ran down the Casino Straight beside the Saint Lawrence River. Both Formula One cars hit 210 miles an hour, the gap no bigger or smaller than it had been for the last five laps. Just *feet* apart. Remy Sabatino, tucked right up behind the race leader, was getting ready…

The challenger was watching Yegor Baryshnikov like a hawk – already thinking ahead to Turns Thirteen and Fourteen, looming in 700 metres.

Sabatino's heart and breathing rates were up. There was a tactical balance to be struck, here: declare too soon and Baryshnikov would be forewarned and able to take defensive action. Leave it too late and he might not react at all, as he might not have to.

Now!

Sabatino dived out from behind Baryshnikov – to the left, clearly stating an intention down that-hand side. Almost as a flinch Baryshnikov reacted, darting that way himself – to head Sabatino off – to block the challenge.

The moment the race leader reacted to the move, Sabatino lifted off – for a fraction of a second. Even with the foot off the power for a moment, the front end of the Ptarmigan dipped slightly, the drag fractionally gaining the upper hand. At exactly the same time Sabatino swung the steering wheel across to the right, the car's front wing sweeping rapidly from left to right behind the car in front, almost brushing its rear tyres. Immediately it was clear, Sabatino floored the throttle once again – aiming to dive the car down the other side of the race leader.

Seven hundred and fifty horsepower exploded out through the gearbox and rear tyres into the surface of the track.

The Ptarmigan's chance now lay in lunging down the right-hand side of Baryshnikov's car.

Three hundred metres to run.

Sabatino willed the car to give its all.

Baryshnikov was only allowed a single defensive move against an overtaking manoeuvre. By launching that feint to the left, Sabatino had forced him to make his one and only permitted retaliation. On their current line, Sabatino should now have the space to be unchallenged into this corner.

Two hundred metres.

Sabatino was drawing level.

Who would earn the right to the line?

Who would brake first?

Sabatino's nerve, line and speed would have to be held right into the corner.

The other car twitched; a tell that Baryshnikov wanted to start turning in, to start setting up for the chicane – except he absolutely did not want to brake sooner than Sabatino … as that could only concede the position.

There was a momentous jolt – the cars banged together.

Through peripheral vision – to the left – Sabatino suddenly caught sight of rapid movement. Baryshnikov was wrestling with his steering wheel – he seemed to be wrestling aggressively with his car. Was he veering away? Clear air opened up between him and Sabatino – which was all the challenger needed.

Now!

Sabatino stood on the brakes. Carrying too much speed through here could be disastrous, inviting an unforgiving rendezvous with the legendary – *infamous* – Wall of Champions on the far side. Even the greats – from Hill, through Schumacher to Vettel – had succumbed to that Wall.

Sabatino turned in, to the right, fighting to hold the line.

The Ptarmigan *was* carrying too much pace.

Shaving the corner, Sabatino bounced in hard over the kerbstones of the first apex. But before the car could be straightened up for the second, there was a huge distraction: a flash of movement entered the extreme left of Sabatino's vision.

In an instant, Baryshnikov was shooting into view – hurtling across from left to right.

After their contact, he had diverged and overshot the right-hand entry to the chicane. Turning in too late, Baryshnikov had overrun that corner, his left wheels soon out on the reinforced grass, which offered far less grip and a greatly diminished chance to slow down. Baryshnikov, cavorting over that run-off, was now cutting straight across behind the apex of Turn Thirteen – still at considerable speed. He was heading back towards the track proper, but on the far side of the chicane. Could he brake, turn and stabilize the car in time?

Sabatino watched the other car cut straight across in front.

Baryshnikov was jabbing repeatedly at the brakes.

Sabatino, desperate not to be rammed by Baryshnikov, also jammed on the brakes, then swerved to the left – hoping to pass behind him, to the rear of the traversing car.

A collision was unavoidable.

Baryshnikov slammed into the Wall. An explosion of turquoise ricocheted off the Wall of Champions immediately below the sign ready to mock its would-be victims. *Bienvenue au Québec.*

Sabatino felt the Ptarmigan fishtail violently as every effort was made to heave the car away from the scattering wreckage: one shard of the razor-like fragments of carbon fibre was all it would take for a puncture. Sabatino couldn't manage it – couldn't avoid running over some of the debris – and did so with both right-hand wheels.

Accelerating away, Sabatino prayed all would stay well for this last lap – to take the chequered flag and so take the win.

Click.

The footage was stopped right there.

The frame was frozen.

Another click.

The picture was being reversed. Someone was rewinding, scrolling backwards through the DVD. It was re-stopped a few seconds later and allowed to run on again before another frame was refrozen.

'*Right there*, Mr Vice President,' declared Chico Amaretti, a middle-aged Italian with slicked-back hair in a sharp suit with thin lapels and no vents, '*right there*, is the moment of impact between the two cars.'

Pointing at the screen, Amaretti added: 'My client states that Ms Sabatino's failure to yield the line was a *deliberate* attempt to destabilize his run into this corner – and thereby gain unfair advantage in the race.'

Amaretti, Yegor Baryshnikov's business manager, affected a wounded expression. 'By committing this reckless act, not only did Ms Sabatino cost Mr Baryshnikov his stability, she also cost him the win. And, by forcing him off the track – so that he would crash into the wall – she seriously put his safety at risk … even his life in danger.'

Remy Sabatino sat at the long table in the stark Council Chamber of Formula One's governing body, already fuming. Representing herself at the hearing, she was sitting directly opposite the seven Council members who were conducting this inquiry. She was barely able to suppress her reaction. Her dark eyes flashed. Her Mediterranean skin was flushed, rendering its olive colouring all the more striking. She breathed in, catching a waft of Amaretti's cologne.

'Baryshnikov rammed *me*,' she declared to the hearing. 'It's obvious. Right there – on the tape. I had the line. *I* did not change direction – how could *I* be the one causing the impact?'

Amaretti gave the impression of a man who ought to be applauded for keeping his patience. 'This council will be well aware that this move of Ms Sabatino's was ill-judged, as well as late – on a corner considered by those who know *not* to be an overtaking opportunity.'

Amaretti sighed, as if to say: 'I'm sorry you don't have the wit to see this, my dear.'

He added: 'In any case, Mr Vice President, Ms Sabatino had *not* done enough – had *not* established enough of a claim to the racing line into that corner. My client and I therefore demand Ms Sabatino be reprimanded and fined; that she forfeit the Championship points awarded to her – unjustly – in Montreal. My client is not vindictive,' said Amaretti, sanctimoniously, 'he just wants to see that justice is done.'

Remy Sabatino was seething. Their lack of imagination was staggering. None of the blazers on that World Motor Sport Council had the vision – or magnanimity – to see the boldness of her move, or even acknowledge the other guy's incompetence. They were calling *her* sharp and reckless. What the hell? Sabatino had caught the race leader with his trousers down, got past him, and taken the win. How was it her fault if Baryshnikov had been taken by surprise, couldn't handle a bit of rough and tumble into a corner and couldn't control his car? Formula One was meant to be the pinnacle, wasn't it? What was the point of motor racing if you weren't supposed to race?

After twenty minutes of circuitous argument, Remy Sabatino was charging down through the FIA headquarters. At the bottom of the stairs she pulled on her Ray-Ban shades and strode out through the main entrance into the overcast day. Press and media were ten deep behind crowd-control barriers all around Number 8 Place de la Concorde. Sabatino's mood wasn't helped by the journalists' attitude and questions.

'What's Baryshnikov's reaction to your unsporting drive in Canada?'

'Are you going to apologize to him?'

'Will you risk the same unsportsman-like drive in Moscow – against Baryshnikov – at his home Grand Prix?'

'How will Russian fans receive you after what you did to their favourite son?'

'Are you – as a woman – really cut out for Formula One?'

Steeling herself, Sabatino bit her lip and simply faced forwards, heading down the narrow alley of barriers between the press and the fans to a car waiting for her at the kerbside.

Within the hour she was at Paris Charles de Gaulle, striding just as angrily across the concrete apron towards the waiting Quartech Falcon. She had since changed, now dressed in a black cashmere turtleneck pullover, slim-fitting black jeans and a pair of black Nike trainers.

White lights flashed at the end of each wing of the Falcon. Red beacons strobed above and underneath the aircraft. She walked up the steps and into the executive jet.

Sabatino appeared inside the cabin; a concerned-looking Bernie Callom rose to his feet. With so much bad blood shed during the hearing, his PR antennae were already on high alert. Seeing her, now, they twitched all the more. Every signal he read was ominous: an inconspicuous wardrobe, the spark in her eyes, the glow of her complexion, the barely brushed appearance of her short dark hair, while her normally expressive lips and mouth just looked tight and pained. Callom attempted to engage her as they took their seats and prepared for take-off. Every effort he made was met with little more than a sullen grunt.

Just after twelve o'clock that afternoon the private jet commissioned to get Remy Sabatino to Moscow in time for the Russian Grand Prix sped down the runway and lifted off into the eastern sky.

The ruling came through, two hours later.

They were overflying Poland, just north of Warsaw at the time. Hearing an alert, the Formula One driver looked down at her phone. Bernie Callom, sitting opposite her, noticed an immediate change in her mood. Before a word was said, he could tell it was bad.

'Remy?'

Sabatino's large pitch-black eyes were still for a moment; then she thrust her phone at him across the low table. The PR man took the device. The email was already open on the screen.

Before Callom registered its content he clocked the sender, "FIA – OFFICE OF THE PRESIDENT". Sabatino declared forcefully: 'I've been stripped of my win in Montreal. They've sided with Baryshnikov.'

Callom couldn't help his innate PR skills kicking in, even sub-consciously. Softening his voice to be barely audible above the gentle whoosh in the cabin, he asked: 'Can you not see this as just one of those things, Rems?' tentatively, bracing himself.

Sabatino was almost shaking. 'Damn it, no! This was a racing incident, Bernie – nothing more. Stuff like that *does* happen all the time, and is not worthy of punishment. That's *not* the point, though, is it?'

She paused.

Sabatino looked him directly in the face. 'Baryshnikov's my *teammate*, for Christ's sake. That bastard ratted me out.'

Callom sighed. There it was; the root of the problem. '*The teammate*,' he breathed. 'You're embroiled in the oldest cliché in Formula One. The teammate – every driver's toughest opponent. Both in the same machine, creating the rawest comparison of ability. All the tougher when you're both in the fastest car. Ptarmigan are a shoo-in for both Championships: you and Baryshnikov are the *only* contenders for the title … there are bound to be tensions.'

Sabatino wasn't going to be placated by any truisms, however well intentioned. 'Ptarmigan won't capitalize on any of this, Bernie, if one of its drivers is so clearly out to shaft the other, not least as Bary-shnikov has a serious issue with me. He *can't* handle it – can't stand being beaten by a woman.'

Before Callom could respond, Sabatino's phone rang. Seeing the Caller ID, he quickly passed it back. 'It's Tahm,' he announced.

Swiping the screen to answer it, Sabatino took the call from her team boss. Callom could only hear Sabatino's end of the conversation.

Sabatino listened for a few seconds and then said: 'Did you know he was going to do this, Tahm?'

There was a pause.

'You're telling me you *didn't* know he was going to the FIA?'
Silence.

'Are you *happy* he did it? … Are you?'
Another pause.

'What? … You're not serious.'

Sabatino's face turned the darkest yet. 'That's really clear, Tahm,' she said with a hint of exasperation in her voice. 'That's perfectly clear – you're so clearly *rewarding* Baryshnikov's treachery…'

Sabatino's face flushed. 'I'm still *second* in the Championship, for God's sake. If it hadn't been for Baryshnikov's bullshit in Montreal, *I* would be leading the rankings right now. The Russian Grand Prix is crucial to me *too*…'

Callom saw Sabatino's expression set harder. She challenged: 'Tahm, *Tahm* … do you think I *sound* happy?' before she rang off.

She stood up. Glaring down at Callom she said: 'Tahm's taking Backhouse away from me. Baryshnikov's race engineer has had to go home, for some reason – not now going to be in Moscow. Nazar's giving him Andy – to make sure "the championship-leading Russian driver has every support in the Russian Grand Prix".'

Callom's eyes conveyed sympathy as well as mild incredulity.

'Baryshnikov attacks me in public. He lodges an objection with the governing body. He testifies against me at an FIA hearing – and then he's rewarded with *my* race engineer. What kind of fucking team is this? You think these are just "tensions", Bernie?'

Callom was about to speak when Sabatino launched off again: 'If Baryshnikov thinks he can beat me – throw me off – with this sort of bullshit interference, he had better be ready.'

Turning away from Callom, she stormed off through the aircraft to the for'ard cabin, yanked open the rosewood door and slammed it behind her.

TWO

An hour on and the Quartech Falcon was entering Russian airspace, crossing the border from Belarus. Callom chose that moment to knock and ask for a word with Sabatino. She would still only communicate with him through the closed door.

'I need you to be ready when we land, Rems,' he said. 'There's quite a reception for you at the terminal.'

They felt the aircraft begin its descent and approach into Vnukovo International Airport, to the south-west of Moscow.

At ground level, a fine haze hung over the airfield, diffusing the light of the afternoon sun; everything was tinted with a soft orange hue. With the humidity around Vnukovo, vapour trails soon appeared from the wing tips of the sleek, brilliant-white Quartech Falcon as Sabatino's plane made its final approach to land. With effortless grace – and seemingly executed as a single manoeuvre – the plane descended, performed a balletic round-out, and lowered itself down onto the runway with the smoothness of a sigh. Once slowed to taxiing speed, the corporate jet made its way to the VIP terminal.

The Quartech Falcon rolled towards the facility that had recently been extended for the president of Russia. Coming to a halt, Sabatino's plane pulled up alongside several other corporate jets already parked there; among them were those of Arno Ravilious, the chief executive of Motor Racing Promotions Limited – the commercial rights holder and therefore the financial powerhouse of Formula One; Ba-Ba Bengeo, the car-mad US rap star who had scheduled a major tour of Russia to coincide with the Russian Grand Prix; and an Ilyushin Il-96-PU, the president of Russia's personal plane – liveried simply with a white, blue and red swoosh of the Russian flag down the side of the fuselage and the single word "Россия" – so understated and yet, at the same time, so grandiose.

At Callom's insistence, Sabatino had changed her clothes. She was now wearing a brilliant-turquoise Ptarmigan jacket with a Nehru collar, white chinos and knee-high boots. Sabatino had stuck with her dark glasses, implying a clear lack of interest in engaging with the world. The moment she appeared at the cabin door, though, everything changed.

There was an immediate crescendo of shrieks and screams.

She couldn't help but look up.

She was overwhelmed.

Above her were huge crowds. Along the front of the nearby passenger terminal, people were two … three … four deep in places. They were stretched out along the roof, along the lengths of several balconies, and pressed up against every inch of the plate-glass windows. Sabatino struggled to take it in. She was confused. Turquoise flags were everywhere – the distinctive colour of her team. Baryshnikov had left Paris earlier and was already in Moscow, she knew that. Flags of this colour, therefore, had to be for *her*. She couldn't help but feel this override her mood. She found herself unable to resist a wave up to the crowds.

Their response was deafening.

Sabatino couldn't understand it. This sort of reception never happened in motor racing, with the rare exception perhaps of Ayrton Senna in Brazil at the height of his popularity. Being the first woman Formula One driver in twenty-odd years, and unarguably the most competitive the sport had ever seen, might be having an effect. A key credential was surely lending some weight: Sabatino had got tantalizingly close to taking the Championship the season before, even in her rookie year. In an edge-of-the-seat showdown in Brazil, she'd missed the title by a solitary point – the equivalent of being 10th rather than 9th in one race across a season of twenty Grands Prix. Despite demonstrating such credibility, though, Remy Sabatino had no presumption of being an accepted part of the F1 landscape; she still felt her presence on the Formula One grid to be very much a novelty.

Except here today – in Moscow – it was the reception that was the novelty. She couldn't believe it: this was more like the Beatles arriving at JFK in 1964.

Followed by Callom, she stepped down the stairs from the plane. As she reached the tarmac she saw an elegant figure walking gracefully towards them. Callom, raising his voice to be heard over the background noise, leant across and discreetly explained: 'This is Oksana Ivanovna Pavlova, the mayor of Moscow.'

Mayor Pavlova, a striking middle-aged woman with short black hair, large brown eyes and a narrow full-lipped mouth, was wearing what looked like a leather flying jacket, along with a mauve scarf, a knee-length skirt and ankle boots.

Needing to raise his voice to be heard, Callom then announced: 'Madam Mayor, may I present Ms Remy Sabatino, the Ptarmigan Formula One Team's number one driver.'

Sabatino smiled and even removed her dark glasses.

'Ms Sabatino?' said Pavlova shaking Sabatino's hand with both of hers. 'Welcome to Moscow. We are *delighted* to have you here.'

Their handshake was celebrated by another deafening roar from the crowds; it echoed around the airport, reverberating off the buildings. Callom was buzzing with anticipation; the PR possibilities of such a reception were enormous.

Mayor Pavlova invited Sabatino to accompany her. When they emerged on the other side of the terminal, the reception was even more astonishing. Pavlova invited Sabatino to climb some improvised steps, up onto the back of a low-loader. A lorry had been turned into a makeshift speaking platform. As she walked up onto its deck, there was another roar hailing her appearance. With the extra height this provided, Sabatino could now look out on an extraordinary sight. Across what should have been a working car park were thousands of people. Mainly young, many of them carried portrait banners of Oksana Pavlova, while most were wearing the turquoise of the Ptarmigan team.

Up on the platform, Pavlova offered Sabatino a generous smile of welcome. She turned to address the crowd using the microphone, amplifier and sizeable bank of loudspeakers rigged up on the back of the lorry.

In Russian, the mayor said: 'Ladies, Gentlemen ... Muscovites,' and was immediately drowned out. She had to wait nearly a minute before it was worth her even trying to speak again. Then she continued in Russian: 'We – you and I, *our* city – have brought the Russian Grand Prix to Moscow.'

In time the sound abated and she was able to say: 'Our livelihood has been hammered by the sanctions imposed on Russia by the grown-up countries of the world. We are paying for the recklessness of the Crimea land grab, the intervention in Ukraine, and the propping up of the monster Assad in Syria. This Grand Prix will at least show one thing – that *Muscovite* Russians are capable of interacting harmoniously with the rest of the world.'

Sabatino couldn't follow the specifics of the message but could easily see its effects: the crowd's reaction was unambiguous.

'Politically, our standing – as a free country – was savaged by the-then president's homophobia at the time of the Sochi Winter Olympics, and the clampdown on political criticism. Our city – *this* Grand Prix – will showcase the *real* Russia. Through it, we will demonstrate Russia's desire to see social freedom, diversity and the unlimited tolerance of our human rights.'

The response from the crowd was emphatic.

Oksana Pavlova chose that moment to turn around and, with an outstretched arm, encouraged Sabatino to step forward. As she did so, Pavlova took her hand and raised their hands together high into the air.

In heavily accented English, the mayor said: 'Ladies and gentlemen, I give you ... Remy Sabatino,' prompting another roar of applause.

Reverting to Russian, the mayor continued: 'This remarkable woman is going to teach this country a great lesson about equality – about the power of merit. I am proud to know a woman showing herself to be at the vanguard of proving that women *can* compete on an equal footing with men ... and that a woman can win.'

There was another blast of noise and excitement from the thousands in front of them.

'Women are going to show this country,' added Mayor Pavlova, 'that change in Russia is demanded.'

The crowd began to chant:

'Zhar-ptitsa! Zhar-ptitsa! Zhar-ptitsa!'

Sabatino had her hand held aloft again by the mayor – to yet another roar of approval.

Bringing the reception to a close, Mayor Pavlova turned and made to give Remy Sabatino a genuine hug, which prompted the biggest reaction so far.

Whatever uplift Sabatino may have felt from the crowd was powerfully tested shortly afterwards.

No more than twenty feet across the tarmac from the low-loader was a very different constituency indeed. A small aluminium barrier had been erected to corral fifty or so members of the press corps. It was plain they were aware of the judgment from the FIA. These journalists bellowed, some of them with thick Russian or at least eastern European accents.

'What's your response to the ruling from the FIA?'

'Are you going to apologize to your teammate?'

'How bad is the rivalry now between you?'

'Do you have anything to say to the Russian people for the way you treated their national hero?'

Bernie Callom hurried forwards to position himself between Sabatino and the press. He declared authoritatively: 'Ms Sabatino won't be giving any interviews, nor will she be responding to the FIA judgment until she's had the chance to discuss things with her teammate, team boss and the team owner.'

The moment Sabatino was back on the ground, Callom graciously but firmly wheeled her round to face the mayor, to whom they paid their respects, before he walked Sabatino straight off to a courtesy car, waiting for them only a short distance away.

THREE

Before Sabatino had time to respond, they were arriving at the VIP helipad. Standing ready on the apron, a sleek executive helicopter was surrounded by a posse of mechanics and ground staff.

Five minutes later, with its rotors at optimum revolutions, the pilot pulled up on the collective to lift the stylish Kamov Ka-62 off the ground. He hovered for a few seconds, as clearance was confirmed from the tower, before he pushed forward on the cyclic, pulled more pitch, and guided the helicopter forwards and up into the air. Sabatino, looking down through the window at the receding airport buildings, saw the huge crowds still milling around them, waiting to wave her off. Masochistically, she couldn't stop herself glancing over towards the press pen, even though most of the journalists had now dispersed. Sabatino dreaded what bile they were about to discharge in their articles.

Callom glanced at his client. 'You haven't seen this circuit yet, have you, Rems?'

Sabatino didn't respond immediately.

She then mumbled: 'Only on the simulator.'

The helicopter continued to gain height into their short flight over the south of Moscow. Callom suddenly saw an opportunity – to provide a bit of a distraction from her thoughts: 'Look down there,' he said indicating through the window, 'you see that brilliant-white cube by the river – the one with the central gold-leaf dome and the four smaller gold domes around it – that's the Cathedral of Christ the Saviour.'

Against Callom's expectations, Sabatino did look out of the window. Seeing her respond, he was quickly encouraged to keep going: 'And that, of course – with the red-bricked walls and the gaudy-coloured onion-shaped domes – is the famous Saint Basil's

Cathedral, right next to the Kremlin. And that's Red Square behind it,' he added, indicating the rectangular area stretching away from them. 'Just the *name* sounds so sinister, doesn't it – let alone how bleak the place looks. Why are Russian governments, of whatever colour, unable to resist using it for their own bit of military willy-waggling.'

Still flying eastwards, they could see the Moskva River's well-pronounced meander through the capital.

'And there, on its own peninsular in the river,' announced Callom, 'is the Zhar-ptitsa Autodrom.'

Sabatino looked down and caught her first glimpse of Moscow's brand-new race track, laid out in the heart of the city. Lit at that moment by its own shaft of sunlight, it made a spectacular sight.

Sabatino studied the complex intently. 'You know, Bernie, I really don't understand this. Russia waits a hundred years, since 1914, for a Grand Prix to come back to this country – which it did to Sochi in 2014; and then, in no more than a matter of months later, they've got a second purpose-built Grand Prix circuit, here in Moscow?'

'I guess some of that could be attributed to Russia's ambition, although much of it seems to have been motivated by politics.'

'You're not serious?'

'I am,' replied Callom. 'The Sochi Grand Prix you mentioned turned out to be a political triumph in Russia.'

'*How?*'

'Don't you remember President Tarkovsky's extraordinary behaviour last year? At the end of that race? He was even in the pre-podium holding room – he was in there with the drivers. That never happens – you never have hangers-on in there. Then he went out onto the podium and presented every one of the prizes. He looked stiff … awkward. So completely out of place.'

Sabatino just shrugged.

'The president was milking the Grand Prix for all it was worth. He seemed to be saying: "Look how involved in this thing I am."'

'And you think that makes it political?'

'Oh, absolutely. Within Russia, that Grand Prix has triumphed as a "fuck-the-West" event. Russia's annexation of the Crimea, its intervention in the Ukraine, the shooting down of MH17 – all isolated the country. Badly. The resultant sanctions hit the country hard. Amazingly, the Sochi GP – known here as Tarkovsky's personal project – *hasn't* been boycotted by F1. So he was revelling in the attendance of the numerous F1 countries – showing that, for all its disapproval of Russia's conduct, the West couldn't stay away – couldn't do without Russia. The president was projecting the international success of that Grand Prix as proof to the Russian people that his stewardship of the Motherland was winning against the outside world!'

'But if Sochi was so successful, why's the race been transferred to Moscow?'

'Because of Mayor Pavlova.'

Sabatino's nod seemed to acknowledge the honour of having been welcomed by her, personally, at the airport. 'Didn't that put some noses out of joint?'

Callom chuckled.

'Whatever did it cost Moscow to get the Grand Prix here, then?' she asked.

The PR man smiled. 'That depends on how you measure it, I suppose – and what you want to get out of it. Financially, it's cost a mint. Commercially, the Grand Prix being in Moscow is seen as a massive boost to the city, because Formula One is recognized as *such* a prestigious thing to host. While politically, the switch from Sochi – to here – has undoubtedly been a significant coup for Mayor Pavlova.'

Their helicopter flew a banked loop around the circuit.

Sabatino studied the brand-new complex. It was hard to see the Zhar-ptitsa Autodrom as anything other than a stunning addition to the Formula One family. Its location was truly magnificent: Nagatinskaya Poyma, a public park, was bounded on three sides by the Moskva River. Other Formula One circuits – Sepang, Bahrain, Abu

Dhabi – may have had the grandiosity, but this latest cathedral to motor racing boasted everything expected of a modern F1 venue. The Zhar-ptitsa wasn't just a generic concrete monstrosity either, as so many of the other new circuits seemed to be. Sabatino could see that most of its elements were designed to say: "Russia". Its buildings – along the pit lane, the balconied hospitality suites above the garages and the massive grandstand along the main straight – all featured distinctive architecture, making each unmistakably Russian. Pastel-coloured walls were offset by white quoin stones, baroque flourishes and mini onion-shaped domes. Sabatino could see that any visual representation of the Zhar-ptitsa Autodrom – from any angle – was meant to render it instantly recognizable as Russian.

Their helicopter began to lose height, hovering in towards the helipad in the middle of the complex. Looking out through the window, Sabatino was struck by the large expanses of woodland preserved from the ancient park now incorporated into the circuit.

'Forests are a big thing in Russia, having a truly mystical place in Russian folklore,' Callom observed. 'As you'll be able to see, the architect has more than achieved his stated aim of melding the track with the landscape.'

They were just about to see the best example of this.

Touching down in the early evening sun, Sabatino and Callom were helped to alight. Moments later the Kamov Ka-62 lifted off again, leaving the visitors – after the receding noise and force of the helicopter's downdraft – to enjoy the setting in relative peace.

Extensive woodland and the Autodrom's buildings were now all around them. They saw immediately how the architect had managed to blend the new with the old. A Capability-Brownski avenue led off from the middle of the complex. Irresistibly, it lured the eye out from the modern – across the river to a vision that, for the rest of the world, would embody a romantic view of Russia: a golden, onion-shaped dome atop the brilliant-white walls of an Orthodox church. A statement of eastern mysticism was there in the Church of Alexander Nevsky. Ancient woodland and this majestic avenue – framing the Orthodox church at the end of it – were all designed to whisk the visitor away to a historical Russia: to the Russia of *Anna Karenina* … Carl Fabergé … Tchaikovsky … *Dr Zhivago* … even the imperial splendour of the Tsars.

FOUR

Walking down the pit lane, Sabatino breathed deeply as she reached the open bay at the front of the Ptarmigan garage. She was anxious about encountering her teammate, Yegor Baryshnikov; not about meeting him, but about doubting whether she'd succeed in controlling herself after his attack on her at the FIA. A public bust-up in front of the team would not be a clever move. She wasn't much looking forward to meeting Tahm Nazar, either; Sabatino was still brooding over the team boss's decision to take her race engineer away from her for this crucial race.

The Ptarmigan bay was immaculate with glossy white-painted walls and a shiny white-painted concrete floor, more reminiscent of an operating theatre than a garage. Casting an eye round inside, Sabatino found it all relatively quiet. Both turquoise Ptarmigan Formula One cars were up on tall jack stands, with every wheel removed. Numerous mechanics attended different parts of each car; the tool most of them carried, though, was a laptop – typically wedged in the crook of an arm. A series of readings were being taken.

Andy Backhouse spotted Sabatino's arrival and made his way over. Her race engineer, a squat British man in his forties with dark thinning hair, hairy arms, and heavy glasses, was keen to break the ice. In his tenor-pitched Birmingham accent he said: 'So sorry to hear about the FIA ruling, Rems.'

Sabatino shrugged. 'It was seriously unjust. I'm going to appeal. I'm far more pissed off knowing that whole investigation was kicked off by Yegor.'

Backhouse replied: 'What?'

She turned to look at him. 'You didn't know that Baryshnikov was behind it?'

'I've been travelling – from Canada last weekend – working all hours to help Yegor's engineers rebuild his car. I haven't been talking to anyone, not plugged in at all.'

Sabatino couldn't work out what to make of this. Bizarrely, it made her feel better. Why should that be? Why should hearing that Backhouse *didn't* know about Baryshnikov's activities with the governing body be in any way comforting? Did it, somehow, bolster her feeling of the underhandedness of it all? Her sense of conspiracy?

'Considering your impending new relationship with him, I'd better not ask you whether you approve of what he did, then,' she said looking at him knowingly.

'What new relationship?'

'You and Baryshnikov.'

Backhouse looked blank.

'Tahm hasn't told you?'

'Told me what?'

'You're going to be looking after Baryshnikov – here, in Moscow – as his race engineer?'

Sabatino could now see Backhouse's own shock at this news: what pleased her was that Backhouse did not look happy about it either.

'I'd better have a word with Tahm,' replied Backhouse, 'but not now – we don't have time. I've arranged for a buggy to take us round the circuit.' And, as though to put all this unexpected news out of his mind, he held out his arm to indicate the way.

Five minutes later, sitting in the electric golf cart, Sabatino was being driven across the start/finish line as they set out on a recce round the circuit. Even their gentle speed created something of a breeze, which Sabatino found refreshing.

'This place may be located in the middle of a city,' said Backhouse as they headed for Turn One, 'but it's absolutely no street circuit.'

Sabatino had gained the same clear impression from her time on the simulator. She knew the track to be one of huge contrasts. Speeds were going to be high, with three flat-out 210 mile-an-hour straights. But *that* was where their challenge lay: to capitalize on those, they would need to set very low wing – to minimize the drag. Except, of course, doing that would drastically reduce the downforce through the undulating, twisty sections – where they'd want maximum grip.

At the end of the half-mile Hermitage Straight, Sabatino and her race engineer drew their buggy to a stop. Behind them, a lowering sun was reddening the sky and coating the landscape with a haunting glow. In front of them was a clear view into one of the key sculpted corners; they were a hundred metres from the entry point of Turn Eleven, a long sweeping left-hander.

This corner, now directly in front of them, was set in a clearing among the trees. They could see the apex of the bend away to the left; the track, there, straightening out before it fell away slightly for a short distance into a tighter right-hander, Turn Twelve. After that, the circuit disappeared again, off into the ancient forest.

Compared with the simulator, this corner was looking very different as she studied it in three-dimensional reality.

Sabatino felt a buzz of anticipation.

She definitely felt there was a possibility here. Plan A, of course, would see her on pole after Qualifying with her being able to leave the rest of the field trailing behind her after the exit of Turn One. But should that not materialize, she would need a Plan B – requiring her to have as many overtaking strategies in her armoury as possible.

It occurred to Sabatino that there could be an unexpected tactical overtaking ploy. She might just be able to create the element of surprise that could seriously wrong-foot an intended victim.

'The track's pretty wide,' Backhouse observed, indicating the approach to the turn, 'but it's not much of a place to overtake; there's barely anything of a braking zone into the corner. Going round the outside wouldn't be advisable, either; very early on you might be all right, but after any number of laps we're likely to see a nasty build-up of dirt and marbles over there.'

Sabatino was listening, but she wasn't agreeing.

Despite her respect for Backhouse, she was not prepared to say anything given his impending transfer to Baryshnikov. Instead, she was studying the topography like a golfer reads a green before a tricky putt. She looked at the surface of the track – its width – its limited braking zone; then she tried to imagine the G-force through here, what effect that would have on the car – on her – on the aerodynamics, on the car's balance front-to-rear; then she took into account the environment around the corner, trying to gauge any effects it might have on wind speed and, most importantly, on temperatures. Mature trees around this section of the track formed something of an organic canyon, which could well induce a microclimate – trapping the air and any warmth here. Sabatino wanted to understand if any of these factors would have a material effect on the working of the aerodynamics, the tyres and the handling of the car through these corners.

Turns Eleven and Twelve, now though, were taking shape in her mind in a completely new way – as an unplanned opportunity: a stunning place in which to launch an unexpected strike, should she need to try and get past a defensive car. It pained her, but she still didn't feel comfortable discussing any of this with Backhouse ahead of his switch to her teammate.

'You have to give the Russkies credit,' said Backhouse, finally distracting her as he pressed the accelerator to continue their recce. Over the whine of the buggy's electric motor he said: 'I take it you've noticed the number of seating and spectator areas they've built?'

Subliminally she had. It had even struck her as a clear distinction of the circuit. Viewing opportunities had been created all the way round. There were the to-be-expected commercial locations, of course – such as the half-mile-long horseshoe-shaped grandstand on the outside of the hairpin and the vast set of stands along the pit straight – but it was the mini-grandstands sited on the outside of nearly every corner that made this circuit unusual. The Zharptitsa Autodrom offered no less than twenty-two such vantage points for a total capacity of a quarter of a million people. It was projecting something very clear about the venue's inclusive attitude to spectators.

'And particularly strange for the commercial world of Formula One,' offered Backhouse, 'they've even got ungated – *unticketed* – access for the public into some sections.'

'Non-paying, you're kidding?'

'Nope. It's an amazingly generous gesture to attract the people of the host city to come and enjoy the Grand Prix. That's one of them up there,' he said pointing to the outside of Turn Eleven, 'that whole bank is one of these communal stands.'

Her eye looked across the large sand-coloured gravel trap on the outside of the corner, over the brightness of the chunky red-and-white tyre wall, then up and over the concrete wall and wire mesh fence, to see – on the far side of the perimeter – a wide staircase of turf terraces cut into a grassy bank, rising to a height level with the tree tops.

'You're saying that all the viewing space over there is *free*?'

Sabatino's passage back through the Zhar-ptitsa Autodrom complex did not end as orderly as she hoped. Backhouse brought the buggy to stop outside the Ptarmigan garage in the pit lane at the precise moment her teammate, Yegor Baryshnikov, happened to emerge from inside. There were several people gathered around the tall slim Russian driver. Before Sabatino could dismount, Baryshnikov's face broke into a challenging but slightly nervous smile. In his pronounced accent, he said loudly:

'At least you could not *bump off* other driver in buggy.'

His entourage was soon chortling.

'There was no "bumping off" in Canada, Yegor,' she replied. 'When you've learned to drive wheel to wheel, you might get to understand what you did … what *actually* happened.'

'Not what FIA believe. FIA say you force me out – deliberately.'

'It's really not my problem if you run away every time someone shows you a wheel, Yegor. I win and beat other male drivers, but *they* don't seem to take my wins as a diminution of *their* virility.'

Backhouse quickly put a hand on Sabatino's arm.

Baryshnikov suddenly looked exposed. A ready response, though, eluded him.

Sabatino knew she had scored.

The Russian driver took a step forwards.

Backhouse quickly intervened, this time ordering both of them to cool it.

Turning to face him, Sabatino said sternly: 'No, Andy, it's just as well you've seen this,' she said cocking a thumb in Baryshnikov's direction. 'You'd better start to embrace the attitude and loyalty you're about to be working for.'

Baryshnikov added more loudly than before: 'Moscow is *my* race. Ptarmigan will be looked after – best – by *me* winning Russian Grand Prix.'

'Then you better *had* win it, Yegor,' said Sabatino as she climbed from the buggy. 'You're in the best car and you're about to have the best race engineer in the pit lane as well. Which means that you will have *no* excuses,' she said and smiled directly into his face.

FIVE

Sabatino woke early the following morning. Despite the detour via Paris from Montreal her body clock was still on Canadian time. She had slept fitfully. She continued to seethe at the outcome of the FIA hearing. Her mind had also been going over the other events of the day before – her various encounters, and, most curiously, her realization that two significant chunks of information had been withheld from a key member of the team.

What on earth was going on?

She felt she needed some air.

Naked, she crossed the splendour of the Kremlin Suite of the Hotel Baltschug Kempinski and drew back the curtains, to look out on the beginnings of the day. She opened the window and let in air that was cool and refreshing. A gentle hum of traffic could be heard rising from the streets below. Four storeys up, she was looking at the gloomy, overcast light that filled the sky. Moscow was doing its best to look grey, moody and brooding in an early morning twilight. It would have succeeded but for the lurid colours of Saint Basil's Cathedral directly opposite – on the far side of the river. To the left of this was the start of the reddish Kremlin Wall and its numerous blocky towers. Then came the copse of gold domes of the various Kremlin churches, which at that angle and distance all seemed to meld into one another. Finally, over to the far left – running away from her – was the long and imposing facade of the Grand Kremlin Palace; its blend of white, cream, gold leaf – and long verdigris roof – emerging through the murky light. For a view of Moscow and a sense of Russia this one window seemed to offer most of what might be needed.

There was a knock on the door. Sabatino picked up a white hotel gown from one of the chairs and pulled it on. She let a liveried room-service waiter into the suite; he was carrying a silver tray and a stack of newspapers.

Once her privacy was restored, Sabatino shed the robe. Naked once more, she sat down at a small table to eat an early breakfast and scan the papers. Her priority was to gauge the fallout from the ruling by the FIA. Like all sports figures, her reputation was her currency. Only on the back of it would she secure and retain size-able sponsorship and endorsement deals. She was anxious to judge whether – and how badly – her brand might have been damaged by the Montreal incident and yesterday's ruling.

She was relieved. The media's reaction to the judgment turned out to be milder than she feared. There were numerous references to the growing rivalry between her and Baryshnikov, although at this stage no one seemed to be taking sides. In the international press, the slight negativity to the incident was limited to the "inside baseball" constituency, most likely represented by that group of journalists she'd heard at the airport. Any such negativity, though, was more than outweighed by the populist journals, all of which focused on the positive – drawing on the public mood indicated by the huge crowds that had greeted her when she landed.

Sabatino even scanned the Russian papers. Not being able to read Cyrillic script, they weren't that informative. She gained a feeling from the numerous pictures of her, though: the inference was of a general anticipation and excitement ahead of the Russian Grand Prix.

Just as its patron intended.

It was, perhaps, a shame that Sabatino had been unable to read the Russian papers; she might have felt better. Their coverage was predominantly about her. Most articles celebrated that, in only the season before, she had broken the twenty-two-year absence of female drivers in Formula One – and that, in fewer than twelve months, she had become extraordinarily close to becoming a motor racing icon. They also pointed out that it hadn't been easy for her.

On Sabatino's arrival in F1, countless commentators and senior motor racing figures had dismissed her presence as a marketing stunt by the Ptarmigan Grand Prix Team. Many considered Sabatino's appointment as a form of politically correct tokenism – affirmative action – positive discrimination. Everything about her credibility was questioned: Whether a woman was up to it. Whether she was physically strong enough. Whether she would have the stamina, car control or technical understanding. A number of tabloids had used barely veiled puns to ask whether Sabatino, as a woman, would even have the balls to compete.

Twelve months on and it was hard for anyone to deny Remy Sabatino's talent. From her first appearance on the grid, she had proved herself to be competitive. And then she started winning, momentously at the Monaco Grand Prix – even as a rookie. That didn't mean the knives weren't still out. It now appeared, though, that some in Formula One felt demeaned by being beaten by a woman. This season, Sabatino's overriding sense was that her new teammate, Yegor Baryshnikov – in the same car and therefore the driver most easily and directly compared with her – was feeling this the most.

Worldwide, spectators were loving the presence of a competitive woman. Across all metrics interest in F1 was up: TV audiences, attendance at races, readership of related periodicals, advertising revenues and sponsorship. A competitive woman seemed to have revitalized an F1 format that had recently been showing some signs of tiredness.

Nowhere had this excitement been more keenly felt – among a whole new breed of Grand Prix fanatics – than here in Moscow. Muscovites were being presented with a quadruple whammy: the prospect of a Grand Prix on their doorstep for the first time; the prospect of seeing the now-iconic female driver Remy Sabatino in the flesh; the prospect of seeing the first of their own countrymen, Yegor Baryshnikov, as a viable contender for the Driver's Championship, currently even leading the rankings; as well as the prospect of seeing the rivalry for the title between these two first-of-their-kind drivers being played out right in front of them.

There was significant excitement ahead of the first Russian Grand Prix to be hosted here in Moscow.

Just as its patron intended.

SIX

Race day came upon the city.

On the grid, a mass of people, equipment and bright colours seemed to smother the twenty-two cars. Either side of the pit straight, the half-mile grandstands were jam-packed. Genuine Formula One fans – as well as the locals swept up by the carnival of the Grand Prix – were in anticipatory mood. There were constant roars from the spectators, surging whenever anyone recognizable appeared.

Few other places hosting a brand-new Grand Prix had demonstrated such mainstream interest for its very first race. Several countries and venues had notoriously shown indifference on their debut, reflected in painfully poor initial crowds: Istanbul Park, Korea, Turkey and Shanghai held some uncomfortable memories for many in Formula One. Moscow's reaction, therefore, was a welcomed relief.

With only minutes to go before the parade lap, Sabatino walked out onto the grid. She was dressed in the turquoise livery of the Ptarmigan Formula One Team and carrying her balaclava, gloves and helmet.

She was in for a surprise.

Sabatino's reception at the Zhar-ptitsa was far more rock 'n' roll than motor racing. The spectators erupted. She couldn't help but look up as the noise boomed out around her.

It was extraordinary.

In reply, her normally sparky eyes flashed even more at the tangible energy from the stands. Against the colour of her Mediterranean complexion and short dark hair, Sabatino's bright smile now radiated delight. She may have been five feet two, but the uplifting effect of this welcome gave her a presence way beyond her stature. Looking up and into the applause from the crowds, she waved and smiled to acknowledge their support. Each time she did so the spectators rose to their feet in response.

On the grid, television crews homed in and swarmed round her. Four presenters thrust microphones into her face. Heavily accented questions were yelled, each drowning the others out. Sabatino managed to catch the drift of one of them. Its tone, though, was in marked contrast to the mood in the stands. Repeating it back, she asked mockingly:

'"Am I going to run my teammate off the road here?"'

The journalist nodded, smirking.

'Why would I do that? I've never done it before.'

'The FIA disagree ... how bad *are* your relations with Baryshnikov?'

'Both of us are racing drivers – both of us are here to race.'

'You aren't concerned about the advantage he has here – being Russian?'

'No one's driven this circuit before, so – *no*. No one has an advantage.'

'What about his home crowd? They always say a home crowd is worth half a second a lap.'

Several of the presenters nodded.

Sabatino smiled back confidently. 'You obviously aren't paying attention, are you – haven't you seen this lot?' she asked and turned to wave up into the grandstands above them. A roar came back in response. Turning back to face the journalists, she said: 'If that's the best Baryshnikov can do at his home Grand Prix, then I'm happy to take my chances!'

She saw some of the TV people smile for the first time. One of them even thanked Sabatino and wished her luck. Nine TV stations were about to use the footage they had just shot, either as a stand-alone interview or as B-roll. That encounter and those few comments were likely to reach upwards of 300 million viewers around the world.

Sabatino made her way to her car at the front of the grid.

All around the front row was a profusion of turquoise. Qualifying the day before had resulted in a front row lock-out: Ptarmigan had secured both P1 and P2. Before Backhouse had been redeployed to look after Baryshnikov, he and Sabatino had worked on the car to achieve the pitch-perfect set-up for her driving style around this circuit. Even with the challenges it presented, they had settled on running exceptionally low wing.

But for a quirk of bad traffic in the last session of Qualifying, which thwarted Sabatino's best time in Q3, she would have been on pole. Even with that misstep she was still fast enough to start the Grand Prix on the front row, having clocked a time six-tenths faster than the car now in P3. Her ambition to get back on top of the Championship leader board was still within reach, except that her most significant rival for it – Yegor Baryshnikov – was today one place in front of her on the grid. And after the points she had lost because of his objection lodged with the FIA and its ruling on the Montreal incident, the Russian was still ahead of her in the overall title race, too. Should Baryshnikov manage to capitalize on his advantage of pole position today, he would extend – and bake in – that lead over Sabatino.

It was, therefore, all to be played for at the world's newest Grand Prix.

Sabatino walked to her car on the front row. Her stand-in race engineer was ready waiting, looking concerned about her delayed arrival. Sabatino smiled her thanks for his patience.

Turning to throw one last wave up to the spectators in the stands above her, which was reciprocated with another sizeable cheer, she turned to her race engineer and focused.

Suddenly, the rock star was gone.

Remy Sabatino, the highly competitive and driven Formula One driver, was now the only persona present.

She was right there – back in the game.

Ready for battle.

The three-minute signal had just been lit.

All the drivers were now going through their last-minute drills. Sabatino, though, almost shuddered – having the strongest feeling that someone was watching her. In full view of the thousands of people in the stands, she knew such a sensation was ridiculous. Except, somehow, she knew she meant Baryshnikov.

Casting an eye in the direction of his car, Sabatino saw she had been right. Despite the blur of activity all around them, he was just standing there, motionless – beside his front wing – staring straight at her. Unnervingly, she couldn't read the expression on his face.

She tried hard to ignore him by looking away and concentrating on her pre-race routine.

Carefully, she inserted her earplugs. Next, she pulled her fire-retardant balaclava down over her head, positioning it to align with the helmet's visor. Then she eased her helmet on, raising her chin to secure the strap. The zip on the turquoise suit was run fully up; the integrity of the fire-protection being ensured as the Velcro was fastened around the neck. The bulky yoke-like Head And Neck Support – HANS – device was looped over her helmet, to rest on her shoulders. Pulling on her turquoise gloves, she massaged the material up into the crook of each finger to ensure minimal loss of movement and greatest sensitivity.

Sabatino was ready.

Lowering herself into her cockpit, engineers were on hand to check her seat harness and then to secure the HANS fastenings – to support and protect the drivers' head and neck. Mechanics were still swarming all over the car, making sure everything on it was ready for the off.

She fired up the turbo-charged 1.6 litre V6.

It created a deafening growl.

Other cars on the grid were doing the same. Drivers blipped their throttles, readying their engines – some seeming to use the growls to gird themselves psychologically for battle.

Each of these cars was capable of producing over 750 brake

horsepower, in a chassis weighing half that of a road-going Mini Cooper. Each car had a package of aerodynamic surfaces that gave drivers the manoeuvrability, in two dimensions at least, of a fighter aircraft. Combatants here at Zhar-ptitsa were expected to lap this track at average speeds of 150 miles an hour.

Around this 3.1 mile circuit – with its feature corners, drops, crests and blistering straights – the dogfight was about to begin.

The modern-day aces were ready.

SEVEN

The one-minute signal was shown. Mechanics, squatting down beside each wheel to mind the tyre blankets – pre-heating all four tyres to reduce the time they would take to reach optimum temperatures out on the track – were soon pulling them away. Then at the run they, along with all the other teams' mechanics, withdrew from the grid, hurriedly pushing their trolleys loaded with all the equipment and alternate tyres back to the pits.

The race director lit the lights on the gantry.

A crescendo of sound screamed out across this south-west corner of Moscow. The cars pulled away – on their pre-race formation lap. Blue smoke appeared from several rear wheels as drivers laid rubber down on the track surface, trying to enhance their grip for the start of the race proper. This being the parade lap, they moved off at a modest pace. Even so, drivers were weaving their cars violently, trying to work higher temperature into their tyres and brakes.

Out in front – the fastest in Qualifying – was the other turquoise Ptarmigan, driven by Russia's Yegor Baryshnikov. The rest of the field trailed behind him around the circuit. Line astern.

Still moving at the modest formation-lap pace, they reached the end of Sector One. This was the beginning of the half-mile Hermitage Straight, which fed in to Turn Eleven. Sabatino was now practically fizzing, particularly given her relatively disappointing position in Qualifying. She had hoped for pole – to be right out in front – but she hadn't achieved it. To take the fight to Baryshnikov, now – and therefore regain the leadership of the Championship table – she would have to get past him that afternoon. After Sabatino's recce in the buggy three days before, she was all the more excited about her potential element-of-surprise move at Turn Eleven.

Right now, she wanted to get up close behind the pole-sitter, to study in fine detail his line through this part of the circuit. Baryshnikov was known for his tactical brilliance, particularly in defence. He could make his car seem four metres wide, seemingly able to shut out any attempt to pass … at least where a pass might be expected. Sabatino knew she was going to have to be imaginative if she was going to get past him.

Her eyes were glued to Baryshnikov's rear wing.

Sabatino was now looking to make the most of the opportunity offered by this parade lap to understand – for the first time – the exact spatial limitations of the track while she had other cars around her. She scrutinized her Russian teammate as he set himself up for the corner.

Even on the parade lap, Baryshnikov had moved over to the left – to hug the inside line of the track.

As expected, Sabatino saw that if he did that in the race, she would have no chance of launching a challenge down the inside – the usual line of attack. Baryshnikov was showing he would be able to block that way completely. She had been right about his style of defence.

Her heart rate surged. She saw that an overtaking manoeuvre *could* be possible here, albeit as a two-stage move.

Instead of trying to pass down the inside of Turn Eleven, she was contemplating the idea of running wide – to the outside, to the right of the racing line and therefore the circuit. The key would not be trying to complete the overtake in Turn Eleven, per se. Her idea was to try and match Baryshnikov's pace through this bend, and end up – if she could – side by side with him *on the exit*. She wouldn't care how wide she might be running at the point where they straightened up: in fact, the wider the better. A wide exit from Turn Eleven could then set her up perfectly for the next corner, where she would automatically be on the inside line after the short straight down into Turn Twelve, giving her a strong claim into that forty-five degree right-hander. *That* was where a challenge proper could be mounted.

Sabatino was conscious that driving wide – off the racing line – was nearly always a risk. Wide parts of a track got "dirty". Out there, dust and debris accumulated which didn't get cleaned by the passage of tyres. Worse, it was where marbles accumulated, the small droplets of softened rubber thrown off the tyres which, on cooling, became hardened spheres. Drive over those and a car became almost unsteerable.

Sabatino made several exaggerated zigzag, snaking manoeuvres. Anyone watching would have read these as a driver trying to work heat into the tyres. Except Sabatino's moves were more pronounced, taking her extra wide – deliberately running out over the green part of the track. Then, as another typical warm-up move, Sabatino stamped on the brakes followed by an immediate burn-out – burst of hard acceleration – all the while making sure her outside wheels were on the "dirt". With heightened sensitivity she was gauging any reduction in grip she might experience when out on this dirty surface. What Sabatino felt through her tyres and steering, though, was putting a smile on her face. She was pumped; this ploy might just work.

She was going to take a shot at Baryshnikov.

She fully expected it to take him by surprise.

This might be the chance for her to pay him back. To even up the score – to avenge the insult of the points he'd robbed her of in Canada.

Three minutes later and the last of the back markers had retaken his place on the grid. There were now just two neat parallel lines of F1 cars on the long start/finish straight. At the very back of them all, a marshal walked out into the middle of the track, confidently waving a green flag.

Race control had its signal.

The combatants were ready.

In his box overlooking the start, the race director – his silver hair tousled by the warm Moscow breeze – looked down his rows of charges. He then watched the clock on his control panel. They were right on time. Firmly, using the heel of his hand, he hit the button.

His countdown was started.

One red light, mounted in the gantry above the start line, came on.

The second red light.

The roar came and went as drivers revved their engines at different times, each going through their own starting ritual. It was like the discordant tuning of instruments before a theatrical performance: the same sense of expectation fuelled the heart rates of those looking on.

The third red light.

The roar intensified, becoming more constant – higher pitched – higher and higher up the rev counter. The noise was reverberating out across Moscow.

The fourth red light.

Everyone's breathing quickened slightly. Everything was about to happen. They were about to see the unleashing of phenomenal power, energy and the force of 15,000 horsepower.

The fifth light was now burning.

The crescendo peaked and plateaued.

A primeval scream of intent.

All the five lights burned. It seemed for an age. Then:

Lights out – they were all *out*.

Go!

The race was on!

Noise translated into movement.

All twenty-two cars of the Formula One grid accelerated forward. Tyres spun, tyres held; the cars, almost in grid formation, hurtled off their marks, screaming up their gears, gaining speed with every yard travelled.

Baryshnikov, from pole – to the left and therefore the clean side of the track – got a cracking start, his Ptarmigan's power translating directly into forward momentum. As soon as he was sure of his grip and rate of acceleration, though, he moved dominantly across to his right – to put his stamp on the rest of the field.

Remy Sabatino, on the front row of the grid in P2, was only just back from the leader, but on the dirty side – not cleaned by the succession of practice laps and pre-race warm-up races. Even so she got away well. But so did Simi Luciano in the Massarella who, although one row back in P3, was on the left side and so did have the advantage of the cleaner surface. Finding better connection with the road, he was very quickly gaining on Sabatino, down her left-hand side.

Then everything closed up.

Baryshnikov was cutting further right, well into Sabatino's field of view.

The black, foreboding shape of the third-placed Massarella was pulling up, directly along Sabatino's left flank.

She was getting boxed in.

They were only a matter of feet apart as they headed into the right-hand corner of Turn One. Baryshnikov struck early for his right to the line, swinging even further right – directly across Sabatino's path. He had the space and the claim to do so. Luciano, never one to miss an opportunity, intimidatingly held his line only inches away to Sabatino's left – not giving her any space – taunting her to brake earlier than she would want.

But she was having none of it.

Into the slow corner – at 90 miles an hour, within touching distance of the cars to the front and to the side – Sabatino resolutely held her ground.

In, through, and round they ran – all emerging on the far side of Turn One, unscathed. Baryshnikov, capitalizing on the clear air and track through the corner, was already pulling away. Sabatino *had* retained P2 but couldn't take anything for granted. A gap opened up between her and her teammate in front, while the one behind – to Luciano – had closed right up to a matter of tenths.

Accelerating into the Gorbachev Straight, Sabatino could almost feel Luciano's Massarella immediately behind her. Buckling down, she worked to establish the rhythm of her car, now that her principal disadvantage relative to the other Ptarmigan and the Massarella had been removed: at the very start of the race she had been forced to cope with the dirty side of the track. Now that the cars were all line astern – with an equal right to the racing line – Sabatino's disadvantage was gone. All of them were now entitled to use the clean part of the circuit, and so she had every expectation of this being far more of a straight fight from here on.

She was already in flat-out pursuit of Yegor Baryshnikov in the other Ptarmigan.

Sabatino was set on nothing less than retribution.

She was out for revenge.

EIGHT

There was a big sky. It always seemed big above the Solent. This expanse of dark blue, almost the shade of sapphire, was broken by the faintest wisps of a high white cloud. One unnatural shape spoiled the sky scape: a lone vapour trail from a transatlantic airliner scored the heavens at high altitude, as it headed out to the west.

To each side of the Solent, headlands and promontories reached down to the water's edge. In the summer haze, only the crest lines of each landmass gave them any shape. Otherwise they appeared like the broad, indistinct strokes of dilute purple watercolour.

Sea, between the south coast of England and the Isle of Wight, stretched away into a bright mist – down towards the Needles – while a high sun created a diamond-like sparkle across the surface of the water.

Dominic Quartano was not oblivious to the escapism of his surroundings, but he wasn't there to savour them. He may have been standing on the quarterdeck of his 300-foot 1930s yacht, *The Melita*, but this chairman and chief executive of Quartech International, the defence business he had founded forty years earlier, was there to do what he loved best: to court a deal.

Quartano was hosting several high-ranking guests. His guest of honour was HRH King Harmeini Al-Buhrani, ruler of Buhran – the Middle Eastern Gulf state and the world's second largest oil producer. Accompanying the king was a sizeable retinue, which included that kingdom's chief of the defence staff, seven senior officers, Buhran's high commissioner to the Court of St James's and three military attachés. To Quartech International, the Buhrani Defence Force already represented a commercial relationship worth in excess of $2 billion dollars a year.

Dominic Quartano had laid on a weekend of special entertainment for his principal guest. The previous day he had taken a box for Glorious Goodwood, the race meeting held up on the Sussex Downs; from it, the king had been able to watch a filly of his win the Nassau Stakes. Quartano had then flown his party in one of the firm's helicopters – a civilian variant of Quartech's hugely successful military Aztec – across to the Isle of Wight for a dinner attended by 200 guests at the Royal Yacht Squadron. Overnight, the king had stayed aboard *The Melita* – giving Quartano a chance to talk privately with him over breakfast, which they had taken al fresco on the quarterdeck. Mid-morning, they were joined by the rest of the Buhrani contingent, ready for the final day of Cowes Week. Rounding off this weekend of hospitality, Quartano was hosting a lunch for fifty in the yacht's stateroom which would be attended by a number of dignitaries including the British foreign secretary, the chief of the defence staff, the president of the Board of Trade and four of HMG's most senior Whitehall mandarins. Over the course of two days, Quartano would have paid tribute to the Bedouin king's passion for horses, Bhuran's history as a seafaring nation as well as fully honouring the country's centuries-long strategic alliance with Britain.

The Melita was lying at anchor directly in line with the RYS, offering those on board a perfect platform from which to watch the regatta. Spread out across the water – towards the mouth of the Beaulieu River on the Hampshire coast – was a flotilla of white sails: the much-anticipated finals of the Flying Fifteens. Explosions of colour sporadically caught the eye on the downwind leg as boats hoisted spinnakers, which, in the hands of such experienced crews, seemed to appear and disappear in the blink of an eye.

Dominic Quartano appeared completely relaxed in this setting. His clothes were utterly fitting for any of the most prestigious sailing centres – from Monaco to Martha's Vineyard. They suggested casual, save that the quality, style, and cost of them were anything but: his dark glasses – top-of-the-range Ray-Bans – were his only concession to "off the peg". His blue checked shirt, white chinos and loafers were all hand-made by the best-known names in Jermyn Street.

Such clothes may superficially have reflected Quartano's at-oneness with such gentrified nautical settings, but it was his heavily lined, lived-in Mediterranean face, piercing blue eyes and mane of silver hair that gave him the presence of someone completely at ease in the social glamour of these places. His charisma, though, wasn't created by anything as trifling as his clothes or his appearance; it stemmed entirely from an air of command. As the founder, owner, and controller of a £50 billion defence business, there were few circumstances anywhere in the world in which Dominic Quartano was likely to be fazed in anyone's company, however exalted their status.

Standing at the guardrail, Quartano pointed out an incident between two boats aggressively rounding the windward mark. He offered the king a powerful pair of binoculars. His guest, seeing for himself, watched the committee boat approach and adjudicate the incident before the Flying Fifteens in question were summarily ruled free to continue.

As the king lowered the glasses, a smartly dressed aide appeared onto the quarterdeck from the large doors of the saloon.

She made her way across.

Discreetly, she attracted Quartano's attention.

'Excuse me, sir – Your Majesty,' she said addressing the king with a shallow but elegant curtsy. 'Mr Quartano, I think you would want to know, sir: Mr Nazar is on Ptarmigan's video link – from the paddock. There's been a terrible accident … at the Grand Prix in Moscow.'

NINE

Lap six and the race order hadn't changed, although everyone felt it was about to. The true speed differences – or delta – of the cars was threatening to tell.

Sabatino and her Ptarmigan were finding their mojo, with a near-perfect set-up for the Zhar-ptitsa track in that day's atmospheric conditions. She was gaining on Baryshnikov.

The two cars crossed the start/finish line. Running at full throttle, they pounded down to Turn One. Baryshnikov – braking late – kept his lead, and was through cleanly. So too was Sabatino, right behind him in P2.

They were now in the Gorbachev Straight.

Sabatino started to gain – little by little, inch by agonizing inch.

Turn Two, a left-right-left, was set in among a clump of trees. Powering through this mini-chicane, the two front-runners were cheered on by the packed grandstands to either side of the track. Sabatino's car, performing magnificently, was instantly responsive; front and rear were in exceptional balance, giving her a particularly fast exit from the chicane.

Baryshnikov, in the turquoise car in front, set himself up for the next corner. This time his line wasn't so clean.

Sabatino smelled an opportunity.

Into the entry of Turn Four the gap was down to 75 metres, which – at 160 miles an hour – was nothing. She had already made her decision. She sensed the time was right. She was going to go for it. She would strike at the end of the Hermitage Straight, into Turn Eleven.

They exited Turn Four.

Sabatino kept pace as the track meandered through a sequence of two-dimensional, and then three-dimensional "S" bends.

Baryshnikov's line was no cleaner: his tightness through two of the apexes was slipping.

Sabatino pushed extra hard.

In no time they were entering the longest straight on the circuit, the half-mile section – named after the Imperial palace and world-famous Hermitage museum.

Sabatino was right on terms.

She was exactly where she wanted to be.

She was not letting Baryshnikov get away: her Ptarmigan's V6 screamed, pumping out as much power as she needed for her move. Sabatino ran up through the gears, hitting 18,000 revs on each upward change.

She got ready to set up her challenge.

First, she was going to cross over into Baryshnikov's slipstream – to get a tow – to take advantage of the hole the race leader's car was already punching through the air. That reduction in drag would allow her to close up even closer behind him. Then, at the last minute, she was going to make her move to overtake. She wasn't going to dive down the left-hand side, which Baryshnikov would expect into a left-hand corner – she was going out wide to the right.

Sabatino would have to time her move, though – waiting until Baryshnikov had fully committed to the corner. The moment he did, slicing left – hugging the racing line to the inside, the fastest route through the corner – Sabatino would set about going round his outside. She had no expectation of getting past Baryshnikov here – through Turn Eleven. Her aim was to get on terms with Baryshnikov by the time she emerged through the exit of this corner. If she managed that, ideally ending up side by side with him as they straightened up, Sabatino would automatically have the advantage of being on the inside line for the next turn, Turn Twelve – crucially a right-hander. *That* was where her business would get done. She would make her move to get by him – there – and take the lead.

Sabatino breathed deeply, preparing herself for the first part of her plan.

Timing was everything.

Wait!

Wait...

NOW!

Her Ptarmigan responded instantaneously. She moved straight across to the left, into the dirty air of Baryshnikov's Ptarmigan. Almost immediately she felt a reduction in drag. In no time, it allowed her to close right in – right up behind the race leader, practically able to touch Baryshnikov's rear wing. Her heart rate soared.

Two hundred metres to run.

The corner – the sweeping left-hander – was looming.

Wait!

Sabatino waited for the split-second moment to time the next part of her move. She had to see the car in front commit itself to the corner first. Only when Baryshnikov had turned in to the left-hander – and could no longer take defensive action against her manoeuvre – would she make her move.

Wait!

Wait!

What if he left it too late? She would be denied the chance – she wouldn't have enough leeway within the confines of the track.

Wait?

Baryshnikov suddenly changed direction.

Without needing to brake, he had sliced off to the left – setting himself up for the bend.

Now!

Sabatino nudged her wheel the other way. At that speed, her car instantly dived out to that side – plunging into the clear air, to the right-hand side of the car in front. The clean air should have altered the car's balance and speed.

Sabatino was hugely relieved. Her Ptarmigan's carriage, attitude and speed hardly changed; its set-up was that good. Sabatino hammered the throttle, the revs skipping repeatedly as she hit the rev limiter. That was of no concern.

Sabatino was gaining on Baryshnikov.

Trigonometrically, even without braking, his change of direction – setting up for the corner – cost him a fractional amount of forward pace. That meant Sabatino was soon well up alongside. Baryshnikov's path, now though, was diverging from hers – glancing off to the left.

One hundred metres.

Now *she* had to turn in, to set up her own line into and through Turn Eleven – round the same sweeping left-hander, although her line was going to be well to the outside.

Dominic Quartano, the corporate owner of the Ptarmigan Formula One Team, was deeply troubled. Excusing himself from the king's presence, he moved inside from *The Melita's* quarterdeck to take the call from the paddock and watch any television coverage there might be on the large HD screen in the yacht's salon.

A replay – an aerial shot of the Grand Prix circuit – was being shown, taken from a helicopter flying directly overhead. It showed the two race leaders emerging through the exit of Turn Ten: Baryshnikov in the first turquoise Ptarmigan was a handful of lengths in front, with Sabatino in the second turquoise car in P2 – both of them accelerating away into the half-mile Hermitage Straight.

'*And here we see the replay again, Ben,*' said one of the TV commentators. '*This time from above. Watch here – Sabatino is about to make her move.*'

'*Indeed, Mike. The move starts some way back. There – you can see it begin. She deliberately moves into Baryshnikov's slipstream. Once she's got herself into it, Sabatino just sits there – right up behind him – getting a really good tow.*'

'*Now we watch her – waiting to pounce.*'

'*And that's exactly what she did* – there – *you can see her dive out – to the* right – *out of Baryshnikov's dirty air.*'

'*It's a really bold stroke – going that way – out to the right, around the outside. But, at this point, it's a flawless move – as we can see, she loses none of the speed she'd been gaining from the tow.*'

'It is *a bold move.*'

'*And then we see she gets a boost to her chances* – there – *as Bary-shnikov appears to slow slightly* – *as he starts turning in to the corner.*'

'*And, of course, that gives Sabatino the invaluable chance to gain some ground.*'

In an instant, the TV producer switched camera angles. Leaving the overhead view, he cut away to a shot at ground-level – to a camera position further on round the track. This perspective offered a view back towards Turn Eleven – as seen from the far side of the corner.

For a moment, the track was clear – the producer having switched a tad too early. The leaders hadn't come into view yet.

The wait wasn't long.

The turquoise nose cone of Baryshnikov's Ptarmigan soon appeared, from the very right of the picture. It turned head-on to face the camera, hugging the inside of the sweeping left-hand corner – running down the right-hand side of the screen.

Moments later the turquoise of the second Ptarmigan's front wing also came into view – as expected – emerging from behind the first, to its outside.

But that's when viewers were taken completely by surprise.

Everyone expected Sabatino to turn head-on to the camera, turning left – to give Baryshnikov chase down the short straight, heading for the foreground of the TV picture.

Except something happened.

The second turquoise shape became a blur as it shot directly from top right to top left – flashing completely across the width of the picture and straight out of the shot to the left.

It hadn't turned at all.

Hadn't slowed at all.

The sight was surreal.

Sabatino's Ptarmigan appeared to have gone straight on … in a dead straight line. Flat out. No attempt to turn … or slow down. At all.

Sabatino had been breathing deeply. Baryshnikov, over to her left, was already hugging the apex of the bend. She braced herself for the drop-off in grip as she was about to venture out onto the dirtier part of the circuit.

Sabatino waited to time her own turn in.

Now!

She turned the steering wheel.

Her brain didn't compute.

It immediately felt odd.

There was suddenly huge resistance.

Mentally, she'd turned the wheel an eighth to the left, expecting an immediate response from the car – and to feel G-force to the right, as she was thrown to the outside of the corner.

But there was barely any change of direction.

Instinctively she tried to turn the wheel further to the left; more effort, surely, would turn the wheel.

She felt no further response from the car's front end.

The Ptarmigan was now going straight on.

Flat out.

She was doing a hundred and ninety five miles an hour.

In the blink of an eye the car was running – tangentially – to the corner. It didn't have long before it would leave the track altogether. On Sabatino's current line, there were fewer than fifty metres before she would reach the edge of the tarmac, marked by the sweeping line of red-and-white kerbstones on the outside of the corner. She hammered the brakes.

Her foot went straight to the floor.

Nothing happened.

Sabatino was now leaving the solid surface of the track.

Her Ptarmigan was still travelling at over a hundred and ninety miles an hour as she went out onto the loose surface of the gravel trap.

In horror, Sabatino lifted her eyes – extrapolating the line of her trajectory.

The scenery ahead of her was getting rapidly larger.

She turned the steering wheel again which responded on the looser surface of the gravel, giving her some left lock – a ploughing effect to offer resistance – to slow herself down.

Sabatino had her first moment of panic.

Ahead of her the bank of red-and-white tyres – stacked in front of the concrete perimeter wall – was looming. Sabatino was sensing the full effect a parachutist would recognize as ground-rush. The same zooming-in sensation applied to the three-metre-high wire mesh fence behind the tyres – and, beyond that – to the shapes and faces of hundreds of spectators lounging in the sun, spread out up the turf terraces of the grassy bank on the outside of the circuit.

Quartano saw the TV producer switch cameras again, this time back to the overhead shot from the helicopter. The tycoon was glued to the screen, along with the rest of the television audience around the world. He saw the unfolding horror of the Formula One car's failure to turn in – and the turquoise Ptarmigan going straight on at that corner.

The camera showed the Ptarmigan shoot off the course – straight across the gravel. Everybody's eyes flitted back and forth, trying to predict where the car was going, and the dreaded fulfilment of that path. People realized that – with the massive speed the car was still doing – a huge impact was unavoidable. Everyone knew deep down they shouldn't really be watching this.

It had to happen.

Wham!

The Ptarmigan smashed into the red-and-white tyre wall at a terrifyingly steep angle.

The front end of the car disintegrated instantaneously – exactly as it was meant to. Carbon fibre in the front wing was pulverized to shards, splinters and dust. The nose cone crumpled. Both suspension systems – the V-shaped wishbones supporting both front wheels – gave way, as the two bulky wheels folded inwards.

But then the real horror began.

With so much kinetic energy still undissipated, it had to go some-where. In the slow motion of the replay, TV viewers watched what seemed to be the inevitable. The Ptarmigan's crumpling nose cone was burying itself in the bottom of the tyre wall.

The energy had to spill over.

The red-and-white tyres were bulging unnaturally.

The car's nose, right in underneath them, could only then act as a pivot.

The back end started to rise.

The Ptarmigan was beginning to rotate, the rear wheels were leaving the ground.

In a split second the whole car was rotating.

It was soon passing through the vertical. At that moment, a rota-tional force developed through the car, having the effect of lifting its front end. What was left of the nose became dislodged from the bottom of the tyre wall, its former pivot point. The car was suddenly free to continue on.

It was starting to somersault.

Now, upside down, the back wheels were leading the inverted car; they were about to hit the wire mesh fence.

This should have absorbed some of the energy. Except the leading limb of the car – the upside-down-and-back-to-front right rear wheel – slammed into one of the upright "I"-sectioned girders sup-porting the three-metre mesh. This stanchion was no match for the force coming its way. Nevertheless, with the car hitting it asymmet-rically, catching only one rear wheel, the upright did put up enough resistance before buckling to spin the front end of the car – clock-wise – swinging it round horizontally and slamming it into the wire almost exactly side on. The turquoise car was now twisting. As it did so, the rear wheel that had caught the stanchion was ripped from the car, its tether snapping like cotton; bouncing off the "I"-sectioned girder, it was shot up high and fast into the air.

For a fraction of a second the mesh bowed significantly outwards.

But under the force of impact, its fastenings were ripped away from the other stanchions to either side. In a moment, the wire itself gave way too, the mesh snapping from top to bottom, whipping apart like a set of double doors being kicked violently open.

These latest forces on the Ptarmigan were not what it was designed to withstand.

Bits burst from the car in a turquoise cloud.

Tethers on the collapsed front wheels, still retaining them like swinging conkers, finally gave up the fight. Viewers saw both wheels catapulted away at frighteningly high speed, twenty-odd kilograms of wheel and brake assembly flying off – hurtling away like cannon balls. Other debris was slung from the car as the airborne Ptarmigan continued to twist and rotate. Carbon fibre – barge boards, radiator pods, large chunks of the rear wing – were all hurled outwards.

What was left of the twisting upside-down car, principally the monocoque – with the driver still inside – was also spinning like a rotor blade as it slammed into the turf at the bottom of the grassy bank. It impacted heavily with the ground. The chassis disintegrated – its components exploding outwards. The engine block broke off, tumbling away separately like a rugby ball, on up the slope.

This hillside was crammed full of spectators.

Sabatino's spinning monocoque crashed into the middle of this block of humanity. People, bodies, were crushed, caught up, rolled under and then hurled away by the rotational energy.

There was still too much momentum.

The remains of the car continued to spin on up the bank, scything down other sections of the crowd.

Finally the car came to rest.

A plume of smoke, dust and dirt billowed out from under it.

The television picture switched back to the heliborne camera. Quartano, along with every other TV viewer, could hardly believe what he was seeing.

From above, the scene on the ground was horrific.

Up the grassy bank were scattered bodies – right up to the point where the residual part of the Ptarmigan had finally came to rest.

At the top of the bank lay the remnants of Sabatino's Formula One car.

All around the wreckage were twisted human remains. From the TV shots it was impossible to count the number of bodies. It was obvious, though, that there were already multiple deaths. Men, women and children, all there to enjoy the spectacle of the Grand Prix, would not be going home.

At the left-hand end of the grass bank was the worst image of all.

Even the ratings- and award-hungry TV producer felt he could show it only once. A two-seater pushchair – along with the mother of its two occupants – was strewn across the grass. This young mother and her two toddlers were not now going home either. One of Sabatino's chunky rear wheels was sitting in the middle of this family, like a bowling ball surrounded by the pins it had just felled.

TEN

An emotional reaction was felt all around the Zhar-ptitsa circuit. Large digital screens had given every spectator an all-too clear picture of what had just happened.

The race director red-flagged the race, ending it there and then. There was no obstruction on the track, but it was obvious urgent help was going to be needed – and the quickest way of getting it there would be via the track itself. He had to keep that access clear. Most drivers reacted the moment they saw the signals, lifted off and made for the pit lane.

The director called up the emergency services. Moments later sirens could be heard blaring out.

Messages were radioed through to the circuit's dedicated air support unit. Immediate evacuation of the casualties to the pre-arranged accident and emergency facilities around Moscow would be inevitable. But normal Grand Prix emergency procedures were designed to support the evacuation and recovery of the drivers, meaning their plans allowed for two or three souls at most. Who knew how many bodies were lying injured across that bank?

The race director flipped through his CCTV feeds to confirm the remaining cars were leaving the circuit. One shot of the Hermitage Straight showed several marshals standing out on the track surface, waving red flags as cars approached the area of the accident. He was relieved to see that those drivers were taking heed.

An ambulance pulled up at the point where Sabatino had left the track. Coming to a stop a doctor and a paramedic crew jumped out. The paramedics grabbed armfuls of equipment before hurrying across the gravel trap to the puncture point in the tyre wall.

At the head of this posse the doctor, looking up, saw a scene evocative of the apocalypse. It looked like a battlefield, as if it had been rent by a bomb. Bodies were strewn right across the slope above him. He couldn't tell how many from a scan of the area. Most were motionless.

At the very top were the remains of Sabatino's car. The canoe-shaped monocoque was lying ignominiously on its side.

There was no movement from the driver, at all.

Sounds of further sirens could be heard approaching from different directions. In a matter of minutes, upwards of thirty medical staff and paramedics were crossing the gravel, converging on the accident.

In race control, the director made and took a continuous stream of calls and radio messages, coordinating the emergency services and the vital help that would be needed on the ground.

Twelve minutes after the crash, a high-pitched whine could be heard. A light helicopter – an air ambulance – was banking steeply over the river, losing height, and hovering in above the trees. It was looking to put down – on the track at the end of the Hermitage Straight – as close as it could get to the scene.

At the crash site, the FIA doctor – Patrick Fairfax – called to a young nurse and asked her to follow him. Carrying an aluminium case, he ran up the bank, leading her towards what was left of Sabatino's car – lying on its side. The doctor knelt beside the monocoque.

He tried to talk to Sabatino.

There was no reply.

Was she unconscious?

Dead?

Urgently Fairfax looked for signs of life. From his pocket, he ripped out his stethoscope and, with extreme care – without wanting to rock her head, for fear of exacerbating any possible neck or spinal injuries – tried to press the diaphragm against her chest. It was not straightforward: her whole body was hanging sideways from the car and there were layers of clothes between the device and her body.

Fairfax heard nothing.

He moved the diaphragm to another part of her chest.

Lower down the bank, another doctor and accompanying gang of medics were clambering through the remains of the concrete wall. This man instructed the paramedics to carry out immediate assessments of all the injuries. A senior nurse was nominated to triage the findings to be sure that clear priorities were set between the injured. On her findings, the remaining medical staff would be deployed to attend the most urgent cases. Splitting up, the paramedics spread out and went straight to work.

Fairfax finally heard something from Sabatino. The faintest of rasps.

Could he be sure? There was a considerable noise all around him – moaning, shouting, vehicle engines, sirens and the helicopter.

Fairfax moved the diaphragm again. She was alive! He said to the nurse: 'We're going to need to turn the wreckage over. Call for help, quickly!'

Several medics responded, running up the hill towards them.

Fairfax was surveying the car and its immediate surroundings. As the help closed in, he directed one of them to his aluminium case. 'Grab a neck brace, will you?'

A moment later he instructed the nurse: 'Hold her head still.'

Extremely carefully, Fairfax tried to feed the plastic restraint up under her neck and then feed the straps round the back of her head. It wasn't going to be anywhere near satisfactory. The FIA doctor quickly addressed the other medics who had just converged. He asked three of them to come and help lift on his side, while urgently directing another four to stand on the other, ready to steady and lower the car once they managed to roll it.

A whine of a turbine engine could be heard overhead. Fairfax looked up. Another helicopter had appeared. This one, though, was from the state-controlled TV company – and there to film the after-math of the crash.

Fairfax bawled: 'Fucking parasites. One of you … go and grab some kind of screen – a tarpaulin, a blanket, sheet, anything.'

Fairfax turned his attention back to Sabatino. On his cue, the six medics attempted to roll what little remained of the Ptarmigan, while Fairfax and the nurse, together, held Sabatino's head and the precari-ous brace, trying to protect her neck against any sharp movement.

Slowly, the car was righted.

A stretcher was brought up and laid on the ground alongside.

One medic made to undo her harness, while another tried to position himself – astride the car where the air intake used to be – gently pushing his hands down behind Sabatino's shoulders, looking for purchase under her armpits. The intent was to try and lift her free of the cockpit.

A sheet had been found. It was held tight by a medic at each corner to form a canopy over the heads of the other medics and the stretcher. Some privacy, at least, could now be afforded against the prying camera circling overhead.

More arms came forward to help support Sabatino's weight as her completely limp body emerged from the car. Six people were needed to extract her from the cockpit. Coordinated by Fairfax, she was finally lifted away from the monocoque and laid down gently onto the stretcher. Awkwardly, the canopy was moved at the same time to try and keep the operation screened from above.

The doctor instructed one of Sabatino's sleeves be removed, to clear the way for a drip. As the inside of her elbow was exposed, the nurse swabbed Sabatino's skin and made to insert a cannula.

Sabatino suddenly stiffened.

And then started juddering.

Violently.

Uncontrollably.

Fairfax dived down and carefully lifted her visor. Peering through the gap, he instantly saw something in the muscles of Sabatino's face.

'She's hypoxic,' he declared urgently but calmly, 'she's swallowed her tongue.' Except that with her helmet still on, and the risk of spinal injury, there was no way he could get to her mouth. 'Get me a scalpel, a trachie tube, gloves, a load of sterilizing wipes. Bring the suction in close … quick!'

Another nurse dived into Fairfax's aluminium case, and extracted a knife. As he took it from her, the nurse asked him: 'Where's the tube?'

Over his shoulder he said: 'Under the tray to the left. Can you work the suction?'

Fairfax, bending back down over the convulsing body, had to remove the neck brace he had just fitted and was now slashing through Sabatino's clothes around her neck and throat – through the turquoise of her overalls and then the white balaclava under-neath. He reached bare skin. Shouting: 'Sterilize!' he held up the gloved fingers of his left hand. Seconds later, a nurse rubbed them down with a sterilizing wipe. Once clean, Fairfax returned that hand to Sabatino's neck and held back the cloth of the balaclava with the fingers of his left hand. Leaning in close to find the right spot, he positioned the scalpel on Sabatino's neck and plunged it straight down and through into her windpipe before slicing firmly down-wards. Using the gloved fingers of his left hand, he stuck them into the wound and splayed them – to hold open the gash he had just made through her throat.

Rasping sounds and short sprays of blood indicated that Saba-tino was now breathing safely through the emergency tracheotomy. Fairfax saw her chest moving up and down.

'Suction!' he shouted.

The nurse handed Fairfax the end of the pump. The doctor quickly stuck it through the gash in Sabatino's neck and tried to extract the blood and any mucous in her windpipe. Handing the suction pump away, he said: 'Trachie?'

A hand appeared holding the tracheotomy tube. Fairfax leant down and, still holding the wound open with the fingers of his left hand, fed the tube down into Sabatino's windpipe.

'She's breathing again,' he declared. 'Can we give her oxygen?'

A short supply was rigged up and the mask placed over Sabatino's throat.

Fairfax had several foam blocks placed and strapped around Sabatino's head to stop any movement in her neck, not knowing what might be broken.

'Right. Let's get her down to the chopper.'

On his command, the stretcher was lifted, the mask kept over her throat and the drip held and carried directly over her arm. All the while, the stretcher party was shielded from above by the sheet held over their heads, supported by a medic at each corner.

The stricken Formula One driver was carried down the grassy bank. Each foot had to be placed carefully; the slope being covered in bodies, body parts, and uneven ground cut up by the impact.

The stretcher reached the edge of the track surface. All this time the helicopter's engine had continued to run, its rotors still turning. It was standing no more than fifty yards away. Sabatino was carried quickly towards it and lifted aboard. Fairfax handed the oxygen mask and the drip up to one of the medics already in the aircraft, before climbing in himself.

The pilot lifted the helicopter into the air. In a matter of seconds it was heading for the circuit's designated emergency hospital, four miles away across Moscow.

Sabatino had been kept alive so far. Her medical support team, though, had no idea of her injuries, let alone any damage she might have sustained to her brain.

ELEVEN

Quartano watched the coverage in the saloon of *The Melita*, stunned by the ferocity of the crash.

He switched the feed to show picture-in-picture; Dr Nazar's face appeared in a window to the bottom right of the screen: 'Tahm,' he said to the caller, 'I'm so sorry – this is awful.'

Quartano, still casting an eye on the main television image, saw a change of shot away from the endless replays of the accident – to an overhead view of the crash site. An army of medics could now be seen swarming across the grassy bank tending the injured. Exactly what was going on, though, was not clear: a number of white tents had been erected, shielding the scene from prying eyes.

In his precise Indian lilt, the principal of the Ptarmigan Formula One Team replied: 'It is quite dreadful. Modern F1 doesn't *have* ghastly accidents like this.'

'How many people are injured?'

Tahm Nazar went quiet. 'There are no official figures. Rumours have it twenty-five are dead.'

'God have mercy.'

'There's no hard news, though.'

'And Remy? How's Remy?'

'We've had it from Race Control – she's been given an emergency tracheotomy.'

'At the hospital?'

'At the crash site.'

'Jesus,' exhaled Quartano. 'I'm going to send you the best medical care. Let me know as soon as you can what she needs. Please report back hour by hour.'

'Of course, DQ. For now, though, I think we're okay. Everyone's stated without reservation that the medical team at the designated hospital is world class.'

'Even so ... what's likely to happen next?'

'No one has a clue. There's pandemonium here.'

'Surely there's a pre-set contingency plan?'

'Indeed – the FIA has called the team bosses to an emergency meeting.'

'But?'

'The scale of this calamity has thrown everyone. No plan caters for twenty-five dead spectators. Counterproductively, the local authority is openly doubting the FIA's ability to handle the crisis management – and so has called its own emergency meeting, which doesn't bode well.'

Quartano grunted. 'Why's that?'

'Because both emergency meetings have been scheduled for the same time in different places.'

'Someone's got to get a grip.'

'They have, which is why – even after such a short time – the call's gone out to the FIA president. San Marino's flying in from Helsinki; should be here in a couple of hours.'

'Well if anyone can hold this together ... Presumably there'll be an investigation; has any formal announcement been made, yet?'

'No, it's still far too chaotic. There's an FIA press conference scheduled for eight o'clock, Moscow time, this evening.'

'Which ought to provide some focus.'

'Except no one can agree on what should be said.'

'Keep me posted: let me know whatever you need. The whole of Quartech is at your disposal.'

'Thank you, DQ; very reassuring. I'll go and participate in the disaster management in any way I can. I'll report back soonest.'

Four miles from the Grand Prix circuit, and now hovering above the car park of the Yeltsin Medical Centre, the helicopter carrying the still-unconscious Remy Sabatino was setting up to land.

Squinting against the downdraught as the aircraft began to put down, a team of white-tunicked medics stood to the side of the car park with a trolley, ready waiting. The helicopter landed on the asphalt and its side doors were slid open.

The hospital's medical team closed in. Sabatino's stretcher was lifted and slid onto the gurney. She was still in her helmet and racing gear. Dr Fairfax was carrying the drip above her right elbow while, with his other hand, he held the oxygen mask as securely as he could manage over the hole in Sabatino's throat.

At the run, the trolley was pushed across the smooth surface of the car park. The main doors of the hospital were being held open. Sabatino was rolled straight through – into the reception area – where a consultant was already waiting to receive the casualty.

Dr Fairfax introduced himself, handing over the drip, mask and pump to the hospital nurses; he explained what had happened, what he had found at the crash scene and what he had administered. Without delay, Mr Pyotr Uglov – the senior trauma consultant in the Yeltsin Medical Centre – issued instructions to several of his staff, and the stricken Formula One driver was rushed away towards the lifts. Before leaving to follow on, Uglov told Fairfax that Sabatino would be taken straight into their emergency assessment room.

Before the lift doors had even shut, Uglov began to assess his patient. While peering through her visor and shining a penlight into each eye, he asked for a pulse.

He was told it was fast and thready.

A nurse was placing an oximeter clip over one of the fingers of her left hand; its wires were quickly plugged into a portable monitor allowing Uglov to gauge the oxygenation of her blood.

It was low, despite the oxygen supplied through the mask.

The consultant leant down and examined Fairfax's emergency tracheotomy. Her airway was still open. There was a significant amount of blood. He asked the person now carrying the pump to suck out what they could.

The hole in her neck, though, was at least allowing Sabatino to breathe.

As the lift doors opened, the trolley party burst out and charged through a set of double doors – also being held open – straight into the assessment room. Immediately it came to a stop inside, the consultant gave his team the go-ahead to execute the tasks he had allocated beforehand.

From different directions, medical staff closed in on Sabatino. Most were carrying scissors, ready to cut through Sabatino's clothes – to clear the way for further examination. One of the first cuts went the length of Sabatino's front, exposing the skin of her chest and abdomen. Self-adhesive tabs were peeled from the backs of ECG electrodes. These were then applied with care – allowing for possible broken ribs – around her heart and lungs. Leads were connected to each of the electrodes and then to the central monitor; before long a beep could be heard marking out her heartbeat.

It was fast and weak.

Another cut was made through her left sleeve. Sabatino's arm was deformed. The skin of her other arm was exposed instead. A nurse fed a blood pressure gauge underneath it. That was wired up to a monitor and its readings, too, were announced to the room.

Sabatino's blood pressure was disturbingly low.

A circular power saw was fired up. One medic held the driver's head steady while its operator sliced through Sabatino's helmet, trying to free her without causing any more damage. Immediately it was away, Uglov examined her mouth, opened her jaw and inserted his fingers to reposition her tongue.

'Pass me the airway.'

Handed a Guedel device, the consultant used the plastic tube to reposition her tongue. It was possible to hear the effect almost at once; the rasping noise through her tracheotomy ceased. Her natural airway was clear again. Sabatino was back to breathing "unaided".

Rather than rely on her natural breathing, though, Uglov decided to keep the artificial airway open, just in case. He secured the tracheotomy tube by applying tapes around the back of the driver's neck.

Sabatino was rendered completely naked. Uglov conducted a systematic examination, looking for obvious wounds and injuries. But he wanted clarity on what internal injuries Sabatino might have suffered. Uglov ordered that she be wheeled off for a full-body scan.

At that moment, at least, the Formula One driver was still alive. Just.

Out on the grassy bank, the swarm of medical personnel were attending the injuries of the spectators. More sirens could be heard approaching the crash site. Four vehicles pulled up on the outside of the Hermitage corner. These, too, were showing blue flashing lights, but they weren't ambulances.

From the leading police car a tall thin man in his early forties climbed from the passenger seat. Short blond hair showed beneath his dark-blue and scarlet peaked cap. Police Colonel Arseny Pudovkin's eyes were set high in his face, and, with such prominent cheekbones, the lower part of his face seemed to bow inwards. They did so to a thin, humourless mouth. His rugged expression, projected naturally by his face, was a large part of Pudovkin's command and control. He wore a pale blue uniform with flashes of scarlet and two gold stars on each shoulder. A 9mm Makarov semi-automatic pistol was holstered on his left hip. In his right hand, Police Colonel Pudovkin carried a bullhorn. Other policemen climbed from their cars and converged on the colonel. He conducted a short briefing. Pudovkin's orders were issued crisply and confidently. Then he gave the word.

His team fanned out.

The colonel raised the bullhorn to his lips, and, pointing the loudspeaker in the direction of the people on the crash site above him, announced:

'This is the Moscow Police. Be informed that this is now a crime scene. Do not touch anything – remove anything – *without* official police authorization.'

To the medics this was outrageous: how could they provide their best care if they could not spontaneously move the injured?

Several lines of blue-and-white tape were quickly unrolled – encircling the area of the crash and the working medics. This was then suspended at waist-height on a series of four-foot plastic poles driven into the ground.

In no time at all, a police cordon had been imposed around them. The Grand Prix crash site had been impounded.

TWELVE

Within moments of the crash, the death toll among the spectators was estimated at twenty-five. With no official denial or confirmation, this number soon became fact. That number, alone, sent the media around the world into a state of frenzy. As a story, this tragedy had everything sensation-hungry news channels could want: A spectacular crash. A world-name celebrity. A dramatic heliborne evacuation. Graphic scenes of devastation and damage. And an already-high but very-possibly rising body count. Correspondents were rapidly dispatched to Moscow, not just by news outlets within Russia but also from across the world.

Television and radio editors were having a field day. To supplement their reports and bulletins, they set about raiding their archives. Every crash throughout the history of Formula One, Le Mans, IndyCar, NASCAR and rallying was worked into the coverage of the unfolding tragedy at the Zhar-ptitsa Autodrom in Moscow. Commentators drew parallels with Ayrton Senna's crash at the Tamburello in 1994. The grotesque conclusion was that, already, the Moscow crash was somehow worse, because spectators had been killed. The 1986 Group B Portuguese Rally and even the Pierre Levegh catastrophe at Le Mans in 1955 were cited. Wolfgang Von Trips's crash at Monza – when fifteen spectators had been killed in 1961 – was considered the closest parallel in the history of Formula One. There was an alarming common denominator to all these disasters, though. There seemed to be an assumption – in referencing these particular crashes – that Sabatino was already dead.

Coverage of the Russian Grand Prix story quickly became all that anyone could talk about.

Fuelling the frenzy was the absence of any public response from the FIA, the venue or the local authority. After an hour, when the first cycle of the news channels had been completed, the television stations were screaming for new commentary and observations. With no new official facts, the inevitable speculation started. Everything about Formula One began to be discussed and criticized – from its governance, its safety regime, to the greed of high-profile businessmen involved with the sport. In hardly any time at all, the media were able to draw an unshakeable conclusion: that Formula One had, for a long time, been an accident waiting to happen.

Long before the press conference – scheduled for eight o'clock that evening – journalists were congregating in the principal ZiL Ballroom inside the main grandstand of the Zhar-ptitsa complex. Fifteen hundred people were crammed into this room. The press corps didn't want to miss out and so were getting in early, to set up well ahead of time. The news hyenas were waiting for something to kick off the next bout of the feeding frenzy.

Within the Autodrom complex, a number of ad hoc meetings were called that afternoon. The two meetings – hosted by the FIA and the local authority – went ahead despite clashing with each other, meaning that neither was attended by a critical mass of the necessary stakeholders. Within the FIA meeting there was much discussion among the powers that be. Divergent ideas came from the FIA, the commercial rights holder and the F1 teams. All seemed completely fazed. In very short order, every discussion became rambling and inconclusive.

Formula One had never had to deal with such a disaster before. It had had its tragedies and losses, but those were mainly confined to its own kind. Never in living F1 history had so many members of the public been hurt. Heated arguments failed to conclude what their response to this tragedy should be, or decide any course of action. One unproductive exchange concerned the press statement and what the sport should be saying. All the discussion, though, was on what it *shouldn't* say. Several stakeholders declared that any indication of remorse would be construed as an admission of guilt, and therefore an admission of liability. Others countered vehemently that, with an understanding that twenty-*six* people were now thought to have been killed, they had to express regret, surely?

Next, they tried to decide what they should announce by way of an investigation. Should they be inviting an independent enquiry, or would they handle a review internally? How would that, though, play with the public? Would it be enough?

Finally, there was considerable agitation over who should front the press conference. This issue was so sensitive – and clearly invoking such emotion – that everyone realized it would need someone with a huge stage presence and gravitas to project the right response. Few of the normally publicity-hungry figures in the sport were keen to step forward. Ironically, there soon developed a readiness to defer to an individual with whom most of them would normally disagree fiercely.

The Marquis of San Marino, the president of the FIA, was already flying in to Russia that afternoon. As head of the governing body, and therefore the organization that set the rules, he was usually seen as a dampener on the other stakeholders' interests: safety cost money; new limitations on the cars and teams, as set out in the Formula, all cost them money; even the attempt to broaden the sport, making it accessible for smaller teams to compete – by influencing the distribution of the proceeds from the TV and sponsorship rights via the Concorde Agreement – cost the bigger teams money. Consequently, the FIA president was typically seen as a negative influence – as a brake on the other stakeholders' commercial interests and freedoms.

But not today.

All such resentments were readily yielded to the authority and soothing power of this patrician figure.

By special arrangement, San Marino landed at the corporately owned Ostafyevo International Airport, not far from the Autodrom. A car was waiting for him there, as was a team of local police outriders.

Whisked through the Sunday afternoon traffic, San Marino

arrived at the Zhar-ptitsa circuit just after six o'clock that evening and asked, without stopping to freshen up, eat or drink, to be taken straight to the room where his FIA team was meeting.

Looking like a 1950s film star, he walked in among the baying rabble of motor racing's key players. Almost instantaneously the mood changed. The room quietened as all eyes turned to him.

In a matter of minutes, San Marino laid out clearly what was needed – how it should be handled and, most importantly, who had responsibility for doing what.

At precisely eight o'clock that evening, the 7th Marquis of San Marino walked into the thronging ZiL Ballroom within the Zhar-ptitsa complex and mounted the dais. He was hit with dozens of bright halogen lights from the bank of TV cameras along the back wall, a stroboscopic barrage of flash guns, as well as a crescendo of voices.

San Marino walked over to stand behind the lectern. He was partially blocked from view by the mountain of microphones secured to each other with gaffer tape. Before speaking, San Marino had the presence to look out into the faces of the multitude: journalists, photographers, sound recordists, cameras and cameramen. To each side, the aisles were six deep with people on their feet.

Appearing completely composed, the president of the FIA – without reference to notes – prepared to address the room. As he removed his half-moon spectacles, the noise levels dropped.

'Motor racing's first response to this horrible afternoon,' he said in English with his soft Italian accent, 'is to look the people of Moscow and Russia in the eye and apologize. We – all of us in Formula One – are devastated by the hurt we have caused to this city. This was *not* what anyone was expecting when you graciously invited us and our sport to come here.

'Our second response is to state that, without reservation, all of us involved in the sport will participate fully in any enquiry called to investigate this tragedy. As a starting point, I undertake to conduct a full enquiry within the International Automobile Federation, appointing independent experts to assess this accident. I am keen to make it clear that, as its president, I will readily surrender the FIA's jurisdiction and powers to any inquiry launched by the Russian people.'

Flashguns were fired in repeated fusillades as thousands of pictures were taken.

San Marino did not want to say more than necessary, for fear of appearing to pad the response or to be waffling, either of which could be construed as evasion or obfuscation. He had already said all he wanted.

Respectfully the room fell silent.

At first.

'How many deaths has Formula One caused?'

'Is Ptarmigan going to compensate the deceased families?'

'Is the FIA going to pay for this?'

'The FIA has failed the Russian people on safety standards – do you expect to keep your job?'

'Are people going to be prosecuted because of this?'

'Can you stay on as president after this?'

'When will you resign?'

'Will you be going to jail?'

San Marino held up his hand. 'Ladies and gentlemen, I have said what I came to say. It is far too early to know what will come out of this. We have to conduct a full investigation first, and then – depending on the facts – draw *informed* conclusions. Only then will we be able to decide what action to take. Anyone found responsible for this tragedy will be held to account. And, yes,' he said firmly, 'if I am considered to have been at fault then, of course, I shall resign.'

Such self-responsibility came as a shock. To most journalists there, more used to dealing with politicians who were far more likely to pass the buck, hearing someone in a privileged position discuss their own future so candidly was a real surprise. Such openness from the FIA president seemed to earn him a considered silence in response.

San Marino used the ensuing calmness to reinforce the authenticity of his presence in the room. Lowering his voice he added: 'Thank you for your time and patience. I intend to talk to you again on a regular basis,' with which he bowed and made a dignified exit.

To everyone's surprise, there was no baying from the room as the president of the FIA left the conference.

Maybe – just maybe – his dignity had calmed the press corps down.

Whatever comfort the Formula One world may have taken from San Marino's handling of the press conference, its effects were all-too short-lived.

THIRTEEN

Sensing the mood of the people's response to the tragedy at Zhar-ptitsa, one individual saw a significant political opportunity. President Tarkovsky, head of state of the Russian Federation, chose to go on television that night and make a statement to the nation.

Broadcasting live at 9 p.m. – deliberately after San Marino's press conference earlier that same evening – the high-cheekboned, Easter-Island features of this lowborn Cossack appeared, face to camera. Supposedly Kennedyesque, he was sitting at his desk in the Kremlin; behind him were the flags of the Russian Federation and the double-headed eagle. The president seemed overly dressed for the part. He wore an outsized black necktie, a dark suit, a sombre-coloured shirt and a very obvious black armband. Most strikingly, the president had a conspicuous lack of TV make-up – to convey the pallor of someone who was still immersed in heartfelt mourning.

Tarkovsky addressed the nation, appearing as crestfallen as Tony Blair had achieved for his "People's Princess" speech.

Tragedy had fallen on Russia.

It was hard to come to terms with such a devastating loss.

There was a message here for the nation.

The country was getting what it deserved: certain people in Moscow had been seduced by glamorous, glitzy things. *Western* things. These people were too ambitious. Too prepared to cut corners. He, their president, undertook to root them out.

Anyone connected with this tragedy was going to pay for bringing hurt to Russia, hurt to Russian citizens.

'Wrongdoing *will* be punished,' he declared solemnly.

He ended the broadcast by stating that he, personally, understood Russia's need to grieve. Consequently, he was announcing a two-day period of official mourning, and that he would represent the nation at a service of remembrance. He had asked for this to be held in the Cathedral of Christ the Saviour. Whatever the cost, he declared, Russia would honour their dead.

'Immediately thereafter,' the president stated sternly, 'I will not stop until those responsible for these deaths have been identified and punished.'

The trauma consultant, Mr Pyotr Uglov, was troubled by two of his findings from the emergency examination of Remy Sabatino. The F1 driver had broken her left ankle and wrist, but these were relatively straightforward injuries and weren't going to present too much of a problem; Uglov ordered that these breaks be set without delay. Several issues emerged from the X-rays and full-body CT scan; the trauma specialist inferred that Sabatino had two serious complications. He was troubled by a severe swelling in the right-frontal lobe of her brain, while he was particularly concerned by a marked shadow across both C1 and C2 vertebrae – suggesting she'd suffered severe compression or torsion damage to her neck.

At great length, Uglov studied all the three-dimensional scans, focusing especially on those of the bones, ligaments and tendons of her spine. He was anxious that none of these injuries be allowed to deteriorate. His preference was to immobilize Sabatino's neck to give her injuries a better chance to heal.

Uglov's other concern focused on any adverse reaction from the patient, should Sabatino surface unexpectedly and in all likelihood start writhing in discomfort; such forces could well complicate the healing process. Uglov's software solution to manage Sabatino's recovery was a mix of fluids – painkillers, diamorphine and a sedative, all administered via the cannula. His hardware solution would have been to fit a neck brace – to immobilize the top half of her body, particularly her neck – except that his preferred device could cause problems of its own; it could even exacerbate the swelling in her skull.

Despite the risks, Uglov did decide to proceed.

It was going to take eight people to fit the thing to the still-unconscious driver.

Six orbital pins on a plane above her eyes were screwed into Sabatino's skull. Then, the circular metal band – the halo – around her head was fitted and bolted to the orbital pins. Five people were needed to lift Sabatino's torso, keeping her spine and neck straight throughout. Uglov fed the back plate of the brace underneath her. Laying Sabatino's head, neck and shoulders back down, the front plate of the brace – resembling body armour – was then laid on her chest and locked with butterfly nuts to the back plate down each flank. Four long rods were fastened to the halo band; these were then aligned with the lugs on the vest, anchored, and bolted rigid. Sabatino's head, neck and shoulders were now completely immobile.

Mr Uglov, with further studies of the exhaustive X-rays, scans and test reports, was satisfied that after the setting of her broken bones and the precautionary use of the halo brace, he had fulfilled his immediate responsibilities to the patient.

Sabatino was wheeled out of the emergency assessment ward and into the intensive care unit, in which she would be monitored – indefinitely – twenty-four hours a day.

Eight hours on from the horrific crash, though, and being kept in an artificial coma via a cocktail of drugs, she had yet to regain consciousness.

There was still no understanding of Sabatino's mental condition.

FOURTEEN

Throughout the night, coverage of the disaster continued to run on Russian television and radio. That exposure, and the repeated clips from the president's national address, made the loss of life that the country had suffered its only focus of attention. All of which contributed to the memorial service becoming that much more poignant; within an hour of its announcement, a crowd was gathering on the streets and pavements around the cathedral.

The high pressure system which had brought the recent summer weather to Moscow meant that the skies above the city were cloudless. While pleasant in the daytime, the same weather system made for cold nights and cool mornings. Which seemed particularly fitting. A chill in the air for that day, of all days, matched the mood around Moscow. It matched the crispness of people's behaviour, attitude and conduct: the atmosphere around the city was almost febrile. Twenty-seven Muscovites, so far, had been slain at the Grand Prix. A feeling of shock continued to pervade Moscow: the whole of Russia was angry.

Overnight, barriers were erected to cordon off the approaches to the Cathedral of Christ the Saviour. Long before most of the city awoke, there was a massive police presence on the streets – deemed necessary from a security perspective. This service was to be held in the heart of political Moscow, a kilometre from Red Square, the Kremlin – the seat of government. Law and order had to be maintained, however distressed the public mood might be. Crowds could not be allowed to get out of hand.

The Cathedral of Christ the Saviour had icing-sugar white walls, the ubiquitous gold-leaf covered onion-shaped dome, four smaller gold domes on their own towers in each corner, and a wealth of baroque flourishes. Apart from its ecclesiastical purposes, this was probably more of a cathedral to the spirit of the Russian people than it was to religion. Its existence, today, owed nothing to the Tsars, and nothing to the godless communists – but almost everything to people power. Built to declare Imperial Russia's gratitude for its survival against Napoleon in 1812, Stalin had ordered the cathedral to be destroyed and replaced by a Palace of the Soviets to glorify Lenin. As a fitting metaphor for communism, the ruined church was never replaced, the regime soon running out of funds. Khrushchev, the populist peasant, turned the flooded foundations of the sacred ruin into the world's largest open-air swimming pool. In the end it wasn't imperial grandiosity or a flawed ideology that preserved this icon; it was people power. After *Perestroika*, a million ordinary Muscovites chipped in to build a replica of the original, resulting in the cathedral becoming more of a monument to the people of Russia than either tyranny or religion had ever managed.

Throughout the morning, additional crowds and invited attendees arrived for the service. Guests made their way up the steps into the church. Among them was a group who seemed particularly ill at ease: the public mood had rounded on Formula One – the sport being held indirectly responsible for what had happened. One of their own had been in the accident which had killed twenty-seven spectators. Far from making a show of being there, the motor racing fraternity were induced to walk inconspicuously into the church, and to be conspicuously solemn.

To Ptarmigan personnel, such feelings of awkwardness were all the more keenly felt. Tahm Nazar, the team principal, felt it right to offer his team's sympathy to the guests. Offering his moral support, Andy Backhouse, as one of the team's race engineers, was anxious to stand with Nazar as he did so. Before the expected start of the service, the two Ptarmigan men chose to position themselves by the main door of the church.

Nazar said to Backhouse: 'I am keen we are visible, but do not want us to appear as any kind of receiving line or welcoming party. Any such appearance would convey entirely the wrong intention.'

Backhouse, looking apprehensive, nodded his approval.

'By the way,' added Nazar in his clipped Indian accent, 'where's Yegor?'

Backhouse looked around. 'I did ask him to be here.'

By the time the mourners were arriving there was still no sign of Ptarmigan's second driver.

Some arrivals, recognizing the Ptarmigan boss, were harsh in their remarks. One walked up to Nazar and spat straight into his face. Nazar did not waver.

At ten o'clock that morning, a large motorcade of black official-looking cars crawled into view along the cleared streets. They processed slowly, pulling up in front of the cathedral. Waiting on the steps to meet the leading car was a Russian Orthodox priest sporting a huge beard and solemn but spectacular robes and headdress. A rear door of the first limousine was opened from the outside by an SBP bodyguard. The president of Russia emerged. A respectful ripple of applause came from the crowds all around the barriers. He acknowledged this reception with a wave of a hand.

Within the motorcade were twenty-seven hearses. As they pulled up, several hysterical shrieks came from the crowds. At the same time, a more modest outpouring of grief began, spreading wider and becoming louder as an army of pall-bearers carried the coffins up the steps, each draped in the Russian flag.

Before the president followed the deceased into the cathedral, a commotion could be heard in front of the main entrance.

A number of policemen had suddenly appeared from inside the church.

Tahm Nazar and Andy Backhouse were still standing by the main doors, preparing to pay their respects to the bodies of the fallen as well as the approaching Russian president.

But that wasn't going to happen.

Police Colonel Arseny Pudovkin, leading the police posse, marched out from inside the cathedral, stood in front of the

Ptarmigan representatives and stated in a heavily accented but comprehensible English:

'Dr Tahm Nazar, I am arresting you – as the head of the Ptarmigan Formula One Team – for the corporate manslaughter of twenty-seven Russian citizens at the Moscow Grand Prix.'

Several burly policemen moved forwards and manhandled Nazar. They slapped handcuffs on him, forcing his hands behind his back. Seconds later they were frogmarching him off the threshold of the church.

Within moments of this commotion, the president broke from the priest with whom he had been walking up the steps of the cathedral and moved across to the barriers on one side – making directly for the bank of television cameras.

There, the president stated: 'I can announce the arrest of the team principal of the Ptarmigan Formula One Team for the corporate manslaughter of our brethren. A charge of corporate manslaughter will also be made against Ms Remy Sabatino, if or when she is fit enough to stand trial. I made a vow to the Russian people,' said the president firmly, 'to make those responsible for our loss pay for this tragedy. I promised you an investigation into this calamity when I spoke to you on television. I declare, now, that it has started. I will hold responsible for this tragedy everyone from the direct culprits, right up to the mayor of Moscow – on whose initiative this catastrophe came to this glorious city.'

Sirens and blue flashing lights were unmissable as numerous police cars hurtled down Komsomolskiy Prospekt. They pulled into the grounds of the Yeltsin Meditsinskiy Tsentr. Climbing out of the leading car, the same police officer – Police Colonel Arseny Pudovkin – strode in through the main entrance of the hospital. There to meet him as previously arranged over the phone from police headquarters was the hospital's general manager as well as the senior medical officer responsible for the individual in question, Mr Pyotr Uglov. Pudovkin presented these two men with a folder of official papers. A court order declared that the hospital was to hold one of its patients, Remy Sabatino, under arrest as she was being formally charged with corporate manslaughter. The hospital was ordered to take on custodial responsibility while she was under their care. Pudovkin called forward four of his officers and, without any consultation, commanded them to continue on into the hospital.

Within five minutes – and standing outside the intensive care unit where Remy Sabatino was being kept in an artificial coma – a security cordon around the injured Formula One driver had been mounted by armed police.

FIFTEEN

After the indignity of his public arrest at the cathedral, Nazar was subjected to further ignominy. A black police van – with no windows – was waiting to receive him in a side street by the church. The Ptarmigan officer was bundled into the back, and the doors slammed shut; he was granted no more grace than if he had been an animal herded into a cattle truck.

Nazar had to brace himself in the back of the van as it sped off; he was hurled about inside as it swung round several corners.

After twelve minutes it came to an abrupt stop, throwing Nazar forwards.

The rear doors were flung open, banging back hard against the sides of the van. A supervizing police major stood in the yard at the rear of the vehicle and ordered him out.

Frogmarched once again, Nazar was manoeuvred into the rear of the Moscow Police HQ off Petrovka Ulitsa. Inside, the Ptarmigan boss was jostled down a flight of stairs to an interview room, in the basement of the building.

Nazar tried to focus on how to handle this. The stakes in this accident had suddenly become alarming high. He realized he was going to need serious assistance.

An unknown officer barged into Nazar's room. Equally abruptly, he barked at the detainee, appearing to be collecting basic personal data. Nazar cooperated until the questionnaire seemed to be completed.

'It is common courtesy,' replied Nazar, 'to offer an arrestee a phone call. Please will you ask the officer in charge if I may make mine?'

The police officer left without acknowledging the request.

Nazar was left isolated for over an hour before another policeman entered Nazar's interview room. This one stayed for a matter of seconds. Nazar made the same request of a phone call to him.

But got no response.

Dominic Quartano, remaining aboard his yacht in the Solent, received news of the arrests in Moscow from a contact at the Foreign and Commonwealth Office. He was outraged. Asking the caller to stay on the line, Quartano dressed quickly, left his cabin and made for his office on the upper deck. Set up as a global command centre, this facility was kitted out with every data- and communication link for him to stay in immediate touch with all Quartech International's business interests wherever *The Melita* was in the world.

A diffuse sun poured in through the large windows. Sheltered water between the Isle of Wight and the south coast of England looked remarkably calm in the early morning mist.

Turning on the bank of flat screens around his office, Quartano tuned each one to a different channel. There was no shortage of coverage. Yesterday's blanket-style broadcasts were continuing. On one of the channels Quartano saw the footage of his Formula One Team's principal being frogmarched away from the cathedral. It was a clear humiliation, making him appear to look like a common criminal. Nazar's arrest was just the sort of dramatic turn to give editors a feeling that Christmas had come early. Big business and powerful people being held to account; all this was a tabloid-minded editor's wet dream.

'Why was that despicable show even necessary?' seethed Quartano.

'For effect,' stated the Foreign Office caller. 'Ptarmigan – Dr Nazar – have been deliberately humiliated … as a way of the State demonstrating its authority.'

'What more do you know about the charges?'

'Dom, we've now heard from the Consulate in Moscow. Dr Nazar and Ms Sabatino have been charged with corporate manslaughter.'

'Christ.'

'I have to say, though, that we are surprised.'

'Why's that?'

'It's a new offence in Russia. No one's been charged with it before.'

'And the penalties?'

'Unlimited fine … and up to twenty years' hard labour.'

'What?' replied Quartano. 'In *this* day and age?'

'I'm afraid so, Dom. We never cease to be amazed by how backward some parts of the world still are.'

Quartano flicked through a few more channels. One of the news outlets had clearly discovered the sanctions available to the Russian courts; it was revelling in their severity, particularly the shock value, having found numerous clips of library footage. One of these showed vast expanses of empty steppe which it showed under the caption "Siberia", while another showed prisoners in a quarry somewhere breaking rocks with hand-held hammers. Adding to the editor's desired impact, the lags appeared unwashed, long-haired and completely desolate.

Quartano said calmly: 'Gerald, I need your help to speak with my people there.'

At the Yeltsin Meditsinskiy Tsentr, armed policemen were guarding Remy Sabatino around the clock. Even Mr Uglov had to show his pass to the two policemen standing outside her door. He loathed this heavy handedness. Despite his objections, Uglov didn't show any dissent in his demeanour, complying fully with police orders. News getting back to the oligarchs at the centre of government that the hospital did anything less than cooperate fully could easily affect budgets, promotions, position, privileges – pretty much everything. No institution in Russia could afford to sour its relations with the federal authorities.

Once through the police cordon and admitted inside it, Uglov saw that Sabatino's room was only lit by artificial light – the blinds having being closed by order of the police. Sabatino was sleeping, lying on her back – immobilized in the neck brace. Her bronze complexion contrasted with the whiteness of the single sheet that covered her. No other covers were needed given the warmth of the hospital's central heating. Sabatino was surrounded by the usual mess of medical equipment and measuring devices. A drip was still inserted in the inside of her elbow, while Uglov had ordered the introduction of a second line, into her neck.

Mr Uglov scrutinized the readouts to check there were no complications before pulling out his penlight torch. Manoeuvring his way through the spars of the halo device, he lifted each eyelid and shone it into her eyes. Expecting no more than the usual involuntary pupil reflex, Mr Uglov was surprised when Sabatino seemed to react physically at all. He felt her flinch at the uncomfortable glare of the light on her retina.

There was the tiniest hint of movement.

An hour later, Nazar was startled by the door of his interview room clanging open. This time Colonel Pudovkin strode in.

'I have a phone call for you,' said the police officer offering up the phone to the detainee. Still with his hands cuffed behind his back, though, Nazar couldn't physically take it. Pudovkin gesticulated urgently to another police officer, who released Nazar's hands. Even while trying to rub his wrists, the team boss was manhandled again as the cuffs were replaced albeit this time with his hands in front of him. Nazar could now at least take the phone from the police colonel.

'Dr Nazar,' said the voice on the other end, barely audible in the poor reception. 'Noel Cooper, here, British consul. I have Mr Dominic Quartano for you?'

Nazar felt an immediate sense of relief.

'Tahm, my dear friend,' said Quartano. 'I am so sorry for all this. Over and above everything, I am disgusted with your humiliation by the police.'

'Thank you, DQ. Twenty-something Russian citizens have been killed. One might understand where some of their attitude is coming from.'

'Insinuating blame before an investigation has even started is monstrous. Listen, Tahm,' said Quartano, 'my telling you not to worry won't help. So this is what I've done: I've appointed Quartech's chief counsel, here, to manage all of Ptarmigan's legal issues in Moscow.'

'Stacey?'

'She's instructing Quartech's solicitors, Brandeis Gertner, to handle everything for you in Russia. Brandeis has a large office in Moscow. One of their English-speaking partners – Sandy McMahon, who has been based there for ten years – is now acting as your counsel.'

'Thank you, DQ. That's very reassuring.'

Tahm Nazar paused while he tried to control a wave of relief.

'I have no idea how long the legal process there will take,' Quartano added. 'But I can't imagine it will be quick.'

Gathering himself, Nazar was able to re-engage: 'I think we are going to need some help, though – over and above the legal, DQ.'

'Name it, Tahm.'

Nazar had to move his position slightly to improve the signal; the basement was hampering the clarity of the line. 'The memorial service was announced by the president on television. My arrest was deliberately stage-managed and, I imagine, covered by the media.'

'You can say that again. You and Remy seem to be the subjects of a coordinated media onslaught.'

'Interesting that you should volunteer the word "coordinated".'

There was silence on the line for a few moments.

Nazar moved again, fearing the connection had been dropped. 'Hello?'

Quartano finally said: 'Yes, I'm still here. What's on your mind, Tahm?'

'Everything by way of a response to this accident, DQ – the presidential address, the memorial service, my public arrest – all seem to have been surprisingly well orchestrated.'

'We can start a fightback through the media, if that's what you're worried about.'

'Of course – except I think we're going to need more than that.'

'Like what?' asked Quartano.

'I don't know exactly, but I think we need ... Matt Straker.'

Quartano paused as he took on the implications of the request. 'Really ... Are you sure?'

'I am, sir, yes.'

'Why, Tahm? Why do you think that? What's wrong?' asked the tycoon, this time his voice showing some concern.

'I don't know for certain, I'm afraid. But I have a very strong feeling. Something about all this really doesn't seem right. Our car was flawless on that circuit, DQ. I mean it was *pitch* perfect.'

'What are you saying, Tahm ... do you think there was some kind of interference?'

'I don't know, sir, I really don't,' replied the Ptarmigan team boss. 'But there's something in all this that just doesn't add up.'

PART TWO

Политика власти

"Politika vlasti"

THE POLITICS OF POWER

SIXTEEN

Tears were welling in the big man's eyes. Not from the brightness of the glare, or even the blinding whiteness of the wilderness all around them. They seemed to be erupting from years of pent-up emotion. Colonel Matt Straker turned to give the big man a hug. It wasn't going to be easy. At minus twenty degrees Celsius, both men were wearing bulky clothes: fur-lined hoods covered their heads; numerous layers of clothing, thermal underwear through to waistcoats padded and bulked out their Gore-Tex jackets. Both men wore over-sized mittens and snow shoes.

A flash – a glint of sunlight catching metal – suddenly brought home the magnitude of this moment. The big man, instead of wearing the same sort of scarlet salopette-like trousers as Straker's, was supported by two spindly shafts of aluminium which reached down from the middle of each thigh to what should have been his boots.

Straker broke from Sergeant Middlemas.

Shuffling himself deftly through ninety degrees – particularly awkward in snow shoes – Straker offered an embrace, this time to Corporal Wendy Mulligan. He looked past her eye patch and the squashed spaghetti-effect of the skin covering the left side of her face – losing himself, instead, in the young woman's unfettered elation. He leant in to hug her, feeling only her right arm round the back of his shoulders.

Straker made to hug all twelve of his team in turn, including the man lying on the sledge; leaning down, Straker said: 'Taffy, I wish you could see this, my friend. You've done it. You've reached the top of the world.'

Their modest celebrations continued, all of them revelling in the personal Everest each had had to scale over the last three months in preparing for the challenge of this two-hundred-mile trip over the polar ice cap. Something, too, showed in Straker's face. His at-rest expression was normally one of intensity, emphasized by the diagonal folds of skin sloping downwards above each eye and the bridge of his nose, which ran in a straight line almost vertically from his forehead to its tip. These striking features were intensified by the darkness of his wiry hair and eyebrows. Today, though, that intensity was softened, if not gone altogether. He smiled warmly, radiating admiration and congratulations to each member of his team.

Straker was feeling buoyed by what he had achieved, but this trek had never been about him. Whatever discomfort he might have felt, whatever stresses he had endured as expedition leader, his outcome paled beside the achievements of the others. They had all coped against the physical odds – as amputees, partially-blinded, or even totally sightless individuals.

Straker may not have been carrying the visible scars of these ex-servicemen, but he was no less haunted by a weight of psychological baggage – at least he felt he had been until this expedition. To his relief, not once during the preparation and execution of this project had he suffered one of his mind-altering flashbacks to his own combat experiences. He felt blessed passing such a milestone. These three months were the longest he had gone without an episode triggered by his extraordinary rendition and torture – at the hands of the Americans – in Afghanistan. Undeniably, immersion in this trek had been a form of therapy for him, too.

Straker brought his thoughts back to the present, ever mindful of keeping his party safe from the hostility of this environment. Everything around them, for now, may look benign – clear skies, brilliant sunshine, no wind – but all of that could turn angry in a matter of minutes. Bad weather was expected from the west within a couple of hours.

'Two more miles,' he declared, and, reconnecting his harness to the sledge, indicated their onward direction of travel. As a few steps were taken, the lines tautened, and the sledge clicked as it unstuck from the snow and was sliding once again.

In the previous valley, Straker had checked their bearing and distance, anxious to confirm they were honouring their route. His main concern throughout had centred on their destination not being an actual place – not being physically identifiable. But as they had heaved their sledge up this snow drift and crested the rise, they all knew they had found it.

Some distance away – out in the middle of the vast expanse of ice – was an incongruous sight. Against the white nothingness visible in every direction was a small blob of colour. A dozen or so people it seemed, in brightly coloured clothes, were gathered in a cluster.

By their presence and location, Straker knew they had reached the Pole.

Having felt tension in the lines behind them, each team member now felt the tension to their front – as the sledge started sliding forwards. They needed to hold its weight, preventing it from running on down the hill below them. Levelling out onto the ice plateau at the base of this ridge, the normal back-breaking strain was re-established; the team of trekkers once more heaved their load across the ice cap in the direction of their RV.

Straker's back ached. His feet stung with pain. Clumping each snowshoe down he was cheered to know their trek was nearly done. Even in this relatively short distance Straker was reminded for the umpteenth time of the fabled fifty-something lexicon of words Eskimo-Aleut languages had for snow. He had no idea what each of them was, or what they all meant, but he now knew why there could be so many. In a matter of yards, the snow under his feet went from powder, to popping crusted powder, to drifting, to rock solid, to translucent. Straker's tours with Britain's Special Forces had involved jungle warfare and long-range reconnaissance; he had always ranked surviving and fighting in tropical or desert heat as the ultimate challenge. This trek had given him a new respect for those specializing in Arctic operations: he had no idea the Cold could be such a consumer of attention and be so threatening.

An hour later the trek party – its sledge and human huskies – closed in on the gaggle standing out on the pack ice. Two plastic poles had been erected: the taller one flying a pennant with the words North Pole written on it. The shorter pole, erected a small distance away, was there to form a gate and so create a finishing line. At the end of eight days and four hours, Straker's party crossed this line.

They had reached their goal.

There were cheers and celebrations all round.

In among the waiting group were several television crews. One of these broke away and made straight for Straker. As he saw them approach, Straker zipped up the bottom part of his hood, almost completely concealing his face.

'Colonel Straker, isn't it?' asked the TV presenter.

'Concentrate on the team,' he said and reached out to nudge the camera very gently away from him to point in the direction of the others. 'This is about the bravery of our ex-servicemen and their cause,' he declared.

'You're the trek leader – and ex-service yourself,' said the journalist. 'What you've done – leading these seriously injured personnel, all the way across the polar ice cap – is extraordinary. Worthy of recognition.'

Straker turned away.

Thankfully, he didn't have to parry any more attention: out of the dead stillness of the air an artificial sound could be heard in the distance. An engine – or engines.

In no time, two vast twin-prop Gemini helicopters – Quartech International's equivalent of the Boeing CH-47 Chinook – swooped in and banked dramatically around the huddle of people standing out on the ice. To prevent those below being blasted by snow as the air cushion reached the ground, the two helicopters put down some distance away.

The pilots did not shut down their engines, though – an indication of the dangers posed by such extreme temperatures, as well as their signalling the clear intention to get off and away again quickly. Bad weather was closing in faster than expected.

All the brightly coloured people were shortly climbing aboard the aircraft. Taffy was helped out of the sledge; its load was then packed into one of the holds along with the sledge itself. Down came the two poles, which were also quickly stowed on board.

A few minutes later the two Geminis were running their engines back up to full power. Everyone felt the airframes judder as the pitch increased and the two aircraft lifted off the ice.

Just in time.

Straker looked out through one of the miniscule windows to the west and saw what he had been working to beat. Instead of the brilliant sunshine and crystal clear air, he saw an ominous bank of brooding gun-metal grey cloud heading in their direction. At least, now, they had the speed to outrun it. Straker took a last look down at the harsh landscape of the ice floes, and finally – privately – allowed himself some satisfaction at what he had helped his team achieve.

An hour later the two Geminis, flying in formation, made their approach into the tented Barneo Ice Camp – the Russian Geological Society base that Quartech was using to operate and monitor their polar expedition. Overhead, the cloud cover was thickening, not yet as dramatically as it had been at the Pole. But it wouldn't be long.

The moment Straker disembarked, however, he was met with something unexpected.

One of the ground staff, who had been manning the forward link with the expedition, hurried straight out from inside the block of tents.

'Matt, Matt,' said the aide, 'you've had an urgent message from Mr Quartano. He wants you in Moscow as soon as you can get there. You need to leave immediately. I've arranged for you to fly out the moment you're ready. We don't want you getting trapped by the weather.'

Straker was surprised at the news. 'Any idea why? What's going on?'

'There's been a terrible crash at the Grand Prix in Moscow. I think you know the driver involved?'

Straker looked the other directly in the eye. 'Not Remy?' he asked.

Straker had hardly any time to think or organize himself. Within the hour he had said his goodbyes, expressing regret he would not be with the team in the "NAAFI" that night to celebrate their success – and was on a plane bound for Longyearbyen.

Waiting for him there – on the Norwegian archipelago of Svalbard – out on the apron, fuelled and ready to fly, was Dominic Quartano's private jet. As Straker climbed aboard, he heard the door shutting behind him and the engines whine into life. Before he had been helped out of his clothes, Straker felt the plane taxiing away. Moments after he had settled into his seat, the Quartech Falcon's engines were at full revs and hurtling him down the runway.

Four hours after reaching the North Pole, Colonel Matt Straker was in the air, en route for the crisis in Moscow.

SEVENTEEN

Straker's plane flew in from Norway and landed at Vnukovo International Airport at seven o'clock the next morning. While being processed by the immigration staff in the VIP terminal, a figure approached him.

'Colonel Straker?' said an unplaceable accent. 'Sandy McMahon. I'm a partner with Brandeis Gertner. Stacey Krall asked us to look after you, for Mr Quartano.'

Straker was momentarily thrown by this striking redhead. He replied: 'Thank you, Sandy, yes.'

The lawyer gestured to a porter, who closed in to take Straker's bags.

Straker watched McMahon intently. Intrigued.

His first impression of her was that of poise; he didn't know how a partner of a law firm was expected to look, or expected to move, but Sandy McMahon wouldn't have conformed to any mental picture he might have had. She seemed to stand and move like a classical dancer. Tall, slim, with a long neck, McMahon had a narrow freckled face, high forehead and fine strawberry blonde hair pinned neatly into a swirl. Holding the senior position of partner in a global firm of solicitors, Straker expected her to be at least, what, in her thirties? Except she looked considerably younger than that, dare he think almost too young: the band of freckles under both eyes and over the bridge of her nose might have had something to do with it. Despite her apparent youth, if Straker had been asked to sum her up there and then, he would have said: elegant. But that had nothing to do with make-up or her clothes; they were simple and plain: no artificial colour showed on her face, and she wore a simple navy blue trouser suit over a white T shirt and low-heeled loafers. McMahon's elegance came entirely from her presence.

'I have my driver outside,' she declared. 'I assume you're keen to get started. I have to say, though, I'm not quite sure with what: Stacey Krall said you aren't a lawyer.'

Straker was now intrigued by her tone.

McMahon gave further instructions to an elderly porter in fluent Russian. Her pale blue eyes glinted; rather than appearing to absorb the world around her, they seemed more to be declaring a direction of travel. They and her voice left no doubt that whatever she was asking for was already too late. Such command was another surprise: Straker was taken by McMahon's air of certainty.

Trying to make conversation on their way to the car, Straker said: 'I'd like to go and see Remy first, please.'

'She's still unconscious, there'd not be much point.'

'That doesn't matter – to me.'

McMahon pulled a knowing face.

'Is there an issue?' Straker asked, sensing that there might be further disapproval from the lawyer.

'I took the trouble to Google you,' she replied as she strode out. 'I noticed that you two were *involved*.'

Straker smiled at her curiosity. 'We had some interference last season from another Formula One team, who'd been sabotaging her car. I was *involved*, as you put it, to combat and rid Remy of that threat.'

'So it was only a professional involvement?'

'Does that matter?' he asked gently. 'Remy and I needed to work closely together – because of that sabotage business. She's great company.'

Straker turned to face her; he found himself intrigued again, this time by McMahon's response. He didn't understand her reaction to his last point at all.

She drew her phone from a pocket. In English, Straker heard McMahon asking someone to arrange permission from the police to visit Sabatino in the hospital. She ended the call.

'Why would we need permission from the police?' he asked.

'Because Ms Sabatino has been arrested,' McMahon replied flatly. 'The police now have her under armed guard.'

'While she's in a hospital – you're kidding?'

'You didn't know?'

Straker shook his head. 'I've been out of reach. Clearly, I need to be brought up to date.'

With no enthusiasm, McMahon said: 'Fine,' as they reached her car. It was already waiting at the kerb. Before Straker could offer to hold the door open for her, McMahon had opened the passenger door for herself and climbed in. Straker realized that McMahon meant business. After he had opened a rear door and was sitting on the back seat, he chose to mirror her lack of warmth: 'Where are we with the case, then?' he asked as they pulled away.

'Things have been deteriorating, with the public mood turning pretty dark. The president raised the level of anger with the memorial service, fuelling it with the very public arrest of Dr Nazar.'

'Tahm's been arrested, too?'

'At the memorial service.'

'Oh, shit.'

McMahon made a point of ignoring Straker's swearing. 'The *way* he was arrested, though – by the police, very publicly – has convinced people he must be guilty. Dr Nazar's humbling at the cathedral, which has since been shown in repeated clips on State television, has offered the public a very obvious scapegoat.'

Straker inhaled with this gloomy summary. 'What – officially, then – happens now?'

'A public prosecutor is likely to be appointed.'

'Before any investigation has taken place, before any evidence has been presented?'

'This would not be the way in most judicial systems, no. You need to realize something, and very quickly: This is Russia. Anything demanded by the president, or the small band of his inner government circle, pretty much happens.'

'You think this is being handled by the *president*?'

McMahon seemed to nod, showing for the first time limited agreement with something that Straker had said. 'Too early to say, for sure; but things happening this quickly – not to mention the presidential TV address and rapid staging of the memorial service – would seem to point to the involvement of high-ish levels of government.'

'Does that mean every aspect of this case will be conducted on presidential whim, or are we going to get some sort of identifiable process?'

She didn't answer the question. 'I'm not sure of your role here,' she replied sharply. 'From the Google search, I wasn't sure how a colonel in the Marines – with a "hero's" DSO – fitted in with a Formula One team?'

'*Royal* Marines,' Straker replied, 'and I'm a director of Quartech, Ptarmigan's owner. Mr Quartano asked me to come over and help.'

'How, though, does a director of *Competition Intelligence and Security* help? And what even is that? Sounds suspiciously like some sort of girl-talk for industrial espionage to me.'

Straker smiled. 'We find it pays to be vigilant, in the defence business,' he said. 'Some of our new ideas cost huge sums of money to develop. We think there's a fair amount of sense in trying to understand the market – before we commit to a sizeable investment – by finding out whether our competitors might be about to launch a similar product. And then, with the massive cost of R&D, we're particularly keen people don't walk off with the ideas we *do* come up with, at least not without paying for them first. All that requires us to remain alert and think laterally from time to time. Typically, it sees me doing a bit of investigative work.'

'All sounds pretty underhand.'

'Tell me, does Brandeis ever use investigators to support a client's position in legal cases and claims?' he asked.

McMahon fell silent.

Straker couldn't resist a smile. 'What I do, then, is no different from what you do. If there *is* a normal in my role, I tend to get involved when something's gone wrong. Underhand – overhand – we only ever mirror what other people are trying to do to us.'

'How can any of that help Ptarmigan here – in Moscow?'

'I've no idea, yet. I imagine there'll be an inquiry into the accident? Or a report on it? And, more than likely, some form of hearing. We might do our cause some good if we can provide our own evidence, particularly if we need to challenge other people's assumptions or claims. Pulling some of that together will probably be my first priority.'

'In that case, I must warn you *not* to use your military background for any kind of *underhand* stuff here – in Russia – colonel.' For the first time McMahon turned to face him, looking backwards between the front seats of the car. She said: 'Even upstanding professionals can very quickly find themselves feeling the rough end of the State.'

Straker looked less than convinced.

'You've heard of the Sergei Magnitsky case, I take it?'

'I'm afraid not, no.'

'Well, you'd be wise to study it and take heed. Magnitsky was an accountant who had been asked to look into allegations of impropriety at a hedge fund here. Having done so, he declared there *had* been impropriety, but ended up pointing the finger at Russian government officials. After his accusations of corruption, Magnitsky was arrested in 2008, held without charge for eleven months, denied medical treatment – despite increasingly poor health – and was found dead in his cell in the notorious Butyrka Prison. An autopsy showed he had a ruptured stomach and had suffered a heart attack. Even the Moscow Oversight Commission, in 2009, declared psychological and physical pressure had been exerted upon him.'

'You're saying he died because he stood up to the government?'

'Or was trying to. Magnitsky was attempting to expose criminals who were, in effect, operating at will – because of the corruption among State officials. So be warned, colonel: the Russian system comes down hard on any opinion – particularly evidence – it doesn't like. I can only advise you to play by the rules: I can only advise you to be careful.'

McMahon was about to speak again when she was distracted by her phone. Answering it, she conversed with the caller in Russian for a few minutes. 'Bad news, I'm afraid. Your permission to see Ms Sabatino has been refused – put down to her medical condition. She's still unconscious.'

Straker showed some concern.

'Also,' added McMahon, 'it appears your role here is all but redundant anyway. Having already impounded the crash site, we've just heard the police are also about to impound what's left of Ms Sabatino's car – on orders from the government.'

'But we'll still have the opportunity to examine them both – the site and the car – yes?'

McMahon shook her head. 'We've been told our access will be denied. The prosecutor is expected to appoint an expert to examine everything. The legal case will be based entirely on his findings.'

'You're kidding? We're to be denied *all* access to the wreckage and crash site?'

McMahon nodded.

'Who's the expert likely to be?' Straker asked. 'Someone at the FIA?'

'Most probably a Russian.'

'This country has no history – hardly *any* credibility – in F1? Who's going to know about this stuff? That would be crazy: Moscow, right now, is full of world-leading motor racing experts – from the sport's international governing body – all here for the Grand Prix, for heaven's sake? How meritocratic or sensible is that?'

McMahon shrugged. 'The authorities here see Formula One and all its associates as complicit in this disaster. The country is wary of the FIA, particularly of any attempt they might make to try and cover up any of their liabilities.'

'How paranoid is that?'

'You're going to have to get used to this,' replied McMahon. 'This is Russia.'

EIGHTEEN

Since the medics had treated the crash victims, and moved the injured and the dead off the grassy bank, all that was left at the crash site were the shattered remnants of Sabatino's car strewn across the hillside. Blue-and-white police tapes still fluttered eerily in the wind, marking out the area of the crime scene. Two armed policemen stood guard, one at the top of the hill and the other at the bottom.

One of them heard the engines in the distance, muffled by the trees.

Along the track of the Zhar-ptitsa Grand Prix circuit, a number of vehicles were approaching. A police car led a convoy made up of a forklift truck, a small flatbed lorry and, coming up the rear, a 4×4 car pulling an open trailer.

At the apex of the now-infamous bend, Turn Eleven, the police car stopped. Police Colonel Pudovkin climbed out. Waving to the forklift truck, he beckoned it to follow him across the gravel trap; he also waved at the car pulling the trailer, instructing it to follow on behind.

At the tyre wall the police colonel was saluted by the guard. Pudovkin barely reciprocated before ordering the policeman out of the way.

Police Colonel Pudovkin assessed the width of the hole punched through the wall by Sabatino's car. He instructed the forklift driver to close in.

Rolling forward in its lowest gear, the forklift driver saw the gap was too narrow – that his truck would hit the edges of the broken wall on either side. He readied himself for an impact. Rather than feel any kind of bump, though, the driver found his machine able to keep going – experiencing little resistance. Several concrete blocks on either side were pushed easily out of place and fell to the ground. He was soon through the wall and emerging into the area at the bottom of the grassy slope on the far side. At the same time, Pudovkin ordered the car and trailer to pull up alongside the wall, on the inside of the circuit.

The police colonel strode up the hill, instructing the forklift to follow him. Climbing slowly, this truck's tyres flattened and crunched numerous fragments of Sabatino's car, even pushing some of them down into the earth, out of sight.

A minute or two later Pudovkin – standing beside the remains of Sabatino's monocoque – gave the signal for the forklift to move in. Riding over a slight mound as it approached, its wheels bounced slightly at the very moment the forks were expected to go beneath the car. The metal blade of the left fork rammed the side of it, piercing the carbon fibre. The forklift driver flinched, selected reverse, and pulled the blade back out of the wreckage. The police colonel showed his impatience at the delay.

A second approach by the forklift was made, more carefully and cleanly this time. The driver pushed on until the monocoque was butted up against the backrest. When he came to raise the load up the mast, Sabatino's car rocked uneasily.

Colonel Pudovkin gesticulated to the driver again, this time pointing back down the slope towards the hole in the wall. To prevent the wreckage rolling forwards off the forks down the incline of the slope, the driver turned the truck tightly, and brought it down the hill in reverse – resting the remnants of the car in the heels of the hoist.

Trundling down the bank, the forklift came back through the puncture point in the perimeter fence and across the gravel trap onto the asphalt of the Grand Prix circuit. Once alongside the flatbed lorry, the driver set about disengaging the monocoque, by tilting the mast. The car, though, didn't move. The driver encouraged it by juddering the forklift backwards and forwards. Sabatino's monocoque began to roll. It ended up tumbling off the forks, dropping down onto the back of the lorry. A number of cracks and breakages could be heard as the carbon fibre absorbed the force of the fall.

Elsewhere across the grassy bank, Pudovkin's team of uniformed officers was scouring the area, picking up shards, fragments and segments of Sabatino's Ptarmigan. These retrievals were simply being thrown over the perimeter wall into the back of the open trailer behind the 4×4.

No one photographed the hillside. No one recorded the locations from where any of the pieces had been recovered.

No one knew where the remains of the Formula One car were about to be taken.

NINETEEN

Their car was still making its way into Moscow, heading towards McMahon's offices.

Straker brought himself back to the case in hand.

'We should start with the basics,' he said, 'start our defence by building a full understanding of the crash. That'll put us in a position to refute – or at least repudiate with conviction – any accusations or claims that might be levelled against us.'

'How will that even be possible if Ptarmigan can't examine the car?'

'We won't be completely devoid of data. Little in Formula One is left to chance these days. Competitive pressures prompt the teams to monitor their cars and performance in microscopic detail. Ours carry over two hundred and fifty sensors. These measure every pressure, loading, temperature, G-force and orientation – in real time. From that data, we should be able to build up a very clear picture of what went on before and during the crash. Ptarmigan also records every inch of video footage, streamed and TV broadcast, put out during a race, enabling us to study our performance and that of the other teams. We'll be able to use that as well to study the crash and to look for clues as to what might have gone wrong.'

'Where's all the data recorded? On some sort of black box?'

'It is, actually, except on our cars there are several components which store them.'

'Not much good if the car has been impounded, and we can't get to them?'

'Agreed, but that's not the whole story. All those sensor readings – metrics – are transmitted from the car back to the team's computers remotely, hence the term: telemetry.'

McMahon's expression lightened slightly.

Straker asked: 'Do we still have access to the Ptarmigan telemetry truck – motor home – or have the authorities impounded that too?'

'No, they haven't – not yet, at least.'

'Good, we should be able to access the recorded data from there, then.'

'And if the motor home *does* get impounded?' she asked.

'It wouldn't be the end of the road. The telemetry doesn't stop in the pit lane; Ptarmigan, like most teams, fires much of its data via satellite link to a master server, back at base. We would still be able to access most of that information through the Ptarmigan factory in Shenington, Oxfordshire. It would be a very different story for the video library, though,' added Straker. 'Our video recordings *do* only stay on the motor home's recorders; Ptarmigan doesn't fire them back – and we have no other copy. If we lost access to the motor home, we *would* lose that source of evidence.'

Remy Sabatino's bed was surrounded by a group of medical staff. Mr Uglov held court and discussed their patient's progress. In the centre of this conference lay Sabatino, on her back – still groggy with her eyes half closed – but closer to consciousness than she had been so far.

'The patient,' declared Mr Uglov, 'is showing some signs of recovery. The effects of the sedative will not fully wear off for some hours. I am happy that her state now allows us to conduct a few more tests, particularly cognitive and brain responses. I want to run these further investigations,' he said handing out a pre-prepared sheet of paper.

Mr Uglov shot a glance through the frosted internal window of the room at the shape of the armed policemen standing guard outside Sabatino's room.

'I intend us to be thorough,' he stated with a clear message in his voice. 'I *don't* want this patient to be vulnerable to medical deterioration when she leaves our care. If the legal fallout from this accident prompts the kind of media turmoil we've seen already, any comment about inadequate medical attention received – or any use of her medical condition to prevent her standing trial – will reflect badly on this hospital. As a medic, of course I want her leaving here with a thoroughly clean bill of health. But, for all our sakes, I do not want the hospital used – or seen to be used – as any form of legal scapegoat.'

Sandy McMahon's phone went again. This call was short. She turned to Straker in the back of the car. 'That was my office. We've just heard from the British consul. We have had our application to the Moscow Police approved. You've been granted – very limited – permission to speak to Dr Nazar.'

Straker nodded.

In Russian, McMahon gave the driver a new set of instructions.

'Where's he being held?'

'In a cell at the Moscow Police HQ, in the Tverskoy District.'

'You said *very limited* – what does that mean?'

'Thirty minutes.'

'What?'

McMahon replied: 'In today's Russia, you're lucky to get even that.'

Matt Straker and Sandy McMahon were dropped off in Petrovka Ulitsa outside the vast taupe-coloured Greco-Roman building of the Moscow Police HQ. Staff attitudes changed instantly the moment McMahon explained why they were there and who they were authorized to see. Straker was all but strip-searched as they were admitted into the police station. One of the officers, aggressively and in very rough English, asked him: 'Are you attached to the killer?'

Straker was taken aback.

'Twenty-eight people are now dead,' added the policeman.

After a further half an hour, which even included the taking of his fingerprints, Straker was escorted with McMahon into the police station, down a set of stairs and into the basement. A row of cell doors faced the corridor on either side. A video camera showing a red light swivelled as they moved. Straker and McMahon were led to the end, where one of the doors was opened. A clang from its bolts rang out harshly, echoing back along the spartan passageway.

Inside, Straker was in for a shock.

He had never seen Nazar look anything like this. He was unshaven. His hair was greasy. His clothes were dishevelled. He looked exhausted. He was sitting, crouched, at the table.

Nazar rose to his feet and greeted Straker, clutching his hand in both of his – the chains on his handcuffs rattling. A policeman stepped forwards and pushed Nazar back to separate them.

'Hey, that's unnecessary,' said Straker.

McMahon hissed: 'Cool it, Straker, do not antagonize these people.'

In an effort to control his temper, Straker focused on introducing McMahon to Nazar and explaining her capacity at Brandeis Gertner and her role for Ptarmigan. Straker pulled out a chair each for McMahon and himself. The policeman was still standing by the door, inside the cell. Straker asked of McMahon: 'Are we not allowed any privacy? You're Tahm's lawyer – he's entitled to confidentiality, surely?'

'Not necessarily in Russia.'

Straker looked irritated.

McMahon turned to ask the policeman: 'Do you speak English?' There was no reply. She repeated the question in Russian.

The man's eyes dropped to meet hers: '*Niet.*'

'He doesn't,' said McMahon.

Straker shook his head, indicating a degree of resignation. 'Tahm, I am so sorry for this tragedy. How are you keeping?'

'Not well,' he replied in his clipped Indian accent. He exhaled and shut his eyes. 'I have no news about Remy.'

'She is alive,' answered Straker.

'We should discuss what needs to happen next, as quickly as possible,' declared McMahon. 'We haven't got long.'

Straker shook his head again before he raised the idea of compiling their own version of the accident and how it might have happened.

'Get the guys to go over the remains of the car,' responded Nazar. 'Have them assess it. They'll be able to get to the bottom of why it might have behaved like that, pretty quickly.'

'We're not going to be able to examine the car, Tahm.'

'What? Why not?'

'The police have impounded it. The court is going to appoint an expert, on whose report it will make its decision.'

'Who's that likely to be?'

'We don't know, yet. Sandy expects it to be a Russian.'

'When we have all the world-class mechanics and technicians already here for the Grand Prix?' said Nazar.

Straker nodded.

'Colonel Straker has mentioned that your cars carry a number of remote sensors. Will their data not be able to tell us about the race up to the point of the crash?'

Nazar nodded.

'So what do you think happened, then, Tahm?' Straker asked.

'Precisely what I, myself, have been wrestling with ever since,' he said. 'Incarceration has at least given me unencumbered time to think things through. Matt – Ms McMahon – I remain baffled. Everything about that car was *perfect*. Remy had shown huge confidence in it. She would never have mounted that overtaking manoeuvre if she had had *any* concerns over the way it was handling. Remy is fearless, but not reckless or stupid. She was at one with that car. Whatever happened at that corner had to have been catastrophic and instantaneous. Once the accident happened, of course, we were all so devastated – and desperate to help – we never had the time to review it. I was then arrested so I've been completely isolated from everything ever since.'

'What do you *think* happened?'

Nazar shrugged. 'There is something strange … something not quite right with all this, Matt. Something fishy.'

At this moment the policeman stepped forward and, although he was speaking in Russian, it was clear he was calling the meeting to an end.

'That wasn't half an hour,' said Straker.

McMahon held up her hand: 'Really best not to aggravate anyone.'

Straker reluctantly stood up.

With increasingly aggressive hand gestures from the policeman, Straker and McMahon were urged from the cell.

Hurriedly, Nazar said: 'Get over to the telemetry truck, Matt, and have Backhouse go through the recorded data with you.'

The policeman's demeanour hardened.

Nazar, his voice rising as the visitors were being herded out into the passageway, said: 'Find out what's *really* going on here, Matt.'

The door of the cell slammed shut.

TWENTY

Straker and McMahon drove away from the Moscow Police HQ in silence. Straker was disturbed by Nazar's demeanour, never expecting to see such indignity visited upon such a proud man. After several minutes of silence he asked: 'How soon can we get him out on bail?'

'We've filed the applications, but we've very little chance of success.'

'I thought this was a charge of *corporate* manslaughter, not against Tahm individually.'

'That's as maybe,' she replied. 'But the courts take the public mood into account. At the moment, the public is not minded to give any quarter for the people considered responsible for so many deaths.'

'We are still applying, though?'

'Of course…'

'We've got to start clearing their names,' Straker stated. 'How soon can we get to the paddock and meet up with the rest of the team?'

McMahon rang her office. She asked her PA to ring the authorities for clearance to enter the Zhar-ptitsa Autodrom. When she signed off she said: 'With absolutely no warning, we've just heard there's going to be a press conference – at the Ministry of Justice.'

'When?'

'Thirty minutes.'

'Any idea what about?'

'Brandeis believes it'll be to announce a prosecutor.' For all her measured demeanour, even McMahon looked surprised.

'I thought we were expecting this?'

McMahon looked unsure of herself for the first time. 'Not this quickly, and not announced by the Ministry of Justice. I don't understand why it's been brought forward and elevated to that institution?'

'Can we get to this announcement ourselves?' Straker asked.

McMahon gave fresh instructions to their driver as she called her office. In no time the car changed direction again, making its way instead to the Justice Department.

Their car pulled up near the Ministry. Both were struck by the size of the crowds gathered on the pavement in front of the building. Straker and McMahon had to struggle to get their car doors open, let alone cut their way through to the main entrance.

At the front doors their entry was officially barred.

McMahon conversed in Russian with one of the uniformed security men. After two minutes of heated discussion she nodded her head in the direction of the doors and beckoned Straker to follow her inside.

Pushing themselves through another mass of people also trying to get in, they were met with a packed crowd in the entrance hall. MacMahon and Straker could get no further into the building. From what they could see, the announcement was going to be made inside the atrium anyway: there was a portable backdrop sporting the Ministry of Justice seal – a golden double-headed eagle – and a lectern, bathed in bright television lights.

Over the heads of the assembled journalists and photographers, Straker surveyed the room. There was considerable hubbub. It suddenly quietened.

A severe-looking man appeared from within the building. He walked up the short steps and onto the stage. As he moved behind the lectern and under the television lights, MacMahon whispered: 'That's the *minister* of justice. He's one of the president's key placemen – an ex-KGB apparatchik.'

'Does this guy always get involved in criminal cases?'

McMahon shook her head.

'How many times does he get as involved as this?'

'That I know of? … Never.'

The minister addressed the room in English: 'The Federal Government, as promised, is taking strong and fast measures to bring to justice those responsible for the thirty deaths at the Zhar-ptitsa Autodrom.'

Some reaction could be heard from the room. The death toll seemed to keep rising, presumably as spectators at the race track succumbed to their injuries. Straker felt that this was acting like an emotional ratchet.

'As minister of justice, I announce that the Ministry appoints … as the federal prosecutor in the Moscow Grand Prix tragedy … Léon Gazdanov.'

Straker had no idea who this was.

But he realized, there and then, it was a significant appointment.

'Good grief!' said McMahon.

Straker looked across at her. It wasn't so much the words as her tone.

McMahon leant in towards Straker. 'Léon Gazdanov is the prosecutor general.'

'Meaning what?'

'He's the most senior prosecutor in the whole of the Russian federal judicial system.'

Straker saw a noticeably short man, wearing a bright blue uniform with gold flashes and brass buttons, appear through a door on the inside of the entrance hall and make his way onto the stage. Léon Gazdanov, with the curtest of nods, barely acknowledged the minister as he strode across to stand behind the lectern.

Straker was given his first opportunity to size up the man who was now, effectively, charged with driving the case against them. From his own experience, he saw his problem immediately: Gazdanov was no more than five feet one. Round-faced, Straker guessed he was in his early forties; Gazdanov had thinning ginger hair, which had been keenly coiffured – shaped to stand some distance from his head – to increase his height and presence, perhaps? Gazdanov's face was fleshy; his features appearing over large. For all that, the man radiated considerable bearing. Medals were strung out in two rows across his chest. Straker wondered what those could possibly be awarded for … in the judiciary.

Straker was getting concerned: Gazdanov's expression struck him as that of a man who looked like he had something to prove.

'The people of Russia have been wronged,' Gazdanov stated in a voice with a rasping nasal edge to it. 'I have been given unlimited resources to bring the perpetrators of this crime – the death of thirty civilians – to justice. I have enough staff backing and support from the courts to make a watertight case, enabling this trial to be held in the Supreme Court of Russia.'

Straker was surprised to hear McMahon actually groan.

'This full application of the judicial system,' continued Gazdanov, 'will give me the confidence to make a quick judgment: I intend to have those responsible brought to justice – and starting their lifetime of hard labour – within four weeks.'

Flashguns were fired off in a continuous volley.

It appeared that Tahm Nazar and Remy Sabatino were now, as individuals, destined to face the full might of the Russian State.

TWENTY-ONE

The injured Formula One driver, still groggy from the effect of the induced coma, could hear distant voices. Sabatino's brain was struggling to process what was going on around her. Her whole left side was extremely sore and uncomfortable. She felt any movement keenly. Her throat was aching like hell.

She was desperate to pee. Trying to speak, no sounds emerged from her mouth that she could recognize as words, because of the emergency throat surgery. She tried slapping her right hand on the bed to attract attention.

But no one could hear her – or they were choosing not to.

Straker and McMahon had to wait some time before they could get out of the Ministry of Justice building. The moment the conference was over, every journalist, photographer and cameraman had scrambled for the door, desperate to get back to base and file their reports of this dramatic announcement.

Straker and McMahon finally managed to break out; they ducked down into a side street to find their car.

'The stakes have become truly alarming,' said McMahon as they pulled away. This time McMahon had got into the back seat of the car and was sitting next to Straker.

As he looked across at her, he realized her demeanour had changed. 'Your reaction in there was quite a surprise.'

'It's the seniority of the prosecutor and the seniority of the court,' she said. 'As a court of first instance, criminal cases are only ever heard at the district level. For the Zhar-ptitsa circuit, that should probably be the Moscow District of Nagatinsky Zaton, in the Southern Administrative Area. If there was a particularly serious case then, maybe, it could be heard at a regional level, within the jurisdiction of the Moscow Oblast – the next level up. But … for the Ministry of Justice to nominate a case to be heard in the Supreme Court – as its court of first instance – is quite extraordinary.'

'Because the case is *that* serious?'

'Legal competences could have had a bearing on what level of court should hear it,' she said. 'The only other instance that I can recall of a case going *straight* to the Supreme Court was the Dubrovka Theatre siege in 2002. In that instance, the surviving hostage-taker – the only one not killed by the Spetsnaz – was tried at the same high level. But that involved hostage-taking – and a clear act of terrorism.'

'The Ministry of Justice is equating the deaths at the Grand Prix with an act of terror?'

'Not necessarily, but it does seem to be ranking this at the same level of significance. A material factor in the theatre siege was the very strong public opinion – which, of course, made it highly political.'

'Are you saying there has been political intervention here?'

'Not for definite. Sending it to the Supreme Court, *and* combining that with the appointment of the prosecutor general himself, though, does take us into some very strange territory.'

'Is Gadzooks a political appointment?'

MacMahon didn't smile. 'Léon Gaz–dan–ov … Politics could well be involved in his appointment. President Tarkovsky has a very strange history of dealings with the office of prosecutor general.'

'Strange, how?'

'Before he reached the Kremlin, the president was head of the Federal Security Service, the FSB – successor to the Cold War's infamous KGB. While there, the-then prosecutor general had been particularly successful in uncovering crime. A major coup had been to expose a network of corruption in government circles, specifically in relation to the awarding of defence contracts and the widespread receipt of backhanders. It was a big story. It *made* the-then prosecutor general. Afterwards, the-then PG turned his anti-corruption sights on Moscow – particularly on the bigger government departments. A big mistake … for him, at least. The high command did not like it. At all. A month later Tarkovsky, as head of the FSB, appeared on television and showed, live on air, a grainy video clip of a man cavorting, naked, with several women in an expensive hotel bedroom. Tarkovsky *claimed* the man in the tape was the-then prosecutor general and that the sex romp had allegedly been paid for by several of the people the prosecutor general had been investigating at the time.'

'You're kidding?'

McMahon shook her head. 'With no further investigation of the video clip, that prosecutor general was hounded out of office. As you might imagine, since Tarkovsky became president, there has been a particular wariness on the part of the prosecutor general's office to do anything to cross him.'

Straker could only shake his head once again.

'It gets murkier,' said McMahon. 'The current prosecutor general, Léon Gazdanov, was appointed – personally – *by* Tarkovsky *after* he became president.'

'So he's a presidential puppet?'

'Not a puppet, exactly – but a placeman, certainly.'

'So you *are* saying, then, that the decisions to use the Supreme Court as the court of first instance, *and* the appointment of the prosecutor general – with all of the complicated history of that office with Tarkovsky – *must* have been motivated by politics?'

'And probably a fair way up the greasy pole, at that.'

TWENTY-TWO

Their car made slow progress through an overcast Moscow. High cloud-cover made for a grey light over the city, giving everything a gloomy feel. Its bleakness seemed entirely appropriate to match the gloom of recent developments – as well as the mood in the car.

'Whatever our analysis of the reasons,' McMahon said, 'the reality is absurd. A four-week lead-in to a trial of this seriousness is ridiculously tight. I'm going to need a lot more help within Brandeis.'

Straker nodded.

McMahon rang her office and asked to be put through to the firm's senior partner. She spent a few minutes bringing the practice head up to date. Given the significance of the announcements at the Ministry of Justice, she was given an immediate undertaking for whatever resources she needed.

They were heading south along Andropova Prospekt, just passing the golden onion-shaped dome and white walls of the Alexander Nevsky Church. As Straker and McMahon crossed the causeway, the view opened up dramatically. Over to their left was the Moskva River. On its far bank was the shoreline of the ancient park of Nagatinskaya Poyma.

Once they drove onto the peninsular, Straker could make out the roofs of the Zhar-ptitsa Autodrom Grand Prix circuit in among the trees. One building shortly dominated the view: backing onto, and running parallel with the avenue, was the ridgeline of the spectacular pit-straight grandstand. Along its entire length flags of over one hundred nations were fluttering gently in the Muscovy breeze. Poignantly, they were all flying at half-mast.

Three-quarters of a mile down the dual carriageway the car started slowing. A major set of traffic lights was ahead; they were pulling into the filter lane. After a short wait they were free to cross. As they turned left, the magnificent entrance to the race track complex was before them.

On the pavement outside the Grand Prix circuit, easily three hundred people were mounting a vigil – carrying banners, flowers, and torches – mourning the deaths. Closer to the gates was another group of people – rougher-looking, most with expensive cameras hanging around their necks. To one end of the press pack was another group manning a bank of TV cameras, all mounted on large heavy tripods, suggesting they expected to be there for some time. The media were present in force.

Approaching the main gate, the car dropped to walking pace. An armed policeman walked forwards holding his hand up, ordering them to stop. McMahon, in Russian, talked with the officer. Straker couldn't understand what was being said, except he could easily hear the tone was brusque and unaccommodating. After three minutes, the policeman pointed at the ground in front the car – ordering them, presumably, to stay put. The official walked back to his control box.

Straker and McMahon remained seated in the stationary car.

'No one is allowed into the place now, without the prosecutor general's permission,' reported McMahon with the first hint of impatience creeping into her voice.

Fifteen minutes later the policeman returned. Something was stated in Russian. McMahon responded, sounding like she was arguing some of the points being put to her. Once again, the policeman left them and returned to his booth.

'He would admit us,' she explained, 'but only if we are accompanied, continually, by a police escort.'

'What? Even during your conversations with the team, even as our lawyer?'

McMahon nodded. 'Yep.'

'Again, no allowance for client-attorney privilege?'

McMahon shrugged.

'"This is Russia"?' offered Straker.

It took McMahon several calls over twenty minutes, including one to the British Consulate in which she asked the consul, himself, to contact the prosecutor general's office, before their car was finally admitted to the Grand Prix circuit. To McMahon's credit, they were no longer obliged to be escorted by a policeman when in meetings within their own team.

The car made its way through the deserted Autodrom complex, aiming for the paddock and the Ptarmigan motor home. With the race abandoned, and the Grand Prix teams long-since departed, there was an empty feel to the place. During the build-up to the Grand Prix weekend, this expansive area had felt quite small, even intimate – as streets had been created between the rows of massively expensive mobile headquarters and hospitality facilities. Now, Ptarmigan's turquoise motor home was the only vehicle there in a vast open space.

Straker climbed out and looked around the area before walking to the doors of the motor home. They hissed open as he and McMahon approached.

Straker was still impressed by this mobile control room, even though it was just as he remembered it from the season before: its inside was decked out in rosewood, chrome and glass, with pale turquoise-coloured leather seating, all edged with navy blue piping. Its finish was a powerful statement of style and quality. It had a different feel, though, when not in operation. Its row of eight workstations, set out down the full length of the truck on the right-hand side, made less of an impression. None of the plasma screens were on and, without the operators, it was oddly quiet. A meeting table ran down the other side of the truck, surrounded by a curved bench.

Sitting round this was a group of people including Andy Backhouse, normally Sabatino's race engineer.

'Matt, thank God you're here,' said the middle-aged, dark-haired Brummie with obvious affection. Stepping forward, he took Straker by surprise; the hardened race engineer even gave him a hug. 'I fear we're going to need even more of your magic this time.'

'Detecting and hunting down a saboteur might be one thing,' replied Straker, 'but this is something very different ... Something far more troubling.'

Uncharacteristically, Backhouse didn't come back with a quip; to Straker, the race engineer wasn't anything like his usual self.

Straker introduced Sandy McMahon. In turn, Backhouse introduced them to the six Ptarmigan members in the mobile headquarters. Last to be presented was Ptarmigan's number two driver, Yegor Baryshnikov.

'You won't have met Yegor, of course,' said Backhouse in his Birmingham accent. 'After Helli left us at the end of last season – following all that crap with Massarella – a seat opened up for Yegor to come and join us from a hugely successful season in GP2. Before that, he was with an IndyCar team in the US.'

Straker shook hands with the tall, slim Russian driver; he was keen to form a view of him. Baryshnikov was a little older than the usual new recruit to Formula One, being in his late twenties.

'Nice to meet too,' said Baryshnikov.

Despite his grammar, Straker was distracted; he had heard numerous stories – from different people – about the Russian's arrogance and self-confidence.

'How's Remy?' asked Straker as everyone was invited to sit at the long meeting table.

'Still pretty groggy, we gather,' replied Backhouse.

'Anyone been to see her yet?'

Backhouse shook his head. 'We've been advised not to by the hospital. Until she's stronger.'

Once they were all seated, Straker brought them all up to date: 'Sandy McMahon is a lawyer, based here in Moscow. Mr Q has instructed her firm to help us with this case. As a first step, we've been to see Tahm.'

'How is he?'

'Not well. We've also just been to a press conference at the Ministry of Justice, where they announced the appointment of a federal prosecutor.'

'Who is appointed?' asked Baryshnikov.

'Léon Gazdanov – the prosecutor general.'

'That's fuck,' said the driver. 'Everyone in Russia know him. He's ego. Wants to make big name.'

Whatever time Baryshnikov had spent in America, thought Straker, it hadn't improved his accent or syntax.

'We're going to have to work extra hard to counter him – to defend ourselves – then,' said Straker. 'Particularly as we've only got four weeks to the trial.'

Everyone's expression around the table changed for the worse.

'Can I suggest we get straight on with discussing what we need to do? Sandy, can you tell us what we are up against? What does Gazdanov need to prove in court to succeed with a charge of corporate manslaughter?'

Without hesitation, she said: 'It's a new charge in Russian law. There is no precedent. The courts have no prior conception of what culpability should look like. For us, this is a negative; in effect, it gives Gazdanov a licence to build any case he wants.'

Baryshnikov butted in: 'And he going to wins.'

'Why do you say that?' Backhouse asked.

'Russian people get revenge. *Must* have revenge. Too many people die.'

'There's meant to be a legal process involved, Yegor,' said Straker; with his eyes still on Baryshnikov he turned to McMahon and asked: 'What does Gazdanov have to *prove* then, Sandy, from a legal point of view?'

McMahon now also looked at Baryshnikov with some concern. 'He has to show that there was negligence. He needs to prove that, with Ptarmigan's full knowledge, things were done – or were not done – which knowingly affected the safety of the car, and which led directly to the accident. *Things*, in this case, would include any malfunction in design, maintenance, repairs, checks, etc. Gazdanov should not find this easy, particularly if he's relying on a Russian expert to investigate the crash.'

'How wrong with Russian expert?' countered Baryshnikov. 'Don't need brains of monkey to know fault. Thirty dead.'

'The law still requires a proper legal argument, Mr Baryshnikov,' said McMahon firmly. 'Mr Gazdanov will have to *prove* what happened ... with evidence.'

'And what about fault? Blame? Ptarmigan must not – run away from – blame.'

'What blame is that, Yegor?' asked Backhouse. 'This was nothing more than a racing incident, for Christ sakes. This was a Formula One fact of life.'

Baryshnikov grunted and shook his head. 'Ptarmigan have to face fact,' he snapped. 'We all know. Remy took risk – *big risk* – going round outside of corner. Everyone know track there dirty. Marbles. Grip, very bad. Knew danger. *Knew* danger.'

'That's total crap, Yegor,' retorted Backhouse. 'What lap were you on, six? On a brand-new circuit! There were piss all marbles out there. And I don't like the insinuation, my friend. Some of us were none too chuffed with the bollocks you pulled in Canada against Remy. Don't try anything like that again here, yeah? Sure you want to win – but win fair.'

'Canada not bollocks,' he said his face reddening. 'I – there – sabotaged. This – here – different. Russians of Moscow – dead. Ptarmigan – *she* – got to face horror of blame. She try to cuts corner. *Again*. She already done it before. Montreal – she criticize by *FIA* for doing it.'

Backhouse replied with a phoney chuckle: 'Well, I guess, Yegor, that means we won't be putting *you* on the stand in the trial.'

The Russian began to look agitated.

Baryshnikov stated: 'Ptarmigan must put up hand.' Then, to everyone's amazement, the Russian climbed to his feet, walked down the room, pressed the button, dropped down the steps, and left the motor home.

TWENTY-THREE

There was an awkward silence as the door hissed shut behind him. No one had expected anything like that. Backhouse, now looking a little sheepish, said defensively: 'Teammates are known to have tricky relationships, but this is the worst case of teammate-itis I've ever seen.'

'We can't believe that reaction is entirely driven by competitiveness, can we?' offered Straker.

'You don't know Yegor Baryshnikov,' replied Backhouse.

Straker looked unconvinced.

McMahon said: 'He's Russian – the first Russian driver – at the first Moscow Grand Prix. Expectations here have been ramped for him in F1. And now there's a national catastrophe, given all the more prominence because of the publicity surrounding him; he could well be feeling the public reaction very personally … and taking it badly.'

Straker exhaled. 'Possibly. But I don't like his vibe – he'd better keep his thoughts to himself. We do *not* want a loose cannon.'

Several heads were nodding.

'While Andy was being somewhat flippant,' Straker went on, casting a mildly admonitory glance at Backhouse, 'I share the concern of putting Baryshnikov in the witness box.'

McMahon stepped in: 'Why don't I have a chat with him? Use the cover of calling it a legal briefing, to try and calm him down?'

Straker nodded. 'Good idea. Let's set that up as soon as possible, please? We don't want him brooding on this for too long, God forbid discussing any of those opinions with other people.'

Backhouse agreed and indicated to one of the team, who turned directly away to call Baryshnikov on his phone.

Straker wanted to bring the meeting back on track. 'With Yegor's claims of blame, and the trial apparently a foregone conclusion, there's all the more reason to prepare our defence *properly*. Sandy, you were saying that Gazdanov would find it difficult to prove negligence.'

'I did, but we never take anything for granted in court, even when we have a cast-iron case. Things can always come up, get blown out of proportion, become a distraction – anything can affect a judgment. But,' she continued, 'when a case is not black and white, the trick for any prosecutor is to try and create doubt. If there is no silver bullet, the prosecution is highly likely to blow up other issues – however small – to colour the defendant in a bad light. None of these kinds of issues would probably amount to anything on their own, but put them all together and they can be presented as an insight into the defendant's background, ethical standards or attitude. If done deviously enough, they can make it impossible for the jury to dismiss the actual charge out of hand.'

'Guilt by insinuation?' said Straker.

'And Ms Sabatino will *not* be well served in this trial by having a disciplinary strike against her with the FIA from her last race. Gazdanov will be all over that, without question.'

'How do we guard against this guilt by association thing?' asked Backhouse. 'How do we defend ourselves against it?'

'Brandeis's advice, we hope, is little more than common sense: preparation for trial has to be thorough. We need to go through every incident that Gazdanov could cite where Ptarmigan – or Ms Sabatino – has been found to have breached a rule or regulation. We need to explain what each offence involved, what it meant, and why it didn't really matter. We need to be able to demonstrate how robust the Ptarmigan management systems are in respect of compliance with the FIA rules, the design process of the cars, the testing procedures, safety procedures, and for monitoring and processing feedback. Any slippage, in any of these, and Gazdanov will smell blood. He will go after every flaw and failure – dissect each one – and make each one out to sound heinous. He will then use them, banging on about the sloppiness of the team, expecting everyone to see that with such sloppiness *of course* the cars were unsafe, that Ptarmigan was cutting corners for financial gain, that it was taking reckless risks, and that – *of course* – any accident can be traced straight back to Ptarmigan's cavalier attitude and negligence.'

It was hardly surprising the mood of the team deteriorated. Straker was aware that morale would need to be high if they were going to face up to the gloomy prospect of this trial, not least in motivating the team in the effort needed to prepare for it.

Retaking the floor, Straker thanked McMahon for her explanations and declared that their fightback was starting right now.

'First,' he said, 'we're going to need to put together a basic description of our cars, their capacity, speed characteristics, how they work, the engineering involved, the dangers involved in producing such machines, the safety measures we have built in to them, and a catalogue of our track record vis-à-vis safety.

'Second, we need a full history of Formula One – the accidents that have occurred, what has been done to prevent them, why there are so few these days, the nature of their causes and what, when they do occur, should be the consequences to drivers and spectators.

'Third, we're going to need a full description both technical – and tactical – of what was involved in that corner, what the risks were, what Remy was attempting, what could've happened, what did happen, and why. We also need to hammer the point that this was completely unconnected with the incident in Montreal.

'Fourth, we need a full analysis – effectively frame by frame – of what happened to Remy's car, why it didn't perform as it should have, and how such underperformance caused the crash; we will also need to show how the car's behaviour during the impact and crash caused the injuries.

'Fifth, to counter every tactic Sandy expects the prosecution might use, we need to trawl through instances where Ptarmigan's compliance has underperformed and infringed the rules, we've made a mistake, suffered an FIA intervention, been reprimanded, been fined or been charged with a crime. We need to show how Ptarmigan responded to each of these shortcomings and demonstrate the grown-up processes the team instigated to prevent a recurrence.'

'Focusing on things like our "mistakes", "shortcomings" and "underperformance" is all incredibly negative,' Backhouse replied. 'You make it sound like we were to blame. We should *not* make this overcomplicated. This was a racing incident. Pure and simple … It was one of those things.'

Straker replied. 'I'm not assuming any blame at all; I just want to be sure that we get our retaliation in first. If, as Sandy says, guilt by insinuation is the likely direction of attack, let's pre-empt *everything* Gazdanov could possibly throw at us. If we do all that analysis, we ought to be able to undermine if not rebut any such accusation.'

'How soon can we get access to Sabatino's car?' asked the race engineer.

'We won't,' said McMahon.

'What do you mean?'

'It's been impounded by the police. The court's going to appoint its own expert to investigate the wreckage.'

'How on earth do we do our own assessment, then – put together credible conclusions – if we can't see the damn car?'

'We have all our telemetry stored in here,' Straker replied indicating with a nod of his head the row of blank monitors down the long side of the motor home. 'We'll have to base our observations on that. We can also study the video footage we'll have captured of the accident. That ought to give us a pretty good idea of what went wrong. If we can find out what did happen, we can then try and work out why.'

TWENTY-FOUR

Throughout the day the blanket of cloud over Moscow had been descending. Internal lights were needed in the Ptarmigan motor home, still parked out on its own at the Zhar-ptitsa Autodrom circuit. Activity in the mobile command centre was now frenetic. All the seats down the right-hand side were occupied, and most of the screens were lit. The team was busy building its body of data to try and prove how well-suited the Ptarmigan cars had been to the Zhar-ptitsa circuit. One group of Ptarmigan staff was collating all the telemetry on the car, not just during the race but throughout the preceding practice sessions. Another was studying the telemetry immediately around the crash. A third group was reviewing all the VT footage of the crash, taken from any angle: in the age of multiple on-board cameras, there was considerable coverage garnered from each of the leaders' cars: Yegor Baryshnikov, Remy Sabatino, and Simi Luciano – the three drivers at the front of the race.

While this research was being gathered, Sandy McMahon sat at the end of the meeting table; working at a laptop, she was preparing the basic frameworks for the legal documents – witness statements and evidence – that they would be submitting to the court.

Straker picked up his phone and, to be sure of his privacy, went through into the private cabin at the front of the motor home. Breathing deeply, he made ready to call Dominic Quartano.

The telephone number pulsed out. Jean, the tycoon's indispensable PA, answered the call: 'Mr Quartano's been waiting to hear from you, Matt,' she said. 'He's asked that Stacey Krall be on the call when you speak. Can I ask you to wait while I get her on the line?'

'Of course,' replied Straker, genuinely pleased that Quartech's in-house counsel would be involved. He liked Krall as a feisty operator;

he would also appreciate her assessment of his findings as well as hearing her stress-test his conclusions thus far.

Seconds later Jean was back on the line. Krall was now in tow. 'I'll put you both through,' said the PA and the line went silent.

'Matt,' came Quartano's well-rounded baritone. 'I've been waiting to hear what you've found. I assume you've made contact with Brandeis Gertner?'

'Sandy McMahon picked me up at the airport. She's been with me since I arrived.'

Krall asked: 'Is she any good?'

'Too early to say. We'll know soon enough: we've had some hefty developments even since I got here.'

'Such as?'

'We went to see Tahm, in the cells under the Moscow Police HQ. He's in a dreadful state. His arrest and treatment since have affected him badly. We were granted no privacy; worse, we were supervized by a policeman throughout the meeting.'

'*What?*' blurted Krall. 'Didn't they know McMahon was his lawyer?'

'Oh, yes, but it got worse than that. Every time we come across indelicacies like that, she declares resignedly: "This is Russia!"'

'Holy crap,' said Krall.

'We've applied for bail, for Tahm and Remy, but I'm told we should have no expectation of it being granted.'

Quartano retorted: 'Why ever not?'

'Public opinion. In the light of the accident, it's toxic. While I was in the police station, I was even goaded by a policeman for merely being associated with the deaths.'

'You've got to do whatever it takes to get Tahm out of jail.'

'Of course, but I should warn you that Sandy's written bail off as impossible.'

'Poor man,' said the tycoon. 'Presumably getting him out will depend on matters elsewhere; what are the other developments?'

'We had a press conference sprung on us by the Ministry of

Justice. Not even Brandeis had been informed, even though the authorities categorically know they are Ptarmigan's representative. That conference gave us several surprise developments. One is the altitude this incident has gone up the food chain of government: the minister of justice, himself, hosted the conference. Second, the minister has appointed the prosecutor general to take on this case.'

'Holy cow,' said Krall. 'How does this case warrant *that* degree of overkill?'

'Oh, it doesn't stop there,' agreed Straker. 'The third googly was the location for the trial: the prosecutor general stated that it will be heard … in the Supreme Court.'

'As the court of first instance?'

'Indeed, while the fourth surprise is the timeframe. The trial's been scheduled to be held within four weeks.'

'You're kidding,' said the in-house counsel. 'What the hell's the rush? That's indecent!'

'I'll come to my thoughts on why all this has happened in a moment. The prosecutor general's actual words were: "I intend to have those responsible for this corporate manslaughter before the Supreme Court of Russia – and starting their lifetime of hard labour – within a month."'

'Holy shit.'

'Unbelievable,' agreed Quartano. 'How can you *hope* to prepare for trial under such time pressure? Have you got the guys going over the car to get to the bottom of the accident?'

Straker braced himself. 'No. And we won't. Remy's car has been impounded. McMahon is pretty sure the wreckage is going to be assessed by a court-appointed expert, probably a Russian.'

Quartano nearly exploded: 'A Russian motor racing expert … that's a contradiction in terms. God help us. Do you want me to push San Marino – to get the FIA to step in?'

'No, sir – not publicly; at least – not yet,' replied Straker. 'One of the reasons the Russians are investigating all this themselves is because they see F1 standards as responsible for the crash. San Marino and the FIA, therefore, are being seen as part of the problem. The Russians are dead against any involvement by the FIA – convinced the FIA's primary objective would be to mount a cover-up of the accident. Bringing them in privately, though, could be very helpful; but let me try and build up a clearer picture of what went wrong first, before we talk to San Marino?'

'Okay, Matt – say when you want ... I'm sure I can encourage his involvement.'

'Ahead of that,' said Straker, 'Andy Backhouse is pretty sure we can piece together most of what we need from the telemetry records, either here in the motor home, or back at the factory.'

'We've got no time to waste – God, Stacey – four weeks to the trial. What do we do for a silk? We've got to have a Rottweiler – and a fast-working one?'

'Oscar Brogan would be perfect,' replied Krall. 'I'll brief him straight away.'

'What about the language issue?' asked Straker. 'The trial's likely to be in Russian, isn't it?'

'Undoubtedly, which makes Brogan all the more perfect,' said Krall with a chuckle. 'Oscar Brogan – né Osip Broganski – is first-generation British: his parents were Russian émigrés.'

'How lucky is that?' agreed Straker. 'Even so, the sod here – of course – is going to be that our response to the legal attack would be far more effective if we could be aggressive, fight back on a similar footing – which Oscar masters without question. But that would kill public sympathy for us. We can never forget that thirty-one people died as a result of all this.'

'It's going to be a tough one to fight,' observed Quartano. 'I'd have every confidence that Brogan would strike the right balance – pitch it right.'

Straker judged this was the moment to bring up his next concern. 'Talking of a tough fight, I should tell you we've had a strange incident with Yegor Baryshnikov this afternoon.'

'What now?' Quartano asked.

'I'd just held a preliminary meeting of the team, introducing Brandeis as our lawyer. Baryshnikov was adamant the trial is going to be a foregone conclusion – that we will lose, not least as Gazdanov had been appointed as the prosecutor. Worse, Baryshnikov firmly placed the blame for the crash on Sabatino.'

'Oh God, no; he's not up to more of his Montreal mind games, is he?' Krall asked.

'I think it's worse than that. Baryshnikov stated, unequivocally, that Ptarmigan should take full responsibility for the deaths. When we tried to disagree with him he pushed back vehemently and ended up storming out of our meeting.'

'What's *wrong* with that man?'

Krall asked: 'Does he want to win *that* badly?'

'For God's sake, don't let him anywhere near the press. If he gets reported saying anything like that, he'll seal Ptarmigan's fate for good.'

'McMahon's going to speak to him as soon as possible – to make sure he knows how important all this is.'

'What about Remy?' asked Quartano. 'Have you managed to speak to her yet? *Her* testimony will be crucial.'

'It will be,' said Straker, 'but, no. Andy was talking to the hospital this afternoon. She *is* now conscious, apparently, but extremely frail. The police have put her under armed guard.'

'In the hospital? Jesus,' said Krall. 'More overkill!'

Quartano asked: 'To keep her captive?'

'Essentially, yes – although I'm glad they are, actually. I would worry for Sabatino's safety if she *weren't* that well guarded. The accident continues to cause great distress. I told you about the goading I received from the police. There were also massive crowds protesting outside the Ministry of Justice this afternoon, and there's a three-hundred-man vigil outside the main gates of the Grand Prix circuit.'

'Sounds almost like hysteria,' said Quartano.

'For sure something's going on. The prosecution, though, is probably this zealous as an institutional response, trying to assuage the public mood. The government seems hell-bent on being seen to do something to avenge the dead.'

'And, now, poor Tahm and Remy are stuck in the middle of all this,' sighed Quartano, 'apparently with the full weight of the State bearing down on them.'

'They are,' agreed Straker. 'Worse, if the charge of corporate manslaughter sticks, they're each looking at twenty years' hard labour.'

TWENTY-FIVE

That lunchtime Remy Sabatino had her first solid food since the crash. Because of the halo device, she had to be propped up on a mountain of pillows. Half sitting, a wheeled hospital-bed tray was positioned in front of her, enabling her to eat lunch in bed. Her motor skills were shaky. She dribbled and spilled a fair amount, but was determined to manage. Swallowing was agony. Even so, she felt better almost at once for having eaten something substantial.

Sabatino was still being kept in isolation, enforced by the armed policemen outside her door. As a result, she had not been spoken to by anyone other than the consultant since the accident – and he'd not discussed anything of what had happened. Nurses were now slipping in and out without speaking to her as if she was toxic. She still knew nothing of the details of her accident. She was confused, sore and wondering why no one had come to see her.

Having ended the call to London, Straker remained in the private cabin of the motor home. There was a knock on the door. He heard a muffled 'Matt' and recognized Backhouse's voice. Straker open the door.

'I think we might have found something.'

Straker followed him into the open-plan section of the motor home.

'What is it?'

'Something,' replied Backhouse pulling out two stools from under the central workstation.

'Perhaps Sandy should see this, too?' suggested Straker, and caught the lawyer's attention. Leaving her laptop, McMahon crossed the motor home and pulled out a stool for herself.

'We've found a fair amount of material,' reported Backhouse.

'This, though, is a very telling clip of the crash,' he said pointing at the computer monitor. He pressed Play.

The coverage began with an aerial view of Sabatino's turquoise car in the middle of the screen. She was exiting Turn Ten, close behind the race leader – Yegor Baryshnikov – in the other turquoise car. The footage showed Sabatino beginning her charge down the half-mile straight. It showed her make her move, closing up behind Baryshnikov, slipstreaming in the lee of his rear wing. Then they saw her dive out to the right – and make her approach to Turn Eleven, the long sweeping left-hander.

Backhouse tapped the keyboard to freeze-frame the film.

Using a two-finger spread he enlarged the image and centred it. The car was facing to the right. It was as if they were now directly overhead, looking straight down into the Ptarmigan cockpit. Filling the screen were Sabatino's helmet, chest, arms and both hands on the steering wheel.

'This here,' said Backhouse, turning to face both Straker and McMahon, 'is just before Remy starts to turn in – turning left – into the corner, yes?'

Straker agreed.

Backhouse nudged the footage on by two frames. 'Now look,' he said. 'You can just see – there – Remy is starting to turn the wheel. Her intent to turn is clear; she's rotating it away from horizontal, her right hand has clearly tried to rise. The car is starting to turn.'

Straker leant in to observe the image more closely.

McMahon did the same.

'At that speed,' said Backhouse, 'with such a direct steering ratio, and given the car's impeccable balance, what Remy did just then *should* have been more than enough to set the car up for the turn.' Tapping the footage on, he stopped a few frames later. 'This is three-tenths of a second on, after she's initiated the turn. Look at her now.'

Straker and McMahon leant in closer.

'Look at her position,' suggested Backhouse. 'From having simply raised her right hand and lowered her left, she's now raising her right elbow – her right shoulder has even moved forwards, off the back of her seat.'

Straker's said. 'So she's exerting herself, is that what you're saying?'

'Exactly. Hydraulic-assisted steering on a Formula One car should be sensitive to little more than fingertip pressure. Here, on a part of the track we would expect to be dirty, and therefore far lighter on the steering anyway, Remy looks like she's trying to heave the wheel over – wrestling with it. She's using her whole arm and shoulder.'

Then, putting his finger on the screen, Backhouse slid the whole frozen image across to the left, until the front of Sabatino's car came into view.

Straker saw it immediately. 'Holy fuck.'

'What?' asked McMahon.

'Look at the front wheels, Sandy,' said Backhouse tapping them on the screen with the backs of his fingers.

McMahon observed: 'So she's turned the steering wheel, but her front wheels are still pointing straight ahead. The car's going straight on?'

'Good God.'

'But that's not all. Look at this,' said Backhouse, this time sliding the frozen image the other way, past the cockpit to bring the rear wheels into the picture. 'We missed this when the film was run at normal speed; we only spotted it in slow motion. Look at this,' he said pointing to Sabatino's right rear, 'something happens for a fraction of a second.'

'A wisp of smoke,' observed McMahon. 'What does that mean?'

'Remy's right-rear wheel is suddenly under-rotating.'

Straker leant back in again. 'Has she braked, there?'

Backhouse shook his head. 'We're still pulling all the telemetry together and so don't know, for sure. But the brake balance favoured the fronts, meaning that if she *had* braked sharply enough for the tyres to lock-up, the fronts should have done so first.'

'If this part of the track *was* dirty, though – as you suggested – wouldn't that account for a tyre losing full grip … and locking-up?'

Backhouse nodded. 'Very possibly, except I don't understand why it did so only for a fraction of a second?'

'What's caused it, then?'

Backhouse looked pained. 'We don't know yet, and won't until we see the loading through each brake.'

'What happens to Remy next?'

Backhouse prompted the film to roll on a few more frames before stopping it again. 'This is another three-tenths on – and, here, Remy's definitely clocked there's a problem.'

Straker could see that Sabatino's arm and shoulder were relaxed again, having returned the steering wheel to the horizontal. 'It looks like she's given up on the front wheels showing any sign of response.'

Backhouse nodded.

'That's pretty significant, isn't it – that degree of resignation? Is she braking now?'

'Again, we're waiting to look at the telemetry.'

'Go on.'

'A driver in that situation *will* hit the brakes, almost as a flinch.'

'And?'

'On a dirty surface, which *this* bit most certainly was, the front tyres would be expected to lock-up pretty easily and, now, be very likely to produce smoke.' Backhouse leant forward to press the space bar to let the footage run on. It did so in slow motion.

Straker strained his eyes to study the image on the screen. Sabatino's car was moving left to right in a straight line. It approached the red-and-white kerbstones on the edge of the track before the gravel.

'There's no lock-up,' said Straker.

'Nor smoke,' offered McMahon.

'Precisely,' said Backhouse. 'And apart from that tiny wisp of smoke from the rear right, none of the wheels lock-up again – even when she gets out onto the gravel. Furthermore, there seems to be no noticeable deceleration, either.'

'Meaning what? That she *didn't* brake?'

'Or that she couldn't.'

Straker was staring at the screen. 'Remy's steering becoming unexpectedly heavy – is that the reason you think she left the circuit?'

Backhouse shrugged. 'She did go straight on – after she'd tried to turn the wheel … twice.'

'So what's *caused* that?' asked McMahon.

'It could be a number of things. The steering column might have been impeded for some reason. If it was, then the steering mechanism would have been harder to turn. The steering of an FI car ceased to be entirely mechanical decades ago, some hydraulic assistance having been permitted under the different Formulas of recent years. To provide that assistance, there's a metering valve set on the steering column, activated by any rotation of it. That causes hydraulic flow into the pistons that apply the assistance. This metering valve is a tiny component and *can* be intolerant. Any dirt getting in there, for instance, could impede the flow of fluid; if Remy's car suffered that, then the steering hydraulics wouldn't have been given any commands, resulting in no help being given to turn the steering column and therefore the front wheels. But those are the things that would be specific to the steering.

'If there was also a simultaneous problem with the brakes, that suggests it might have been the hydraulics. One pump serves all the hydraulics on our cars. If that had failed then, automatically, the hydraulics in the steering would fail, as would the calipers in the brakes. It might have been that one of the hydraulic tubes burst: these things are only the thickness of a pencil but can still withstand the pressure of two hundred atmospheres. A burst in that system, carrying the fluid around it, could have caused an instant loss of power. Any such failure would kill the power-assistance, making the steering heavy *and* affect the brakes.'

'So hydraulics seem to be the common denominator?' suggested Straker.

'Do these systems fail often?' asked McMahon.

Backhouse shook his head. 'Hardly ever, but we could never say never. It's entirely possible there could have been a catastrophic failure in any of the components, completely without warning. Around a Grand Prix circuit – particularly at race pace – the stresses and strains are immense. Who knows? A bad bump, a collision, a contact with a kerbstone – any or all such incidents could shock the system enough to cause a failure.'

Straker asked: 'How do we narrow it down, Andy – to pinpoint the actual cause?'

'Normally we would go over the car. We would examine each and every component, and check everything … but …'

'… we can't get access to the wreckage,' confirmed McMahon.

'We are, though, gathering all the telemetry across the car. We'll just have to hope we can find other clues to give us an idea.'

'We've *got* to know what happened,' said McMahon gravely, '*and* have a solid explanation for this. Any kind of mechanical failure would leave Ptarmigan hugely vulnerable to accusations of mechanical underperformance, design underperformance, management underperformance – and, therefore, corporate underperformance. I can't stress this enough. Identifying the reason for the failure of the car is *critical* to defending ourselves against the charges of corporate manslaughter.'

TWENTY-SIX

Remy Sabatino may have felt better after a modest go at her first proper meal since the accident, but she was now getting bored. A television was mounted on the far wall. Awkwardly she used what limited movement the halo brace allowed to look around her bed and bedside table, trying to find the remote. She couldn't see it. It must be in one of the drawers, she realized, but didn't have the mobility to check. When the next nurse attended her, Sabatino croakily asked for the remote. The medic barely nodded before leaving the room.

Ten minutes later the senior staff nurse appeared. Sabatino repeated her request to have the television on, again asking for the remote. The nurse shook her head. 'The doctor says not to watch television,' and dropped two celebrity magazines onto the bed tray in front of her.

Sabatino replied: 'Why not? How could watching TV do me any harm?' The nurse had already turned her back and was opening the door to leave.

There was no further response to Sabatino's questions.

'What on earth is going on?' she rasped to the empty room.

Later that afternoon Remy Sabatino was subjected to a further series of tests. Her strength seemed to be improving, but she was constantly reminded of her accident by the intense pains running down her left flank.

Helped up into a half-sitting position, Sabatino found herself able to concentrate on some of the articles in one of the trashy celebrity magazines, if only for short periods at a time. Because of the residual effects of the coma-inducing drugs, she didn't notice that the editions she had been given were at least three months old.

Matt Straker turned to face the race engineer. 'What you have found, Andy, seems to have narrowed down the apparent cause of the crash. It gives us something to focus our research on.'

Backhouse nodded. 'As well as gathering the telemetry, I've now got the guys going through all the records of the steering mechanism, the brakes and the hydraulics – the history of each component involved, when it was made, when any of the elements were replaced, who did the work and when they were last tested. That way, we can hopefully demonstrate our system was young enough and proven enough to have been trustworthy. I'm hoping that we can show – if it *was* a component failure – that we were not wrong to have had faith in it for the race.'

'Would the issues you've spotted have any consequences for the crash itself? How the car went on to behave? How it might have affected the spectators as it broke up?'

Backhouse shrugged. 'I doubt it, but now that we suspect what might have gone wrong, we could take a look.'

They all turned back to face the screen.

Backhouse pressed Play. The video clip ran on.

Straker re-watched Sabatino's reaction to the steering failure. The car was shown reaching the outside of the bend, where it bounced violently over the red-and-white kerbstones around the outside edge of the corner and headed off across the gravel trap.

'Steering and brakes are completely ineffectual across this sort of loose surface,' Backhouse explained, 'although Remy does do something unusual.'

Straker said: 'Oh, yes?'

'She reapplies the lock from the steering wheel.'

'While she's on the gravel? Knowing it wouldn't have any grip?'

Backhouse nodded.

'Why would she do that?'

'Because it's doing something.'

'What does that mean?' asked McMahon.

'Remy was hurtling forwards, effectively out of control.

Instinctively, she should be braking right here – except that, on this loose gravel, any brake pressure would *surely* result in locked-up wheels. But, look, she's not even doing that – all four wheels are still rolling.'

'So it *did* look like the brakes failed?'

Backhouse shrugged. 'We'll have to wait to read the tea leaves. But if she's not getting any deceleration from the brakes, and you've nothing left, you might try anything to slow down; hence it looks like she's turned the steering wheel to try and use the angle of the front wheels as a some sort of retardant.'

'So the steering *is* working *here*?' McMahon offered. 'No longer heavy?'

'On loose gravel, Sandy, the steering probably would turn.'

'And how much effect did doing this have?' Straker asked.

'Nothing significant.'

Straker examined the screen closely. 'But by turning the wheels she meant to create something of a plough effect?'

'Pretty much.'

'At that speed, Andy, wouldn't the gravel, stones, dust – whatever – ruck up in front of the wheels? Spray outwards?'

Backhouse nodded.

'Why isn't it, then?'

Backhouse's face showed genuine surprise.

He peered in closer to study Straker's observation.

He ran the footage back and forward several times, to make sure. 'Well, I'll be…'

As the footage of the crash was run on, the next occurrence was the car striking the tyre wall.

Backhouse stopped the footage again. 'This is how the crash became so catastrophic,' he said, 'how the subsequent damage was done.'

The frozen frame showed the Ptarmigan at the moment it made contact with the tyres. 'We can see here, very clearly, the speed of her impact,' said Backhouse. To make the point, he ran his finger across the screen from where Sabatino had left the track to her point of collision. 'Modern circuits have sizeable run-off areas, across which cars are given a chance of slowing down, long before they come into contact with anything solid. Formula One has instituted massive improvements to this idea over the years. Early on, it was simply straw bales lining the track. Then we saw speed traps made from wire netting held up by fence posts, which had to be abandoned because some wretched drivers were nearly decapitated. One of the crucial breakthroughs in safety, where space is tight, was the development of the Armco barrier. In more spacious circuits, there was a move to wide, loose-lying gravel traps – designed to slow cars down with minimal forces of deceleration. The most modern circuits nowadays have large expanses of asphalt, where the cars can slow down over much longer distances.'

'But?'

'The Zhar-ptitsa appears to comply with all those modern safety standards, but it doesn't quite, somehow.'

'That's a little cryptic,' said McMahon. 'In what way?'

Backhouse responded: 'They've used tyres, rather than the more modern interlocking Tecpro barriers and, most significantly, they've used a gravel trap here, rather than the more recent preference of an asphalt run-off.'

'So?'

'Remy went across that gravel trap extraordinarily quickly.'

'Why wouldn't she?' asked the lawyer. 'How fast was she going when she left the track?'

'Probably a hundred and eighty-plus miles an hour.'

'So she was *going* to be going fast,' added McMahon.

'No question,' countered Backhouse. 'But my point is that a gravel run-off should still offer *some* deceleration. It should do something to slow a car down, even one going this fast. I'm saying it didn't seem to offer her *any*. The gravel did almost nothing to slow the speed of the car.'

Straker latched onto this observation. 'Could that be connected in some way to the lack of gravel spray we saw as Remy turned the wheel?'

Backhouse pulled a face. 'Possibly. It might have something to do with the way the trap was made? The type of gravel they used? The depth of it, perhaps?'

Straker was silent.

'Then,' said Backhouse, 'there's the angle of impact. Current design, where possible, constructs barriers, walls and perimeters at a very shallow angle to the track. A car is meant to glance off on its initial contact with something solid, or at least merge with it slowly, so as to slow the car down without a sudden impact.'

'And here?'

'The outer concrete wall, and the tyre buffer in front of it, are at a pretty steep angle to the direction of travel.'

'So the impact was going to be more severe?'

'Exactly.'

'Is that a design flaw, or just an unlucky fluke?'

Backhouse shrugged his lack of strong opinion. 'Turn Eleven is far more of a curve than a corner. There's more than enough room to brake beforehand if the drivers wished, allowing them to decelerate without destabilising their cars. This is not a corner that most in Formula One would expect drivers to come off at.'

'Doesn't that rather back up Yegor Baryshnikov's comment, then, that her attempt to go around the outside was *not* expected: that she *was* taking a huge risk – doing something beyond the expected safety of the circuit?'

'Maybe. All I'm saying at this point is that Sabatino's impact was faster and more severe than I would have expected it to be. Before she got there, hardly any of the energy of the car had been dissipated, which meant that this crash was going to be more violent – go on for longer – and go further – than it ought to have done.

'And then we come on to the other "break" with modern circuits. Tyres instead of Tecpro barriers.'

'What difference would that make?'

'Tecpro dissipates more of the energy away laterally, and doesn't reassert itself after impact anything like as much.' At this, he nudged the video on, one frame at a time, until it showed Sabatino's rear wheels lifting off the ground. 'There,' he said, 'do you see the tyres? Having been compressed by the impact, they are now bouncing back – reasserting themselves. I think that force, pushing back and down on the nose cone, was why the back wheels were lifted off the ground, and why the car started to rotate.'

Straker scrutinized the picture. 'We'll definitely need to check this further. We could challenge the circuit's design during the trial. At this stage, though, what effect could a steering failure have had on the dynamics of the car?' he asked.

Backhouse looked at each wheel and the nose cone assembly. 'By eye, I couldn't say there was anything different at this point; we can try and confirm some of this when more of the detailed data comes in. At the point of impact, the front wheels are centred, back in the middle of their lock.'

Backhouse cued the video again.

Sabatino's car was now rotating through the vertical and starting to somersault. Once again the film was stopped and studied, but without significance.

It was restarted – again in slow motion. A few moments later it was Straker who leant forwards and froze the frame. He'd done so after the inverted car had slammed into the "I"-sectioned upright and had begun to swing round horizontally. 'What about here? Does anything untoward happen to the front wheels, now, because of a steering failure?'

After Backhouse had peered at the image for a few seconds he said: 'Not that I can see.'

On it went again, right through to the point when the car was spinning on up the grassy bank, scything through the people on it.

'Does it look like a potential steering failure made it any more likely that Sabatino's car would hit or kill any more spectators during the actual crash?' Straker asked.

Backhouse said: 'Not that I can tell from this. My key observations, from what we *have* seen, remain the speed of the car across the gravel – and the angle of impact with the tyre and concrete walls.'

They let the video footage run on. It then became an aerial shot, taken from the helicopter circling directly overhead.

Suddenly Straker's attention was held.

'Andy, Andy,' he said quickly, 'back up – back it up.'

Backhouse touched the slider on the screen.

The clip was replayed. The camera was focusing on a broken part of the wall. Straker tapped a key and froze the frame.

'What?' asked Backhouse.

Straker, using a two-finger spread, enlarged his selected area of the image to fill the screen. 'Take a look at that...' he said.

Backhouse peered in.

'Does that look normal to you?'

Backhouse's eyes narrowed, moments before he shook his head. 'Good God, no. No, it does not.'

TWENTY-SEVEN

Sandy McMahon was distracted from their video analysis. Her mobile had just gone off. Answering it, she was told that the Yeltsin Meditsinskiy Tsentr had just rung her office in Brandeis Gertner. Apparently, Remy Sabatino's condition was improving – and Mr Uglov, the consultant in charge, had declared the injured Formula One driver fit enough to be interviewed by the police.

When McMahon passed this on to Straker, he became agitated. 'We've no idea how ready for this she is – no indication of her condition. We have got to speak to her before any interview is held.'

MacMahon agreed.

'Given the legal stakes and sensitivities, it's imperative she has legal representation there – particularly if the police are as brutal with her as they have been with Tahm. Is Remy really going to be robust enough for all this so soon after such trauma? Sandy, these people aren't going to interview her – they are going to *interrogate* her. She'd be hugely vulnerable to intimidation, to being tripped up – to being prompted into saying something incriminating.'

McMahon launched into a rapid round of phone calls and email correspondence with the Ministry of Justice, the British Consulate and the hospital – urgently trying to secure Remy Sabatino's right to legal representation.

After an hour of protracted negotiation, McMahon managed to achieve a result. Once again it needed an intervention by the British consul, personally, directly with the prosecutor general. Talking over the loudspeaker on the phone in the private cabin of the motor home, the consul said: 'I'm afraid I had to go quite far. I hadn't meant to, but the intransigence of these institutions on all this is staggering. I made the point emphatically to Gazdanov himself, that the eyes of the world were on this case. I said that any hint of legal nihilism – anything less than a full, clear, equitable process – would have serious international consequences. But that didn't seem to bother him.'

'How *did* you swing it, then?' asked Straker.

The consul said: 'In desperation, I'm ashamed to say, I brought up the Magnitsky scandal. That did work, though; it was the only thing to knock him back. That and the likelihood of more UN sanctions.'

'*Magnitsky* did it?' Straker said.

'It seemed to. Their attitude in this Grand Prix case, though, is unprecedented,' said the consul. 'There is a zealotry involved; I've never known anything like it. Anyway, you now have permission to go and see Ms Sabatino before the police do. I can only advise you make the most of your time with her, as I wouldn't want to say how many more chances you'll get.'

Straker thanked the consul for his efforts.

They disconnected the call. Straker said: 'Let's go to Remy straight away. We don't want to miss the chance to debrief her – and to warn her of what's about to happen.'

They headed into central Moscow. The day's overcast light was still unbroken by the blanket of low cloud. It rendered every view sullen and drab. Straker looked out of the window as they made their way west through southern Moscow along the Third Ring Road.

'It was extraordinary to hear the prosecutor general's reaction to the consul bringing up your example of the Magnitsky case.'

'I'm not surprised it had an effect on him,' McMahon replied. 'It *would* have been a provocative point. That case was a huge issue here.'

'And the consul mentioned sanctions: I hadn't realized the UN went that far.'

McMahon nodded: 'Oh, yes – it all went a very long way. December 2012. The US Congress even passed the Magnitsky Act, imposing significant restrictions on US citizens and companies interacting with key Russian officials. The biggest impact was that it prevented named Russians – senior people – from using the American banking system.'

'Did that work?'

'Disproportionately well, actually, and not to the detriment of the Russian economy, that time. Most of the senior government figures had sizeable wealth abroad. That Act of Congress froze those assets, targeting pretty effectively the political class that was probably responsible for the Magnitsky death in the first place. Hence, I imagine, the sensitivity when the consul raised it in his conversation with the prosecutor general. Diplomatically, though, the Magnitsky Act served to recalibrate the world's view on the integrity and reliability of Russia's institutions. And to those of a certain age, it was an uneasy flashback to the Soviet Russia of the Cold War.'

Their car pulled up outside the hospital. In reception, the permission they believed they had been granted to see Sabatino was flatly refused. Once again, numerous calls had to be made – back through the British Consulate, and from there to the prosecutor general's office – before their request was finally granted. It took thirty minutes for this tortuous communication trail to bear fruit.

Eventually, it was Mr Uglov who appeared in reception to authorize their visit. But his approval was heavily qualified. They had to fill out detailed forms before they were allowed any further into the hospital; even when those had been completed, several of their entries were challenged or elaborations were demanded. Only after that did the consultant let the visitors up to Sabatino's room.

Straker's concern was compounded when their way was barred by the two armed policemen standing guard directly outside her door. Further records were taken of his and McMahon's ID before they were allowed through.

At last Sabatino's door was opened to them.

Straker led the way in.

He wasn't sure what to expect. The reality of her state struck him hard. In a closed room, the curtains still drawn under orders from the police, Sabatino was lying on the bed, lit by a harsh overhead fluorescent light. Monitors, drips and tubes attached to needles in her right arm were arranged haphazardly around her bed.

It was Remy Sabatino's encasement in the halo brace that hit Straker hardest: its ring bolted to her skull, and the four spars anchoring it rigidly to the body-armour-like vest, created a harrowing image.

Lying under a single sheet, folded back to her waist because of the body armour, Sabatino wore a hospital gown to cover the rest of her torso. Straker saw the plaster casts on her left leg and arm. He saw the tracheotomy tube protruding from her throat – and the small patch of diffuse blood that was showing through the cloth-like straps around her neck. His expression fully reflected his shock.

Straker wasn't sure that Sabatino was yet aware of his presence. He studied her eyes and realized she was in a semi-stupor. Gently, he said: 'Remy?'

Her eyes swivelled towards the voice. Sabatino breathed: 'Matt!'

She moved her right hand across her body – the tubes from the drip flapping – to touch his arm.

The warmth she derived from seeing someone familiar showed immediately in her eyes; tears started welling. 'What are *you* doing here? I've not seen anybody – no one's come to see me – not Tahm, Andy, Yegor. I've been completely isolated.'

All Straker could do, thinking of the legal situation they faced, was to squeeze her hand and offer some comfort.

'I have no idea which hospital I'm in, or where I am. I'm just relieved to be in one piece … well … sort of.'

Straker continued to hold her hand, longing to provide support for as long as possible. It was clear that Sabatino was completely oblivious to what had been going on.

Straker looked across at McMahon who tilted her head sharply in the direction of the armed police in the corridor outside.

'Remy, I don't know how much time we are likely to have with you, so I need to bring you up to date quickly – in case we get thrown out of here.'

Sabatino smiled, expecting this to be some sort of joke.

'I need to introduce you to Sandy McMahon,' he said.

The lawyer stepped forward into Sabatino's field of vision.

'Sandy's with a firm of solicitors here in Moscow. DQ has appointed her and Brandeis Gertner to look after you and Ptarmigan.'

'A solicitor – to look after me?' she rasped.

'Remy, it seems you've not been told anything about your accident.'

Sabatino acknowledged the point with silence.

'Things have become rather complicated. Are you up to this?'

Sabatino's eyes showed a hint of concern for the first time.

Straker moved in closer and sat on the bed beside her. 'You had a terrible accident – crash, at the Grand Prix.'

She smiled as if to say *tell me about it*.

'You went off the track – at high speed. You hit the tyre wall, went through a concrete wall and fence, and ...' Straker paused, '... landed in among a group of spectators.'

Sabatino's face fell. 'Oh God,' she said. 'Were any of them hurt?'

Straker braced himself: 'Remy, thirty-one people were killed.'

Without saying a word, new tears were welling in her large dark eyes. In a matter of moments they were running down her cheeks. She stuttered: 'Thirty ... one ... people ... *dead?*'

Straker squeezed her hand again.

Sabatino did not speak. Her eyes rolled up, her whole body seemed to slump and, then, with her face crumbling, she let out a heart-wrenching, uncontrollable howl. All her pain – all the discomfort she had endured for the last few days – all the attempts she had made to be brave – all her struggles to recover – all were set at nought. Her trials, efforts and the challenges she'd set herself – all her little triumphs – meant absolutely nothing against the horror of anybody dying.

Sabatino was now sobbing, her breathing becoming deeper – more rapid – and uncomfortable under the body armour of her brace. Straker put his other hand on hers, trying to provide any form of comfort. Sabatino howled again, tears pouring down her cheeks. She needed to sniff, to keep her airways clear. Straker continued to hold her hand, thinking it best simply to let her react as fully as possible, to help her start to come to terms with this news.

From across the room, McMahon approached the bed. 'We are sorry that this has come as such a shock,' she said.

Taking his cue, Straker said: 'Remy, Sandy and I need to talk a few things through with you, as the Ptarmigan situation – here – is pretty serious.'

Sabatino's attention was held for a moment, distracted from the deaths.

'Ms Sabatino,' said McMahon. 'As Colonel Straker has explained, I am a solicitor and have been asked to look after you. Dr Nazar has been arrested. The government here in Moscow has charged Ptarmigan and him with corporate manslaughter for the deaths of the spectators at the Grand Prix. You, yourself, have been placed under police guard while you remain in the hospital.'

'*I'm* under police guard?' She paused. 'Does that mean … *I* am also under arrest?'

McMahon shrugged. 'Sort of,' she said.

'What does that mean, Matt?' she asked, sniffing severely – prompting Straker to reach for some tissues sitting in a box on her bedside table.

'The authorities have declared that they want to put the two of you on trial – for the deaths that occurred at the race,' stated McMahon.

A look of concern crossed her face.

'The trial has been announced very publicly, because of how fiercely the public has reacted to the accident,' said Straker. 'Public feeling is running so high that the president of Russia has got involved. A prosecutor has already been announced.'

'Colonel Straker and I are looking into what might have happened. I gather the colonel is highly effective as an investigator; I am confident we can construct a powerful defence.'

Straker looked down into Sabatino's eyes. 'Andy and I have already made a good start,' he said. 'But we're going to need you, though – as soon as you can – to tell us everything you can remember, to help us understand what might have happened, and what might have gone wrong to cause you to crash where you did.'

There was suddenly a noise from outside her room.

The policemen were moving about outside. Agitated discussion could be heard taking place in the corridor.

'I have tried not to remember too much about it,' said Sabatino.

'I understand,' said Straker.

'I think I was attempting to go wide,' Sabatino went on hesitantly. 'I was going round – wide – and was ready for the track to be dirty. But when I got out there,' she said, sniffing again, 'the steering went.'

Voices again came from the direction of the corridor. 'Sandy, could you go and see what's going on?'

The lawyer nodded.

'What did the steering feel like, Rems?' Straker asked.

'Not normal, at all,' she said. 'I remember starting to turn. And then feeling huge resistance. The wheel wouldn't move. Then I hit the brakes – and, in a millisecond, I was hurtling across the gravel.'

Straker could hear McMahon's voice discussing something animatedly with someone outside the room. He was concerned that a halt could be called to their visit at any moment. 'Did you feel the brakes kick in? – I know this must be painful.'

Sabatino breathed deeply, trying to dismiss all her emotions from her thoughts. 'I can't remember, Matt,' her voice cracking slightly. 'I really can't,' she said trying to cast her mind back – trying to think of something to help her and Ptarmigan's cause. 'My memory's so patchy.'

'Was there anything that happened to you or the car in the race *before* that manoeuvre? Anything that didn't work as it should? Do you remember hitting anything – a kerb, another car? Was there anything that could have upset the workings of the car that morning, before the incident?'

'No,' she said. 'The car was *perfect*. Best I've ever known it. I was ready to take Yegor in that move. I remember everything was going exactly as planned.'

'What do you think caused the resistance to the steering, then, Rems?'

Sabatino fell silent, trying to concentrate.

More voices were audible outside. The door was banged hard and swung inwards. 'Was there anything else that happened that afternoon – or during that manoeuvre – that struck you as strange?' he asked.

Sabatino's face screwed up in concentration. 'I don't know … I really don't, Matt,' she said with tears in her voice. 'I don't know whether I'm remembering or imagining things.'

'Doesn't matter,' said Straker.

'I think … I don't know … there might – *might* have been some kind of jolt – as I began to turn in.'

'What kind of jolt?'

Straker's attention was suddenly caught by the door flying open and Mr Uglov striding in. 'You're going to have to leave,' declared the consultant. 'Your visit's over.'

McMahon was following the doctor back into the room, having appeared to have been pushed out of his way. 'What's going on here?' demanded the lawyer. 'We've had permission – through the British consul – from the prosecutor general's office.'

Mr Uglov seemed unmoved. Shouting through the doors of the room in Russian he seemed to be issuing instructions. Moments later the two policemen came charging in, brandishing their weapons.

McMahon moved past Uglov and leant in over Sabatino.

The patient seemed a little taken aback at seeing the lawyer's face up so close.

'At no time should you say anything to *anyone* here,' McMahon instructed her. 'Do not discuss anything to do with the crash, or Ptarmigan, with anyone, even the medical staff. Remember, any of them could be called as a witness. Matt and I will be fighting your case as hard as we can. Please try and put all this out of your mind – easier said … I know.'

As McMahon was giving her urgent briefing, the two policemen had walked up behind her. One of them was issuing instructions. She straightened up and turned to face them.

Straker took advantage of the distraction.

Quickly digging into his pocket, he pulled out his phone and, without looking down, turned it off and shoved it into Sabatino's hand, closing her fingers around it. He then pulled the blanket up over the phone. Bending down, he appeared to be kissing her; instead, he was whispering: 'Take this. Turn it on only for a few minutes every four hours – eight a.m. to eight p.m. each day – and wait for any instructions or news. To save the battery, turn it straight off again after you check for messages. If anything happens here that you're worried about – text Andy straight away, yes?'

Tightening her grip around the phone, Sabatino felt some relief that she might at last have a link to the outside world.

A few minutes later McMahon and Straker were being physically escorted out of the main entrance of the hospital.

TWENTY-EIGHT

Standing outside the front of the medical centre in the twilight, neither Straker nor McMahon knew how to react professionally to what had just happened. It was so far removed from anything they might have expected. If anything, the lawyer was taking it worse.

'This is intolerable,' said McMahon. 'Either one hand of government doesn't know what the other hand is doing, or they are maniacally changing their minds.'

Straker was quiet, trying to weigh it all up.

'Aren't you appalled?' she asked him.

'I take it this incident has finally taken us beyond the stock response of: "This is Russia"?'

McMahon wasn't happy at her own line being used back at her.

Their car drew up. Both climbed in to the rear. Pulling away, it headed towards the centre of Moscow.

Straker spent some more time looking out of the window. As he turned to face McMahon, though, he was intrigued: for the first time that day she looked as if she was ready to defer to him.

In response, Straker offered: 'We need to try and see what has been going on for what it might mean.'

'I don't understand.'

'We need to put all this in perspective,' explained Straker. 'The accident at the Grand Prix was horrible ... dreadful. It would be perfectly natural – and expected – for there to be a negative public reaction – a public outcry.'

'So?'

'We need to consider what a rational and proportionate response to that *ought* to look like, even if it was horrible.'

McMahon looked as if she didn't know whether that was a rhetorical point or whether she was meant to hazard a response.

Helping her out, Straker went on: 'No aspect of the "system's" reaction to this tragedy, so far, could be considered as anything close to "normal". None of the authorities' actions could be described as "expected". A humiliating arrest and a Black Maria? Impounding the wreckage and the crash site, denying us the chance – and the best experts – to examine them both? Initiating legal proceedings ahead of any investigation?

'At the same time, some of their actions could only be described as overkill: appointing the country's most senior prosecutor? Escalating this case to the highest court in the land? Holding the trial in four weeks?

'While some of the "system's" other actions seem almost vindictive – such as denying both the accused legal representation, and even countermanding permission to see your clients when such permission had been granted?'

McMahon didn't offer a challenge to any of these observations.

'I am prompted, therefore, to wonder ... Why?' said Straker. '*Why* is nothing about what has happened since the accident "normal", let alone reasonable? Why has everything been so exaggerated?'

With the continued lack of pushback from McMahon, Straker paused.

'You know,' he said in a softer tone, 'when things occur in line with expectations, no one thinks to question them. But in an investigation, whenever something *unexpected* occurs, my curiosity is always piqued – because things very rarely happen without a reason. In this case, it is not just the exaggerated occurrences that have me curious, but the combination of them. How can there have been so many here – one after the other?'

McMahon was still silent. The legal part of her brain was desperately trying to question Straker's logic. 'Are you suggesting that, because the sequence is so extraordinary, you think they are *linked*?'

'Doesn't the sequence surprise you: how likely is such an unbroken chain of such disproportionate occurrences from different institutions?' he asked. 'If they didn't happen randomly, then – logically – it means they would *have* to have been orchestrated.'

McMahon found herself inhaling. She would never have let her mind leap from F to Z like this in one go. 'But that's ridiculous,' she said. 'If they were orchestrated, it would have to imply that they were intended? Why on earth would someone *want* all this to happen?'

Straker went on: 'God knows why ... for some sick reason? But it isn't impossible, is it?'

McMahon shook her head less tentatively than she felt.

'So if – for whatever warped reason – the institutional responses *were* intended,' Straker said, 'none of them could have happened without the accident having occurred in the first place.'

McMahon looked at him incredulously. This time, her legal instincts didn't allow her to follow him from F to Z: 'You're not serious?' she asked. 'You're not saying that you think ... the accident ... was *premeditated?*'

Straker maintained direct eye contact. 'That deduction would not be inconsistent with everything that's happened since,' he said. 'Besides, Tahm and Remy both stated that there was nothing wrong with that car. Something, then, must have happened to it. My starting point in this investigation, therefore, is now clear: we have to establish what that might have been.'

'How can you ever hope to do that, when the car and crash site are impounded?'

'Andy Backhouse has a fair amount of data in the motor home and we can do a lot more analysis of it.'

'What if that isn't conclusive, though ... isn't enough?'

They continued to make their way through the Russian capital as the last of the light was fading.

Straker shifted in his seat. Softly, he said: 'We might need to get proactive.'

'What does that mean?'

'We might just have to take a look at some of this for ourselves.'

'No, no. *No*,' she replied vehemently, suddenly sounding surer of herself. 'Don't even contemplate going anywhere you shouldn't. I am, officially, warning you – right now. *Don't.*'

'As I understand it,' Straker replied, 'part of the circuit abuts municipal parkland, which is open to the public.'

'Communal ownership and access would be completely superseded by police orders,' McMahon said. 'Anyone found anywhere *near* any police-impounded items will be in serious trouble – in all likelihood, arrested. Encroachment on anything to do with a legal case carries the clear penalty of contempt of court.'

'Which means what?' Straker asked, showing a hint of impatience.

McMahon answered: 'Five years' imprisonment, no questions asked.'

TWENTY-NINE

Straker's frustration with the case was mounting, but it was nothing to the hammer blow they were about to suffer.

Every aspect of this affair – so far – had fallen to their disadvantage. The system appeared to be marshalling itself against them. Straker felt damned if they were going to be prevented from getting to the truth but, realizing he was not going to get any support from McMahon for his suggested action to counter this, he stopped talking.

In the ensuing silence, a gabble of Russian filled the Brandeis car; their driver was listening to some sort of talk radio station.

Straker, having not eaten since arriving in Russia however many hours earlier and been busy non-stop, wanted to find his hotel, order a decent slug of room service and take a high-pressure shower before working out what he was going to do next. 'Do you know where Quartech's putting me up?' he asked as the car reached Kremlevskaya Naberezhnaya. They were heading east on the embankment along the north bank of the Moskva River, below the walls of the Kremlin.

Still sounding wary at Straker's intent to be proactive in the investigation, McMahon said: 'We've put you in Ms Sabatino's room – in the Hotel Baltschug Kempinski. Ptarmigan still have the booking; it seemed an efficient substitution, at least while she's still in hospital.'

Just before Saint Basil's Cathedral, the car navigated the slip road to make a right turn over the bridge and head south over the river.

Without any warning, McMahon barked at the chauffeur in Russian.

Almost flinching, the driver leaned across and turned up the radio. Straker wondered what was going on.

He heard the matter-of-fact tone of a news bulletin. In the background were the unmistakable sounds of rapid camera clicks.

'What's all that about?' he asked.

McMahon held up her hand to silence him so she could hear. Her face told Straker that some serious news was breaking. The broadcast went on. A voice could be heard, sounding like the man was reading a prepared statement. His intonation only rose as he came to finish speaking. Then, a different voice – more natural, but more hesitant – could be heard.

Suddenly it dawned on him.

Straker suddenly realized who it was.

No wonder McMahon was concerned.

The second man's voice continued for nearly two minutes before the reading voice was back again. In a matter of seconds, the bulletin was over and a woman, presumably in the studio, could be heard moving on perhaps to the next item.

Straker's heart sank. 'Is that what I think it is?'

McMahon nodded, realizing Straker might have caught the gist: 'Yegor Baryshnikov has just declared himself for the prosecution.'

'Holy fuck,' he growled. 'That bastard's gone and ratted us out. What the hell is his testimony going to do to our chances in this case?'

They pulled up outside the five star Kempinski Hotel.

Normally Straker would have enjoyed the splendour of the lobby, the modern chandeliers along its length, the mezzanine level and the flowing staircases edged with wafting wrought-iron decorations leading down to the intricate tile-patterned floor. The impression of the Hotel Baltschug Kempinski should have been calming. But Straker's mind was somewhere else entirely.

McMahon accompanied him to reception, to ensure the transfer of the room from Sabatino was efficient, but Straker was in a hurry to get to a television to see more news of this defection. Their receptionist apologized but said there were no television screens in any of the communal areas of the hotel; it was suggested they use the one up in his rooms. Straker asked McMahon if she wanted to see the bulletin too. They were accompanied up to the fourth floor by one of the concierge team.

Up in the sumptuous suite, the concierge went to work in the television cabinet. After a minute or so, *Russia-1* appeared on the screen. There was a news bulletin in progress; it was clearly about the Formula One defection. The remote was handed to him by the concierge; Straker thanked him as he left.

The news report was worse than they feared.

Wherever the press conference had been held, the room was packed. Gazdanov was one of the voices they had heard on the car radio, the one sounding like he was reading a prepared speech, because he had been. Gazdanov looked like the personification of smug, revelling in every moment – soaking up every photon of the limelight. Baryshnikov's demeanour, by contrast, was unexpected. Not the abrasive person the driver had been in the motor home. He looked timid, nervous.

'What's Baryshnikov saying?' Straker asked.

McMahon's response conveyed some of her own surprise at the man's tone and bearing. 'That he is proud to be a Formula One driver, but prouder … more proud … of being a Russian. He feels concerned … no guilty … that Ptarmigan, his team, had caused … inflicted … such pain … hurt? … to the people of Russia.'

Straker studied Baryshnikov's face as he spoke. The Russian's eyes were darting left and right. He was speaking with a distinct lack of fluency, the reason perhaps why McMahon was having such difficulty interpreting him.

Gazdanov retook control of the press conference. 'Russia is proud of her national motor racing star,' translated McMahon, 'especially as Mr Baryshnikov is putting Russia's interests before his own and the commercial interest of his team.'

Questions were then yelled at the prosecutor general from the packed floor of the room.

'*Da*,' barked Gazdanov in reply, 'Mr Baryshnikov is now a major witness in the State's prosecution of this crime.'

'Yes, we expect Mr Baryshnikov to give Russia the inside story of the Ptarmigan team – so, *da*, the State can be absolutely sure of succeeding in its prosecution of the culprits.'

The coverage of the press conference ended.

Straker felt as though he had been kicked in the guts. Baryshnikov's defection changed everything. His mind was whirring. His first thought was: How the hell do we defend ourselves now? Anything that Ptarmigan puts up as an argument in the trial – irrespective of its merit – could be flatly contradicted by Baryshnikov. And which version was a Russian jury going to believe?

Straker's brain was whirring. Ptarmigan may not have discovered anything concrete in their investigation so far, but his suspicions had been building that something unusual was going on. This defection was only enhancing those feelings.

He would have to reconsider his opinion of all these Russian institutions: clearly with the Baryshnikov defection, they were showing a readiness to be invasive – to go even as far as recruiting witnesses from the other side.

Straker reached a conclusion, but then had reservations about what it meant. He did not want to appear alarmist – and yet at the same time he didn't want to be naïve.

Sandy McMahon was about to speak when Straker swiftly held a finger up to his lips. He then beckoned her to follow him to the door. Straker led her out of the suite and closed the door behind them.

Once out in the corridor, McMahon said: 'I feel terrible I never got to speak to Baryshnikov – as we discussed I would in the motor home.'

Straker looked up and down the softly lit landing to make sure there was no one there. He replied: 'Forget it. You couldn't have made any difference. That defection has not happened since our meeting today; it's been brewing for much longer than that. Thankfully, we never discussed anything meaningful about our defence while he was with us.'

McMahon looked around. 'What the hell are we doing out here?'

'I don't want us to say anything significant in there. I want to change rooms.'

It took a moment or two for the sinister inference to register. 'What? Why … you don't …?'

'Just think about how the authorities have behaved for a moment, Sandy. They've done everything they can to thwart us, even enticing Baryshnikov away. They've shown the lengths they will go to. Would they have been able to find out where Remy was staying? Of course. Why wouldn't they, then, have wanted to keep tabs on her, too?'

'You don't think they've interfered with her room?'

Straker's face told her the answer.

'But she hasn't been in there since the crash.'

He shook his head gently. 'We have no idea *when* – whatever all this is – began. It could have been weeks in the planning. At the risk of appearing paranoid, I want to switch rooms.'

Twenty minutes later the hotel had responded to Straker's request and set him up in a smaller suite one floor down; the new accommodation was reassuringly grand and still boasted a similar view out over the river and the Bolshoy Moskvoretsky Bridge. What took the transfer longer than expected was the need to pack up Sabatino's kit, which was still scattered around the Kremlin Suite.

'I'd offer you dinner,' said Straker as they stored the last of Remy's items in the wardrobe, 'but I'd better brief Quartano.'

McMahon nodded her understanding with some sympathy. 'Not likely to be an easy conversation. Oh, and I nearly forgot this,' she said pulling a mobile phone from her pocket complete with its charger. 'It was by the bed upstairs; I assume it's Ms Sabatino's?'

She placed it on the bedside table.

'I'll be here to pick you up at, what, 7:30 tomorrow morning?' McMahon added, except Straker now seemed distracted; she was thanked almost automatically for all that she had done that day as Straker walked her to the door.

The moment McMahon had left the new room, he set about quelling his apprehension at calling Quartano. How the hell was the tycoon going to react to their latest news – to this act of betrayal?

As if he didn't know.

Straker turned all the major lights off in the room and stood by the window; the view was the same as the one upstairs: he was looking out over the floodlit towers and domes of Saint Basil's Cathedral and the stark blocky shapes of the Kremlin. He breathed deeply, collecting his thoughts. The room was stuffy. He needed to open the window.

In a cooling Moscow breeze, Straker prepared himself and dialled. He was connected straight away.

Straker explained to Quartano the latest developments involving the Baryshnikov defection, expecting him to explode at any moment.

At first Straker was unnerved.

Quartano seemed remarkably calm. Had this, thought Straker, gone so far that replying with a sense of humour was the only sane thing to do?

Quartano asked with a hint of levity: 'Is this one of your Machiavellian masterstrokes … have you encouraged a loyal lieutenant to defect to the enemy … to gather intelligence?'

'Not this time, I'm afraid, sir, no.'

Straker waited for the tycoon to realize that his benign supposition was false.

It didn't take long.

'The low-life,' roared Quartano. 'He's fucking screwed Ptarmigan. He's screwed his colleagues. The gutless low-life. Does that man have no shame? First he rats out Remy to the FIA after Montreal – and now this!'

Straker didn't have anything to say; from previous experience he knew it was best to lean back and let the anger play out. Quartano ranted on: 'He's fired, as of *now*. He'll never work for me again. Period. Is that understood? Stacey Krall can serve him his severance papers, right now.'

When Quartano realized that Straker wasn't responding, he regained some composure. 'Sorry, Straker – sorry. What the hell do we do now? We're so completely fucked.'

'We do seem to be facing an overhang of institutional barriers, sir.'

Quartano grunted agreement. 'Who now hold *all* the power.'

Straker inhaled deeply. 'Contrary to appearances, Mr Q, I would doubt whether everything on the Russian side in this case is quite as definite and certain as the institutions and authorities would have us believe.'

'I don't understand?'

Straker lowered his voice: 'We need something – anything – to create a chink. We need to find something, however small, to start questioning, challenging, or God-willing undermine any of the ploys the Russian authorities are pursuing against us.'

Quartano sighed heavily. 'Where would you even begin looking for that?'

'It's likely to require something bold,' said Straker quietly, 'particularly now, of course, that anything Ptarmigan might say in court can be countermanded by Russia's favourite son and patriot.'

'Oh, Christ.'

Straker smiled to himself. He suddenly felt the time might be now: 'Well, sir, this is what I've been thinking…'

Straker took a shower and got into bed. His mind was still whirring. It didn't let him sleep. It wasn't long before he even feared falling asleep. Haunting him, above all, was Sabatino's reaction to the deaths at the Grand Prix – the way, unprompted, she had responded so emotionally and sympathetically to the horrific news that people had died. Then he thought of the guilt the Russian State officially wanted to lay on her: his mind was contemplating the consequences. He couldn't rationalize the mounting restrictions and limitations which the Russians were putting up against them. Any one of those impediments would be an insult to justice and a fair trial. Having them all bearing down on their case was quite absurd. Under these circumstances, Straker couldn't see their defence now being anything other than inadequate against the charges.

The next morning, McMahon re-appeared at the hotel five minutes earlier than expected. But Straker wasn't there.

She asked if any messages had been left for her.

There weren't any.

She asked reception to ring his room.

There was no reply.

She asked to have his name paged through all the restaurants in the hotel.

After a sweep of them all, as well as all the public areas on the ground floor, there was no response.

McMahon returned to her car. She tried Straker on his cell phone but then remembered he had left it with Sabatino in the hospital.

As the car pulled away, McMahon had to admit – if only to herself – that she was more than just a little concerned.

THIRTY

Straker had awoken at three o'clock that morning. He had barely slept, more like drifting in and out of consciousness – dreading a return to the horrific flashbacks of his rendition and torture. It had taken him years to grapple with the psychological effects of his treatment at the hands of the Americans in Afghanistan, having suffered the intelligence equivalent of friendly fire. He thought his immersion in the polar expedition had offered him a distraction from those disturbances, and yet here he was – after only one day in Russia – in danger of sliding straight back down again.

His rough night soon turned to anger. To preserve his own sanity, Straker had to act. But what? What *could* he do?

Straker turned on the lights in the spectacular rooms of the hotel and set about channelling his anger. Firing up his laptop, he searched for a Google Earth shot of the city. He was looking for satellite images of the Zhar-ptitsa Autodrom. The best of those available had been taken during the construction of the circuit. Straker saved the picture in a PowerPoint slide. He then searched "Russian Grand Prix" and scanned the resultant entries. He found what he was looking for: a diagram of the track offering labels and a legend for all the elements making up the race track complex. Cross-referencing that with his satellite image, Straker was able to insert text labels into his slide. As it took shape, he could identify what he was looking for. Better still, he had a clear idea of the terrain directly around his objective.

Straker thought about the kit and equipment he might need. A key requirement would be a record-taking device. He decided his phone would be ideal, but then swore – realizing he had left it with Sabatino in the hospital. Then he remembered McMahon had retrieved a phone from the suite upstairs. Straker examined it.

Being a Quartech one, it was the same make and model as his own; for what he wanted, its camera, 240fps video and data store would be fine. Having been left on its charger, there was no need to worry about battery life.

Straker thought about his cover.

Unpacking his suitcase, he pulled out his running kit and the small rucksack he always carried while travelling. He played with a combination of clothes before deciding on the look he wanted to project. He realized he needed a couple of additions to his kit. Looking through the room he couldn't find exactly what he was after but, at the foot of the wardrobe, he managed to find a couple of white plastic laundry bags. These were stuffed into the side pouches of his rucksack. Half an hour later, Straker was dressed.

Armed with the key details he had downloaded onto Sabatino's phone, he was ready to go. McMahon's words, though, kept ringing round his head:

Contempt of court … Five years' imprisonment.

Slipping out of his room, Straker made for the servants' staircase. It was an echoey well, stretching from the basement right up through the building to the sixth floor. He waited just inside it – listening for any voices or footsteps. He made his way down cautiously – not wanting anyone to know he was leaving the hotel.

Dropping down onto the ground floor, he found a door into a utility area at the rear of the building. Thankfully, there was no one there either. A number of lights were on, but whoever had needed them was away from their work. Straker walked swiftly through to a glass-panelled door. This had to be an outside wall: darkness and the orange glow from a streetlight showed through the frosted glass. Straker dreaded it being locked. He tried the latch.

Shit!

It was stuck fast.

Straker flinched. A clang rang out behind him. He did not want to be discovered in here, not at such a suspicious time of the morning. Gripping the handle again with more force, and pushing the door in against its jamb, he tried it again. Thankfully it clicked open; layers of paint, rather than a lock, had caused it to stick.

There were more sounds behind him.

Slipping through the door, Straker pulled it shut behind him and quickly ducked down below the level of the glass.

The middle-aged laundry manager had just re-entered the room. He had caught sight of someone dressed as a jogger slip out from the back of the building. The Cossack's immediate thought was: thief. Not wanting to be accused of anything himself, should something have been stolen, he hurried to the phone on the wall and reported the sighting to hotel security.

Straker, meantime, was out in the cold dark Moscow air. Walking along the back alley, away from the Raushkaya Naberezhnaya, he emerged onto Sadovnicheskaya Ulitsa. At that time of night the roads were virtually devoid of traffic. He headed on, across the Bolotny Ostrov, before reaching the waterfront on the south side of this island in the Moskva River. He had to wait five minutes before seeing a taxi. Climbing into the back, Straker asked for the Saint Alexander Nevsky Church: at four in the morning he would be a memorable fare and did not want to reveal his precise destination. Straker planned to be dropped some distance away.

As the car made its way through the Russian capital, Moscow seemed to be as eerie as his long-held preconceptions of it. Cold War images were hard to forget. Wide streets, the imperial splendour of landmark buildings, the brutality of Stalinist architecture. For its twenty years of post-communist existence, Straker had a sense – or at least could find it easy to imagine – that one form of harsh politics or another lay only just below the surface here.

Twenty minutes later, travelling through the more mundane parts of Moscow, Straker's cab reached his destination. It pulled up beside the beautiful onion-shaped dome and brilliant-white walls of the Alexander Nevsky Church, all of which, in the darkness, was being bathed in brilliant floodlight.

Straker climbed out into the cold morning air. Waiting for the taxi to be out of sight, he took in the area around him. Next to the church, running north/south, was the dual carriageway of Prospekt Andropova. This stretched off into the dark. Traffic was a little busier here, but still sparse compared to his experience of it the day before.

Straker readied himself. He concentrated and got himself into "character". Now dressed as a jogger – loose top, long tracksuit bottoms, running shoes, backpack and woolly hat – he could pass for any urban fitness freak on any street anywhere in the world.

Setting off, he jogged away down the pavement beside the dual carriageway, over the causeway – across the Moskva River – towards the Nagatinskaya Poyma Park.

After a quarter of a mile, now fully on the peninsula, he pulled out Sabatino's phone and turned it on. Looking at the map he had compiled, he orientated himself, scanning the lie of the land around him. He was pleased: he was very near his Start Line.

In the gloom, it was hard to see. But he found it.

At an angle of forty-five degrees or so from the road, a narrow overhung footpath led off into the trees. Discreetly, Straker cast one last eye up and down the pavement he was on, saw there was no one within the limited view offered in the dark, and headed off into the murkiness of the forest.

In among the trees it was even darker, with no ambient light from any of the buildings or the city penetrating the undergrowth. In such blackness, its meandering course could easily have been disorientating.

Five minutes on and Straker found himself breaking through a treeline onto a broad mown-grass avenue, running left to right in front of him. The sky above the clearing was greyer, even with the heavy cloud cover – rendering it here slightly less than pitch black. A light breeze rustled the tops of the trees. There were no other sounds – no human sounds nearby; just a muffled rumble of traffic away in the distance.

Straker looked up and down the avenue. Moving out into the middle of the ride he looked along it to the left. At the far end of his sightline, across the bend in the river, was the floodlit Alexander Nevsky Church – where he'd just been dropped by the taxi.

Straker scanned down the avenue in the opposite direction, to his right. The clearing headed off – deeper into the park, deeper into the darkness. That was the way he was going.

Straker was keen to move on.

He stayed in close to the treeline, tight to the right-hand side, as he jogged on for a quarter of a mile.

It appeared as nothing more than a shadow in the gloom.

Up ahead, to the left of the avenue, he could make out a shape. Something not out of keeping. Then he knew he was in the right place; he could hear the sound of plastic tape gently crackling in the breeze.

Straker dropped to walking pace.

Behind the police cordon was a man-made mound – fifty-or-so yards long running along the same axis as the left-hand edge of the avenue. The top of the bank was level with treetops all around. Its shape had been smoothed, sculpted, turfed and mown. Looking up and down the avenue again, to make sure he was still alone, Straker moved in even closer. The strip of plastic police tape was now right in front of him.

He ducked under the tape and climbed up the slope of the mound.

Straker reached the crest.

Expecting to see something of the Zhar-ptitsa Autodrom Grand Prix circuit in front of him, all he got – in the darkened gloom – was an inkling. Straker could only rely on his rod cells to see at that point. Everything was an indistinct black and dark grey.

He looked over the top of the whole Grand Prix complex, to see whether there was to be any imminent lightening of the darkness. Close to the level of the horizon he could make out the first dark-grey hint of dawn. Arriving on site considerably earlier than expected, Straker realized his study of the ground – in this light – was going to be a challenge. Waiting for more light was not really an appealing option. More light increased the risk of his being seen.

And that could lead to Straker being discovered – without authorization – in the middle of a police-impounded crime scene.

THIRTY-ONE

Standing on the top of the bank in the dull Moscow morning, Straker lowered his eyes to the grassy bank below him.

This, then, was the scene of the infamous crash.

Thirty-four people – at the latest count – had been killed right here.

This was where Sabatino had had her miraculous escape and been lucky enough to survive. Would she now be able to escape twenty years' hard labour? That thought, alone, motivated Straker to push on with his mission.

As the night slowly lifted, the horror of the scars left by the crash emerged through the gloom. First, there were the black gashes in the grass and turf directly below him. Then Straker could see some of the debris thrown from the car, missed by the police in their clearance of the site. A few minutes later, an outline of the wire mesh fence began to emerge, no longer appearing as a fuzzy grey stripe edging the circuit. With this marginal clarity came sight of the puncture wound through the mesh: the two severed ends still hanging slack, tapering out from the point of rupture. Then he could see the remains of the concrete wall. Rubble was strewn in a semicircle out from the hole that had been punched through it.

Straker readied himself to start his detailed assessment. Suddenly he was not alone.

There was an unexpected arrival.

He heard it first.

An engine, over to the right, from behind the trees. Straker dived to the ground. Following the course of the Grand Prix track, a car – travelling quickly – emerged from the woods, straight towards him. Straker swore. He'd been caught out in the open. A row of lamps above the vehicle's cab cast a huge beam ahead of it, lighting up each side of the cavern-like swathe as it moved between the trees.

Straker shielded his eyes. He almost felt the light beam wash over him.

How could he have not been spotted?

Then: Shit!

The car's engine note was dropping – a fall-off in revs.

Was it stopping?

They *had* seen him.

With relief, Straker heard the engine note start to increase again. The car had rounded the bend and was carrying on around the track.

Straker lifted himself off the ground. He had to get on with this. A pen and notepad were pulled from his pocket. Orientating his sketch to the east, he drew the layout of the scene.

Half left, stretching into the dark, where the car had just gone, was the end of the Hermitage Straight. Straker mentally plotted how Sabatino had charged down this – directly towards him. She should have then swept left – left to right, as Straker was looking at it – round the gentle curve, to head down the slight slope – away from him, half right as he looked at it – towards the next turn. Instead, Sabatino had careened on dead straight, leaving the track to land directly at his feet.

With the slowly improving light, Straker could begin to see more detail of the gravel trap on the outside of the bend.

And that was why he was here.

Straker did not want to become a silhouetted shape on the top of the mound. Dropping a short way down the forward slope of the dew-covered grassy bank, he set about recording a variety of angles and distances from there.

Ten minutes on and the sky was properly turning to grey. It gave the area a ghostly feel. Straker was soon ready for his next stage. Turning side on, to prevent his feet slipping on the damp grass, he made his way to the bottom of the slope, towards the gravel trap on the outside of the corner. To get there, he would have to climb through the hole in the fence – the point of impact.

Straker sidled down and reached the wall just to the left of the breach.

There, he had to navigate his way round one end of the ripped wire mesh hanging from one of the uprights. This end of it, like the one on the other side, splayed outwards. Straker had to place his feet carefully, anxious not to disturb anything. When he looked down to do so, though, his heart rate surged.

A cursory glance of the mesh had allowed something to catch his eye.

What had he seen?

He had to double-check to work out what it was.

Something wasn't quite as it should have been. Straker squatted down to take a closer look. Directly in front of him he could see the ripped end of the mesh. He lowered his head and looked even closer.

Having pulled his phone out of his pocket, he raised his head above the height of the wall – to be sure the track was clear in both directions – and turned on the camera. In the lee of the wall he had to risk using its light. He fired off a shot and examined it in the player closely afterwards. It was too fuzzy. Being so dark, it would need a concerted effort to hold the camera steady to produce a clear enough photograph.

He tried again.

This one was better.

Straker checked again over the wall. The track was still clear. He fired off several more camera shots. With a quick review of these, he realized he had captured what he needed.

Straker rose to his feet. The light level had increased, to a kind of twilight: although still dim, a grey hue made everything visible. That would help with any further photography, but would also make him more visible. Looking over to the eastern horizon – just above the trees – Straker could see the sky there had turned to a very pale yellow.

In its light, he studied the grassy bank behind him, which he could see much more clearly now. It was easy to understand how several hundred spectators had been comfortably ranged across this grassy slope. Straker sketched and scribbled down detailed notes of these dimensions in his notebook. He then found his way round the end of the mesh and made for the hole. Again, he had to be careful where he put his feet. Breeze blocks were strewn all over the ground.

Straker inhaled.

His heart rate raced again.

Why now?

Another anomaly?

His brain made a more rapid computation this time, assisted by one of the observations he had made while watching the video of the accident. Prepping the camera, Straker checked the race track for any unwanted presences, looked up the bank behind him, and zoomed in. This time, even in this light, the camera had caught the shape without question. He fired the shutter.

Straker then saw something else.

The breeze block he had just photographed was far from unique. Squatting down he studied the pile of rubble. There were … two – three – four – five – six … God, how many of them were there? It could be dozens.

All exactly the same.

Straker, in his excitement, hovered his camera over the debris and took numerous pictures. He bent down to get an even closer look. One of the breeze blocks was right in front of him. He found himself reaching out to touch it. Along one edge was a grey-brown material – cement? Mortar? Somehow, even in this gloom, it didn't look quite right. Switching the camera to video this time, he extended a finger forward to touch the edge of the block as he filmed.

Amazingly, the grey-brown stuff was soft. And moved to the touch.

What?

Straker scraped a fingernail along the edge and found he could dislodge the material easily. He lifted the small sample away from the block and held it up to his nose. It smelled instantly familiar.

He pocketed his phone, pulled out his handkerchief and wrapped up his sample.

Careful to leave no signs of any tampering, Straker found a splinter of carbon fibre on the ground and, like peeling an apple, used his thumb and hand to smooth over the section from which he had just lifted his specimen.

Straker was pumped.

He checked the track once more. Light levels were rising quickly. Straker found himself standing beside the disfigured "I"-sectioned upright, its distortion indicating that it had been the one impacted by Sabatino's rear wheel as she somersaulted. The stanchion was bent outwards from the collision. Straker saw it was coated in a plastic weather-proofing material. When yet again something caught his eye.

Straker looked in closer.

Checking quickly left and right along the line of the fence, he realized the next-nearest upright was the other side of the gap. He crossed over to it. On this one, the top section of the wire had been ripped away in the force of the impact, while the lower section of the mesh was still in place, held there by what looked like wire loops – ties. Straker leaned in close and peered at the post. He hadn't been wrong. He photographed the wire around the top and then at the bottom of this "I"-sectioned upright. Returning to the one bent in the crash, Straker photographed that one too – top, middle and bottom.

It was now clearly morning.

Straker's retinas were switching from black and white to colour: colour was emerging from the landscape.

He needed to be extra vigilant now.

Checking over the wall, Straker readied himself for the last, risky part of his reconnaissance. Walking out through the hole, he gained admittance to the inside of the circuit, where he stood for a moment on the edge of the gravel trap. Holding completely still, he listened.

He then walked out onto the gravel. In the stillness, he was concerned a crunching noise under his feet would be obvious. As he placed his feet and applied weight, though, there was hardly any noise at all. Straker was already smiling. His hunch had not been wrong.

Looking down to check, his feet were on the top of the gravel – with virtually no sinkage into the stones.

Straker flipped the rucksack off his shoulder, unzipped one of the pockets and pulled out one of the white laundry bags taken from his hotel room.

He squatted down and, still being careful not to leave any signs of intervention, tried to scoop up a handful of the gravel and sand. It almost hurt his fingers as he scraped the surface. He managed to dislodge a small amount, which he picked up and then dropped into the white plastic bag. Rolling it up on itself, to resemble a sausage, he stuffed this into his rucksack, zipped it up and pulled it back onto his shoulders.

Straker moved further out across the expanse of the gravel trap, making for the red-and-white stones on the outside edge of the track. He suddenly felt very exposed. Light levels had properly risen: the first sign of sunlight was striking the tops of the trees around the circuit. Anyone casting a casual eye now, even from some distance away, would have seen him easily. Straker walked on, though – out onto the asphalt.

Once there, he used his phone again to take numerous pictures, aiming to construct a panorama of several shots to be pieced together later as a mosaic. Finally, he took a number of photographs of the exact line Sabatino had taken – tangentially off the track – across the gravel, through the hole in the wire fence, and up onto the grassy bank.

Suddenly there was a sound.

Straker heard it from behind him. What was that? An engine?

Shit!

Straker was right out in the open.

He needed to get off the road – and out of sight – fast.

He pushed off, ready to run for the closest point of the perimeter fence, over to his right. He ran directly across the shorter expanse of gravel trap. Instantly, though, he felt something was different. His feet were sinking into and sliding in the gravel. He could hardly gain any kind of traction, his footfalls giving way through the sand and stones. He ran on though, exerting more effort, concentrating on keeping his balance. Reaching the perimeter, he forced himself to do one final thing while his brain screamed at him to get the hell out of there.

Another sound – this time ahead of him, the other way down the track. Despite the surge of adrenalin, he bent down and grabbed a fistful of gravel. Wrestling with the rucksack still across his shoulders, he heaved it round, slid down one of the zips and tried to ram as much of this latest gravel sample into it as he could.

Straker had to move, even while twisting round to close the zip.

Instead of mechanical sounds, Straker suddenly heard something unexpected. Something dreaded.

Dogs!

His heart raced.

Out of the corner of his eye he saw a vehicle breaking into view. Its engine was roaring. Despite that noise, he could still hear the other engine coming from the other direction. Wasn't its engine racing too?

Then, taking Straker completely by surprise, was another sound altogether.

Rifle shots.

They started firing.

Firing at him.

THIRTY-TWO

Several shots rang out.

What the fuck were these people doing?

Straker was still some distance from the hole in the wall. He ran down the line of red-and-white covered tyres.

A burst of automatic rifle fire echoed off the mature trees all around. Rounds from behind struck the ground at his feet, throwing up mini-explosions of gravel.

Shit, these people were serious.

Straker needed to throw them off their aim – present the most difficult target he could. As he sprinted, he darted from side to side – running in a pronounced zigzag pattern – just about making it to the hole in the wall.

As he went to dive through it, several rounds pinged off the breeze blocks on either side. Chips of concrete were spat into the air. Straker felt a number of stings down the left side of his face.

Fuck!

Straker now had a dilemma. His most direct escape was straight up the grassy slope and over the crest line into the avenue beyond. But that would present an easy target to the firers behind. Instead, the moment he was through the wall, he swung round to the right and, bending double, dropped his body below the top line of the concrete wall. It seemed to work. He was out of sight and behind some sturdy cover.

But where now?

Twenty or so yards ahead Straker could see the treeline edging the bank. He would be able to get there, still using the wall for cover. But then where would he go? The undergrowth beyond looked impenetrable. More shots pinged off the top of the wall above him. They made his decision for him. Straker pushed on – awkwardly still bent double – heading for the treeline.

He closed in on the foliage. His hunch had been right. The undergrowth was heavy. Insanely thick. How could he possibly get through it quickly? Raising his arms in front of his face, Straker leant forwards and lunged into the dense mass of branches.

Behind him he could hear the second vehicle pulling up on the edge of the track. Doors were opened and slammed shut. Voices were raised. The dogs were getting louder. Although struggling through the dense foliage, Straker was at least now out of the circuit. They wouldn't pursue him any further – on the outside – would they? They'd only want to drive an intruder off their premises?

Whatever their intentions, Straker knew he would be a lot safer by getting away. He fought the tangle of branches all around him. The palms of his hands, the front of his forearms and shoulders were being lacerated by some fearsome thorns. It took a huge effort, and the blocking of considerable pain, to move through this undergrowth.

He ploughed on, aiming for the turfed avenue he had used to gain access to the place. Thorns were shredding his tracksuit and puncturing the skin. How much further? It couldn't be that far to the track, could it?

Voices could still be heard behind him. They were soon drowned out by the dogs. The barking was getting louder. It meant they were giving chase, didn't it? Had they picked up his scent? How far behind him were they? Were they going to come out through the wall after him?

Straker stumbled out from the undergrowth, finally breaking the treeline into the long grassy avenue he had jogged down to get there. Now sprinting flat out, he headed off along the ride in the direction of the Alexander Nevsky church. He could see the beautiful gold onion-shaped dome glowing in the early morning sunlight across the river ahead of him.

Crack – thump.

A rifle round pinged past his head.

Straker had to get out of their line of sight. He darted diagonally across the avenue, throwing in a couple of zigzags to disrupt the shooters' lay.

More shots rang out.

These people weren't content with just getting him off the circuit. They were now firing at him in a public park. What did that mean? Who were they? They couldn't be a private security firm: they wouldn't have authority to fire weapons in a public space, would they? Didn't shooting at him out here mean these people had to be police? How could the police be reacting so excessively to an intrusion into the circuit? More rounds were fired at him. Just before he dived into the treeline on the opposite, left-hand, side of the avenue he heard: crack – thump.

Then he heard the dogs. Baying dogs. They must be out in the open now – in the avenue. Their cries were getting louder. They had to be loose.

Shit!

Straker ran on under the trees, this stretch of ancient woodland boasting mature trees with a coherent canopy overhead: the undergrowth here was much thinner. Straker was able to make much better progress. But if the dogs were now loose, they, too, would be able to cover the ground quicker through this section of the forest.

Straker heard them directly behind him.

They were giving chase. Their bark bounced off the trees, reverberating between the sizeable trunks. It made for an eerie sound.

Straker broke through another treeline into a small clearing. A picnic area and bower. Permanent wooden tables and benches were dotted around. At that time of the morning it was empty, of course. With full exertion, Straker sprinted straight across it, spotting a narrow overhung single-track path leading out from it on the far side – offering him an exit. As he ran on, the dogs were still behind him. They'd be hunting by scent. Straker was still in serious danger of being caught.

The narrow lane away from the picnic place continued on through the trees.

It kinked slightly right.

Straker could now hear the traffic on Andropova Prospekt ahead of him. There would be humanity there. Would his pursuers go on shooting at him in such a public place? Even if they didn't, Straker feared no such restraint would apply to the dogs. He realized he would have no comfort from them, even if he reached a place in full view of the public. Passers-by wouldn't intervene against such menacing animals. All the dogs needed to do was catch him and bring him down. His pursuers could then saunter up and apprehend him at will, even if they weren't firing at that point. What the hell would that mean?

Contempt of court … Five years' imprisonment.

Reaching the end of the narrow path, Straker finally broke out of the woodland into an empty car park beside the dual carriageway. He saw a noticeboard with its own little roof, a large doggie-mess bin and a low rack for bicycles.

Three were parked there. Straker ran to the first and gave it a yank. A sizeable chain held it fast. He tried the next. Same thing. Then, looking at the third, he didn't even bother – realizing the front wheel had been deliberately removed.

Spinning round, Straker sprinted straight towards the main road. He had fifty yards or so to run. Traffic had built up in the time since he left the avenue nearly an hour before. He reached the verge. The baying dogs sounded as if they were closer than ever – louder than ever, heard easily above the noise of the cars.

How far back were they?

He daren't look.

Straker reached the pavement beside the road. A constant flow of cars was zooming by in both directions, either side of the central reservation – nose to tail down all four lanes. Straker realized he could never outrun the dogs along the pavement – in either direction – along the side of the road.

Crossing this dual carriageway was his only line of escape.

He would have to take his chances.

Turning to face the road, Straker studied the traffic hurtling towards him from the left, trying to work out how to time his moment. This was the northbound carriage – heavier with traffic as workers from the suburbs headed for their offices in the centre of Moscow. There were barely any gaps. It was solid.

Then Straker saw his chance.

Now!

He dived out into the road – immediately behind a passing lorry. There were five car lengths between it and the next car. With a horn blast, a jab at the brakes and a swerve, that car only just managed to give him the space to cross. But Straker had only crossed one lane. He was standing on the white line dividing the two lanes in the middle of fast-moving traffic.

Straker looked behind him.

One of the Rottweilers had made it as far as the kerb. Its eyes were flashing. Its mouth open. Its teeth bared, slobber flowing from its mouth. The dog had locked on to him, but realized there was danger from the cars. It seemed hesitant.

Cars hurtled past Straker, only inches to either side. Watching the oncoming flow of cars again, he prepared to dive forwards across the next lane towards the central reservation. He held his breath.

Now!

He lunged forward. But mistimed his move. His foot slipped on the smooth asphalt; it didn't give him anything like the expected amount of purchase. He had committed himself, though – was it going to be enough?

Thwack.

The bulky wing mirror of a passing BMW walloped Straker as he tried to get out of the way. It clipped him badly, catching him on the wrist, catapulting the left side of his body round. It threw him off balance. His momentum across the lane was baulked. He hadn't cleared the traffic. His presence induced an ear-splitting screech of tyres as the next driver panicked, slamming on the brakes, swerving violently – trying to avoid him.

Straker fell forwards, heavily onto the rough and littered ground of the central reservation. The pain down his left arm and side was excruciating. He tried to scramble to his feet.

Straker looked back across the carriageway through the blur of the passing cars. He could see the dogs, standing hesitantly on the far kerb, with the same sort of look as if they were plucking up courage to dive into water.

Straker tried to face them down. He whistled, beckoning them on. One of the dogs' attention was caught. Seeing its quarry, it seemed unable to process two pieces of information at once. Catching sight of its prey meant that its instinct kicked in. Without any further hesitancy, it dived forwards to give chase.

A blast of a horn was heard.

Another screech of tyres.

There was a massive – dull – thud. More screeching tyres. The bulk of the Rottweiler had been hit, its corpse struck by the bumper of an estate car. In an instant it was scooped up by the radiator grill. The hundred-pound dog was soon rolling up the bonnet towards the windshield. In a spray of blood it walloped the glass. Even the safety laminate was no match for the might of the impact, which shattered the windshield. It didn't break, but – acting as a ramp – it sent the Rottweiler's body up and onto the roof. With no resistance from the expensive metallic paint, it slid the full length of the car and fell off the back.

The dog went under the wheels of an eighteen-wheeler right behind it.

As more vehicles whooshed past, Straker could see the effects of the impact between the flashes of cars speeding along the two-lane carriageway. Blood, guts and bits of bone from the dog were flattened or broken off by passing cars.

Straker realized he was still far from safe. Climbing over the steel barrier down the middle of the central reservation, he clutched his left side and prepared to cross the remaining two lanes of the road.

Being the southbound carriageway, the traffic here was nowhere near as heavy. A break emerged. Straker pushed off hard against the kerbstones – like a sprinter off the blocks – propelling himself across. This time there were enough gaps. He made it, his chest heaving with relief as he finally reached the far side.

Straker was now across, having somehow put a clear barrier between him and his pursuers. He hoped dispatching one of the dogs would be enough to put the others off. Only an animal devoid of any self-preservation would give chase now. Straker seemed to have eluded his pursuers. Even so, he wasn't going to leave anything to chance.

Heavily clutching his left flank and limping badly, Straker was soon running awkwardly to get as far away as possible.

But he was still out in the open – and had a long four miles to get back to his hotel.

THIRTY-THREE

Sandy McMahon was still concerned at Straker's absence from his hotel that morning. Now being driven to her office, she was running down the side of Red Square. Her thoughts were jolted by her phone ringing. McMahon looked at the caller ID. It was simply a number. No name. She didn't recognize it.

Formally, she answered: 'McMahon, Brandeis Gertner.'

She could hear a loud background noise. Traffic? Then a car horn.

'Sandy, it's Matt,' came a raised voice from the other end. Straker sounded strained – out of breath.

'Where are you? I've just left your hotel.'

McMahon heard a groan.

'Are you all right? You don't sound it.'

'Not really,' he breathed.

'What happened? Where are you?'

McMahon heard a street name and a landmark. She had to ask her driver which part of Moscow it was in. She asked: 'What are you doing *there*?'

'I've got some evidence,' he wheezed.

'You sound dreadful. Are you sure you're okay?'

'No,' he said. 'I'm hurt.'

Twenty minutes later McMahon's Mercedes pulled up to the kerb by a small town park near the Avtozavodskaya Hotel. She spotted Straker sitting on a wooden bench, leaning over to his left, a seriously uncomfortable expression on his face.

Climbing out, McMahon crossed the pavement. 'God, what happened to you?'

He gave no reply.

She had to help him to stand.

Straker, with McMahon taking a fair amount of his weight, shuffled across the pavement to the open car door, groaning as he lowered himself into the back seat. McMahon rounded the back of the car and climbed in the other side.

'What the hell happened?' she asked.

'I was hit by a passing car,' he said, keeping the explanation as uncomplicated as possible. 'Have you got any painkillers?'

After a question in Russian, the driver reached across and produced some from the glove compartment. Straker swallowed a handful dry.

'We need to get you to a doctor,' she stated.

Straker grunted. 'No. Need to get to the motor home – there's something you all have to see.'

McMahon made a phone call to her office at Brandeis Gertner. She instructed a fee-earning colleague to clear a visit to the Zhar-ptitsa Autodrom.

Going against the rush-hour traffic, they made good progress through Moscow.

McMahon's phone rang a short while later.

'Good,' she said ringing off afterwards. 'For some reason we've achieved quicker authorization to enter the circuit this time. We can go straight in. How are you now?'

Straker nodded more freely then he would have done fifteen minutes before. The painkillers were beginning to work.

Helped by McMahon, Straker climbed awkwardly up into the motor home. He found the Ptarmigan team already assembled. It was a quarter to nine.

'God, Matt, are you all right?' asked Backhouse looking at Straker's dishevelled state.

He didn't answer. Pulling Sabatino's phone from his pocket, Straker said: 'I want to show you something. Can we link this up to one of the screens?'

Backhouse's expression changed markedly: 'Why? What have you found?'

A minute or two later Sabatino's phone was connected up. Everyone gathered around to look.

Straker explained slowly: 'I only had snatched conversations yesterday with Tahm and Remy. Both, though, were utterly clear in their opinions: there was nothing wrong with Remy's car.' He paused to breathe, Straker's face contorting as the movement in his chest pained his ribs. 'Neither did Tahm have any reservations about where she had been trying to go – wide – at Turn Eleven. He saw nothing wrong with her attempting to go round the outside. In view of what happened, then, the crash didn't seem right. There was an inconsistency – a conflict – between their opinions and what happened.

'So this morning, I "went for a run".' Straker didn't turn to face McMahon. 'I ran through a public park,' he said as the map he had cobbled together appeared on the screen. 'By chance, I happened to get close to this point here,' he said, and pointed to the grassy bank.

'Isn't that the crash site?' asked McMahon in a strained tone.

'While in the public area,' Straker continued, 'I was able to examine the point of Sabatino's impact,' with which he showed them a photograph. The first image looked down the bank towards the fence. 'This is the line of her approach to where she crashed,' he said, pointing further up the image to the end of the Hermitage Straight. 'She got to here, expecting to turn left' – indicating to the right across the image as they looked at it – 'and round Turn Eleven. Instead, as we know, she came straight off,' he said running his finger straight down the picture, 'going straight on at the corner, over the kerbstones, across the gravel trap, to hit the tyre wall – here – did her somersault and came through the wire mesh fence, hitting it right – here – puncturing the perimeter, and came to rest about where my feet were when I took this.'

All eyes were glued to the screen.

'On my "run",' Straker continued, 'I wanted to look at one

specific thing. To get there, I had to drop down the grassy bank and go through the hole in the fence.'

There was an air of expectation in the motor home.

'Getting there, I had to place my feet carefully,' he said, flicking to his next image. 'I had to keep looking down. When I did, I caught sight of the ripped end of the mesh. You're all engineers: tell me, what forces acted on the wire when Sabatino struck it?'

'Tensile,' said Backhouse.

'Stretching it, then,' summarized Straker. 'And what happens to wire when you stretch it?'

'It gets thinner and thinner.'

'And ...?'

'Ends up snapping at the thinnest bit.'

Straker nodded as if this was merely confirmation. 'And you *would* expect that effect to be evident at the point where Sabatino hit the wire?'

Backhouse nodded.

'What do you make of this, then?' asked Straker as he clicked the next photograph and enlarged the image.

It showed the ragged edge of the wire fence.

'Good God,' bleated Backhouse. 'Every other strand of that mesh has a thick – *flat* – end.'

Straker nodded with a reassured smile.

'Meaning what?' asked McMahon, still uneasy at Straker's reconnaissance of the police-impounded site.

'That mesh had been partially cut,' said Backhouse. 'The strands that were left connected *did* stretch under the forces of impact – you can see, here ... and here – their ends tapering down to a point – meaning they were so stretched they eventually thinned down to nothing and broke. These wires – with the flat ends – show that they were *not* stretched. They played no part in slowing Sabatino's car – because they had been cut beforehand.'

McMahon's face changed with this unexpected analysis. 'Are you saying this fence was weakened?'

'And that's not all,' said Straker in reply flicking through more images on the phone. He selected his close-up of the intact "I"-sectioned upright – the stanchion next to the impacted one. 'Look here,' he said pointing to the middle of the upright. 'See the ties – the fastenings – used to fix the wire mesh to the upright?'

There was a series of nods.

Straker switched to the next close-up. 'Now look at the top of this same upright. The tie here is missing – presumably ripped away under the force of Sabatino hitting the fence?'

McMahon leant in for a closer look.

'Look at the paint under it,' said Straker. 'Do you see? It's been scraped off; the tie and the post putting up something of a fight before breaking and being ripped away. Now,' said Straker pulling up his next image, 'this is the stanchion she actually hit – right in the firing line of the impact. Take a look at it. Tell me what you see.'

'There's one scrape mark there,' pointed Backhouse, 'in the middle of the post.'

'How many ties should there be?' asked McMahon.

Straker flicked the image back to the previous "I"-sectioned upright. 'This is the clean stanchion.'

'Five.'

'So where are the other ties on the impact post?' McMahon asked.

'Exactly what I'd like to know,' replied Straker.

'Fuck me,' said Backhouse. 'Were they cut too?'

'I could see only one tie – of a possible five – on the upright in the middle of the impact point.'

'What would that do to the fence?' asked McMahon.

Backhouse answered: 'Cutting every other strand of the mesh and removing the ties which were meant to hold it to that post would significantly reduce the fence's ability to withstand an impact.'

'Meaning it would give way easier?'

'Precisely.'

'So you're saying that the fence *was* weakened, then?'

Straker looked at Backhouse and then at McMahon.

'Deliberately?'

Straker saw from McMahon's face that his evidence was starting to make its point. He flicked on through his collection of images. 'This is a picture of the breeze-block wall in the perimeter fence,' he explained, showing an intact section of it some distance from the hole. 'When a breeze-block wall breaks, the blocks – themselves – normally give way before the cement in between them does.'

McMahon's expression seemed to say: "So?"

'Look at the breeze blocks on the ground, lying around the debris-side of the impact.'

Several pictures were flashed up and flicked on.

'Christ,' said Backhouse. 'They're all completely intact. Unbroken.'

Straker nodded.

'Why would that be?' McMahon asked.

Straker re-consulted the iPhone and tapped on one of his video clips; he pressed Play. In very dim light, it showed a breeze block in the middle of the screen. Straker's hand could be seen in the shot, placing a finger on the cement along the edge of the block.

Straker's fingernail ran along the cement edge of block dislodging the material easily. Straker stopped the clip. He shuffled awkwardly, trying to retrieve something from his pocket. Unfolding his rolled-up handkerchief, he held up some of the brown material they had just watched him scrape from the concrete block. 'Here,' he said, 'take a look,' and offered McMahon the sample.

She squeezed it. It moved easily between her fingers. As would a child, she automatically lifted it to her nose. 'What smell *is* that?' she said as if trying to recall something familiar. 'Isn't that plasticine?'

The others also smelled it and then showed their agreement.

'Blocks in this wall were just "held" together with the adhesive power of *plasticine*!' stated Backhouse.

'The blocks were little more than balanced on top of each other.'

'Good heavens,' said McMahon.

'That's not all,' said Straker. 'None of these discoveries were even the reason for my "run". The real purpose was to take a look at the gravel trap.'

'You breached the premises – actually trespassed,' McMahon declared.

Ignoring her, Straker lifted the phone again and, shuffling through a few more of his pictures, said: 'Here,' showing the photograph he had taken while standing out on the track. 'When I walked across here,' he said indicating the direct line Sabatino had followed across the gravel, 'there was no give in the gravel.'

'Meaning what?' asked McMahon.

'Run-offs are meant to help a car slow down, without dramatic deceleration,' replied Backhouse. 'They're made of gravel and sand. The tyres are meant to sink into the surface, to slow the cars down gently.'

'On Sabatino's line to the perimeter,' replied Straker, 'my feet hardly sank into the stones and sand at all.'

'Extraordinary,' said Backhouse. 'It backs up what we were saying when we watched the video yesterday.'

Straker nodded. 'Precisely why I went for my "run".'

McMahon looked quizzical: 'What *had* you seen on the video?'

'That Remy didn't seem to slow at all as she crossed the kitty litter – er, gravel trap.'

'Why would that be? Was that unusual?'

'Empirically, yes.'

'Did you look at other parts of it?'

'Of course,' replied Straker. 'While out on the track, I was "interrupted" – and needed to escape. I ran from the circuit, here,' he said pointing at a spot on the screen, 'straight across the gravel – to about here – being the closest point of the perimeter fence. Across *this* stretch of sand and gravel my feet were slipping and sliding about all over the place – sinking well in, giving me no purchase at all.'

'You're saying the strip of gravel – directly in line with Ms Sabatino's departure from the track, then – was different?'

'I am,' said Straker who then shifted in some discomfort as he lifted the rucksack up onto his lap. Pulling out the white laundry bag he said: 'This is the gravel sample I took on Remy's line, while this,' he said jiggling the rucksack and rattling the loose gravel inside, 'was the gravel I took from my escape route.'

'Why do you keep saying "escape" and "escape route"?' asked McMahon.

Backhouse watched Straker wince as he lifted the rucksack up onto the table. 'Is that how you got hurt – in your "escape"?' asked the race engineer.

'No, I got hit by a car.'

'On the track?'

'Out on the main road.'

'As a result of the "interruption" you mentioned?' Backhouse asked with a smirk on his face.

McMahon was clearly not finding this amusing. 'Colonel,' she said, 'may I have a word with you a moment?'

Straker and McMahon moved through the motor home into the private cabin at the end. She shut the door behind them. Lowering himself awkwardly into one of the chairs, Straker sat, leaning on a small circular table trying to support his left flank.

'What you have done is beyond reckless,' she said. 'You should *pray* no one saw you. You could have so easily compromised our case. Not only that, you could have been arrested, found in contempt of court, sentenced to God knows how long in jail.'

'Jail, *sch*mail,' spat Straker. 'People didn't just see me, Sandy – they fired at me.'

'*What?* … What do you mean?'

'Fired at me – they shot at me.'

'You were *shot* at?'

'Rifle and automatic fire, Sandy.'

McMahon's terms of reference for this case suddenly seemed to be shattered.

'I was shot at – with sustained fire – for nothing more than walking onto a race track!'

Trying to recover her authority, McMahon said: 'If we're to fight this case properly, we have to comply with the rules of the court. There's no reason to breach city ordinances, deliberately violating a court order to trespass on territory the police have impounded and placed out of bounds.'

Straker replied: 'Unless we do things like that, Sandy, we're going to lose this case.'

'Not necessarily.'

'Of course we will,' Straker exhaled. 'Don't you understand? Even if this was ever about justice and the state preserving citizens' rights of law and order, it's certainly not about that any longer.'

'Yes it is,' answered McMahon. 'That's why the Ministry of Justice …'

'… Sandy,' he said firmly, 'Tahm and Remy said there was nothing wrong with the car.'

'Machines *malfunction*,' she countered. 'Nazar and Sabatino's assertions carry no weight in law. Subjective, self-serving opinions have no value as legal argument.'

'I don't care. They are no longer subjective to me. What I found this morning – the cut wire, the missing ties, the plasticine in the breeze-block wall and the tampered-with gravel trap – all make one thing abundantly clear: a car was expected to breach that fence. Therefore, Remy's crash was … *not* … an accident. My intelligence – garnered this morning – therefore, is utterly consistent with Tahm's and Remy's assertion that there was nothing wrong with the car.'

McMahon looked momentarily lost. 'What you "found" this morning is – legally – useless,' she said. 'It's inadmissible. We can't use illegally gathered evidence in court.'

'I don't care.'

'That's the second time you've said that. Why not?'

'Because it tells us, without question, that somebody wanted this accident to happen – something we did not know for sure earlier.'

McMahon, for all her profession's readiness to take any view in an argument for the sake of a fee, was thrown. She tried to think of a rebuttal, but couldn't; had the sinister implications of Straker's last comment thrown her too far, perhaps?

'What this morning has absolutely done,' he went on, 'is to help define our immediate course of action. We have found the first tiny chink in the accusations and legal processes that have been launched against us. My recce has given us a clear indication of what was intended to happen at that Grand Prix, even though we are yet to understand fully how it happened, let alone why. We have made a breakthrough. We now know we should be looking for whoever is behind all this: we now know we need to look for a *who*. If we can identify this person, we might then – crucially – have the chance to understand the *why*.'

McMahon said nothing.

'The other key corollary,' said Straker, 'is the clear realization of the malice involved, something else we weren't aware of before.'

'What do you mean?'

'For someone to have doctored that corner in that way – fully expecting the car to be going that fast, and knowing there would be spectators behind the point of impact on that fence – means the perpetrators *knew* exactly what the consequences would be.'

'You mean injuries?'

'At that speed – on that corner – they could not have been in any doubt the consequences would be serious.'

'That there would be deaths?'

Straker nodded. 'Whoever's behind all this, Sandy, wanted to see people die.'

'Who could *ever* want that?'

'God knows, but that's what we've got to find out,' said Straker. 'Now that we do know that someone did, though, we should be in no doubt about the malevolence of the people we're up against.'

THIRTY-FOUR

When Straker shuffled back through into the main part of the motor home with McMahon, he found the Ptarmigan team members looking at him expectantly. There was a very different atmosphere. Backhouse pulled up a stool. Still favouring his left side, Straker heaved himself up onto it.

Backhouse asked: 'Any thoughts on what you want us to do now?'

'Yes,' he replied. 'Sandy has pointed out that none of my discoveries this morning is admissible in court. What I have discovered, though, tells us one thing very clearly. Someone wanted a car to crash through the fence at that point. Of course, that's far from how the world sees it; it's certainly not how the Russian people see this accident. Our job, now, is to come up with a convincing explanation of what actually happened – which would also get Tahm, Remy and Ptarmigan off the hook.'

'How the hell do we do that – with all the obstructions we've encountered so far?' asked Backhouse.

'Our intelligence gathered this morning should convince us of a key factor. That when Remy says the car was faultless, and Tahm says there was nothing wrong with her attempt to go round the outside of Baryshnikov, we should believe them.'

The faces round the table changed quickly.

'So, our investigation starts with trying to understand how she could still have come off the track.' Straker held up his hand to acknowledge the difficulties. 'I know we don't have access to the wreckage but, Andy, you're piecing together a picture of the car during the race, yes?'

Backhouse nodded.

'Let's crack on with that, then, and pull together every scrap of telemetry data you've got.'

'Okay.'

'I'd also like to analyze the gravel samples,' he said turning to McMahon. 'Does Brandeis have access to a decent lab here?'

'I'll ask. It's not something we do as a matter of course.'

'If you don't have any luck, we can always fly them home. Next,' said Straker, 'could we download my photographs and video? They could be useful in the investigation.'

One of the young Ptarmigan team volunteered to take that on; Straker handed him Sabatino's phone.

Addressing the whole gaggle, Straker said: 'Getting those things going would be a good start. Before we disperse, I want to talk about Yegor. I want to know how you all feel about his defection?'

Their faces darkened once more.

'Does anyone feel his defection to the prosecution was a surprise?'

'Yes,' answered Backhouse. 'I *was* surprised, actually.'

'Really?'

'Yes.'

'Go on.'

'Baryshnikov is a competitive, self-centred, driven, egomaniacal … arsehole. Some drivers need those qualities to win.'

'But?'

'I *am* surprised that he sold the team out.'

'Even after causing such trouble for Sabatino at the FIA after Montreal?' asked McMahon.

Backhouse nodded. 'This is very different for one overarching reason, Sandy. Have you spoken to Quartano about Yegor's defection, Matt?'

Straker nodded.

'What did he say?'

'He was seething. Said Baryshnikov would never work for him again – was going to get Quartech's in-house counsel to serve his severance papers right away.'

'Pretty much as expected, then?' said Backhouse. 'That means Baryshnikov is *finished* with Ptarmigan – as of now – mid-season.

Think what that means for the man's earnings? More than that, think what it means in terms of the car he's giving up? Ptarmigan, this year, is the best machine *by miles* – in a league of its own. With little doubt, Ptarmigan's going to win the Constructors' Championship. One of our drivers is going to be World Champion. No driver would give up *that* seat lightly. And that consideration is long before one thinks about the damage he's done to his reputation. Teams need and demand loyalty. Ratting out Ptarmigan is hardly going to enamour him to the other teams in the pit lane, either. Who's going to hire him now? Baryshnikov's all but ended his career doing this.'

Straker looked Backhouse straight in the eye. 'Precisely, Andy. So why the hell *has* he done it?'

There was silence.

McMahon volunteered: 'We're in Russia. His home Grand Prix. The deaths at the track – of his own countrymen – have affected him in a different way to the rest of us. Perhaps he's taken it more personally than others. He will have come in for considerable pressure from the Russian press, media and public opinion – particularly in putting right what's been done?'

Backhouse shook his head. 'Baryshnikov is far too ambitious for any of that to matter a fig.'

Three of the Ptarmigan team reacted at the same moment.

Something had caught their eye.

Movement.

It wasn't difficult to see with the motor home out on its own in the middle of the concrete apron.

Police cars and armed policemen on foot were closing in on the motor home quickly from all sides. How many of them were there? Thirty? Forty? Fifty?

'Jesus,' exclaimed Backhouse. 'What the hell is this?'

Sandy McMahon shot to her feet. Running down the motor home, she pressed the release button and dropped down the steps towards the door before it had fully opened.

Straker snapped painfully to his feet. '*Christ*,' he said, 'they're here to impound the truck. Andy, quick! Start uploading the video footage from all the on-board recorders.'

In an instant, every Ptarmigan member spun round, ran to a console, fired it up, and was selecting video files – triggering their upload to the Ptarmigan mainframe.

'Hurry,' said Straker, 'we're going to get chucked out of here at any minute.'

Down on the asphalt, Sandy McMahon surveyed the police officers as they approached. She said firmly and loudly in Russian: 'What is the meaning of this?'

One policeman caught her eye. He was striding out in front. A 9mm Makarov pistol was holstered on his left hip.

'I have orders to impound this truck,' declared the officer.

The other policemen formed an imposing semicircle around McMahon and the door of the motor home.

McMahon responded: 'On whose authority?'

'By order of Prosecutor General Gazdanov,' was the reply. 'You are to evacuate the vehicle at once and hand over the keys.'

'Who are *you*?' she demanded. 'And where are the court orders?'

McMahon held out her hand expectantly.

'I am Police Colonel Pudovkin. And here are the court orders,' he said handing over the papers.

McMahon took them.

Pudovkin made to move towards the motor home.

'As you were, colonel,' she said sharply. 'Before you act, I am entitled – even under Russian law – to read a court order and challenge it, if I wish.'

Colonel Pudovkin was halted.

Straker was impressed. McMahon was conducting herself with considerable confidence. She appeared unmoved by the circumstances. Straker, though, could see signs of the tension she was feeling: several veins were showing proudly in her neck.

McMahon read the order, slowly and thoroughly.

Pudovkin's expression revealed that, in being halted, he was having to contend with a loss of face induced by the lawyer, as well as being shown up in front of his own men.

Straker looked again down the inside length of the motor home. Backhouse was darting from console to console, urging his team to upload as many of the team's videos as they could. How much longer would they have?

Straker switched back to McMahon outside, dreading that she was about to be overruled.

It looked like she'd come to and was reading the last page.

Pudovkin said: 'I order that you step aside.'

McMahon raised her hand 'Not so fast, colonel.'

The policeman's hand was moving menacingly towards his left hip.

McMahon was folding the sheaves back into their original configuration.

Pudovkin took a step forward.

Straker looked back at McMahon. Her pale red hair was set off even more by the adrenalin-induced glow of her skin. Straker couldn't take his eyes off her – how could he describe the effect? With her colouring and complexion she seemed to have developed an aura.

Colonel Pudovkin was now beginning to fidget.

McMahon said: 'Gentlemen, this court order is invalid. To be effective – under federal law – it must be an original document, which this is not: this is a scanned copy. A copy can be valid if it bears the stamp of the Ministry of Justice, which this scan does not. This piece of paper, therefore, is *not* an authentic court order. It does *not* give you – or your men – the power, legally, to impound this vehicle. Any attempt you make to enter it, gentlemen, will be an *il*legal act.' She politely offered the court papers back to the police colonel.

Pudovkin was very obviously thrown by the lawyer's conclusions.

He could have charged on – but there was something convincing about this woman's authority.

Spinning round, Pudovkin walked away from McMahon, barging out through his wall of policemen – shouting an order over his shoulder. The phalanx of policemen was soon following the commanding officer back to their cars.

Backhouse banged the door release which hissed open, letting McMahon back up into the truck.

'Sandy, mate!' bellowed Backhouse. 'That was bloody *great*. Way to go.' He offered her a glass of whisky from the motor home's secret stash. Others team members clapped enthusiastically, stepping forward to shake her hand.

She smiled at their appreciation and downed the shot of single malt in one hit. When Straker caught her eye, he said: 'That was phenomenal, Alexandra. *Brava!*'

She nodded.

Straker announced to the team: 'Thanks to Sandy, the first shot of the fight-back has just been fired.'

THIRTY-FIVE

More glasses of whisky were poured as the showdown was celebrated. Straker found himself unable to participate fully, though. He
was deeply concerned. The authorities had shown a clear intent to
confiscate Ptarmigan's motor home. Either the prosecution wanted
access to the data stored in its computers and video banks, or – as
with the crash site and car wreckage – they wanted to deny Ptarmigan use of its own data for its defence against the charges. Were these
Russian institutions going to stop at nothing in this case?

McMahon moved towards Straker.

'Sandy, that was magnificent,' he said. 'Talk about coolness under
fire?'

'I think we can all see that we're now up against something verging
on the unreasonable?'

Straker nodded his acknowledgement; compared with her attitude and comments in their private conversation earlier, that was
quite a concession.

'Those sods will be back, though,' said Straker. 'We must assume
we are destined to lose access to all our video files in here. We initiated a panic upload, while you were facing down the police. We'll
get it finished. To have some security, though, we'd better move the
fight-back out of the motor home right away. Can we transfer everything to Brandeis – relocate to your offices – and have access to your
mainframe?'

'Sure.'

'Let's get that going right now, then,' said Straker.

By a quarter past eleven, Straker could finally relax. McMahon's car
was leading three taxis – carrying the remaining Ptarmigan personnel – out of the main gates of the Zhar-ptitsa Autodrom. They had

managed to strip the motor home of data, and were okay now to abandon it.

'I've got us a conference room in the Brandeis building,' said McMahon. 'We'll set that up as your HQ.'

'Good, thank you.' Straker groaned involuntarily from the discomfort of his injuries.

'I've also arranged for the company doctor to see you. There's more wrong with you than you think.'

'We've got no time to lose,' he said. 'We may have preserved the video research material, but we need to download all the telemetry from the Ptarmigan mainframe – which will require some pretty hefty bandwidth – and there are several other lines of enquiry we need to initiate ...'

'I'll sort the bandwidth. Let me have the other lines of enquiry: I'll get them going while you're being looked at. What else do you want?' she asked, opening a page on her iPhone to take notes.

'Yegor Baryshnikov seems very close to being a son-of-a-bitch,' he said, 'and so I *was* surprised by Backhouse's response to his defection. After ratting Remy out with the FIA in Montreal, *I* wasn't surprised he switched sides at all.'

'He's got form,' agreed McMahon. 'Maybe Backhouse is just in a state of denial?'

Straker pouted. 'That's as maybe, but Andy's reaction was a surprise. As I said before, in any investigation, I love coming across surprises – because they so rarely occur without a reason. A surprise offers a clear invitation to look into something further. Backhouse's opinion, therefore, has me intrigued.'

'But it is only that – an opinion.'

'Yes and no. Backhouse's comment about Baryshnikov being finished with Ptarmigan was spot on. I spoke to Quartano last night, after Yegor's defection.'

'You're sure that *Baryshnikov* would know Quartano's likely response?'

'Oh God, yes. He'd know he was finished with Quartano; the Big

Man is renowned for having a less-than-zero tolerance of disloyalty. But Andy's point about his career with other teams is unquestionable. His career is buggered. I take it you know what the top F1 drivers get paid?'

'A fair amount?'

'Millions a year, which he's now lost. But Backhouse's other point is probably the more significant. Apart from the money, drivers wouldn't willingly give up as good a shot as this to win the Championship and – let's face it – achieve immortality. For any of those reasons, therefore, Baryshnikov's actions have to be a surprise. So *why's* he done it? Why? … The sacrifice is huge. Hang on a minute; I take it he hasn't been subpoenaed by the courts or something, has he?'

McMahon shook her head. 'Not that we know of.'

'For Yegor to give up what he's given up, then, means he must have got something substantial in return – he must have got the authorities to make it worth his while. Either that or they've got some serious hold over him.'

McMahon said nothing in reply.

'Do you remember Yegor's tone and body language during his defection press conference?'

'When he seemed to be stumbling over his words?'

'That wouldn't have been noteworthy had he been speaking in English – but he was like that in *Russian* … that isn't like Baryshnikov at all, is it?' Straker groaned again. 'Can we get hold of a recording of that conference? I want to give it another look.'

McMahon made a note in her phone.

'I think we should also look into the mechanics of Baryshnikov's defection.'

'What do you mean?'

'How was the defection handled? Who contacted whom? When? There may be something in that process that could offer clues as to why he's ratted us out.'

'Like what?'

'When was the first contact made between him and the authorities, for instance? If it was yesterday afternoon, that would tell us one thing. If contact had been made – say – before we ever got to Moscow, that would tell us something different entirely.'

'You think this could have been set up that far back?'

'Doctoring that circuit didn't happen overnight, Sandy. Who knows how long all this has been in the planning?'

'How could we ever find that out, though?'

'Contact with Baryshnikov would have to have been discreet. He's far too well known around here for anything to have been done in public, or by him walking into a public office somewhere. There must have been communication, though – probably by email? Phone? SMS texts?'

'I suppose that's possible, except we don't have powers of intercept. How do we get hold of that sort of information? We'd never be able to subpoena the Russian Postal Service, the telephone companies, or any ISP here.'

'Baryshnikov has a Ptarmigan phone. That means he has a Quartech phone … email address and email account. He uses our comms and internet platform.'

'To which Quartech – Ptarmigan – would have access?'

'Precisely.'

'Can we get at those records easily?'

Straker looked at his watch and worked out the time difference in London. It was late enough to make a call. 'My hyper-efficient researcher back at Quartech's HQ will be able to.' Pulling out Sabatino's phone, Straker dialled a number from memory – his office in Cavendish Square. Karen was in and answered immediately. Straker chatted briefly with his research assistant for a few minutes, their not having caught up since Straker's departure for the Arctic.

Three minutes on he reported: 'Karen will download all Baryshnikov's comms records into a spreadsheet and send it over.'

McMahon was impressed.

Straker exhaled painfully as he tried to get himself into a

comfortable position. 'The next strand I want us to research,' he breathed, 'is the Zhar-ptitsa Autodrom. We need to know everything about it – and everyone involved with it from the very beginning.'

'Why? What's your interest there?'

'We now know the crash wasn't an accident, so we *have* to conclude there was an intended outcome? An intended victim.'

'Okay?'

'So, then, who do we think the victim was meant to be?' asked Straker. 'We currently have a number of victims. The spectators – who were injured and killed. Remy – who nearly died. And now, after the crash, Ptarmigan is a victim – corporately, along with its most senior director.'

'Okay.'

'What's the likely effect of this crash going to be on the Zhar-ptitsa Autodrom, though – to its business and standing?'

'Crippled it, I'm guessing.'

'It certainly has been seriously damaged. Might *that* have been someone's intention? Perhaps it was meant to hurt someone who's involved with it? So, let's find out who owns it? Who runs it? Who's invested in it? Who wants to make money out of it? And, now, who might be losing money because of it? Any one of those people could have been the intended victim.'

'So are you suggesting that Ptarmigan may not have been an intended victim at all?'

Straker shrugged.

'Looking into all that is going to be a big job. I'll have to set up a research team to pull it all together.'

Straker nodded. 'But,' he said, 'if you do bring anyone in, I want to brief them, personally. And I do *not* want any of them to know why they are looking.'

'Brandeis is trustworthy,' she said. 'Client confidentiality is the bedrock of our profession.'

'Do you think the authorities know Brandeis Gertner is involved in this case?'

'Of course.'

'How far have the authorities gone in respecting boundaries so far, Sandy?'

McMahon didn't answer.

'I'd rather be careful, then – and keep all our key information and conclusions on a very close hold. "This is Russia" could easily apply to the authorities' respect for your staff.'

THIRTY-SIX

Their car descended into an underground car park. They were now beneath the Imperatorskaya Tower in the business area of Presnensky District, to the west of Moscow. Heaving himself out from the rear seat, Straker was led across the well-lit concrete to the lifts. He and McMahon rode up through the building to the Brandeis Gertner offices, hosted on the top five floors.

'We'd better get you to the sickbay,' McMahon suggested as she took another look at Straker.

'I want to see the room you've got for us as our command centre first.'

Reluctantly McMahon relented.

Walking out onto their destination floor, Straker found a well-appointed – but not ostentatious – reception and meeting area. Its decor would have been recognizable in any cosmopolitan business centre anywhere in the world. A male receptionist emerged from behind an elegant desk and led them down a wide corridor to the conference room, which had been set aside for Ptarmigan at the far end.

Inside it, Straker was struck by two of its features. One was its size – easily ten metres long and six or seven metres wide, with a substantial boardroom-style table down its length. The second was the plate-glass window occupying the entirety of the long outside wall. From twenty floors up, it offered an exceptional view to the east, out over Moscow. Straker could see the meandering Moskva River curve its way into the distance, passing the sinister shapes of the Kremlin in the middle distance.

'What other facilities do you need?' McMahon asked.

'A number of phones, and several access points to the computer mainframe. A bank of printers would be also useful.'

'Okay.'

'The sooner the guys get set up and start analyzing the telemetry on Remy's car, the better.'

'All that will be arranged. And, through here,' said McMahon leading Straker to one of the short ends of the conference room, 'we have a smaller adjoining space – for your HQ – for privacy and for sensitive stuff.'

This was an unremarkable room, although it had a central circular table and a smaller plate-glass window set in its smaller outside wall.

'This is good – can it be locked?'

'Yes,' she said, and, removing the pair of keys from the door, peeled one off and gave it to Straker. 'I'll keep the other.'

'Are those the only two?'

'I'll make sure they are.'

'Could we have a couple of computer links set up in here too, as well as a large display board mounted against that wall – so it can't be seen from next door? A collection of stationery would also be good.'

McMahon picked up the landline phone and passed Straker's logistical requirements on to her PA. Hanging up, she said: 'Now let's get you to the doctor.'

The doctor assessed Straker's injuries, pronouncing them painful but minor. He strapped Straker's left wrist and shoulder. There was not much he could do for his other injury which he diagnosed as a couple of broken ribs. Straker was given some hefty painkillers, which, he was told, should keep the discomfort at bay.

Forty minutes on and Straker was back in the conference room. Andy Backhouse was supervizing six Ptarmigan team members now arranged around the boardroom table, each set up with a keyboard and computer screen. A bank of printers had been set up towards one end of the table, several of which were busy printing pages off. Straker presumed the collation of the Ptarmigan telemetry data had begun.

'This is excellent,' he offered to McMahon. 'Thank you for getting this up and running so quickly.'

'We're having to juggle some of our in-house links to the UK,' she explained. 'Ptarmigan's bandwidth demands are pretty high, as you suggested. We should have a dedicated high-speed data connection to Shenington operational within the hour. And in here,' she said leading him off towards the smaller HQ room, 'we have the other things you asked for.'

Straker was pleased. Mounted directly onto the side wall – hidden from the conference room next door – was now a three-metre wide whiteboard. Computer access had been made available through two work stations set up on the small table. There was also a mass of new pens and paper carefully laid out.

Picking up a large black felt-tip pen from the collection of stationery, Straker walked across to the whiteboard and wrote four headings across the top, dividing the board into quarters: PTARMIGAN | CAUSES OF CRASH | BARYSHNIKOV | ZHAR-PTITSA AUTODROM.

McMahon said: 'I've called a meeting of my research team looking into the Autodrom for half an hour's time, if you'd like to brief them?'

Straker said: 'Good, but not in the Ptarmigan rooms, please. In the meantime, I'll check in with my office – to see where we are on Baryshnikov's phone, email and text records.'

Karen, as normal, had exceeded Straker's expectations. His assistant had prepared the spreadsheet as discussed but had also sourced a copy of Baryshnikov's personnel file, sent across from Ptarmigan's headquarters in Oxfordshire. Straker delved straight into the telecoms data – keen to see what sort of information was available.

Volume-wise, the number of calls and texts Baryshnikov had made was not excessive – possibly four- or five thousand over the previous six months. Straker cast an eye down the incoming and outgoing calls. He quickly noticed significant duplication. Using Excel's Sort Data function, he ranked the numbers – so duplicates would form vertical blocks in one of the columns. He was mildly encouraged. This showed there were far fewer unique numbers than it had seemed when they were all jumbled up; Straker estimated there to be about eight- or nine hundred in all. Sorting the data this way also drew attention to several unfamiliar country dialling codes.

There was one prefix that he was keen to check on. Via Google, he looked up the international dialling code for Russia. Going back to his column of sorted numbers he saw a sizeable block of a hundred or so starting with its +7 country code.

Drafting a reply email to Karen in London, Straker asked the Competition Intelligence and Security team to research these. He wanted to identify each of the callers and the called, if possible. First off, he suggested they Google them all – to eliminate obviously disinterested commercial operations such as hotels, restaurants, airlines, shops – a process that might also, if they were lucky, even identify some institutional numbers. For the remaining unknown ones, he asked that each number be called directly to question their identities. Straker pressed Send.

He then wrote up some notes for the research he wanted into the Zhar-ptitsa Autodrom. By the time he had finished, McMahon was back in the command centre.

'The research team is ready for you, Matt – in a room down the hall.'

McMahon led Straker off to another meeting room. Four executives were already sitting around its small table. First, Straker was introduced to Anatoly Pokrovsky, whom McMahon described as one of her solicitors and the Brandeis colleague she had appointed to head up the research effort. Pokrovsky was easily fifteen years McMahon's senior. He was stick thin with ever-moving eyes behind a pair of thickish wire-framed glasses. He was prematurely thinning on top and had a pale – even pasty – complexion. Overall, Straker gained from him an impression of gaucheness; Pokrovsky did not appear to be particularly confident or at ease with himself. In a profession where even rudimentary interpersonal skills were necessary, Pokrovsky's relatively junior rank – to McMahon's – could perhaps be attributed to his social awkwardness.

'As part of the defence against the corporate manslaughter charges that Ptarmigan is facing,' Straker announced, 'we need to research some factors around the crash at the Grand Prix.'

The faces around the table looked expectant. All of Moscow knew Brandeis Gertner was involved in this high-profile case. There was a sense from the researchers that they were about to enjoy the privilege of becoming "insiders" in the impending trial that the whole country was talking about.

'These are the aspects of the Zhar-ptitsa I am keen to look into,' Straker said as he handed each of them a page of his typed-up notes. 'I would like a full timeline of the Autodrom's development and existence; this means everything from the initial bid to host the Grand Prix, which was presumably made to the business that runs Formula One – Motor Racing Promotions Limited; I'd like to know all about the people – or organization – that put the bid together; how the bid approach was announced; how the venue was chosen; how the land was bought; who granted the planning permission; which companies were involved in the development of the Grand Prix circuit; how all this was financed; who designed the track; which companies did the building work; which entity operates the complex now; and a list of all suppliers, companies, and people with regular access to the Autodrom.'

At no point in this briefing did Straker say why he was looking into the Autodrom in this much detail. These Brandeis people may have been subject to client-attorney privilege, but the hackneyed phrase "this is Russia" nagged at Straker's confidence. He wasn't prepared to assume – or expect – the norm, here, for a moment.

Straker looked into the faces around the table for acknowledgement of their tasks.

'I am happy you produce your findings as each segment feels

complete, Mr Pokrovsky. No need to wait until it's all done. Let's see what you can find.'

Straker walked with McMahon back towards their conference room command centre.

'Thank you,' he said to the Brandeis lawyer. 'We've got our defence planning up and running encouragingly quickly. Let's just hope we can find something that gives us an insight into the *who* behind this case.'

THIRTY-SEVEN

When Straker re-entered the command centre, Andy Backhouse broke from a group huddled round a computer screen.

'We've pulled together a full set of telemetry and video coverage of the leading cars over the Grand Prix weekend – including pre-race practice, Qualifying, the parade lap, the laps preceding the crash.'

'And?'

'As far as we can tell, there are no oddities. Remy's own take on the car does bear out – that there didn't seem to be any impact or mechanical failure during that time.'

'Have you enough data to be certain?'

'We could go into more detail, but I'd be confident the malfunction we're talking about would be obvious, even in headline-level data.'

Straker nodded at the assumption. This conclusion may not have told Straker anything new, but it did enable the process of elimination to begin – allowing them to focus specifically on the issues and periods of time that could matter. 'What about the immediate lead-in to the crash?'

'That's what we're working on now.'

'Good, Andy. While I've got you here, let me give you a quick overview of the investigation,' he said and indicated to Backhouse that they go into the inner HQ.

Straker closed the door behind him.

'I'm going to restrict access in here to you, Sandy and me.'

Backhouse looked surprised. 'Any particular reason you're keeping such a close hold?'

'Something weird is going on here. I don't want us to take any chances. After the Baryshnikov defection, we have no idea how far the Russian authorities will go to find out what we're up to. We don't need to make it easy for them.'

On the whiteboard Straker wrote a list under the heading CAUSES OF THE CRASH: *Practice*, *Qualifying*, *Parade Lap*, *Laps 1 to 6*. Then, picking up a red pen, he drew a diagonal line through each of them. He left *Hermitage Straight* uncrossed.

'What's the significance of the ZHAR-PTITSA AUTODROM heading?'

Straker answered: 'For the infrastructure around Turn Eleven to have been interfered with so much, someone must have had access to the circuit.'

'Okay.'

'Who could that have been? One of the staff? An outsider? If it *was* an outsider, who let them in? I want to understand all the commercial, operational and personal connections with the Autodrom. At the very least I want to know who had access to the site.'

'Good stuff. Why the BARYSHNIKOV heading?'

'Who knows? I'm intrigued by your assertion that defecting to the other side was *not* what you would have expected from him.'

Backhouse looked concerned.

'No, no – take the credit,' said Straker noticing Backhouse's expression. 'Any kind of hunch, particularly if something doesn't seem quite right, is always a godsend in an investigation.'

Almost unnoticed, afternoon merged with evening in the Brandeis command centre. The gloomy overcast Moscow day gave way to a murky Moscow dusk. Fluorescent lights in the conference room seemed to make the darkness through the plate-glass window come quicker. Before any of the Ptarmigan team had realized it, night had fallen. From their eyrie at the top of the Imperatorskaya Tower, the view of Moscow was now made up of a mass of silhouettes, an occasional floodlit church or government building and lights burning in windows across the city.

Straker had spent the afternoon working his way through management emails from the Ptarmigan factory, editing them for inclusion in the witness statement. He was pleased. There was some thorough background material to help reinforce the robustness of Ptarmigan's management and operating procedures. A number of electronic folders had been set up to assimilate, index and collate the information he had requested. As Straker went through them, he transferred selected emails into the relevant folders.

McMahon reappeared in the room just before seven o'clock carrying a bundle of files. 'Pokrovsky has come up with some initial findings on the Autodrom.'

Straker pulled out a chair from under the table for her. While she was arranging the files on the small table, Straker re-closed the door.

'They've found some things about the entity that mounted the bid,' she said.

'Excellent.'

'Guess who was the first person to go public with the idea of a Grand Prix in Moscow?'

McMahon paused for effect before handing Straker one of the files. He took the document; even as he opened it he could see – from the contents page, the index tabs and the elegant layout – how professionally her team had put this together.

'Tab 1,' McMahon said.

Straker flipped the page over: 'Yegor Baryshnikov?' he read with a sigh.

McMahon grunted acknowledgement.

'Good grief … When?'

'Four years ago.'

'In what capacity? I can't imagine him as an organizer or entrepreneur?'

'It seems he was little more than a figurehead.'

'How did he start negotiations, then? Who did he approach?'

McMahon leant forward and flicked over Tab 2. 'He wrote an open letter in *Pravda*, addressed directly to the president.'

'High-profile stuff.'

'And pretty unsubtle.'

'Why?'

'For the previous three years,' she said, 'the president had been in negotiations, personally, with Motor Racing Promotions Limited to host the reinstated Russian Grand Prix in Sochi, down on the Black Sea.'

'Would Baryshnikov have known about that bid?'

'Tab 3.'

Turning over the page, Straker saw a collection of newspaper articles, each summarized in English. There were several screen scrapes from the websites of State institutions as well as references to State-controlled TV and radio news bulletins. 'Okay, so how could Baryshnikov *not* have known about the Sochi bid? And, when he wrote that letter, he would have been well aware that the Sochi Grand Prix was the president's baby.'

McMahon nodded emphatically.

'Why on earth, then, would Baryshnikov have been arguing for a switch to Moscow?'

'Quite,' replied McMahon. 'From what little I've read this afternoon, hosting a Grand Prix is highly prized. It's also clear that negotiations with Motor Racing Promotions can be notoriously complicated.'

'So Baryshnikov's counterbid could *only* have been disruptive – prejudicial, even – to the ongoing Sochi negotiations?'

'It would have to have been, wouldn't it?'

'Why the hell did he do it?' Straker asked. 'Naïvety? Arrogance? Did he do it off his own bat – was he put up to it?'

There was a knock on the door.

Straker answered.

An elegantly dressed young woman appeared and apologized for the interruption: 'I thought you would want to know, Sandy.'

'What's up?' she asked.

'Andy Backhouse has just had a message from Ms Sabatino. She's texted him saying that there are policemen "swarming" all over the hospital. She thinks she's about to be questioned about the accident.'

'Holy crap,' said Straker.

'Thank you, Nadia,' said McMahon. 'I'll be right there – can you get me the British consul, urgently?'

The aide pointed at the small sideboard in the room. 'He's on the phone for you right now – line two.'

THIRTY-EIGHT

Straker rode with McMahon across Moscow to the hospital. They had no idea if another intervention by the British consul would have an effect this time.

'Remy cannot be interviewed about the crash,' said Straker. 'Her condition's far too frail. She'd have to be still in shock. She only heard about the deaths yesterday – and from us. You saw how she reacted to the news. Have these people no sense of perspective?'

'How do we stop her being interrogated if the consul can't get the prosecutor general to see reason?'

'At the very least you've got to be with her. How could the police even *contemplate* this without ensuring Remy has legal advice?'

They rode in silence as their car headed across town.

Straker's mind whirred through the case and the unthinkable consequences of Sabatino inadvertently saying something incriminating; what if the police were out to trap her? He found himself visualizing a courtroom, an ambitious results-hungry prosecutor, a jury of ordinary Muscovites wanting someone to pay for the deaths of their brethren.

He and McMahon had to stop this interrogation. The risks were far too high.

A word out of place, a comment made too lightly, even an error of memory could result in twenty years' hard labour. Unwittingly, words from someone still coming to terms with their injuries could so easily undermine their case...

'Undermine!' he said. 'I've got it – I might just have got us an angle!'

Reaching the Yeltsin Meditsinskiy Tsentr within thirty minutes, they were braced for the likely obstructiveness. On arrival, McMahon requested a meeting with Mr Pyotr Uglov.

'Please tell him,' McMahon said in Russian to the receptionist, 'that Ptarmigan will call him as a witness in the forthcoming trial unless he comes to see me here, right now.'

Uglov did appear a few minutes later.

'Thank you for seeing us, Mr Uglov,' she said softly in Russian, hoping to neutralize the tone of her summons.

The consultant nodded perfunctorily.

'As Ms Sabatino's lawyer, I am deeply concerned that she is being subjected to a police interview.'

'The police have made up their minds,' said the doctor. 'I am told that this case is of the highest national importance. It has been impressed upon me that as Ms Sabatino is such a key figure in the investigation and the trial, she needs to be interviewed before she is coached to fabricate her memories.'

'Please tell me, doctor, when did you inform Ms Sabatino that she had been involved in killing thirty-four people?'

There was a pause while Uglov considered his answer.

'Had you even told Ms Sabatino of those deaths – before *our* visit to see her – yesterday?'

He shook his head.

'How would you describe Ms Sabatino's mental, psychological, even *emotional* condition now – within twenty-four hours of learning that she had been involved with the deaths of thirty-four people?'

Almost as an admission of guilt, Uglov replied quietly: 'I am not a psychiatrist. Even so, how could I not say: distressed?'

McMahon nodded gently in an acceptance of his admission. 'I have to confess, while readily declaring that I am no medic myself, I would guess the same.'

McMahon then asked: 'Since Ms Sabatino learned about the deaths in her accident, Mr Uglov, has she been seen by a psychiatrist?'

The consultant shook his head.

'Received any form of counselling?'

Another negative.

'I want to be very clear, Pyotr,' she said using his first name for the first time, 'given Ms Sabatino's condition, this police interview is wrong. I can't speak for the medical considerations, of course, but – morally – I am unable to see this interview as anything other than unjust: *nespravedlivyy.*'

Mr Uglov didn't seem unnerved by McMahon's assertions, if anything he gave an impression of accepting them.

'Let me be clear again, then, doctor,' McMahon added, her tone shifting subtly, 'if this interview proceeds, I will have no choice but to call you as a witness in the trial – and have you cross-examined.'

Uglov recoiled slightly.

'I will have you questioned on your medical procedures. I will have you questioned about the validity of your clinical stewardship of Ms Sabatino as a patient. I will have you questioned about why you didn't tell her about the deaths; why no clinical assessment was made of any effect that such news might have on her; why you offered her no treatment – support, even – for any effects on her mental or emotional state; why you gave permission for your patient to be submitted to a crucial, legally significant, interrogation with no clinical understanding of her readiness for it. I will have you questioned on whether you would feel – if *you* were in Ms Sabatino's condition – that you, yourself, would be ready to answer such questions; and whether you would expect yourself to give balanced answers in such circumstances. I will have you questioned on whether you believe such answers would be psychiatrically reliable.'

The consultant looked increasingly pained. After several seconds of awkwardness, he said to McMahon: 'Come with me,' and strode off towards the lifts.

They rode up the three floors in silence.

Straker saw the trauma specialist was tense. What did that mean?

They reached their floor. Uglov charged out, striding on ahead down the austere echoey passageway with its harsh fluorescent strip lights and smell of disinfectant.

As they rounded a corner, they could see the armed policemen standing guard at the end of the corridor. Straker wondered how they were going to react. Would they even be let through? Wouldn't the officers bar their way?

Uglov suddenly broke into a run. He turned round and encouraged Straker and McMahon to do the same.

The consultant shouted forwards to the police.

Straker turned towards McMahon with a quizzical expression.

'Emergency, emergency. Patient in trouble,' she translated.

It seemed to work.

Uglov was soon barging into Sabatino's room. In the moment of apparent medical urgency, the police had stepped back, letting the other two in behind him.

Once inside, the consultant started talking loudly and gesticulating. His outburst may have been in Russian, but Straker heard the tone and read his body language: he was clearly calling a halt to the interview.

Sabatino was in the bed propped up on a bank of pillows, wearing the halo brace with the tracheotomy tube still in her throat. Two men in suits were hovering over her, one to either side. Because of where they were standing, Sabatino wasn't able to see into the face of either interrogator. Her eyes, though, were flashing this way and that between them.

One of the men turned round to face Uglov. He looked indignant, his stature expanding rapidly to mirror that of the clearly agitated consultant. He moved away from the bed, heading towards Uglov.

'What is the meaning of this?' said the policeman

'Your interrogation has to stop.'

'You have no authority. This is a federal inquiry.'

The other man didn't stop trying to question Sabatino. Over the hubbub between Uglov and the other policeman, Straker strained to hear what he was asking her.

'You haven't answered my question,' said the second interrogator in heavily accented English. '*When* did you agree to the rally with the mayor?'

But Sabatino was not listening; her attention was now held by Uglov, who was getting increasingly heated.

'I am declaring the patient unfit to endure an interview,' announced the consultant.

'How could you change your mind in the space of an hour?' barked the first interrogator. 'No more than an hour ago you declared her to *be* fit enough.'

Uglov was resolute: 'I have since consulted with colleagues.'

'Irrelevant,' said the policeman. 'Your earlier medical opinion will be submitted to the court.'

'Then I will submit a signed statement, countermanding whatever we might have discussed informally. I will testify against any statement you take from Ms Sabatino today. I will give my professional opinion that I was wrong in letting this interview proceed, and that I should not have been coerced by the police into giving permission.'

'If you say that in court, you will look ridiculous. We will *make* you look ridiculous.'

'I have no doubt,' replied Uglov. 'But my questioning of the patient's medical state *will* diminish Ms Sabatino's answers in the eyes of the jury. Her answers, today, will not serve your case, gentlemen. My patient deserves the time to heal and to come to terms with the emotional effects of her accident.'

Silence fell on the room.

No one moved.

Soon Mr Uglov moved across to Sabatino's bed and reached for the readouts from the machines monitoring her condition. The moment he looked down at one of them, he stretched across to the wall and struck the alarm. Over his shoulder he said to the policemen: 'Her heart rate and blood pressure are disturbingly high. She's showing considerable signs of stress.'

In barely fifteen seconds or so the doors flew open and several nurses poured into Sabatino's room. McMahon translated some of the ensuing discussion.

As the medical staff approached the bed, the interrogators were crowded out. They realized their interview was over and, angrily, they began to leave.

Straker was encouraged by their departure but was now concerned by the medical attention Sabatino was receiving. From what the medics were doing, this certainly didn't look like any kind of wheeze. One of the nurses was hurriedly administering something into the line in the patient's neck.

Sabatino seemed overcome. Tears were welling in her eyes.

Straker, moving to reach between two of the nurses, made to touch her lightly on her right hand. She smiled up at him through the tears.

'Thank you,' she said as pillows were rearranged behind her back. 'How did you get here? How did you get them to stop the interview?'

'Your text came through just in time,' said Straker. 'Don't worry about any of this now, Rems. Rest yourself. Just concentrate on getting better.'

Straker was anxious to see her settle. He knew he should fight it, but he couldn't stop himself; he was desperate to ask her a question about the interrogation: 'Rems, one question – then we'll leave you in peace.'

She made a face of acceptance.

He asked: 'Why on earth were those men asking you about a rally with the mayor? And which mayor were they talking about?'

THIRTY-NINE

Driving away from the hospital, Straker sat in the back of the car looking out of the window, staring at the darkened streets of Moscow, preoccupied by the scene at the Yeltsin Medical Centre. What the hell was going on? He couldn't stop turning that monstrous interrogation over in his mind. One element of it had firmly taken root, though: that question from the police about the rally.

'Sandy, what do you know about Remy appearing at a rally with the mayor of Moscow?'

She looked surprised. 'Absolutely nothing. Rallies are illegal in Russia. The president's cracked down on political opposition. Rallies are banned. There are strict and heavily enforced limits on public assembly. The mayor *couldn't* have held a rally.'

'What would the police have been talking about, then? They appear to be focused on a "rally" for some reason. Can we look into this?'

McMahon rang her office and asked Pokrovsky to find out anything about such a rally. Her conversation continued.

Catching Straker's curiosity, she then said: 'Good grief. We'll come back and hear what you've got straight away.'

Straker and McMahon headed straight back to Brandeis's offices. Riding up in the lift, he finally broke his silence.

'We only ever seem to be surprised by developments in this case,' he stated testily. '*We* haven't done anything, yet, to take the initiative.'

'Court cases tend to be like that,' McMahon said. 'Claimants, defendants, accused are all at the mercy of the legal procedure and timetable.'

Straker shook his head. 'That may be true, except none of the

incidents mounted against us in the last two days have been proce-
dural. They've all been the other side acting at our expense.'

Walking into another of Brandeis Gertner's small meeting rooms,
Straker found McMahon's research team already assembled.

'What have you got for us?'

Anatoly Pokrovsky spoke for the group. 'We've been looking
at the corporate personnel involved at the Autodrom – and have
found out the name and composition of the entity that approached
Formula One to make the bid.'

'Sounds promising,' said Straker.

'I think we should say up front, though, that there are some
pretty strange aspects to it,' said Pokrovsky as he handed Straker the
piece of paper.

Straker read aloud: 'Moscow CTO? What is C–T–O?'

'If pronounced "Sto",' replied the researcher in a full Russian
accent, 'it means "a hundred".'

Straker looked quizzical.

'We think it refers to a length of time. At the time this bid was
made, it had been exactly one hundred years since the last Russian
Grand Prix – held in Saint Petersburg, in 1914.'

'That long ago? What's strange, then, about Moscow 100?'

Another piece of paper was handed over.

Pokrovsky said: 'There were four individuals involved with
Moscow 100 at the time of the bid. One of these, the highest-profile,
was Yegor Baryshnikov – as we told you this afternoon.'

Straker nodded. 'Presumably having the leading Russian racing
driver on board would be a valuable asset to such a bid?'

'It is, which is why we have been intrigued by some of the news
we have discovered since. Baryshnikov was ousted from the board of
Moscow 100 at the end of last year.'

'Ousted? He didn't just resign?'

There was a shake of the head. 'We haven't been able to discover
any reasons. The "strange" bit, though, is how what happened to

him fits in with other things we *have* uncovered about Moscow 100.'

'And what are those?'

'Of the three other board members, one was a man called Feodor Olyshenko. Olyshenko was as influential as it got, having been a past president of the RAF – the Russian Automobile Federation.'

'Another big name – presumably having the head of the sport's national governing body as part of this bid would add weight, I imagine. Was he still on the board of the Automobile Federation at the time?'

'No. He'd been fired from the RAF shortly before he got involved with Moscow 100.'

'Fired as president?'

'And the board.'

'At the same time?'

'In a fairly dramatic way.'

'Fired for what? Impropriety? Some sort of scandal?'

'We'll let you draw your own conclusions,' replied the researcher. 'We have found out that he was fired on the direct instructions of the president.'

'The president? The president of what?'

'The president of Russia.'

Straker's face instantly gave away his surprise. 'What the hell was the president doing intervening in the management of a sport's governing body?'

The researcher handed over another piece of paper showing a photocopied newspaper cutting. 'Olyshenko was opposed to the country's bid for the Grand Prix going to Sochi,' Pokrovsky explained, 'Sochi, of course, being the other venue…'

'…which was being championed by the president?'

'…indeed, and which did end up hosting the first modern Russian Grand Prix in 2014. It seems that throughout Olyshenko's time as head of the Automobile Federation, he – very publicly – withheld his and the RAF's support for the race going there.'

'Do we know why?'

There were shaking heads on the other side of the table.

'What else do you know about this difference of opinion … this showdown between Olyshenko and the president?'

'Not much more at this stage,' said the lead researcher.

'Can we look into it further? This clash is extraordinary, isn't it? Something very odd must have been going on between them?'

'Indeed.'

'It would be really useful to go and have a chat with Olyshenko. He could help us get to the bottom of this. Can we find out how to get hold of him?'

'I'm afraid that won't be possible,' said one of the researchers.

'We can't find his contact details?' asked McMahon.

'Oh, we know *exactly* where he is.'

'Well then?'

'He's in the cemetery at Vagankovskoye.'

'What?' said McMahon. 'How did he die?'

The researcher replied: 'We're not sure. Olyshenko was fifty-six. It appears he acquired a disease that killed him … inside three weeks.'

'He hadn't been ill before then?'

The researcher shook his head. 'Remarkably fit. Olyshenko was known to run several marathons a year.' Pokrovsky handed over a newspaper cutting showing a photograph of Olyshenko crossing the finishing line of the Moscow Marathon: a respectable time of 2 hours 57 minutes showed on a digital clock above the finishing arch.

'What else can we glean from this bidding entity, Moscow 100? Who else was on the board?'

'Deputy Vladimir Kosygin.'

'Deputy meaning what?' asked Straker.

'It's the styling of elected members of a government here,' explained McMahon. 'It can be applied to politicians at the city, regional or federal level.'

Pokrovsky nodded in confirmation. 'In Kosygin's case, he was an elected member of the Moscow City Duma; he represented the United Russia Party.'

'And so, presumably, was on the Moscow 100 board for his local connections.'

'We assume so – his patch did encompass the Nagatinskaya Poyma Park, where the Autodrom was built. Kosygin stood and had been re-elected for the same single-seat constituency for the last twenty years, pretty much since *Perestroika*. He had built up a significant personal following – and a sizeable majority – even outperforming his party's showing in neighbouring seats.'

'So a good local worthy, then. Do we know anything else about him?'

'Yes. He, too, was removed from the board of Moscow 100.'

'Why?'

'He lost his position as deputy.'

'So he ceased to be useful, politically?'

'Maybe, only there is something else slightly weird about him, too …'

'Go on.'

'After twenty years' service, and countless election wins in his district, Kosygin was de-selected from his seat and dropped by the United Russia Party at the end of last year.'

'Not voted out?'

Pokrovsky shook his head. 'There was no public election; he still had eighteen months of his term left to run.'

'Was there a local squabble? Some sort of scandal?'

Pokrovsky looked a little sceptical. 'Talk around Moscow has it that there was direct intervention by the United Russia Party high command…'

'…and the leader of the United Russia Party,' said McMahon, 'is – of course – President Tarkovsky.'

Straker exhaled. 'Wow,' he said. 'Is there any chance of talking to *this* guy – Kosygin?'

One of the researchers replied: 'We can look into it.'

'Okay. Who is the last board member?'

'Menashe Rosenthal,' said one of the researchers. 'He was a Muscovite – a businessman – who ran a sizeable construction and property company around western Russia.'

'Hang on,' interjected McMahon. 'You're using the past tense ...?'

'Yes.'

'What did *he* die of?'

'We haven't been able to find out.'

'How old was *he*?' McMahon asked.

'Thirty-nine.'

'Holy shit!'

'Was Rosenthal a petrol head,' asked Straker, 'or a businessman?'

'He was a property man, so his property expertise would have been useful to Moscow 100,' replied Pokrovsky, 'but I'd say Rosenthal was a genuine petrol head. He'd amassed one of the largest private collections of supercars in Russia.'

'So we're saying,' stated Straker, 'that of the four people involved in the bid for the Moscow Grand Prix, three were forcibly removed?'

There were nods.

'You've also discovered that *two* of the four board members are dead, having died relatively young from unexpected – and, as yet, unidentified causes?'

More nods.

'In addition, you've uncovered a serious difference of opinion over the choice of venue for the race, rooted – we think – in bad blood between the RAF, the Sochi bid, and the president of Russia?'

Further nods.

'And the president of Russia – *himself* – got involved in the internal politics of the sport's governing body ... removing the then-president of the RAF, not only from the presidency but from the board as well?'

Pokrovsky nodded.

'Good God, Anatoly, no wonder you flagged these findings up as "strange".'

FORTY

Straker returned to his small HQ in the Brandeis offices. Walking across to the whiteboard and standing directly in front of the heading ZHAR-PTITSA AUTODROM, he wrote "Moscow 100" underneath. Beneath that he wrote a list: *Yegor Baryshnikov – Ousted, Feodor Olyshenko Ex-President RAF – Ousted (Dead)*, *Deputy Vladimir Kosygin – Deselected* and *Menashe Rosenthal – Businessman (Dead)*. He turned to face McMahon.

'How weird *is* this?'

A knock was heard on the door jamb.

Andy Backhouse, the race engineer, was standing there with a laptop in the crook of his arm. 'I think you need to see this.'

He shut the door behind him.

In response, McMahon said: 'What have *you* found?'

'We've now managed to download and analyze the telemetry from Remy's car – directly before the crash.'

The three of them gathered round the computer screen.

'I've pulled together all the key data measured and recorded on the car.'

'As it happened?' asked McMahon.

'In real time, yes.'

'And?'

'I'm not sure, and wouldn't be certain – or able to prove anything – without examining the wreckage. However, you remember we noticed the anomaly of Sabatino's steering into that corner – that she had started to turn the wheel and then it looked like it had suddenly become heavy?'

The other two nodded.

'Right, well take a look at this,' said Backhouse and pressed Play on the laptop.

The screen showed a forward-facing view from an on-board camera mounted above Sabatino's helmet; it also showed the top of her steering wheel and her hands. They could see the back of Baryshnikov's car directly in front of her. The impending left-hander of Turn Eleven was in the distance at the top of the picture. The two cars were running at full throttle along the Hermitage Straight. As a blur, the surface of the track flashed by underneath, disappearing out of shot through the bottom of the screen.

'Now watch this,' said Backhouse. 'Remy is about to duck out of Baryshnikov's slipstream, across to the right. There! As you see, the car responds perfectly – performing everything needed to make that move. Remy only needed to make tiny movements with the wheel.'

Straker watched the footage as Backhouse let it run on. 'Okay.'

'Now we see Baryshnikov start to move over the left of the track, as he sets himself up for the left-hand corner. This, though, is where it gets strange.' Backhouse pressed a key on the computer. The image froze. He tapped another key. Blocks of numbers, graphs and columns of data scrolled down, overlaying the stilled video image.

'I've managed to sync the car's telemetry with the video timeline,' he explained. 'Here,' he said pointing at one small graph, 'we have the hydraulic pressure for the car's entire system. Here, in this block of numbers,' pointing to another column of figures, 'we have the output from a torque sensor on the steering column.'

'Is that the metering valve thing you mentioned yesterday?' Straker asked.

'No, that's over here. The torque data is different; it comes from a sensor which measures the amount of twisting force being applied when the driver turns the steering wheel.'

'Okay.'

'And, here,' said Backhouse pointing at three groups of numbers in turn, 'we have data on other hydraulic valves in different parts of the car – the steering, the differential and the brakes.'

'Sorry,' said McMahon, 'what's that middle one you said?'

Backhouse said: 'Don't worry, I'll explain as we go.'

McMahon nodded.

'The key thing,' said Backhouse, 'is that we're looking to measure four very different – and completely unrelated – states of the car, yes? The "twist" of the steering wheel and then the three sets of hydraulics relating to the steering, differential and brakes.'

Straker nodded.

'Now,' said Backhouse, 'watch this.'

Backhouse tapped a key followed by the space bar.

The picture moved again but this time in slow motion. They saw that all the numbers, data and graphs overlaying the image started changing.

'As you can see, these metrics are all moving in real time, measuring their specific states of the car?'

McMahon nodded.

'Right, look at this,' said Backhouse pointing at the data relating to the torque sensor. Straker would not have been able to explain exactly what he was looking at, but he could see that one of the numbers was rising – and then increased dramatically.

'That's a torque spike,' Backhouse explained. 'It's showing the force that Remy was applying to the steering wheel. And it fits, exactly, with the wheel suddenly becoming heavy.'

'As she tried to heave it?'

'Precisely.'

'So *did* the hydraulics fail?' Straker asked.

'That's what we thought, until we saw this.' Backhouse backed the film up by a few seconds, pressed the space bar again and let the film run on. 'I want you to look here this time,' he said holding his finger on the line of the graph. 'This measures the overall hydraulic pressure across the entire car. As you can see,' he said keeping his finger in place, 'right the way through Remy's two attempts to turn the wheel – and then as the car leaves the circuit – the overall pressure in the hydraulic system never faltered. It stayed constant throughout.'

'So it wasn't a hydraulic failure, then?'

Backhouse tapped the space bar and, using the slider, returned the film to a point before the corner. 'That's what we thought – until we saw this.' Backhouse ran the film again in slow motion. 'On this pass, I want you to watch these two sets of data – which show the state of the metering valve and the hydraulic valves in the pistons, which steer the front wheels.'

McMahon and Straker both leant in.

'At the point where the torque sensor reading starts to rise,' Backhouse explained, 'we want to see that the two sets of hydraulic valves in the steering opened. That would be consistent with hydraulic assistance being asked for and then being applied to help with the turn. So, here is Remy turning the wheel,' he said pointing out the torque spike again, 'and look – there! – at the reading from the metering valve, it's working perfectly. But – there! – *look* at the valve in the steering pistons. It's completely closed – shut down to zero.'

'Meaning?'

'That there's suddenly no hydraulic assistance ... at all.'

'So the hydraulics *did* fail?' offered McMahon.

'Yes and no.'

'Was the piston valve "misfiring"?'

Backhouse shook his head. 'No, not exactly as ... wait ... *there* ... do you see? The piston valve is not stuck. It's suddenly back to being fully open again – exactly where it remains for the rest of the crash. Which explains how Remy *was* able to steer when she was out on the gravel.'

'So,' offered Straker, 'the overall hydraulic system was working 100 per cent, the torque sensor was 100 per cent, the metering valve was 100 per cent and the hydraulic valve on the steering pistons was 100 per cent – except for a fraction of a second at the moment she's trying to turn?'

'But that's not all,' he added. 'You remember we spotted that hint of smoke from Remy's right-rear tyre?'

'Which we thought could have been a patch of dirty track, her being on the outside of the circuit?'

Backhouse nodded and said: 'Except it wasn't anything to do with a dirty surface.'

The race engineer switched screens, showing a different view of Sabatino's approach to the corner; he'd reverted to the overhead shot. 'I want you to look at the timeline, here, before we go back to look at the telemetry.'

'Okay.'

Backhouse ran the tape. They watched for the wisp of blue smoke. 'There,' he said freezing the video, 'can you see? The timecode shows that it happened at 22.61.44.'

'Okay.'

Switching the images, Backhouse toggled back to the on-board footage above Sabatino's helmet, which still showed the data overlaid in numbers, graphs and columns. 'Okay, we'll now run this forward,' he said as the footage moved and the timecode clicked on. 'There,' he said, tapping the space bar, 'I've stopped it at 22.60.01 – so just before we see the puff of smoke, yes?'

Straker and McMahon nodded.

'Look at this,' said Backhouse as he pointed to another block of data. 'This is *another* valve reading, this time for the differential. I'll explain that in a minute. Watch this, though,' he said as he tapped the space bar to move the film on in ultra-slow motion. '22.61.20 – the valve half opens. Also, please note Remy's hands – that she makes no attempt to touch this dial here on the face of the steering wheel. Then, at 22.66.44 – look – the valve reading shoots up.'

'Meaning what?' asked McMahon.

'That, once again, while the overall hydraulic pressure across the whole car remained constant, the differential valve went from half opened to fully opened. Meaning it had been activated hard.'

'And the significance of the differential?' Straker asked.

Backhouse paused the footage. 'Okay,' he said, 'I need you to think about a car on a circle.'

'Okay.'

'While on a circle, the wheels on either end of any axle will want to travel at different speeds – the outer one wanting to run faster than the inner one.'

'Because it's got further to go?' offered McMahon.

'Exactly. Now imagine trying to deliver power to the drive wheels in a corner, when they are each going at different speeds? The power delivery from the engine needs to be asymmetric, delivering a different level of power to the different drive wheels, depending on the specific circle each one is on, yes? On most cars, this is delivered using a set of angled gears – a differential – or a mini-gearbox, if you like, built into the middle of the rear axle. Still with me? Good.

'Sometimes, though, this can allow all the power to go to just one drive wheel – think of how one wheel can spin when your car gets stuck in the mud? We want to prevent that – and we do so by a device that enables us to lock the differential, sometimes referred to as a diff-lock.

'But … joining the wheels together can then produce *another* complication – and that relates to the readiness of an axle to turn. If an axle *is* fixed, like on a go-kart, there is always a conflict between the wheels on either end of it through a corner as they are both forced to turn at the same speed; this effect dramatically inhibits the whole axle from turning. We certainly do *not* want that effect on a Formula One car; and so, rather than have a diff-lock that's either straight on or straight off, we put a clutch in the middle of it, which can be varied by the driver using a dial on the steering wheel. This enables us to adjust the joining and unjoining of the rear axle all the time – into, through and out of corners. We call this facility a limited-slip differential; and it, too, is operated by hydraulics.'

'So what happened here – to Remy?' asked Straker.

'As I showed you a moment ago,' Backhouse replied, 'Remy's differential clutch had been half activated into that corner.'

'Because she had started to turn?'

'Precisely. But, at 22.61.44 – without, if you remember, any sign of Remy touching the dial on the steering wheel – the hydraulic valve is suddenly activated with near-maximum force.'

'Which means?'

'Her rear wheels *had* started to rotate at slightly different speeds, because she'd started rounding the corner. At the moment the wisp of smoke appeared, the differential was fully locked, the clutch having been slammed shut.'

'Forcing both rear wheels – suddenly – to rotate at exactly the same speed, presumably?'

'Correct. The right rear adjusting the most – suddenly under-rotating – hence the wisp of smoke from the tyre. Normally on a corner, with the weight shifting to the outside, the outside wheel is loaded – so it would be the inside one that would change speed. But here, the inside wheel was still on the clean part of the track, while the outside one was on the dirty – with less grip – so it was the *outside* wheel that adjusted this time.'

Straker was shaking his head. 'You know, Remy did mention that she felt a jolt … maybe the right rear locking-up was something to do with it?'

'Very possibly.'

'What does all this locking-up mean?' asked McMahon.

'Well, Sandy, two things. First, at that precise moment, the car will have been destabilized by the momentary lock-up in one rear wheel – and, second, because the rear axle was now effectively "fixed", it would *immediately* show much more resistance to turn.'

Straker suddenly looked dark.

He was about to speak, when Backhouse held up his hand.

'But that's not all…' The race engineer triggered the footage again. In slow motion, he let it run on beyond Sabatino's two steering attempts.

'After Remy realizes she's not going to turn in time, we come to the brakes,' said Backhouse. Moving his hand to point at another set of data, he said: 'This is the reading from sensors measuring the pressure on the brake pedal; as you can see – *there* – she's just hit the brakes … pretty hard.'

'Presumably not an unexpected reaction, under the circumstances?' offered McMahon.

'Absolutely not,' replied Backhouse. He paused the film.

Straker said. 'Everything all right, Andy?'

The race engineer looked troubled. 'I need to show you something else, something strange.'

'Go on?'

'I need to explain what would be considered normal, though, before you can see the significance of this for yourself.'

The other two nodded.

'Let me give you the big picture. I can always go into more detail afterwards, if you want me to?'

Both Straker and McMahon nodded again.

'Okay, under the current Formula – the rules – F1 cars have to run hybrid engines and their size is relatively small. The quid pro quo is that we are permitted to augment the power of the engine by "recycling" some of the energy it produces. In fact, to be competitive we *have* to do this. Recycling is done by connecting a generator to the engine – an Energy Recovery System – called MGU-K...' Having said that Backhouse put his hand straight up in apology, indicating some of the detail was not essential to their understanding. 'This device generates electricity, which can then be stored in batteries on the car for subsequent use; that stored electricity is actually fed back through the same generator – turning it into an electric motor – to assist the engine during subsequent acceleration.

'But, the process of generating that electricity takes considerable effort, producing significant reverse torque – sorry – resistance. It would seriously slow the engine down – and the car – if we used the generator all the time; it would *kill* performance. However, we make a virtue of the resistance it does create while generating electricity – when we want to slow the car down. Instead of losing energy that would otherwise be lost as heat in the brakes, we "harvest" some of that energy for recycling by engaging the generator; and we use the resistance that it creates, then, as part of the braking system. But the car-slowing attribute provided by the harvesting only works on the drive train – the back wheels. Are you with me so far?

'I now need to explain how this interacts with the brakes. The brakes on an F1 car – front and back – are operated by fairly conventional hydraulics. But to make the most of the useful deceleration characteristics of the energy recovery generator, we end up trying to combine these two very different braking systems – both with very different variables – and expect them to work at the same time. To manage all this and get the most out of both for the drivers, we have to have a smart add-on to the cars' existing engine management system – to fine-tune the different contributors to the braking process.'

Backhouse looked at the others and thought he had probably given them enough background. 'So, with that rough outline in mind, what we should *expect* to see during deceleration is Remy hitting the brake pedal. Immediately after that, we should see the hydraulic-operated front brakes respond. Then, depending on a number of factors – the brake balance front-to-rear, the temperatures in the front discs, the response of the car, and a whole load of other things – the smart add-on to the ECU, the car's computer, should activate the energy recovery generator to start harvesting, which would also contribute to slowing the car down. Finally, as a balancing item, so to speak, we would then expect to see the hydraulic system on the rear brakes kick in, particularly given how fiercely we might expect her to be trying to decelerate at this point.'

'So what happened at Turn Eleven, Andy?' asked Straker.

Backhouse now looked like a man in mourning. 'Remy did hit the brake pedal, as I showed you before – as measured by the pressure recorded on the pedal itself. But if you look over here,' he said pointing to a different set of numbers, 'her front brakes didn't respond: the hydraulic valves stay completely closed – *inactive*. Most bafflingly, the ERS generator did not cut in, either. And finally, as shown here, there was no fill-in or backup braking from the hydraulics on the rears.'

'Meaning her brakes didn't work?' said McMahon

The race engineer shook his head.

'*At all?*'

Backhouse's eyes conveyed his answer.

'So, if I've followed you,' said Straker, 'during this extremely short period into the corner, the overall hydraulic pressure across the car remained constant. One hydraulic valve, though – in the steering – stayed *inactive*, causing the steering wheel to be heavier than expected, as shown in the torque spike on the steering column. At almost the same time, the hydraulic valve within the differential on the rear axle – which should have stayed partially activated – activated fully, without any instruction from Remy, locking that axle which would not only lock-up the outside wheel but also cause the car to behave like it wanted to run on in a straight line. And, at the crucial moment, the three elements of the braking system, if I've understood you correctly – the hydraulics in front, the energy recovery generator and the hydraulics on the rears – all failed to activate, meaning, effectively, that she had *no* brakes?'

The race engineer shook his head in agreement.

'None of which should have been expected or intended.'

'Fuck, no,' said Backhouse. 'At that speed, even the slightest unexpected happening on the car will have a disproportionate effect, throwing the balance and control for the driver.'

'Christ,' said Straker. 'How did those valves and systems get to *do* each of those things?'

Backhouse replied: 'Cars can fail at any time – components can fail – drivers can make mistakes, so one shouldn't rule out a "normal" failure of some kind. But, all of these elements are unconnected. For them to behave like this – with things "going in different directions" at the same moment – is almost impossible by themselves. Mathematically, the probability of them doing that randomly – in that sequence – is so remote as to be dismissed.'

'So are you saying that these valves and systems were *instructed* to do those things?'

Backhouse nodded. He paused. 'They would have to have been.'

The room fell silent.

'What's up, Andy?' Straker asked.

Backhouse said: 'I am trying to be objective, but what troubles me is that any attempt I make to interpret the actions and timings of these hydraulics and systems leads me to a pretty ugly conclusion.'

McMahon asked: 'Which is what?'

'That they would form the perfect combination of interferences if you *wanted* that car to leave the track at that exact point.'

All three of them were stunned.

Silence returned for several moments.

Then Straker asked: 'How are those valves and systems controlled ... normally?'

'All by the engine management system, the ECU. The instructions to control each of those valves can *only* come from that on-board computer. In which case, the ECU must have been interfered with in some way; the software must have been tampered with.'

'You mean sabotaged?' asked McMahon.

Backhouse shrugged.

Straker asked: 'How does that happen, Andy? Would it have to have been done by someone needing to get close, physically interact-ing with the car – or could it be done from a distance: could we have been hacked?'

'Matt, I really don't know,' said the Brummie. 'I've never seen anything like this before. We need to look at everything, and be alive to every possibility until we get to the bottom of it.'

'How quickly can you do that?' asked McMahon.

'At the moment, not ever ... not until we get to examine the wreckage ...'

Straker said: 'Even so, Andy, it looks like we're clearer, now, on *what* was done? But without access to the wreckage, we can't fully get to know the *how* – and so we won't get to know the *who*.'

McMahon's eyes suddenly widened. 'Oh my God,' she said. 'What if this was done by someone in the team? What if someone within the *team* sabotaged the car?'

FORTY-ONE

Realizing they were now dealing with a concerted intent to do Ptarmigan harm, Straker and McMahon worked on into the night. A takeaway pizza arrived at nine o'clock.

Making them aware that they weren't alone in working late, McMahon received an email from Pokrovsky shortly afterwards.

'Anatoly's managed to track down some footage taken when Ms Sabatino arrived at Vnukovo Airport,' she announced dabbing her mouth with a paper napkin.

'What's the significance of that?' Straker asked.

'He's sent it up because there was a large crowd there to greet Ms Sabatino when she landed, which included the mayor of Moscow. Anatoly says it's the closest thing he could find to a "rally".'

Straker leant in to study the clip. McMahon clicked the link. A clip of poor quality mobile phone footage was soon running. Whoever had filmed it was standing in the car park at the back of the terminal, in among the crowd – about twenty people back from the low-loader and a little over to the left. The shot offered a slightly side-on view of Sabatino and the mayor as they stood on the back of the lorry.

McMahon turned up the sound. It was just about possible to hear Mayor Pavlova's speech, except it was in Russian. Then Straker saw McMahon's look of concern.

'What's up?' he asked. 'What is she saying?'

'Pavlova is declaring that she helped to bring the Grand Prix to Moscow.'

'Okay?'

McMahon translated: 'A showcase for Russia, the Grand Prix … she criticizes Tarkovsky's homophobia … the Grand Prix will demonstrate … the country's desire for social freedom, diversity … tolerance of human rights.'

McMahon stopped talking as the crowd roared its approval.

Then, on the screen, Straker saw Mayor Pavlova offer and take hold of Sabatino's hand and raise them both high into the air. McMahon translated:

'This remarkable woman is going to teach this country a great lesson about equality – about the power of merit.

'Women are going to show this country that change in Russia is demanded.'

The crowd, once again, showed its enthusiastic approval.

'Good grief,' said McMahon.

'What's wrong with that? It all sounds pretty innocuous. Just a bit of puff – bigging-up Russia.'

'Oh, it's not that innocuous – and it's not just what's being said,' McMahon replied as the clip ran on.

The person taking the footage chose that moment to hold the mobile higher above the heads of the crowd and to pan round behind them.

'Look at the *size* of this gathering,' said McMahon. 'I had no idea it was as big as this.'

'Is that big?'

'Yes ... if there's a legal ban on *any* form of public assembly.'

'You're saying this was an illegal meeting?'

'Hell, yes.' McMahon hesitated for a moment. 'It's pretty clear why Pavlova held this gathering there, though – to try and confuse her crowd with passengers coming or going to the airport, except the numbers are far too big. Look at the platform Pavlova's on – it's pretty improvised, but deliberately mobile, wouldn't you say?'

The clip ran on. The crowd was then heard starting a rhythmic chant. Even on the video, the clarity and volume became audible enough:

'Zhar-ptitsa! Zhar-ptitsa! Zhar-ptitsa!'

Straker strained to discern the words: 'Is that them celebrating the Tsars – like the Grand Prix circuit?'

'No, no,' she said shaking her head. 'Zhar and Tsar may sound alike, but Zhar-ptitsa's nothing to do with the imperial family. It's a reference to a Russian myth. Zhar-ptitsa translates as the Firebird … an eye-catching female creature … supposed to have majestic plumage that glows red, orange and yellow.'

'So the Grand Prix circuit's named after some sort of fairy tale?'

'Oh, it's far more than that,' admonished McMahon. 'The Firebird legend has endured for centuries – because she's a symbol of hope … a kind of longed-for messiah. The Firebird is only ever implored to bring the people good fortune. In Russian folklore, the Zhar-ptitsa is always invoked to come and save the country … particularly in times of crisis.'

McMahon rang Straker's room at seven o'clock the following morning. 'How ready are you?'

'Just leaving.'

'Stay there – I'll come and pick you up. I'll be there in ten minutes.'

'Why, what's going on?'

'A press conference has just been announced.'

'By whom?'

'The prosecutor general.'

'About what?'

'Ms Sabatino's car,' declared McMahon. 'Word on the street has it that Gazdanov's going to announce the cause of the crash.'

'Like hell he could ever know that,' he said. 'Christ. What time is this thing … and where?'

'Eight o'clock at the Autodrom. And, get this – they're holding it right in front of the Ptarmigan motor home.'

'Talk about loading the dice.'

'The prosecutor general wouldn't be doing this if he didn't feel it strengthened his case.'

Straker, thinking through some of the ramifications to their defence, responded: 'If this is about the car and, possibly, technical, we should have Andy Backhouse there as well.'

'Leave that with me. I'll be with you at a quarter past.'

McMahon's car pulled up in front of the Baltschug Kempinski Hotel and Straker climbed straight in.

'Andy Backhouse is on his way to the press conference,' she reported as they pulled away. Heading for south-east Moscow and the Zhar-ptitsa Autodrom, they made swift progress, going mainly against the flow of rush-hour traffic.

McMahon's phone went. She took the call.

'Pokrovsky and his team are ready to discuss their next set of findings. They've got some stuff on the property aspects of the Autodrom.'

'Can we have them ready to go through it all the moment we're back from this conference?'

At the Zhar-ptitsa Autodrom, the crowd for the press conference was huge. As billed, the location and backdrop was the Ptarmigan motor home. A trestle table had been set up in front of it, draped with a cloth bearing the seal of the Ministry of Justice. On it was the usual profusion of press and television microphones. A low morning sun bathed the area in a soft apricot light.

Three men appeared and stood behind the table.

One of them was Yegor Baryshnikov.

'I guess we shouldn't be surprised he's here,' hissed Backhouse 'They've wasted no time in capitalizing on the gutless turncoat.'

Léon Gazdanov, the prosecutor general, announced in English: 'Ladies and gentlemen, as promised, we are building the evidence of the case against the perpetrators of the atrocity at the Moscow Grand Prix.'

He turned and signalled.

Another man appeared from inside the Ptarmigan motor home carrying two small objects. These were brought to the middle of the table and placed down on the blue cloth in full view of the press. Camera shutters clicked as the moment was recorded.

Gazdanov continued: 'Now with the expertise of one of Ptarmigan's own staff – a Russian patriot, who has chosen to put his country before his own professional interest – the Ministry of Justice has analyzed the data stored on the black boxes of the car that crashed.' The prosecutor general waved Baryshnikov forwards to the bank of microphones.

Baryshnikov, pulling a piece of paper from his pocket, began to read from a prepared statement. Also in English, he announced in his heavy accent: 'I can confirm what Prosecutor General Gazdanov has just said. From my analysis, I have inferred that there was mechanical failure on the part of the Ptarmigan car. This, in my opinion, induced the loss of control at Turn Eleven of the Zhar-ptitsa Autodrom and that, consequently, there is a direct causal link between Ptarmigan's negligence and the deaths of the spectators.'

Flash guns were fired off in a near-continuous fusillade.

'How can he utter such bullshit?' said Backhouse, loud enough for those around him to hear.

'Hang on, Andy – calm down a second. Keep listening. We need you to stay rational.'

Backhouse swung round to look at Straker as if he was about to throw a punch.

Calmly Straker asked: 'Didn't you tell me that only the FIA could access those "boxes"?'

In an instant Backhouse's mood seemed tempered, as if Straker had flicked a switch; as the point sunk in, he nodded emphatically.

Behind the trestle table, the prosecutor general had retaken control of the press conference, almost pushing Baryshnikov to one side. The prosecutor seemed to be preening himself, ready to answer questions.

Straker leant across and said: 'So, Andy, I want you to ask Gazdanov this…'

Backhouse listened to what Straker was suggesting. And then nodded.

'But you need to ask him about the FIA first, before you ask the big one, yes?'

Again Backhouse nodded his agreement.

Turning in to face the conference, Backhouse waited for the

prosecutor general to finish his current declaration, so he could time his moment. It wasn't going to be easy – twenty journalists were already screaming their follow-up questions.

Backhouse tried to ask his questions twice but was drowned out on both occasions.

Suddenly, there was a deafening ear-piercing whistle. With four fingers in his mouth, Backhouse had produced a shrill Top C at well over 120 decibels. No one could ignore it. People turned round to see where this shriek had come from. The ensuing quiet was just what Backhouse needed.

'Mr Prosecutor,' he said, 'Birmingham Broadcasting here – can you confirm something for us? Have the FIA been engaged in decoding the "black boxes" as you called them?'

'We have not needed to involve the FIA,' said Gazdanov. 'Mr Baryshnikov has provided the answers for us.'

Backhouse quickly looked at Straker who gave him a half smile. Turning back to face the speaker, Backhouse declared as loudly as before: 'Mr Baryshnikov is well aware – as you should be before any trial of Ptarmigan or its people, sir – that *only* the FIA has the passwords to access those "boxes". Unless the FIA have unlocked them first, anything you or Mr Baryshnikov says about the data on them is completely bogus.'

Léon Gazdanov did not look amused. His expression hardened: he half shut his eyes and started gesticulating dismissively. 'We do not need input from the *F–I–A*,' he said, pronouncing the initials as if he had an unpleasant taste in his mouth. 'The FIA are as much to blame for the deaths of Russian citizens here as Ptarmigan. They were the so-called "experts" who signed off on the safety standard at this circuit. We do not want a biased opinion, or them trying to cover up their negligence. We now have better than an FIA expert, we have an insider – Mr Yegor Baryshnikov – from the heart of the very team that is to blame. He knows all the facts … *and* the truth.'

Gazdanov looked out across the conference, pleased that most of the journalists were keeping their heads down, suggesting they were recording his comments. 'So, thank you, Mr Birmingham, we have all the information we need to secure a clean – and quick – conviction.'

Suddenly Straker leant across to Backhouse and whispered something in his ear. He felt the race engineer nod again before Backhouse bellowed: 'Mr Prosecutor, could we please hear confirmation of your statement from Mr Baryshnikov?'

Gazdanov paused for a moment.

He was obviously thinking about the consequences of this request.

The prosecutor general then indicated to Baryshnikov that he should step forward.

Baryshnikov seemed to look at Gazdanov askance before answering: 'We have data to form picture,' he said and looked down.

'What about your access to the "black boxes"?' yelled Backhouse.

Straker was now studying Baryshnikov's face until his eyes hurt.

The Russian Formula One driver looked up and scanned the faces at the back of the crowd. 'On my mother life,' he said and paused. 'We have data.'

Gazdanov reacted quickly, all but pushing Baryshnikov out of the way.

'Forget the FIA and forget the black boxes,' bellowed the prosecutor general. 'We have an insider from the team to tell us all the truth. We can confirm, now, that – without doubt – Russian justice will be done.'

FORTY-TWO

Straker was fizzing when he, McMahon and Backhouse walked away from the press conference.

'Well done, Andy,' he said as they walked back to their car. 'Stating the need for the FIA to be involved in reading the data loggers – the "black boxes" – won't have been lost on some of those journalists. Hopefully, we can start prompting a little more scrutiny of such pronouncements from now on. It may not have much of a bearing on the legal position,' he said to McMahon, 'but we need to demonstrate that in relation to evidence the prosecution will be held to some standard of reality.'

Straker was encouraged that McMahon seemed to approve.

'Okay then,' said Straker as their car pulled away, 'what did you both make of Baryshnikov's performance?'

'What do you mean?' asked Backhouse.

'Think about it for a moment. A pretty obvious oddity ... Why didn't Yegor draw attention to who you were when you asked your question – why didn't he identify you as one of the Ptarmigan team? Wouldn't Gazdanov have made hay with that? Surely he would have launched into a diatribe against you, if he'd known. Surely he would have denounced you – saying you weren't a journalist – that you had a direct interest in Ptarmigan – that you were biased, and declared that you were only there to distort the conference and the course of justice?'

McMahon seemed to register what Straker was saying.

'And then, did you hear Baryshnikov's speech?'

Backhouse said: 'What about it?'

'Like *hell* he wrote that himself,' said Straker. 'It was grammatically correct, for one thing. He's nowhere near that fluent in English in normal conversation. Didn't you hear the vocabulary he used?

Words like "analysis", "inferred", "induced", "causal link" … I've only met him once, but from that one encounter I would have to ask: Are those really expressions that Baryshnikov would use?'

Backhouse agreed they *didn't* sound like Baryshnikov's normal vocabulary.

'And then there was his body language – his demeanour?'

'Eh?' grunted Backhouse.

'Sum up Baryshnikov for me,' said Straker.

'Confident.'

'Sure of himself.'

'Cocky.'

'Arrogant.'

'Son-of-a-bitch.'

Straker nodded before asking: 'How comfortable did Baryshnikov seem to you during that press conference?'

'Hardly any of those things,' answered Backhouse. 'But who cares, Matt – I sodding well hope he is *un*comfortable having ratted us out.'

'So you agree – he wasn't behaving as he would normally?'

'Why should we care?'

'For this very simple reason: Did he look like a willing participant to you?'

The others didn't answer.

'There was also one particular phrase he used,' Straker added, 'that seemed so completely out of place.'

'Which was what?'

'"On my mother life"?'

The others looked blank.

Straker looked slightly impatient for a moment. 'What's the significance of that? Do you know?'

The other two shook their heads.

Straker answered: 'He said it as part of his answer to your question about the "black boxes". What if I told you that he seemed to look me straight in the eye as he said it?'

They arrived at the Brandeis offices twenty minutes later. Up on the meeting-room floor, Straker and McMahon peeled off to a separate meeting room down the corridor. They found Pokrovsky and two of his researchers already there. Having closed the door, Straker and McMahon sat at chairs around the table.

'We think we have some potential leads,' said the research leader.

'Good,' replied Straker.

'But, we've also hit a number of dead ends.'

'Okay.'

'We've been looking into the venue for the Zhar-ptitsa Autodrom. We've looked into the previous ownership of the site. We have tried to look into the transfer of the land, and the planning permission sought for – and granted – to build the Grand Prix circuit complex. We have found some information on the property development company that built the complex, and some on the current operating company that runs the circuit.'

'Sounds good,' replied Straker.

'Let's look at the site first then,' offered Pokrovsky. 'Its location, the Nagatinskaya Poyma Park, was public property – a common, effectively – until the Grand Prix circuit came along. Word has it this park was signed over to the Moscow Grand Prix via a 999-year lease.'

'Is that kind of arrangement usual in Russia?' Straker asked.

A folder was produced and handed to him. 'As a lease, yes. Of a public park? No. Because of our continually changing political and governmental histories, we can't say yet that there is a "usual" in Russia.'

'Fair enough. Has a transfer of common land into new ownership ever been done before?'

'Not that we can find.'

Straker nodded. 'To which entity, then, was the land transferred?'

'That's not in the public domain,' replied Pokrovsky. 'But we are pretty sure the lessee was Moscow 100.'

'At least that would be consistent with what you found earlier?'

'What we didn't know earlier is that there was no public consultation or announcement ahead of this transfer.'

'Who would have the authority to sign common land like this away?'

Pokrovsky shrugged. 'The park itself falls into the Southern Okrug – or administrative district. We would be surprised, though, if any local politician at that level of government had the power to dispose of public rights and ownership of such an ancient park as this. The Southern Okrug is little more than a small suburban municipality.'

'Who did give the authority, then?'

'We don't know – because we can't get to see any lease agreement. None of this documentation is in the public domain, either. Office rumour, though, points to City Hall.'

'As an institution?'

Pokrovsky shook his head. 'We believe – and, forgive us, having only been able to read between the lines of what I was told by a contact there – it was the mayor of Moscow.'

'Do we know what price was put on the land?'

'That information is not public,' replied Pokrovsky. 'Canteen gossip, again – from City Hall and the Southern Okrug – has it changing hands at around ten billion rubles.'

'Sounds a lot?'

'About a hundred million pounds.'

'So a substantial sum of money. Have you been able to discover how the purchase was funded?'

'That's where we grind to a halt. We reach a dead end. And it happens to us every time we try and find out about the money.'

Straker was now smiling, which Pokrovsky clearly found disconcerting.

'However hard we look into the financial aspects of the Autodrom,' Pokrovsky continued, 'we get nowhere. The funds for the purchase, the capital for development, the running expenses – every time we ask about the money, we hit an impenetrable wall of silence.'

FORTY-THREE

Straker and McMahon walked through into the inner sanctum of the Ptarmigan command centre.

'Need I ask what you make of the "wall of silence"?' McMahon asked. 'Another of your welcome surprises?'

Straker smiled knowingly. 'The structure of the Autodrom has — clearly — been set up to conceal the identity of the backer.'

'How can we ever hope to penetrate the corporate veil, then?'

'Quite clearly, desk research isn't going to do it, because none of the records seem to exist in the public domain.'

'So?'

'Have we had any luck in getting hold of that politician on the board of Moscow 100 — Deputy Kosygin, wasn't it? He would *have* to know about the money, wouldn't he?'

McMahon nodded and put a call in to her office downstairs. A minute or two later she reported: 'One of Anatoly's team has been trying to reach him. They're going to call me back.'

Straker pulled a face.

'Don't we need to be careful who we discuss any of this with?' asked McMahon. 'Someone has clearly taken determinedly against Moscow 100, bumping off two of its board. Whoever's behind this seems to attract some pretty violent opposition.'

Before McMahon could react, her phone rang. She listened silently: 'Anatoly says Deputy Kosygin is refusing to meet us.'

'Damn. Does he say why?'

'Let me put this on speaker.'

'Hi, Anatoly,' said Straker. 'Does Kosygin say why he doesn't want to meet?'

The researcher said: 'He seemed okay to meet us, at first.'

'So what happened?'

'He asked what we wanted to talk about.'

'What did you say?'

'I had to tell him Moscow 100.'

'And that put him off?'

'He said he was nervous even talking about it on the phone. If someone had the power to deselect him from the Duma, what else did they have the power to do – particularly after the suspicious deaths of Olyshenko and Rosenthal? Kosygin sounds seriously worried.'

'We have *got* to talk to this guy, Anatoly,' said Straker. 'He's the only chance we've got of penetrating your financial "wall of silence". Tell him we're trying to flush out the people behind the attacks on Moscow 100 – and bring justice for his colleagues who died. Also, try telling him that we'd be happy to meet him somewhere neutral. Somewhere out in the open.'

'Okay,' replied Pokrovsky. 'I'll try him with that approach. Do we have any other incentives, if that doesn't work?'

Once the call was ended, Straker said: '"On my mother life" is a phrase that's still bugging me. Is that a well-known idiom in Russia? In the Orthodox Church, perhaps?'

'Not that I know of. I could think of several phrases the Russian church might throw up, but that wouldn't be one of them.'

'Why the hell did he say it, then?'

McMahon looked at Straker. 'Perhaps we should look at this more literally?'

'Maybe … let's try something else. Hang on.'

Opening the door of the inner HQ, Straker looked out across the main command centre. Activity was still intense with people working at each of the workstations. 'Andy? Can we borrow you for a sec?'

Backhouse came into the smaller room.

Straker shut the door behind him.

'You know Yegor reasonably well. Do you know anything about his mother?'

Backhouse shook his head: 'Nothing at all. I have no idea. The pit lane is hardly the place for "sharing".'

'Can we find out?' asked McMahon.

Straker nodded. 'Andy, I've been sent his personnel file – it's on the confidential Ptarmigan system. Could you have a look through it?'

'I can get one of my researchers to do it,' offered McMahon.

'Not on something this sensitive, Sandy – it really ought to be a company officer.'

Backhouse nodded and left the room.

McMahon's phone rang again. Seeing who it was, she put the call straight onto speaker: 'Anatoly?' she said. 'Any news?'

'Yes,' said the Brandeis researcher. 'Kosygin has – reluctantly – agreed to meet you.'

'Great work,' said Straker.

'He's suggesting the Komsomolskaya Metro Station – meeting on one of the underground platforms.'

'When?'

'He's offered to be there – next to platform two, on the main concourse – in forty-five minutes.'

McMahon looked at her watch. 'We should just about be able to make it.'

'Can you confirm with Kosygin, Anatoly, that we'll be there? Wait a minute – how are we going to recognize each other?'

'I've already asked him that. He's wearing a dark suit, yellow tie and is carrying a pale orange leather briefcase.'

'Excellent work,' said Straker. 'Let's just hope he shows up.'

Straker, turning to face McMahon, couldn't help but notice her pensive look. 'What's wrong?' he asked.

'Kosygin is a civil servant, and works near the White House. He lives in the Nagorny District.'

'So?'

'The civil service buildings are in the north-west of Moscow, while his home is in the south-east – further south even than the Autodrom. Both are on the Zamoskvoretskaya Line.'

'So our rendezvous, I'm guessing, is off his patch?'

McMahon nodded. '*Way* off. Komsomolskaya's north-east, a completely different line altogether.'

'Perhaps he's got a meeting up there?'

'Or, maybe, he's just really concerned … and is really playing it safe?'

FORTY-FOUR

McMahon and Straker climbed out of their car onto the pavement outside the Komsomolskaya Metro building. Given what they now knew about the interference with the Moscow 100 board and Deputy Kosygin's apparent nervousness, Straker felt he ought to be more careful. He started by applying some of his 14 Int Company fieldcraft. Without drawing attention to what he was doing, he scanned the area. There was a bustle of lunchtime activity around the underground station; as far as he could see, no one was worthy of suspicion.

As Straker made to go in, he couldn't help looking up – finding it hard to believe he was actually looking at a railway station. In front of him was an unexpectedly grand building. Six Corinthian columns supported a deepish frieze, above which was an intricate cornice. Topping off the building was a beautifully proportioned octagonal dome and cupola.

'This is an underground station?'

McMahon, heading straight into the station, said: 'The Moscow Metro is absolutely one of a kind – very special. Very grand.'

Straker had to agree. 'The phrase "civic pride" comes readily to mind.'

'Oh, yes – but you haven't seen anything yet,' she said as they found themselves weaving between a mass of travellers emerging from the station.

Even inside the entrance hall Straker saw something of the extraordinary architecture. McMahon bought them a notional ticket, to afford them access to the platforms.

As they descended the escalators, Straker was nearly overwhelmed: a high barrel ceiling, chandeliers – no trace of any industrial fluorescent lighting – buttermilk yellow walls, white plaster baroque-like flourishes, grandiose murals, and an expanse of polished-granite floors. It all seemed far more like a church – palatial, even – than a railway station. Straker couldn't help mouthing the word: 'Wow!'

But he had to pull himself away.

They were approaching their rendezvous.

Straker needed to concentrate.

Stepping onto the floor of the concourse, Straker, once again, scanned the crowd gathered across it.

McMahon muttered: 'You think he'll even come?' as they walked between the long row of pink limestone pillars. She appeared apprehensive. 'What if he chose this place because he *is* being watched or being followed?'

'Then we had better be careful.'

Beyond the pillars, on either side, were the two platforms. Trains were pulling in and out every few minutes. People were coming and going constantly.

There was no sign of anyone resembling Kosygin's description.

A train pulled in over to their right. Another mass of humanity poured out onto the platform.

Finally Straker saw something.

A man was standing – on his own – in the lee of an octagonal column at the far end of the concourse. He was holding open a newspaper.

Straker nudged McMahon. 'Think that's our guy?'

'Yellowish tie … pale orange leather briefcase … very possibly?'

Straker scanned the area again, looking for anyone out of place. With people expected to be moving through the station, anyone standing still ought to catch the eye. When Straker was sure there was nothing unusual around them, he walked McMahon slowly towards Kosygin. They moved off the main concourse to stand behind one of the pillars.

'Mr Kosygin?' asked McMahan in Russian.

The man looked up. He gave off an expression of alarm. Kosygin was in his mid-fifties, five feet something with thinning and obviously dyed hair and a receding hairline. He had a round, fleshy face – even fleshier through his being at least three stone overweight. Kosygin looked them up and down between snatched glances between the pillars, out into the concourse, and then the other way towards the nearest platform.

Straker said: 'Thank you for seeing us today,' which McMahon translated.

Kosygin barely nodded. Sweat was beading on his forehead. His face was flushed.

'Would you like to go somewhere else to talk?' Straker offered.

'No,' came the reply. 'Talk here – and quickly. I am nervous someone is watching.'

'Okay, Mr Kosygin. Please feel free to leave us whenever you want to.'

Straker was pleased to see Kosygin's stance ease very slightly.

'We are here representing the Ptarmigan Formula One team. As you may know, some of our staff are being charged with corporate manslaughter – following the accident at the Grand Prix.'

There was a nod.

'We would like to know more about the Zhar-ptitsa Autodrom. We think it could be helpful in pursuing justice for your lost colleagues and to our defence.'

Kosygin looked surprised.

'You were involved with Moscow 100 – as the bid was being put together, yes?'

Another nod.

'We understand why you are nervous. Two of your colleagues were removed from that board.'

'We were all removed – the driver, the ex-president of the Automobile Federation, the local businessman and me. Two of them were removed – permanently,' said Kosygin. 'They are *dead*.'

There was a loud and sudden bang away to the right.

Kosygin flinched at the noise.

Straker looked over in that direction. On the far side of the concourse a litter trolley had collided with a metal bucket; the noise, though, had bounced around and over the barrel ceiling, the acoustics making the sound seem much louder and much closer. Straker put a hand on Kosygin's arm to try and reassure him. The beads of sweat on Kosygin's forehead returned.

'We have learned that the land, the Nagatinskaya Poyma Park, was bought by Moscow 100 on a 999 year-lease?'

A nod.

'And that the amount paid was around ten billion rubles?'

A shake of the head.

'No?'

'Five billion.'

'Thank you. We understand that the Nagatinskaya Poyma Park was public property – a common. Who in the government signed it over to Moscow 100?'

Kosygin's face froze, as if he was weighing up how much to divulge.

Straker's pulse rose in response – he suddenly got the feeling they were about to discover something.

Kosygin exhaled. 'The mayor of Moscow – Mayor Pavlova.'

'Okay,' said Straker; at least Kosygin *was* telling them things they didn't know. 'We can't find anything about who was behind the development of the Autodrom, though; can you help us?'

There were a couple of exchanges in Russian. McMahon relayed: 'Moscow 100 subcontracted the building work to a consortium of local builders.'

'So did Moscow 100 stay in charge throughout the construction?'

For the first time Kosygin's expression changed, from apprehension to the slightest hint of pride.

Straker smiled. 'How much did the overall construction cost?'

'Eighty billion rubles.'

Straker looked impressed. Breathing deeply, Straker prepared to ask his big question. 'Can you tell us anything about who put up the money for the circuit?'

Kosygin suddenly looked on edge again.

A train pulled into the station, making a considerable sound. Its noise reverberated under the arches. Another mass of people flowed through the concourse.

Kosygin blinked a couple of times. 'You must *not ever* say that I told you,' he said, with a pleading look on his face.

Straker replied with an expression of sincerity.

'I am only telling you,' said Kosygin, 'so justice might come for Feodor Olyshenko and Menashe Rosenthal.'

Straker nodded.

'Their deaths were never explained.'

Straker nodded and touched Kosygin's forearm again by way of extra reassurance.

The politician's eyes darted this way and that before he spoke again.

Kosygin then half-whispered a name.

This time, Straker didn't need to wait for the translation. Even over the noise – over the hubbub of the underground station – Kosygin's pronunciation was clear enough.

Except, now, it was Straker's turn to manifest the leaden fear of dread.

Even so, McMahon repeated the name.

The silence between them seemed to last an age.

'Thank you, Mr Kosygin,' said Straker, his tone barely able to disguise his reaction. 'We are very grateful to you for your time, and for everything you *haven't* told us,' he said with a conspiratorial shake of his head.

McMahon now looked at Straker with surprise. How could this meeting be coming to an end so soon? Kosygin, too, seemed surprised the meeting was ending; but at least he seemed relieved. Without acknowledging them any further, or even shaking hands, Kosygin picked up his briefcase and slunk round the large column, slipping out onto the main concourse.

McMahon turned to Straker: 'Why are you letting him go? Are you all right? You look like you've seen a ghost?'

Straker blinked a couple of times before peering round the other side of the pillar, making sure to keep his body concealed behind it. He was watching for Kosygin's back as the former politician made his way across the polished granite through a mass of people towards the foot of the stairs.

Straker scanned the entire area again.

He kept watching.

Kosygin reached the bottom of the steps.

On the far side of the concourse, beside one of the pink limestone columns, Straker had spotted a figure looking down, consulting a mobile phone. That figure was now looking up.

He saw it starting to move.

As Kosygin reached the top of the steps, the mysterious figure accelerated – bounding up the stairs after him, bumping into several people as he ran.

Then Straker saw him do something disturbing.

Before disappearing from sight, the follower turned back to face the concourse – and then pointed directly across at the pillars from where Kosygin had emerged.

It was a clear signal.

To another watcher in the crowd?

Straker froze. 'Shit.' He tried to triangulate the possible sight lines to and from the second watcher. Would that second man have seen them meeting Kosygin? Straker wasn't sure; he shouldn't have been able to see them in the lee of the pillar. But just in case, Straker quickly thought about possible misdirection.

'Don't react,' he said firmly as he leant in closer towards McMahon. 'Kosygin's got a tail,' and made immediately to kiss her fully on the lips.

McMahon recoiled and stiffened.

As his explanation dawned on her, Straker could feel her relent slightly.

Between kisses he whispered: 'Keep calm – *we're* about to be watched,' and made to kiss her again.

McMahon broke contact, twisting her head to the right. '*We* are? Where? By whom?'

'Don't look. Someone's about to come through the pillars to my right,' he said leaning further forward, this time to give her a hug.

Straker strained his peripheral vision, trying to see whether the second watcher had followed the signal. As he pulled back and kissed McMahon tenderly on the end of her nose, Straker looked into her eyes, still trying to sense everything around him.

Through the extremity of his peripheral vision he became aware of a figure looming into view – through the row of pillars, over to his right.

Straker re-embraced McMahon with a full-on-the-lips kiss, pushing her back against the pink limestone column.

This time it was McMahon who snatched a glimpse over Straker's shoulder. Disengaging herself, she moved her head beside Straker's and whispered. 'He's searching the area. Doesn't look like he's looking at us.'

They maintained the hug.

Seconds later McMahon said: 'He's moving away.'

Straker whispered: 'Stay in character,' and, raising an arm to lay across her shoulder, he turned her away from the pillar. Maintaining his eye contact with McMahon, Straker steered them both towards the open door of the train waiting alongside the adjacent platform. The two of them walked under the magnificence of the murals, the white plaster work, and the buttermilk-yellow ceiling towards the waiting train.

'What can you see?' McMahon asked as she looked up into his eyes.

'No one who looks like they've found someone.'

Then taking Straker by surprise, McMahon smiled deeply – uninhibitedly – and reached up to kiss him this time. She pulled back and smiled.

Unexpectedly, Straker was captivated.

Her smile was really deep, deep enough to show the gumline

above her teeth. To Straker, her smile was completely eye-catching. Her teeth were porcelain-white, and, for the first time, he noticed that each eyetooth was slightly prominent showing her smile to be natural – real – not plastically perfect. Such mild imperfections even seemed to imply a hint of impishness. Straker couldn't take his eyes off her mouth, her smile – almost to the point that staying in character was becoming a distraction.

They stepped on board the train.

As they turned left, to sit in one of the rows of seats, Straker forced himself to grab a backward glance through the open doors between the pillars and back across the concourse. As far as he could tell, the man wasn't there.

Finally the doors started closing.

The train started pulling out.

Straker and McMahon were away.

FORTY-FIVE

In the tunnel, Straker turned to McMahon: 'I'm so sorry for being that invasive; I should have warned you – about possible misdirection. I hope your other half will understand.'

McMahon smiled again, as naturally as she seemed to earlier.

Straker couldn't stop his eyes going back for more.

'My husband won't be thinking of anything but himself, as usual, wherever he is – chasing law students in a Dublin bar, most likely. I can't believe your wife would be too content… ?'

Straker smiled. 'It looks like Google's let me down, then. Mrs Straker is now Mrs Double-Barrelled something or other – has taken silk – and is highly unlikely to be giving me much thought, either.'

'So it looks like we've both been screwed by lawyers?' she said with another smile. Her face then fell. 'Where did you learn that kind of deception?'

'The kissing thing … nowhere. I'm afraid I made that up on the spot.'

'No, not that – the spying stuff?'

'It's not unconnected to my time with the Royal Marines.'

She wanted to know more but, reading his tone, refrained from asking, feeling she might be prying.

McMahon's face fell further – as if she was feeling dirty. 'It's really not nice – the thought of being followed.'

'If those watchers were any good, I shouldn't have been able to spot them. The ones you *need* to worry about are the ones you don't see.'

'Them – *plural?*'

'Oh yes, there was more than one. One was watching Kosygin, and followed him out of the station. He gave a signal, as he left, to someone else out on the concourse. It was the second guy we were trying to avoid. He didn't seem to make us, though.'

'Who *are* these people, Matt?'

'No idea.'

McMahon's expression now showed concern. 'I hope Mr Kosygin is going to be okay.'

Their train continued on through the tunnel.

Even though the sound all around them could easily drown out her voice, McMahon asked him quietly: 'What was that reaction of yours, back there, to the name he gave us? What's the significance there?'

Straker inhaled before he whispered: 'Avel Obrenovich.'

'Yes, and?'

'Avel Obrenovich,' said Straker, 'is a Class 1 – Grade "A" – shit.'

McMahon flinched at the ferocity of his reply. 'Who is *he* then?'

Straker leant in towards her so he wouldn't be overheard: 'The man is Russian. Oligarch, a multibillionaire – owns a vast oil and gas company. Ptarmigan knows him, though, as the owner and sponsor of the Massarella Formula One team. *He* was the arsehole behind the sabotage of Ptarmigan last year – those incidents I told you about, which nearly killed Remy and her then-teammate.

Straker went on: 'Obrenovich is ruthless. During that spate of sabotage, we uncovered an attempt by his people to grab control of – pretty much steal – Formula One's commercial entity, Motor Racing Promotions. And, now, it seems he's involved in the Grand Prix circuit in Moscow.'

'Could he have something to do with the crash, then?'

'Who knows? But I have a foreboding sense that this situation will become a whole lot murkier if Obrenovich is involved. He has a proven antipathy to Ptarmigan, to Quartech, and, above all, a hatred of Dominic Quartano – resenting his financial genius. It was Ptarmigan, ultimately, that thwarted Obrenovich's plans that year.'

'Sounds like it was *you* who did that,' McMahon replied. 'You'd better take care, then, if he is that ruthless.'

Their train slowed down, approaching the next station.

Straker became alert to their surroundings once again.

Encouraging McMahon to move slowly, they ambled off the train just as the doors were closing. Straker cast a discreet eye up and down the platform. As far as he could tell, there was no sign of a third presence.

They made for the exit.

Once more, Straker couldn't help being struck by the architecture. Prospekt Mira was a station as beautiful as the last, but in a completely different way. Its pylons – either side of the concourse – were white marble, topped with flower-patterned bas-reliefs. Its highly polished floor resembled a chessboard; overhead, its chandeliers lit up the striking diamond-shaped plaster design that covered the entirety of the semicircular ceiling.

Straker continued to scan the crowd and their surroundings for tails.

Emerging above ground and back onto the street, he moved them into the lee of a building, out of sight. McMahon telephoned her driver to have him pick them up.

Ten minutes later their car drew up to the kerb on Mira Prospekt, a hundred yards south from the station. The two of them got in. The car pulled off straight away.

Straker had not been able to spot anyone watching them.

A man, though, had emerged from the station. He had made a phone call – all the while watching them from a distance. As the Brandeis car pulled away, he was able to pass on the make, colour and number plate of the Brandeis Mercedes.

Straker and McMahon felt able to relax for the first time since meeting Kosygin. Discovering that Avel Obrenovich was involved in the Russian Grand Prix was the biggest breakthrough in the investigation so far.

'But if Obrenovich did put up all the money,' said McMahon, 'why on earth would he orchestrate the crash? It doesn't make any sense. Surely it – let alone the deaths – would *devalue* his investment in the circuit? How could he ever benefit from such a tragedy?'

'I am not sure yet,' admitted Straker. 'There could be any number of possibilities. Maybe it's a property play? Moscow 100 gains control of a sizeable piece of prime land in the heart of the city. He gets rid of the board of directors one by one, giving him control. A big enough tragedy causes the venue to be abandoned as a race track; the site is then turned over to property development, which would easily be worth a multiple of the sums he's already invested.'

Straker then added: 'There could still be a significant benefit from a Formula One earnings point of view. F1's TV and commercial rights are colossal, measured in the billions. At the end of each season, those earnings are shared out between the teams according to their success: the higher a team's standing in the Constructors' rankings, the bigger their share of those revenues. Maybe Obrenovich has taken a gamble: his team is lying a poor second to Ptarmigan in the Championship this year, with little chance of getting past us. If Obrenovich found a way to put Sabatino out for the rest of this season – through injury, or better still if he could disrupt Ptarmigan in the ball-aching distraction of a court case – he might create enough of an opportunity for his Massarella drivers to take advantage. A destabilized Ptarmigan could be just enough help to see Massarella close the gap in the Constructors' rankings, helping them to win the Championship. The financial benefit of *that* to Massarella and Obrenovich would be huge and, very likely, outweigh any short-term devaluation of his investment in the Autodrom.'

'How could someone *go* to such lengths?'

Straker shook his head: 'It was a mindset beyond my imagination – I would never have believed it existed at all until I exposed Massarella's bullshit last year. If Obrenovich is still smarting from that defeat – looking for revenge, even – then who knows what he is capable of doing?'

'I can now see why you reacted so strongly to hearing his name connected to the Autodrom.'

'If he *is* involved, though, something significant does change,' said Straker, 'and possibly to our advantage. If an element of this crash stems from Obrenovich being out for a bit of old-fashioned unprincipled sportsmanship, it would definitely bring part of this crisis under the jurisdiction of the FIA.'

'Because his involvement would indicate a competition-related element to the crash?'

Straker nodded. 'It would give the sport's governing body a clear mandate to be involved – and to have an interest in it.'

'And you think that would help?'

He grunted "Yes". 'It would bring its president – Bo San Marino, a straight-up man with huge integrity – directly into the case. He, and the FIA, would *have* to take sides. I think, therefore, the time is now right,' he said, and took out Sabatino's phone. Straker dialled a number and waited for the connection. 'Jean,' he said, 'Matt Straker. Is Mr Q about?'

In no time Dominic Quartano's PA had located their boss and was patching Straker through.

'You won't believe what we've discovered,' Straker said, as he set about explaining their afternoon.

Quartano listened attentively to Straker's update.

'So Avel Obrenovich has reared his ugly head again.'

'It seems that way.'

Quartano exhaled audibly. 'What's the plan now?'

'Earlier, you asked whether we should involve San Marino,' replied Straker. 'I said yes, but only after we had managed to build up more of a picture.'

'Uhuh.'

'I think we are now ready, sir. I'd like to brief San Marino. I think the FIA *should* now be playing a role in this fiasco.'

'I'll have a word with him. Do you want me to mention the Obrenovich connection?'

'I think he'd have to be forewarned, don't you?'

FORTY-SIX

Straker and McMahon arrived back at Brandeis's offices and walked into the Ptarmigan HQ just before two o'clock that afternoon. The place was buzzing with groups of people at work in different parts of the room. Out over Moscow, shafts of sunlight were breaking through gaps in the cloud, highlighting different patches of the city.

Backhouse saw them return; he walked straight across to greet them. 'How did the meeting go?'

Straker held out an arm, indicating that the three of them should go through into the inner sanctum before they discussed it. Once the door was closed, Backhouse stated: 'Oh, by the way, Matt, we've just had the lab report back on the sand and pebbles from the gravel trap. It's pretty much as you suspected. They've identified a clear film of cement around the stones in that sample you took from the direct line of Remy's crash, while the stones in the other sample – taken away from the crash route – are completely normal.'

'So that *would* be enough to alter the properties of the gravel?' asked McMahon.

Straker said: 'Most certainly. The car wouldn't sink down into it, which it should do to create drag; instead, the cement coating would create something of a crust, causing the car to run over the top of it far quicker.'

Walking across to the whiteboard, Straker picked up a large-tipped magic marker and wrote "Doctored Gravel" under the heading ZHAR-PTITSA AUTODROM.

Backhouse then asked: 'How did you get on with Kosygin? Did you learn anything?'

Straker turned to face the race engineer: 'Andy, I'm afraid it's déjà vu, all over again.'

'Why, what's happened?'

Turning back to face the whiteboard, Straker explained over his shoulder. 'The driving force behind the Autodrom,' he said as he wrote out the name under the heading ZHAR-PTITSA AUTODROM, 'is none other than … Avel … Obrenovich.'

'Holy shit, no.'

Straker said: 'At least it fits, Andy. He's Russian … has an interest in Formula One … we know he's an arsehole … and he's got form.'

McMahon may not have known that much about Obrenovich, but the vehemence of the exchange between these two was making quite an impression. 'Does that mean,' she asked, 'that he might have been behind the deaths of the Moscow 100 board members?'

Straker shrugged. '*Cui bono?*' he asked. 'Removal of the directors, whether by coercion or death, would have the clear effect of concentrating control of the Grand Prix circuit in his hands, would it not?'

There was silence in the small inner HQ.

'There's also something else,' said Backhouse, with a heavy almost-resigned tone as he walked over to the whiteboard. 'Obrenovich's involvement brings a whole lot of connectivity much closer to home.'

McMahon asked nervously: 'In what way?'

Picking up a red pen, Backhouse clicked off the top and, circling one name, drew a line from that loop across the board to circle another name, so connecting two of the elements from different columns. 'Baryshnikov!' he declared wearily. 'Don't forget that Yegor Baryshnikov used to drive for Obrenovich. Baryshnikov was a Massarella team test driver up until the end of last season.'

'No.'

'Yep. He drove for Obrenovich's team in GP2, and was on the Massarella Le Mans team, driving there the year before last.'

Straker exhaled. 'This can't be that dirty, can it? The idea that Baryshnikov is working for Obrenovich – to sabotage Ptarmigan's chances in the Championships here in Russia?'

McMahon asked: 'Do you think it could have been *Baryshnikov* who interfered with Ms Sabatino's car?'

Backhouse shrugged. 'It's not impossible, is it? As teammate, he would have unlimited – *unchallenged* – access to all parts of the team, including her car. Doctoring it, or placing an intrusive device on it, would not be difficult. We won't know for sure though, unless we get to examine the damn wreckage.'

Straker added: 'If that's not going to happen, then the next best data source we have on the crash are the "black boxes". Which is why, if the police won't let us near them, we've got to get them analyzed some other way; somehow, we've *got* to get the FIA involved. I've already talked to DQ and asked him to get me a meeting with San Marino.'

Backhouse nodded. 'Good. Any idea when that might happen?'

'DQ's coming back to me. Sandy, in case we do get what we want, could you ask Pokrovsky to do me a background note – ahead of a possible meeting with San Marino? I want to be fully briefed on Obrenovich before then.'

McMahon typed instructions straight into her phone.

'Have you got anywhere with looking into Baryshnikov's family?' Straker asked.

Backhouse indicated the small table in the centre of the room. The race engineer opened a file lying on it. 'Baryshnikov does have some family in Russia. Specifically, his mother – Mrs Tatiana Baryshnikov – lives here in Moscow.'

Straker walked over and sat down to look at the findings. He read out: 'She lives in a place called Barvikha?'

McMahon corrected his pronunciation and said: 'It's one of the richest suburbs in Russia. It's in the Odintsovsky District, fifteen or so kilometres out to the west.'

Backhouse reported: 'Mrs Baryshnikov moved there last year. Her previous address was an apartment in the centre of the city.'

McMahon said: 'That sounds like a pretty big step up, if she moved from there to there. For a house in Barvikha, you're talking serious money – few houses would change hands for less than five million euros.'

'Courtesy of her son, do we think?'

'Tying in with his contract at Ptarmigan?'

'Or,' suggested Straker, 'with his leaving the Moscow 100 board?'

'Christ, that would be dirty.'

'Does Baryshnikov's file give us anything more about the mother?'

Backhouse nodded. 'A fair amount, actually. Strangely, one thing is very obviously mentioned – above all others.'

'Oh yes?'

'She's on home renal dialysis.'

'Wow, that's pretty specific.'

'It is. But his file makes clear that the mother has a serious kidney condition.'

'Why would Baryshnikov's personnel file specify that?'

'He's filled it in under the "In Case of Emergency" section. Baryshnikov's HR file shows he's been called away to her a few times in the recent past, at very short notice. He's rushed home to see her on several occasions this year. She's clearly not a well woman.'

'Interesting,' said Straker. 'Does the file give a telephone number for Mrs Baryshnikov?'

'It's emblazoned across that "Emergency" section I mentioned. Here we go: +7 495 142 9873.'

'Is that landline or mobile?' asked Straker.

'Landline,' answered McMahon. '495 is the Moscow exchange.'

Straker slid across behind a computer keyboard, logged on and clicked open the spreadsheet of Quartech telephone data that Karen had previously sent over showing Baryshnikov's communications. Running his finger down the screen: '495 142 … 495 142 … 495 142.' Finally, he said: 'Got it. No surprise there are hundreds of calls to that number.'

Straker then noticed something else: 'Wow, that's odd,' he said.

'What?'

'The duration of the calls to that number is hugely variable – between twenty and forty minutes, while, weirdly, a large number of others are only a matter of seconds long. Hang on.'

Straker clicked the Sort Data button once again, but, this time, looked to rank the information additionally by date. 'Well, well – look at that,' he said. 'Calls between Baryshnikov and his mother are extensive and chatty – up until the twenty-first of July,' he declared. 'From that date on, their duration falls right off. No call *since* then has lasted more than a matter of seconds.'

'What does that mean?' asked McMahon.

'A call lasting a few seconds must mean that no one's speaking, or the calls are going to voicemail, doesn't it? Or the caller's hanging up.'

'Something happened to Mrs Baryshnikov?' offered Backhouse.

'On and since the twenty-first of July,' suggested Straker.

McMahon leaned over to check the column of figures for herself. 'The mother certainly wasn't answering her phone from then on.'

'Were there *any* proper calls after the twenty-first of July?'

'Nope. None.'

'Could that be because of a medical emergency?'

'Possibly. Hang on – hang on … *shit!*'

'Shit what?'

'When was the Grand Prix – the twenty-third of July, wasn't it?'

Backhouse nodded.

'Good God…' said Straker, '…it appears that Mrs Baryshnikov has not been answering her phone since two days before the Moscow Grand Prix.'

FORTY-SEVEN

Straker's face broke into a smile. 'How inviting is *that*?'

'Another of your surprises?' said McMahon shaking her head knowingly.

Straker asked keenly: 'Can we call the number for Mrs Baryshnikov, right now, Sandy? And see if there's any reply?'

'Okay.'

'But let's do it with an ID withheld number?'

Again McMahon nodded. 'I've got an unidentifiable mobile in my desk. I'll have it sent up.'

While they were waiting, Straker reached for his phone and called his assistant in London.

'Karen, how are you getting on with ID'ing the numbers in Baryshnikov's telecom records?'

'Pretty well, but it's taking time.'

'Appreciate that. I might be able to make it slightly easier. We can set a narrower search for the team: can you focus on Baryshnikov's calls in the four weeks leading up to the twenty-first of July?'

'A much smaller task. I'll pass it on straight away.'

McMahon's PA brought the unidentifiable phone to reception.

Back in the small HQ room, McMahon looked up the number for Mrs Baryshnikov from the Ptarmigan HR file and dialled.

'It's ringing,' she declared.

It kept ringing, with no answer.

Suddenly the call went through. McMahon swallowed; in Russian, she asked: 'Could I speak to Mrs Baryshnikov, please?'

The lawyer's eyes were flashing. 'Who am *I*?' she repeated. 'A friend.'

A pause.

'She can't speak? I'm sorry – I hope she's okay? Is she there, though?'

Another pause.

'What's that to do with me? As I said – I am a friend. I've not heard from her in a while. I was anxious she was okay. Who are you, then?' McMahon asked. 'A relative? A friend of the family?'

Straker couldn't follow the Russian but the expression on McMahon's face and her tone told him the conversation was getting awkward.

'He's rung off.'

'*That* sounded pretty odd.'

'Was very weird.'

'What's going on?' Straker asked.

McMahon shook her head. 'I've no idea. That guy sounded strange.'

'Strange, how?'

'Staccato. Blunt. No charm – no people skills.'

'Not a member of the family, then?'

McMahon shook her head. 'And not a servant, either – you'd never have someone like that answering the phone for you.'

'Not a doctor or medic?'

'Hardly, with *that* bedside manner.'

'A plumber, then? An odd-job man?'

McMahon's face told them she didn't think so. 'His words were: "You can't speak with her".'

Straker pulled a face. 'That's interesting. Not: "She's not here", but "You can't speak with her"?'

McMahon nodded. 'Doesn't that suggest she *was* there, then?'

Straker's phone went. He answered the call. "Quartano" he mouthed to the others.

'Mr Q?'

'Matt, I've been on to San Marino. He *will* see you, but not in

Russia. He's still in Finland. He can see you, in Helsinki, the day after tomorrow – for breakfast in his suite at the Hotel Kämp.'

'Good.'

'I'm going to put you over to Jean, who'll talk you through the arrangements she's made.'

'Matt,' said Quartano's PA, 'I've booked you a room in the same hotel as Lord San Marino. Your flight leaves Sheremetyevo International Airport at ten forty-five tomorrow evening. I've just emailed you your ticket and boarding pass.'

'Oh heavens – to which email address, Jean?'

'Yours?'

Straker now hoped Sabatino had not lost possession of his phone to the police in the hospital. 'Could you send them to Remy's phone – and only hers – from now on?'

Straker explained his itinerary for seeing the president of the FIA to Backhouse and McMahon.

'That's positive, isn't it?' asked the lawyer.

Straker nodded. 'It's a pain being out of the country, but I should be back by early afternoon the day after. I'm going to need the briefing material on Obrenovich, though, fairly pronto.'

That evening, back in his hotel, Straker was taking a bath, using the time to think through the investigation. But he was soon distracted. Sabatino's phone started ringing. He could hear it next door. Climbing out, without grabbing a towel, Straker walked dripping wet into the sitting room, leaving clear footprints across the deep-pile carpet.

He saw the number ID'd on the screen. 'Sandy?'

There was no reply.

Straker strained his ears. He couldn't hear anything.

'Sandy?'

He suddenly heard staccato breathing – a series of juddering breaths. With a hint of urgency Straker asked: 'Sandy? What's wrong? Are you all right?'

'No,' came a bleated reply followed by what sounded like sobbing.

'What's up? Where are you?'

Again there was silence.

Something was seriously wrong. 'Tell me where you are – I'm coming right over.'

Twenty minutes later Straker's taxi pulled into Sretensky Boulevard and the driver was looking out for the numbers of the houses. They ran along the north side of an extensive municipal park before finding their destination. Quickly climbing out, Straker found himself in front of some ornate wrought-iron railings and an intricately decorated set of gates. Looming over him was the facade of a pre-revolutionary mansion block, just catching the last of the day's sun. But he didn't stop to study it any further. Leaving the park behind him, Straker hurried through the gates and along a short pathway decorated with an abundance of carved stone. He was about to take in the large front door – its door handles and grand brass entry panel – when his attention was distracted.

Sitting on a low wall, hunched over, was the unmistakable figure and strawberry blonde hair of Sandy McMahon. Straker ran forward; she was clearly in a state of distress.

'Sandy?' he asked gently.

Slowly her form unpeeled. She looked up. 'Matt,' she said as she then shot to her feet and, taking him by surprise, flung her arms round his neck, leaning heavily into him.

Straker enveloped her shoulders with his arms. Immediately he felt her sobbing.

A few seconds went by. He said quietly: 'What's happened?'

Straker felt her shudder.

'I've been burgled.'

Straker hugged her even closer.

'*You're* okay, though – not hurt?' he asked, placing a hand on the back of her hair.

Straker felt a shake of her head.

'Has anything been taken?'

McMahon sniffed. 'I don't know. Haven't been inside. I ran the moment I saw the front door.'

Moving both hands onto her shoulders, Straker eased her away so he could look into her face. Her complexion was pale; her eyes were wide and staring; her mouth and jaw were taut.

'Do you want to leave, or should I go in and take a look?'

McMahon didn't know.

'Stay here, then, I'll go and check things out.'

Without looking up, McMahon nodded.

Straker, removing his jacket, eased it over her shoulders. He helped her sit back down on the low wall beside the entrance.

Straker emerged onto McMahon's landing three minutes later. With his senses on full alert, he made his way down the wide corridor to her apartment at the far end.

Even at a distance he could see her door was ajar, swaying slightly in the breeze.

As he closed in, Straker saw the signs of a forced entry. A substantial splinter hung from the door frame; it could only have been jemmied. Directly below, other slivers were scattered across the carpet. Straker stopped, listening out – trying to sense if anyone was still inside. His ears hissed as he strained to hear.

As far as he could tell, there were no signs of activity within the flat.

Nudging the door gently inwards, Straker kept listening. Inside, he began to make out some of the layout. There was a generous entry hall with intricate plasterwork across the ceiling and an artful almost imperial-styled coving around the edges. Two doors led off from the hall, each doorway decorated with a heavily moulded architrave. Leading with his shoulder, Straker moved on a few paces. That gave him sight into the kitchen. While large, it didn't look to have spaces big enough to conceal anyone, whether hiding or lying in wait. Straker looked through the other door. This led into the sitting room: a large well-proportioned space with a high ceiling and a chandelier hanging from what looked like a plaster rose in the centre. He could see a marble fireplace at the far end. Down the long wall, two sizeable shuttered windows looked out over the park. It was a dignified room with elegant furniture.

Surprisingly, nothing inside seemed to be disturbed.

Straker moved on into the room. In an instant he was caught off guard.

One of the curtains billowed out, causing him to flinch.

His pulsed raced.

Darting swiftly across to the wall beside it, he studied the floor beneath the curtain – for any signs of a presence. Judging there was none Straker pulled the left-hand drape to one side. There was nothing there; the billowing had come from a half-opened window directly behind it. Still with his body facing the room, he leant over his shoulder and peered out through the opened window. He could see he was three storeys up above the pavement below. There was no balcony, no ledge to either side, no obvious pipework running up the side of the building – and it faced onto a public park. Straker ruled out the window as an exit point.

The intruder, therefore, could still be inside.

Straker moved away to check out the rest of the flat.

Another closed door led off the sitting room. Swiftly, in one movement, he twisted the handle, pushed the door inwards – concealing himself to one side – waiting for the door to fly back against the inside wall.

He waited, listening.

Again there were no signs of any presence.

With his back flat to the wall, Straker peered round and into what was McMahon's bedroom. There didn't seem to be anyone in there, either.

Straker ventured into the large room; everything, though, was immaculate – not a thing out of place. He moved over to open a door which led into a stylish en suite bathroom. Once again there was no one in there – and, still, everything seemed undisturbed.

Straker was beginning to wonder what this was about. Had the burglar been disturbed? Had the neighbours been alerted by the noise from forcing the front door? He couldn't work it out.

But as Straker walked back into McMahon's bedroom, he saw – on her bedside table – something unexpected and out of place.

Something that conveyed a very clear message.

Something giving all this a particularly sinister meaning.

FORTY-EIGHT

Two minutes later Straker had dropped back down to the front entrance of the mansion block. McMahon looked up anxiously as he appeared through the large front door. She sensed something was wrong.

'It doesn't look like anything's been damaged,' he said trying to offer some reassurance. 'Do you, though, ever leave your windows open?'

'Never.'

Straker nodded. 'And I take it this wouldn't be yours,' he said as he held his hand forward.

On his outstretched palm were the broken turquoise fragments of a four-inch long die-cast model of a Ptarmigan Formula One car.

McMahon's face froze.

McMahon did not take Straker's proffered arm when they emerged onto her landing. Instead, as they made their way down the corridor to her apartment, she put her arm round his waist and pulled herself to him.

Straker felt McMahon stiffen as she saw the signs of the break-in; he sensed she was feeling all this as a personal violation.

Straker led her into her home. McMahon's eyes flashed this way and that. Straker manoeuvred her across to her sofa.

McMahon continued to look lost. Hesitant. Uneasy.

Walking into the kitchen, Straker searched the fridge and a couple of her cupboards before reappearing with a bottle of wine and two glasses. Expecting her to recoil, McMahon surprised him by accepting one of the glasses he'd poured.

'At least they don't seem to have damaged anything.'

Straker nodded. 'When you're ready, it wouldn't hurt to check your credit cards and passport.'

McMahon, taking a large gulp of Sauvignon Blanc, managed a smile. 'Because "this *is* Russia", I always carry them on me.'

Straker smiled back.

McMahon looked into his eyes. 'Who the fuck *are* these people, Matt?'

'Their leaving that model car,' he said, 'has to mean they've got something to do with the case.'

'So what *was* this, then? Some kind of warning?'

Straker nodded firmly. 'I fear so, particularly with the model being deliberately broken. But, Sandy, this takes your role well beyond any legal obligation to Ptarmigan as a client. Quartech would not hold you to this case, if you wanted out.'

'What about the trial? I can't quit now – how can I quit? What about Ms Sabatino? Dr Nazar?'

'They're our responsibility, not yours.'

McMahon smiled unexpectedly.

'What?' Straker asked.

'You know, before you got here I was quite sure you'd be one of those macho thugs – all brute force and cockiness.'

'And I've disappointed you?'

'No, no,' she countered. 'I've been genuinely moved. Numerous times I've wondered how you still keep motivated with all the shit that's been thrown at us. You never seem fazed, ever. You just keep going.'

'What choice is there?'

'Oh, there are plenty of choices,' she said. 'They may not be honourable, but they're definitely out there. Except you just keep on battling, whatever the circumstances. It's affected me. You've prompted something unexpected: you make *me* want to keep going, too.'

Straker shook his head. 'You mustn't do anything you don't want to. There's no need to decide about this in a hurry, anyway. You need a long relaxing soak – I'm going to run you a bath.'

Half an hour later Straker was sitting on the sofa having pulled the curtains in the sitting room and turned on some of the lamps.

McMahon appeared from her bath, wrapped in two white towels.

Straker looked up. The moment she walked in he realized he had a problem; he was desperately fighting the urge to stare. McMahon's pale red hair was now loose, tousled and falling partly across her face; he found himself fantasizing that this was how she might look having just woken up, first thing in the morning. That allure was intensified with the cuteness of the freckles over her nose and across her cheeks under each eye. Her skin was glowing from the warmth of the water. Her bare arms, shoulders and back declared the slenderness and tautness of her body. And, as she walked gracefully, Straker caught glimpses from her thigh down – through the gap in the towel around her waist – of her slim, long legs.

Straker had to fight to stop absorbing every part of her.

McMahon moved over to sit next to him on the sofa.

Some of the spark had returned to her pale blue eyes. 'I'm not going to quit the case,' she declared quietly, 'I couldn't do that. But, given recent developments, I do have one *new* condition.'

'Which is what?'

'That you must make me feel safe.'

Straker's dark eyes intensified. 'Sandy, I can't guarantee your safety.'

'That's not what I asked for,' she said with a hint of the legal in her tone but with a provocative smile. 'I said that I wanted you to make me *feel* safe.'

Straker smiled. 'I don't know how to do that.'

'That's the surprise about you,' she replied. 'Because it's something you do without trying – just as you did at the Metro station. As of now, for instance, I want you to make me feel safe in this apartment again.'

Straker looked confused.

'Make me feel safe. Stay the night with me.'

Straker studied her, trying to gauge what she was saying.

'What's wrong?'

'I'm not sure that's a good idea,' he said. 'Not with you dressed like that; not with you looking like that.'

McMahon's expression suddenly looked more defiant than at any time since discovering the break-in. 'Why, what's wrong with how I'm dressed – how I look?'

'Oh there's absolutely nothing wrong with how you're dressed or how you look, that's just it.'

'So?'

'You're asking too much,' he said. 'I just don't think I have that much self-control.'

McMahon's face changed again. Gone, though, was the anxious victim of a burglary; gone was any distress – nor was there any sign of the feisty lawyer. Straker sensed that Sandy McMahon, the person, was in front of him for the first time.

Lowering her head, she then looked up as if from under her eyebrows. 'You really don't think you could control yourself?'

Straker shook his head.

McMahon's smile showed the gumline again above her imperfect but porcelain-white teeth.

'Really?' she breathed.

FORTY-NINE

After spending the next day in the Brandeis command centre processing Ptarmigan's emails for the witness statement, it was time for Straker to leave for Finland. He made his way down through the Imperatorskaya Tower. McMahon's car was waiting for him in the basement car park. Straker climbed in and he asked the driver if he knew their itinerary.

'Your hotel, and then the airport, isn't it, sir?' came the heavily accented reply.

The car moved off across the smooth concrete surface and made to climb up the ramp to ground level.

The traffic in the Presnensky District was more congested. Twilight was turning to night. Lights were burning in every direction. For the first time that day Straker felt tired.

Nevertheless, he set about thinking through the investigation. Had they made any progress? He really didn't know. They certainly hadn't yet made any material difference to their chances at trial.

Inevitably, his mind returned to the main thing that had been bugging him: the deliberate attempt by Avel Obrenovich to conceal his involvement in the Zhar-ptitsa Autodrom. Why had he done that? He was a Russian – known to be involved in Formula One – and rich enough to back it financially. Why had Obrenovich gone to such lengths to stay anonymous, then sacked all the directors from the board of Moscow 100 – possibly even seeing to it that two members of that board were killed?

Straker's thoughts turned to Kosygin, the ex-politician. He had been a nervous wreck. Why had he been in such a state? Was that because of Obrenovich, too? Straker considered some of the negatives. Several calls had been made to Kosygin's phones, to thank him for the meeting and to check he was all right afterwards – but they had all gone unanswered. What, if anything, did that mean?

Straker suddenly thought of the figure tailing Kosygin, the one he had spotted on the far side of the underground station. What kind of surveillance was that? Was that also something to do with Obrenovich?

And then he thought about McMahon's break-in and the symbol that had been left on her bedside table … the broken model of the Ptarmigan F1 car. Did *that* have something to do with the odious Russian oligarch?

Straker's concern was mounting.

The car came to a halt at a set of traffic lights.

His driver was indicating to turn right. As the car moved forwards and started to turn, Straker's thoughts induced him to stay vigilant. What might these people do next?

Almost involuntarily, Straker snatched a glance behind through the rear side window of the car.

All he could see was a collection of bright white headlights in the gloom.

Nothing stood out.

They drove on for a quarter of a mile before they slowed for the next set of lights. This time his driver was indicating left. Again Straker used the change of direction to scan the cars down the road behind him.

Then he twigged.

There was something there.

A small scooter, three cars back – occupying the same distance behind him on both occasions. The whole purpose of a scooter in a city was, surely, to beat the traffic – to enable the rider to weave in and out of slower-moving cars, wasn't it? Few scooter riders would subject themselves to travelling at the same speed as the slow cars all around them.

Straker waited for one more change of direction.

When he looked backwards again, he was pretty sure.

The scooter was still there – maintaining its position a discreet distance behind the Brandeis car.

'Dimitri?' he said to the driver. 'When we get to the hotel, I'm just going inside to pack. Could you wait for me – out in front of the main entrance?'

Straker's car pulled up on the sweep of the Hotel Baltschug Kempinski and stopped under the grand portico. Not looking around, Straker climbed from the car and walked straight inside. While careful not to give away his alertness, he listened out over the background noise of the free-moving traffic along the waterfront, trying to hear a noise that might give away his tail.

Sure enough, it came.

It was definitely out of place.

A small two-stroke engine was audible, running slowly right to left behind him. The Doppler effect indicated it was clearly slowing down.

Passing through the glass doors of the porch, a side window allowed Straker a fleeting view out onto the road fronting the river. The scooter was trundling by, its driver peering over his shoulder back in the direction of the hotel entrance.

As Straker showered, he thought about ways to deal with that tail.

The effect of the shower was refreshing, making Straker more comfortable – to the extent he was happy not to replace the bandages.

Straker prepared to leave. On one of the tables was the usual file of hotel facts, internal numbers and notices. Leafing through it, he managed to find what he wanted: a page giving details of private functions that could be held at the Baltschug Kempinski.

Picking up the phone by his bed, Straker rang Reception and asked for a taxi – but for it to collect him from the ballroom entrance.

He was told it would be there in five minutes.

Straker moved over to the window of his bedroom and looked down. Sure enough, there was the scooter, parked up on the roadside opposite. Waiting.

Straker left his suite and made his way down to the ballroom entrance of the hotel. Its glass-panelled doors allowed him to see out onto the side street.

Straker waited until he saw the taxi pull up directly outside.

In a matter of seconds, he was able to open the rear door of the taxi and climb straight in. Once inside, he glanced up and down the street. He was comfortable there wasn't a watcher on this side of the hotel.

As the car pulled away, Straker leant back against the rear seats – so his head would be behind the solid sloping part of the roof, preventing him from being spotted from the outside. It did still enable him to see that the Brandeis Mercedes was waiting for him – parked up on the hotel forecourt as requested. Directly opposite it was the scooter – its rider sitting astride, wearing a helmet, watching the front of the hotel and Straker's car.

The taxi merged with the traffic.

Straker rang McMahon: 'Can you ring Dimitri in about half an hour,' he asked, 'and tell him that he can come back to the Brandeis office?'

'Why, what's happened? Aren't you going to Finland?'

'Nothing's wrong. I was followed from the office. I've taken a taxi to the airport instead. I've left the scooter – that was following me – watching your car outside the front of my hotel.'

'You were *followed*?'

'I'm afraid so. We're going to have to be careful. From now on, you've got to change cars – or at least travel by taxi.'

McMahon paused.

The line went silent.

Then, her voice sounding strained, she asked: 'Who the hell *are* these people?'

FIFTY

Straker didn't drop his guard at the airport, either. Climbing from the taxi, he scanned the drop-off zone and kept looking around as he walked on into the terminal building. He was pleased to see the place was crammed full of people. While queueing for security, Straker conducted several scans of the crowds and building, and was comfortable there was no one there for him. Only when Straker was through security and airside was he able to relax.

In the departure lounge, he found that McMahon had emailed Pokrovsky's background note about Avel Obrenovich. He transferred the Brandeis report to his iPad. Throughout most of his hour-and-three-quarters-long flight, he read and thought about what it contained.

AVEL OBRENOVICH

Avel Obrenovich, 57, is an oligarch. *Forbes Magazine* lists him as the twenty-fifth richest man in the world, and the third richest in Russia, with a fortune valued at $25.8 billion.

Obrenovich, along with the other oligarchs, emerged during the corrupt sell-off (privatization) of state assets under President Yeltsin. A lack of transparency or formal bidding process saw assets sold off at massive discounts to their real values – the so-called voucher privatization programme. Insiders got prior warning of impending sales and lodged bids themselves, or sold information to individuals or consortia who did. Billions of rubles were made overnight by those acting on such inside information. Blatant corruption inherent in this process earned it the nickname of the "kleptocracy".

Obrenovich, from a lower-middle class family in Volchansk on the steppes to the east of the Ural Mountains, got into the Ural Federal University in Yekaterinburg where he studied chemistry. Aged 32, Obrenovich was an established but not-very-successful geological surveyor for the state-owned Trans Uralian Oil Company ("TUOC"). It is thought his department was approached by the Ministry of Energy (Minenergo) in Moscow to prepare a national schedule of all the oil assets owned by the Ministry ahead of possible privatizations. Somehow, possibly through a school friend sitting as a deputy in the Legislative Assembly of the Sverdlovsk Oblast Duma, Obrenovich discovered the price at which tracts of his own company were to be sold off. The prospective discounts to net asset value (NAV) were unarguably substantial.

Obrenovich sought to make a bid for himself, choosing to fund it by bank debt. Allegedly, to facilitate his funding, he offered to cut the manager of the local Urals branch of the United Bank of Siberia in, personally, for 20 per cent of the equity if he secured approval for the loans. Obrenovich's bid at the equivalent of $50 million was successful.

With most such sell-offs, there proved to be a number of systemic factors of undervaluation at work. Post-privatization, the kleptocrats were able to exploit sizeable arbitrage opportunities: valuations for these sell-offs had been based on domestic Russian prices; once in private hands, inventory held by these companies could then be valued or sold at international prices for a sizeable premium. Most of these former state assets were immediately revalued to multiples of their purchase prices: from $50 million, the Trans Uralian Oil Company was revalued – a matter of only days after its acquisition – to a figure in excess of $300 million.

Things then get murky. Using the Trans Uralian Oil Company as his vehicle, Obrenovich then bid for another oil company to be hived off, based in Ukhta, in the nearby Komi Republic. It is thought he put the police chief there on the payroll. On the day the bids were closed for Ukkom Oil its managing director's house was raided and the man himself arrested by the police on charges of fraudulent accounting. In a state of apparent panic, Minenergo rapidly accepted Obrenovich's bid, seeing Ukkom without a boss to be in urgent need of management. The charges against the managing director proved to be groundless. Three other examples of similar "irregularities" can be found in the acquisition history of Obrenovich's business portfolio. Twenty years on, his oil assets – trading today under the name Obrenovich Oil & Gas (OO&G), having acquired numerous other businesses in the energy sector – are currently valued at $20.2 billion.

Obrenovich was one of the few plutocrats to resist President Putin's "Grand Bargain" with the oligarchs – designed to rein in their power; Obrenovich also refused to contribute to Putin's Stabilization Fund, which he referred to publicly as the president's slush money. Ever since, Obrenovich has been persona non grata – a status which has persisted under President Tarkovsky. It is thought Obrenovich has not set foot in Russia for ten years.

Urban legend has it that he interfered with two teams of inspectors sent to conduct a government audit of OO&G's Russian assets; the leader of one was found in a local hotel room with three prostitutes, while a key investigator of the other was found to have half a kilo of cocaine in his suitcase – having been driven to the airport in a courtesy car supplied by Obrenovich Oil & Gas…

Obrenovich has rarely been short of controversy. The manager of the local Urals branch of the United Bank of Siberia, to whom Obrenovich had promised 20 per cent of the equity in the initial privatization, disappeared – without trace – while holidaying on the Black Sea in 1996. In 2007, the banker's widow famously sued Obrenovich in New York for $4 billion, the value of the shareholding she claimed she should have inherited from her husband in Obrenovich Oil & Gas. Obrenovich offered her $10 million to go away, coincidentally a sum equivalent to 20 per cent of the original Trans Uralian acquisition. She rejected it on the basis her husband was a shareholder in the holding company, not a subsidiary, and that the original $50 million TUOC was anyway valued at $4 billion today – setting the minimum value of her claim at $800 million. Obrenovich's legal approach was to trash the character of the dead man, and then his widow – citing alcohol abuse, irregular accounting, tax evasion, associations with known criminals – all of which she denied. Breaking down in court and contradicting herself several times, probably under the stress, the judge described the widow as an "unreliable witness" and threw the case out.

Today, Avel Obrenovich lives in Monte Carlo and, on the back of his interest in motor racing, has bought and owns the Massarella Formula One Team. Most of that team's costs are claimed against tax, filed by Obrenovich Oil & Gas as a marketing expense.

Anatoly Pokrovsky

Straker thought that Avel Obrenovich sounded like a right charmer.

If you wanted "greedy", "unscrupulous", or "ruthless", this oligarch was a viable candidate. Straker soon felt that as a suspected perpetrator of the crash at the Grand Prix, Obrenovich could easily have him heading in the right direction.

Straker landed in Finland late that night. Carrying only hand luggage, he was out through immigration quickly and riding in the back of a cab towards the centre of the city half an hour later. The short journey into the middle of Helsinki had him arrive at the Hotel Kämp just after midnight.

A message was waiting for him at Reception. San Marino was confirming their breakfast meeting at 7:30 the following morning.

Shortly after arriving in his room, Straker turned in. Before falling asleep, he sent McMahon a text: *Hope your flat was in one piece this evening?*

FIFTY-ONE

At half-past seven the next morning Straker knocked on the door of the Mannerheim Suite. The Seventh Marquis of San Marino opened it personally and greeted him warmly.

'I am glad you could come,' he said as he closed the door behind Straker. The FIA president added: 'The tragedy of the Russian Grand Prix is a very sorry business. I am so sorry for you all.'

San Marino's 1950s movie-star looks seemed a little less charismatic than usual, possibly reflecting the gravity of the matter in hand. Even so, he put Straker at his ease, inviting him to sit at the small table in the middle of the sitting room. Breakfast was already laid up, complete with silver service on a crisp white linen tablecloth. A liveried waiter stepped forward to hold out a chair for him. But Straker didn't sit immediately.

To his surprise a third place was set.

In a far corner of the suite a lavatory could be heard flushing. Shortly afterwards a door was opened.

'Colonel Straker,' he said, 'I have taken the liberty of inviting another guest to our meeting. I don't believe you've met before – please let me introduce you to Mr Avel Obrenovich.'

What? Straker screamed to himself.

What the fuck is *he* doing here?

What kind of stitch-up was this?

From all that he knew about Obrenovich, this was little less than a betrayal by San Marino of Straker's confidence.

The Russian was walking towards him.

Straker wondered how much his expression might be giving away his reaction.

Soon standing in front of him was a distinctive rather than a good-looking man.

Obrenovich appeared to be older than expected, perhaps in his mid-sixties. He was roughly five feet eight, a good six inches shorter than Straker, with a markedly angular face. His forehead, nose and chin all seemed to protrude to a point. Beady, penetrating eyes were deeply set in his skull, while his receding hairline resulted in a size-able bald patch. What hair he did have, on either side of his head, was long and greying.

Straker almost had to force himself to shake the man's hand.

'It is interesting finally to meet Ptarmigan's strategist and master tactician,' said Obrenovich quietly, which Straker took to be sarcastic. The Russian had a deep voice and spoke slowly in a Russian-tinged – but cosmopolitan – accent. 'I have been looking forward to meeting the man who dismantled Mr Van Der Vaal's – let's call it – "scheme" last year. That was seriously impressive of you.'

Straker had no idea how to react to this.

Surely Obrenovich should have been pissed off with Straker? After all, he had outed the oligarch's team boss at Massarella for his nefarious intentions; Van Der Vaal had been using Obrenovich's money, name and trust to pursue an illicit power grab of Formula One's commercial arm, not to mention sabotaging Ptarmigan's racing cars with violent results. Yet Obrenovich seemed to be offering him gratitude. How could this be?

The Russian then added: 'The mock defection you engineered, and the compelling case you mounted against Van Der Vaal's activities, were the work of a keen mind and a bold strategist.'

Straker continued to struggle with this.

Obrenovich was being so completely at odds with his expectations. For some kind of reassurance, Straker turned to San Marino. The president of the FIA appeared completely comfortable with Obrenovich's compliments.

The other two men took their seats for breakfast. Hurriedly, Straker tried to recalibrate his opinion of everything that had gone on over the last year, let alone what had been going on in Moscow since the accident at the Russian Grand Prix. If this was the *real*

Obrenovich, Straker's investigation would have to be completely reset to zero. How could this Obrenovich be behind the Zhar-ptitsa sabotage and crash?

Unless, of course…

Straker suddenly realized he would have to revise his entire pitch to the FIA president.

San Marino said: 'Colonel, or may I call you Matt? Dominic Quartano told me that you have some information – gleaned from your investigation into the tragedy at the Moscow Grand Prix?'

Straker couldn't shut one thought out of his mind: How could he be sure that the Russian at this table *was* as divorced from last year's sabotage, or as detached from Van Der Vaal's unethical activities, as he was making out?

'Please forgive me,' he said to San Marino. Then, looking at Obrenovich, Straker said: 'I have some highly sensitive findings from the crash, which, I believe impact – if not directly involve – Mr Obrenovich. After Ptarmigan's experiences with his F1 team last year, it's not easy for me to see Mr Obrenovich as a neutral figure here. I believe some reassurance would not be unreasonable, given our "mutual" history.'

'I understand fully, Matt,' replied San Marino. 'Please let me assure you that Mr Obrenovich enjoys my full confidence.'

Straker looked at the president as he spoke, and then at the Russian. Obrenovich's appearance – his angular features – could so easily have been read as lean and hungry. Straker was now floored. He was about to discuss things – highly sensitive matters, concerning the legal fate of two colleagues as well as the Ptarmigan Formula One Team itself – in front of a man he suspected until only five minutes before of foul play in the proceedings.

Obrenovich said: 'Bo, I am happy to let you two speak privately, if you would prefer?'

'It's up to you, Matt,' said San Marino. 'I have offered you my confidence in Mr Obrenovich. I will leave it up to you.'

Straker turned to face the president. He realized he had to rely on his own judgement. To help him, could he rely on San Marino? Could he rely on *his* vouching for the Russian? The stakes were so high.

Straker breathed deeply.

'Gentlemen,' he said, 'I have information that will alter your perspective on the deaths in Moscow.'

He paused.

Then, Straker stated: 'Remy Sabatino's crash was no accident,' and looked straight at the Russian.

Obrenovich said nothing.

'I appreciate that such a claim – from someone associated with Ptarmigan – could be dismissed as convenient,' Straker went on. 'But I have significant proof. Both Tahm Nazar and Remy Sabatino have declared themselves 100 per cent happy with the reliability of that car, as well as the tactical manoeuvre that Remy had been attempting at Turn Eleven.'

Straker lifted his laptop on to the tablecloth. Firing it up, he displayed on the screen the overhead shot of Sabatino's cockpit, which showed her two attempts to apply left lock to the steering wheel; he also pointed out the wisp of smoke from the car's right-rear tyre.

'There are several occurrences in the hydraulics which have had us vexed. At this critical point into that turn,' said Straker, 'an unusual sequence in the working of the hydraulic valves – in the steering, differential and brakes – rendered the car unsteerable and unstoppable into that corner.'

Straker proceeded to show them the on-board CCTV footage with the telemetry data overlaying the image underneath.

San Marino made a request with a nod of his head for a closer look at the displays. Straker swivelled the computer round to face him. San Marino leant in further to scrutinize it all, running the footage on to study the sequence for himself.

'The authorities have impounded the wreck of the car,' continued Straker, 'so we cannot conduct our own technical investigation, or our own validation.'

Having finished his closer scrutiny, San Marino swivelled the computer round to face Obrenovich.

Straker, deciding to continue, added: 'With little other chance to investigate the crash or the remains, I took the risk of conducting a close reconnaissance of the crash site myself. I found clear complementary evidence which shows that this crash was highly engineered and intentional.'

Straker now had both men's attention back on him again.

He went on to explain the firmness of the gravel trap, validated by the lab report of the cement coating; the plasticine in the breeze-block wall, playing his video which showed how easily he could move and dislodge it with his fingernail; the missing fence ties that should have been holding the wire mesh fence to the uprights, which he evidenced with the still photographs he had taken; and finally, he showed them the cut sections of the wire mesh fence, again using his photographs as proof.

'All of these,' Straker declared, 'from the interference in the car's hydraulics – right through to the tampering with the wire and perimeter wall at the circuit – show quite clearly that there was a pre-determination for Remy Sabatino to leave the circuit at high speed and to impact with that section of the fence. And, with the public spectating area directly behind it, it can only mean that there was a clear intention on the part of the saboteurs to cause injury and death.' Straker had directed the last point to San Marino. He needed the president to buy in to his conclusions before the next stage of the exposition.

'Well then, Avel,' said San Marino to Obrenovich, 'it seems to look pretty much as you thought.'

FIFTY-TWO

'*What?*' Straker asked.

'Mr Obrenovich had suspected that something must have gone on.'

Straker found himself trying to take stock. Questions were ricocheting around his head. 'If you suspected something "had gone on", how come no one's been in touch with us?' Straker's tone was harsher than he had intended. 'Any suspicions you had around the crash could have had a material impact on our response to the charges that Ptarmigan and my colleagues are facing.'

Straker found himself staring at Obrenovich: all his suspicions of the man were fully re-ignited.

The Russian remained impassive. 'It's complicated,' he said.

Straker retorted: 'How is the truth ever complicated?' He felt impatient to ask a whole raft of questions.

There was silence around the table.

He stared at Obrenovich, who still said nothing.

With no dialogue forthcoming, Straker chose to wade in, putting the oligarch firmly back in the guise of a suspect: 'I want to know about Moscow 100. How is it that you removed four members of the board from your corporate vehicle? How is it that two of them have died subsequently, despite being suspiciously young?'

The Russian sighed. 'This is what I mean by things being complicated,' said Obrenovich. Slowly and calmly he added: 'I can assure you that I had nothing to do with the removal of board members, and certainly nothing to do with their deaths.'

'You were the principal shareholder and investor in Moscow 100: surely you had a say in the management and board of that company?'

'Commercially, yes,' he said. 'But I had no say in the politics.'

'What? How does politics come into play?'

'Politics infuses everything in Russia, colonel. You haven't been there very long if you haven't worked that out.'

'How did *politics*, then, remove and kill two of your Moscow 100 directors?'

Obrenovich lent forward. 'I think ... colonel ... Bo ... I need to put all this into some form of context.'

Straker simply stared at the oligarch.

'Russian politics are dire,' said Obrenovich calmly. 'They have been deteriorating for some time. It started, for real, with President Putin's manipulation of the constitution. You might remember that, in 2008 and 2012, he swapped roles with Dmitry Medvedev – between the presidency and the premiership, and then back again after one term – to circumvent the constitutional time limit on how long Putin could serve as president of Russia? The so-called tandemocracy? That was also accompanied by Putin's attitude to opponents and criticism, a period which saw the death of the accountant Sergei Magnitsky; the suspicious death in London of the former Russian secret service agent, Alexander Litvinenko – mysteriously poisoned by polonium 210, a chemical element simply not available to non-government agencies; the hounding of Putin's former political ally Boris Berezovsky; and the shameful assassination of the opposition leader, Boris Nemtsov. All these placed an unbearably high price on political criticism. As a result, political opposition in Russia had been all but obliterated. Following that, we had the Tarkovsky succession, a transfer of power which was seen as blatantly corrupt ... a coup, for want of a better word. Its lack of legitimacy having been compounded ever since by more and more restrictive laws. In parallel, this latter period has seen a clampdown on public assembly – accompanied by the arrests, farcical trials and imprisonment of journalists critical of the regime.'

Straker felt the need for caffeine and reached for his coffee. 'How does any of that affect the Grand Prix?' he asked.

'Because I wasn't prepared to sit by and watch all that happen,' said Obrenovich. 'I wanted to do something, politically, to address the corruption of the Russian state.'

Straker's hand stopped halfway to his mouth. 'What?'

'My way of being politically active has been to contribute size-able sums of money to fund opposition politicians. I wanted to see Russia save itself from an inevitable slide back into a Tsarist/Stalinist dictatorship.'

'I'm with Colonel Straker here, Avel,' said San Marino. 'How is that relevant to the crash at Turn Eleven?'

'Because,' replied Obrenovich, 'Formula One, in Russia, took on a massive political significance. The idea of hosting the first Grand Prix there for a hundred years was a matter of huge pride to the Russian people. The president latched on to this mood, and sought to make political hay out of it. Except that, very quickly, the event became seriously at risk of being tainted.'

'How come?' asked San Marino.

'In the same way the Sochi Winter Olympics had been tainted,' answered Obrenovich, 'by corruption. With those Games, the back-handers, the cosy deals, the theft of state funds all occurred on a vast scale. The Sochi Winter Olympics are rumoured to have cost \$51 billion. Did you – or anyone – see \$51 billion worth of facilities or competition infrastructure at the time of those Olympics? So where did all that money go? When it was suggested that a Grand Prix might be held in the same place, no one doubted for a moment that it wouldn't be taken advantage of in the same way.'

Pokrovsky's findings about the former president of the Russian Automobile Federation opposing the Grand Prix going to Sochi were beginning to echo in Straker's head.

'For these reasons,' Obrenovich went on, 'Feodor Olyshenko – the RAF president – was adamant that any Russian Grand Prix should be a worthy tribute to the sport as well as to Russian integrity. That was why, throughout his leadership of the Federation, he was against the race going down there.'

And there it was, thought Straker. 'No wonder, then, that Olyshenko's objection saw him in a head-on collision with the president,' he volunteered. 'Sochi was widely known as the president's baby.'

'It was,' said Obrenovich, 'except that this clash took on much more significance, because of Formula One. There were plenty of others nervous of the Grand Prix going to Sochi – Arno Ravilious of Motor Racing Promotions, for one,' said Obrenovich. 'When news got out that he had had an informal discussion with Baryshnikov and Olyshenko – about the race going elsewhere, somewhere other than Sochi – nothing less than a political earthquake occurred in Russia.'

'You're saying that Formula One interfered in Russian politics?' said San Marino.

'Not wittingly, Bo,' answered Obrenovich, 'but the moment Yegor came back with the possibility of an alternative Grand Prix venue to Sochi, other things started to happen. The pivotal one being that Moscow mayor, Oksana Pavlova, saw a huge political opportunity.'

'From a *Grand Prix*?' asked San Marino disbelievingly.

'Oh yes,' said Obrenovich firmly. 'Bo, if you are a young country, the prestige that can attach to hosting a Grand Prix is colossal. Mayor Pavlova definitely thought so. The mayor of Moscow is very obviously two things. One, she is a liberal democrat who hates the despotic developments in Russia under Putin and which have worsened under Tarkovsky. Two, Mayor Pavlova is highly competent as a politician, which means that she is highly ambitious.'

Straker finally managed to drink some of his coffee.

'Mayor Pavlova latched onto the idea of a *Moscow* Grand Prix for a whole range of reasons. She saw that it would be a coup to host it in Moscow, the nation's capital. It would show the country that her mayoralty was capable of winning a world-class event to the city. It would enhance Pavlova's reputation as a doer. And, most significantly to Pavlova, winning the Grand Prix – away from Sochi, stealing it out from under the nose of the Russian president – would be a big power play in national politics, clearly bolstering her standing as a serious political player.'

San Marino looked at him: 'Avel, you can't be serious?'

Obrenovich looked defiant. 'Why ever not?'

'A Grand Prix *cannot* carry that much significance,' countered the FIA president.

'In Europe, Bo – and the thirty-odd possible circuits to host Grands Prix around the continent – the considerations for hosting a Grand Prix are principally commercial. In Russia, the prestige of hosting this race took on a far more potent dimension.'

Straker might have been ready to accept some elements of Obrenovich's analysis, but vast gaps remained in his understanding. He said: 'I still don't see how we get from that sort of power play – to thirty-four dead spectators at the trackside.'

FIFTY-THREE

'Once again, colonel, you go straight to the root of the issue.' Obrenovich took another sip of coffee. As he replaced the cup he said: 'I, too, am anti-corruption – anti-despotism. I was against Vladimir Putin, I was against his cosy duumvirate with Dmitry Medvedev, and I was against Tarkovsky's stitched-up succession to the presidency. I am against Tarkovsky's ever-closed administration – and I am against his clampdown on the media, public assembly and free speech.'

All this time, Straker was desperately trying to gauge Obrenovich's sincerity.

The Russian declared: 'I wanted to take action against this political malaise. As a consequence, I became the largest supporter of the opposition leader, Boris Nemtsov. Gratifyingly, Boris showed himself to be highly effective – and started attracting some serious support. The moment he gained traction in the 2011 election campaign, though, he found himself *banned* from appearing on TV. Election officials refused to register his Popular Freedom Party. Then the State – in other words the Kremlin – levelled allegations of fraud against him. Finally, Nemtsov was assassinated.

'After that, my life was changed – catastrophically. It kicked off with harassment. My house was frequently broken into, even though nothing was taken; it was the State's way of saying: "Look how we can invade your space and yet there's nothing you can do about it." They loved getting in, taking phones off the hook – leaving little mementoes. For some reason, leaving windows open was one of their favourites. Then came their policy of *demonstrativnaya slezhka* – demonstrative pursuit; they would follow me everywhere – very obviously – as a clear form of harassment and intimidation.'

Straker suddenly realized he would have to rethink another aspect of his investigation: specifically his observations of the surveillance they'd endured back in Moscow.

'This intimidation was constantly ratcheted up,' said Obrenovich. 'My commercial activities in Russia were, then – and have been since – constantly investigated; they suffer unending interventions: raids by balaclava-wearing tax inspectors from the FSB's Economic Security Directorate are the Kremlin's favourite. Such harassment has caused me severe financial losses. Finally, I started receiving death threats to the extent that I had to get my family out of the country.

'But that was exactly the kind of political oppression I was trying to put a stop to. So I was not deterred. If anything, having been driven into exile, it spurred me on. But I had a problem. Which politician could I back after Nemtsov was murdered? There weren't that many around offering too much promise.

'It soon became clear that the politician most worthy of any attention was Oksana Pavlova, the mayor of Moscow. So I decided to step up. Since Nemtsov's assassination, I have been bankrolling her entire political operation. To me, she is the only viable challenger to President Tarkovsky.

'I saw the City of Moscow winning the Russian Grand Prix as the starting gun for Pavlova to become a national political contender,' said Obrenovich. 'With my F1 connections, I saw a material opportunity to use a Moscow Grand Prix as a platform to launch Mayor Pavlova – not just here in Russia, but as a world figure. I wanted her to be seen internationally as a new leader the West could believe in – a person through whom the world could believe in Russia again. A politician – a leader in waiting – ready to take over as president of Russia. At this moment, gentlemen, Oksana Pavlova is Russian democracy's last best hope.'

Straker found himself sighing as another piece of all this was making a little more sense. Under his breath, he said: 'The Zharptitsa, no less?'

Obrenovich smiled, acknowledging the connection Straker had

just made. 'So, I put Russia's leading racing driver, Yegor Barysh-nikov, up to calling for a Moscow Grand Prix. I paid for his open letter, advocating it, to be advertised all over Russia. I convened and fronted the meetings with Arno Ravilious at Motor Racing Promotions Limited to negotiate the award of the race to Moscow. I put up the money to fund the bid and then to finance the development of the Grand Prix circuit. I also managed Mayor Pavlova's PR around the Moscow Grand Prix, so that it would maximize the political impact for her.'

While Obrenovich was talking, it brought to mind something that had been bugging Straker since their dramatic intervention to halt Sabatino's interrogation by the police in the hospital. That baffling question put to her by one of those police officers:

When did you agree to the rally with the mayor?

Straker wondered if that was how all this fitted together? Did that association begin to explain why the State was coming down so hard on Ptarmigan?

Straker, though, had to make further connections. 'You didn't explain how "politics" prompted you to remove the directors of Moscow 100.'

'I didn't remove them,' said Obrenovich sharply, reaching unhurriedly for a croissant from a basket on the table.

'But you were the financial backer – you held the controlling interest in Moscow 100, didn't you?'

'Except that, one by one, I lost my board and control of that entity. It was eventually neutered – rendered inoperable.'

'How come? As the principle backer, with the reduced board, corporate and voting control would collapse back on to you, surely?'

Obrenovich shrugged with a world-weary sigh. 'Voting, *schm*oting,' he said. 'This is not some cosy little Anglo-Saxon jurisdiction, colonel. In Russia, corporate power pales in the face of *krysha*.'

Straker frowned. 'Sorry, what?'

'Protection money,' said San Marino. 'Tribute … extortion … organized crime.'

Straker's eyes widened, not just at the subject being raised, but that San Marino should already know about this.

Sounding weary, Obrenovich added: 'The Russian economy is like no other. You are no doubt aware of the privatization "process" which occurred under Yeltsin?'

Straker nodded: 'The kleptocracy and the emergence of the oligarchs.'

'Whatever the shortcomings of that stage in the transition, from the old to the new Russia, the thefts from the system were barely half of the ongoing problem for the emergent Russia. The resultant oligarchs became extremely powerful. But they owed their positions entirely to the corruption in local, regional and national government. Consequently, they had no reason to change the nature of the culture that had gained them their assets in the first place. It was in the oligarchs' interests to preserve that corruption, throughout all levels of State administration.'

'Weren't you one of them?' Straker asked.

'Don't believe everything you have read about me, colonel. Far more significantly, the result of this corruption in government is that Russia has not developed an impartial civil service in the way that settled regimes have done in the West. Russia's administrative machine, if we could call it that, is not that at all. Russian governance is controlled by corrupt officials. Immediately after the collapse of communism, the economy was in such a fragile state that an administrative vacuum developed. Anarchy could have so easily ensued. Instead, a consolidation took place. In the same way that companies hived off by the State were consolidated by the oligarchs within their different economic sectors, so another "organization" consolidated in the same way – but this one happened to be operating within all the strata and regions of corrupt government.

'Officially, the KGB – the secret intelligence service of the Soviet Union – was disbanded in 1991. Succeeding it – in the post-communist era – was the FSB. For the first few years, the FSB was trying to find its feet, its role. That was until 1999 when an unknown former lieutenant colonel in the KGB – and a favourite of President Yelt-sin's – was put in as head of it: one Vladimir Putin. Later in 1999 Yeltsin moved Putin on, making him prime minister, so he wasn't at the FSB for long – but it proved long enough. Putin had used his short time in that position to insert hundreds of *siloviki* – former KGB agents with an intelligence or military background – into countless government posts: governorships of provinces, cities, even state-owned companies. Via this network of FSBers, a consolidation occurred comprehensively – at all levels – all over Russia.

'Today, fifteen years on, that consolidation is truly breathtaking. One individual has succeeded in drawing together all of what gov-ernment machinery there was, pretty much under his own personal control. But, whereas the KGB had been an arm of the Commu-nist Party and supposedly answerable to a clear ideology, the FSB is completely free from any such political control or restraint. At best, the organization is amoral – driven entirely by the goals of keeping itself in power and enriching its members – at worst, it is barely distinguishable from an organized crime family. The man who mas-terminded that consolidation, and who heads the FSB today, is the most powerful man in Russia.'

'So a kind of mafia don?' offered Straker.

Obrenovich smiled condescendingly. 'Vadim Kondratiev is no mafioso. His organization outstrips Lucky Luciano's Commission of 1930s America, because it has more cohesion than a federal pact between equal members. Kondratiev's power is as omnipotent as Carlo Gambino's was as boss of bosses of New York in the 1960s and 70s, except Kondratiev doesn't just control one city – Kondratiev's reach is national. His influence is far more the impregnable position that J. Edgar Hoover established for himself as the director of the FBI in the US, having a quasi-blackmailing hold over everyone and every institution of government. Vadim Kondratiev gives the impression of being Russia's chief civil servant, a government administrator. But what he heads is an utterly corrupt organization. And he's achieved the greatest licence and camouflage for a criminal one could ever imagine. He is a crime boss *masquerading* as a civil administrator. Nationally, he controls everything – he's a one-man Banzhaf Index: he controls every decision, all government procurement, all infrastructure spending, anything to do with government payroll – who gets hired and who gets fired – the army and intelligence services; let alone the law, the police, the courts and the judges. Indeed, today, the judicial system has become so corrupted that a state of legal nihilism exists. It is an utterly predictable despotic mindset: "For my friends, everything – for my enemies, the law," except in Russia the "law" has been utterly perverted – it is staged entirely for show – while being completely manipulated and bent. There is, now, even the ludicrous practice of "telephone justice" – where, irrespective of the evidence presented at trial, verdicts and sentences are handed down directly from the Kremlin.'

Straker was staggered by Obrenovich's revelations. 'How the hell haven't we heard of this man in the West?'

'Because Vadim Kondratiev uses the presidency and the Kremlin as his cloak. He has effectively bought their cooperation. Let me tell you how. Through Kondratiev, President Putin was rumoured to be the richest man in Europe, owning double-digit stakes in Surgutneftegas, Gazprom and a Swiss-based oil trader, Russoil. At the time he left office, those stakes were valued at more than $40 billion. And this is where Kondratiev comes in. The critical thing any despotic leader needs before he can ever leave office is an assurance that he will be free from prosecution and that the possessions he has acquired while in office are legitimized. Kondratiev is able to guarantee both those things; that was how Putin had the confidence to retire when he did at the end of last year. Very much part of that deal, though, was that Putin had to accept and endorse Tarkovsky as Kondratiev's choice as his successor for president. The whole succession, therefore, was a stitch-up. Kondratiev has brought the presidency and the Kremlin completely under his personal control. And both institutions are used to conceal his presence.'

'How does he get away with all this?' asked San Marino.

'By the threats of *krysha*,' said Obrenovich with a sigh, 'which he applies with ruthless intimidation and violence.

'*Krysha*, colonel, is a particular brand of Russian social cancer. It's a form of protection racket: a kind of extortion. It describes the process of extorting money from any entity in Russia. Today, 80 per cent of businesses in Russia are forced to pay it – or they suffer violent consequences.

'And to your point about being unknown in the West, it doesn't hurt that – via *krysha* – Kondratiev controls the media, too. This was started by Putin. One of Putin's first acts as president in 2000 was to shut down NTV, the only independent TV station in Russia: it had dared to be critical of the Second Chechen War and Putin himself. It was soon raided by "tax inspectors", of course, and shortly afterwards forcibly taken over by Gazprom, a pro-Kremlin organization. Putin then brought in "broadcast guidelines" for all media, all of which are still enforced today by Tarkovsky: under these, the State does not tolerate any investigation of corruption or abuses by top officials; it has instituted a "blacklist" preventing opposition politicians and entities from appearing on air; and there is even a ban on satirical programmes making fun of government figures. The State casts a culture of fear and control, particularly over the television companies. It's because of Kondratiev's grip on Russia's television and newspapers that I needed to invest such huge sums of money in social media campaigns.

'Everything in Russia is said to be under "State" control; but it is, in effect, under the control of this man, Vadim Kondratiev. *No one* dares to speak out against him or the regime.'

'So what was the *krysha* reference you made, then, in connection with your control of Moscow 100?'

Obrenovich replied: 'Kondratiev was behind the Winter Olympics in Sochi, as well as the Russian Grand Prix going there too. It is rumoured that he had, personally, acquired all the land around the venue. He apparently pressured the banks to lend to the development vehicles, which, of course, he also controls. Then he took backhanders from all the contractors and suppliers. The scale of this made his interest in the Games substantial: if the Sochi Olympics cost $51 billion, and he managed to skim off just 1 per cent, we're talking about half a billion dollars going into his pocket. The reality was probably far closer to 10 per cent.'

Straker said: 'So Kondratiev was smarting because of the money he was going to lose by the Grand Prix moving away from Sochi?'

'Not entirely. For him, the money – which wouldn't have been anywhere near as substantial – wasn't the full issue with the race going to Moscow.'

'No?'

Obrenovich shook his head. 'It became much more significant than money. What actually mattered was the prospect of the Grand Prix going *anywhere* else. For the first time since Kondratiev had come to "power", he had lost something *far* more costly. He had lost *face* within Russia. Losing the Grand Prix from under his control in Sochi was the first time since Kondratiev's rise that anyone had stood up to him.'

'So it was Kondratiev who made these *krysha* threats against you and the Moscow 100 venture?'

'All the way through the project.'

Straker turned to San Marino: 'Did you – the FIA – know about these power plays in Russia before the Grand Prix was awarded to Sochi, or even before it was switched to Moscow?'

San Marino was about to answer when Obrenovich said: 'No, he didn't.'

'I don't know whose integrity or diligence is impugned by that omission,' Straker retorted. 'The risks of these Grands Prix in Russia were not fully understood. Someone should have known. But you've still not closed the gap, Mr Obrenovich, between the snub of Kondratiev losing a Grand Prix – and a sabotaged race track with thirty-four dead spectators?'

The Russian answered: 'Kondratiev's mob moved, wholesale, against the Zhar-ptitsa Autodrom. As you have said, all the board members of Moscow 100 were threatened and removed.'

'So the president's interference in the management of the Russian Automobile Federation – and the removal of Olyshenko – was a separate incident to this?'

Obrenovich shook his head. 'Absolutely not; all of those actions were instigated by Kondratiev. *No one can govern in Russia, at any level of government, without Kondratiev.* The president has to do whatever Kondratiev tells him.'

'And the deaths of Olyshenko and Rosenthal?'

'I would only be speculating.'

Straker looked aghast as the implications became clear.

'And then,' Obrenovich continued, 'Moscow 100, as the organizer of the Grand Prix, was threatened ... with *krysha*. Kondratiev attempted to extort no less than a hundred billion rubles from the Autodrom.'

'Which is what?'

'A billion pounds.'

'For what purpose?'

'To stop the race.'

'Or what?'

'Suffer the consequences.'

'Holy shit,' exhaled Straker. 'Was it paid?'

'That amount was meant to bankrupt the circuit, or – if I was to put up the money – to take a huge toll on my finances. *Krysha*, on that scale, was a clear threat to me and a warning to any backer of political opponents in Russia. At the same time, any disruption of the Grand Prix would have the desired political effect of embarrassing the mayor of Moscow – denying her any kudos from the race – even tainting her public standing.'

'Did you pay it?' Straker repeated.

'The size of the *krysha* was also meant to be a powerful message to anyone looking to challenge Kondratiev's authority in future. He was affronted by the Grand Prix being taken from under his control. He was looking to get even.'

Straker looked the oligarch directly in the eye until he held his attention.

Then he asked: 'Mr Obrenovich, did you pay it?'

Meeting Straker's stare, Obrenovich replied: 'I don't give in to terrorism.'

'Jesus,' replied Straker. 'You didn't pay this *krysha* protection money – and you let the race run anyway?'

For the first time Obrenovich looked slightly uncomfortable.

'A doctored corner at the race track and the deaths of thirty-four Muscovites was a direct result of this threat?' said Straker.

Obrenovich stayed silent.

Straker sighed. 'Gentlemen, this is a monumental fuck-up. Apart from the slaughter of innocent spectators, we have further innocents still at risk. Two staff members of Ptarmigan – completely disinterested in this political bullshit – are facing corporate manslaughter charges and twenty years in jail, all while being at the mercy of a corrupt regime run by a crime boss – whom *you* have antagonized. I want to hear your ideas for resolving this and for getting Tahm Nazar and Remy Sabatino off the hook and out of that godforsaken country.'

FIFTY-FOUR

Obrenovich appeared to be thrown for the first time during the meeting.

'Well?' asked Straker.

'It is not going to be easy,' replied Obrenovich.

'I don't care. Two innocent victims need to be cleared of any legal wrongdoing.'

'I, myself, am at risk,' he said. 'There's an open warrant for my arrest in Russia. I'm now in exile, hence meeting you here in Finland. Since the deaths of Alexander Litvinenko in London, and Boris Nemtsov in Moscow, I live in fear for my own life. Who knows what the Kremlin – the FSB – are capable of doing?'

'What bearing does that have on Ptarmigan?' snapped Straker. 'Your situation is a function entirely of your own doing. My interest lies solely in getting the innocent Ptarmigan people out. What are you going to do to help rectify this?'

'What *can* I do?'

He turned to San Marino. 'What about the FIA? What can *you* do to help?' he asked.

'Whatever we can,' replied San Marino. 'We would be willing to testify and validate your claims, but the FIA has been excluded from all the Russian authorities' investigations so far. The safety standards we supposedly signed off for the Autodrom have been branded as part of the problem.'

'I was thinking of something more strategic, Mr President,' said Straker. 'You could send a very clear political message.'

'Like what?'

'Officially withdraw the Russian Grand Prix from the calendar – from any venue – until justice is done. Withdrawing international endorsement would attract significant attention to the internal corruption within Russia and help swing the balance of public opinion.'

'I will certainly consider doing that,' San Marino replied. 'If you're sure that doing so wouldn't just inflame the situation?'

'It would be helpful to know that we might have such a potential move in reserve, if needed.'

San Marino nodded.

'There's also something that could benefit Remy Sabatino's case.'

'Go on.'

'Even if there ends up being no change in the outcome, the FIA could at least announce a review of the ruling against her in Montreal. Any doubt expressed on that finding would surely lessen some of its negative impact on the trial.'

Straker left the Mannerheim Suite, his blood boiling at the political straits Ptarmigan now found itself in. He took the lift down to the ground floor and headed out into the bright Helsinki morning. He was desperate for some fresh air and the chance to think. Striding along the pavement of the Norra Esplanaden, he saw a patch of green opposite and made his way into the park. Straker breathed deeply, trying to cleanse himself of his anger. After some time he was ready to ring Quartano's office in London.

His PA answered the call: 'I'm sorry, Colonel Straker,' she said. 'Mr Quartano asked me, specifically, to tell you he's in conference with the foreign secretary and can't be disturbed – not even for the Moscow situation. He *will* speak to you as soon as he is out. What time would suit you?'

Straker explained his itinerary, and suggested a time later that evening: 'It doesn't matter how late, Jean, even with the time difference.'

Leaving Helsinki within the next two hours, Straker set about flying back to Moscow.

His anger returned.

How was Ptarmigan's position in Russia anything other than hopeless? It appeared, now, that they were up against the might of a shadowy, ruthless crime boss able to control all aspects of a corrupt Russian government. Most alarmingly, this man could completely manipulate the judicial system against them. How could Ptarmigan ever hope to win out against that?

Despite the apparently impossible odds, Straker was damned if he was just going to resign himself to their inevitable fate.

What, though, could he conceivably do to counter such over-whelming opposition?

On the flight out of Helsinki, Straker found himself motivated to think. On a legal pad, he began playing around with his favourite planning tool: a mind map. For all the elements he now knew to be involved in this crisis, Straker wrote down words and encircled them: *President Tarkovsky, Crush Opposition, Avel Obrenovich, Mayor Pavlova, 34 Deaths, Moscow 100, Massarella F1 Team, FIA, Yegor Baryshnikov, the Zhar-ptitsa Autodrom, Circuit Operator, Ptarmigan, Remy Sabatino, Tahm Nazar, Corporate Manslaughter, the FSB, Prosecutor General, Supreme Court, Police Impounding Evidence, Legal Nihilism, Telephone Justice* and, finally, *Vadim Kondratiev.*

Nothing came to him … looking at these elements face on; Straker realized he would have to think laterally. He started drawing connector lines between the loops where he knew there to be links. In very short order the mind map looked like a spider's web. The interconnectivity was staggering. So much was linked or associated with everything else.

One name, though, seemed to have more connections than any of the others.

Vadim Kondratiev.

Which made sense, didn't it?

Wasn't he the spider in the middle of all this?

As he headed back to Russia, Straker realized he would have to be more vigilant than ever. Having spotted the motor scooter tailing him from the Brandeis office to his hotel on the way out, Straker felt sure that – whoever these people were – they would be onto him again the moment he reappeared at Brandeis or his hotel. If someone like Kondratiev was behind all this, though, what else was possible? Was Obrenovich himself being followed while in self-imposed exile? Would "they" even know about Straker's meeting with him in Helsinki?

Straker landed back at Sheremetyevo International Airport.

Even while still airside, he was alert, studying everyone he could see around the building.

He was approaching Immigration.

He felt his pulse rate rise.

A number of policemen stood behind the row of booths in passport control. Trying to affect indifference, Straker adopted the world-weary body language of the international commercial traveller. Inside the booth was a no-nonsense border guard. Straker slid his passport through the slot under the glass.

In a matter of seconds Straker thought his investigation was over.

Practically snatching the passport, the immigration officer bent it back on its spine before slapping the digital section of the passport down onto the UV reader. The computer terminal beeped. The guard rubbed the face-down page backwards and forwards, before tapping a couple of keys on the keyboard. It beeped again. He took it off the device.

Straker wondered what was wrong. Why wasn't his passport being accepted?

He watched with alarm as the guard leant across his booth and pressed a red button.

'Wait!' came the instruction in his direction.

Shit – had there been an alert put on his name?

The door at the back of the kiosk opened and a uniformed official stepped in. It wasn't a policeman. Was that grounds for relief?

The supervisor moved the positioning of the passport on the scanner himself, and pressed a series of keys. Again the computer beeped.

Was it a malfunction, or was there something more sinister behind this?

Another attempt was made with the passport on the reader. Still no dice.

One of the immigration officers picked up the landline phone. A conversation ensued. The caller turned to look at Straker while the man answered some of the questions he was asked.

Christ, thought Straker – *it's all over. These bastards aren't going to let me back in. Maybe ... it could be even worse.*

Three minutes went by.

The call was ended.

The caller leant down and whispered something in the other man's ear. With no further consultation, Straker's passport was thrust back through the slit at the bottom of the glass. He was instructed to pass.

What the hell was that all about?

As Straker emerged through the row of booths, he saw the line of policemen straight in front of him. To his relief they remained inactive.

But as Straker walked towards the baggage reclaim and exit, he saw two men – in plain clothes – peel away from beside an office door and start walking after him.

What the hell was this? Who were *these* people? If the incident with the passport was official, wouldn't a response to a flagged passport be by the authorities? Wouldn't that involve a response from the uniformed police? Who were these, then, if they were in plain clothes?

Straker's mind whirred as he rode the escalator down into the baggage reclaim area. With just hand luggage, he didn't need to attend any of the carousels, so he could make straight for the customs channels. He soon realized his followers had increased their pace to keep up with him.

What should Straker do? If he tried to lose them, he would reveal his awareness of them, which would only arouse suspicion. Wasn't it better to act as if he were unaware: whoever these people were, they obviously knew he was now in the country. Weren't they also going to know his business and associations? Straker deduced he was far less likely to compromise himself if he acted in ways they might expect.

Out on the pavement in front of the terminal, Straker queued briefly for a taxi. Climbing in, he gave instructions for Brandeis's office in the business district – and set about keeping tabs on his tail.

FIFTY-FIVE

'What do you mean you were tailed from the airport?' McMahon asked incredulously when they met in Ptarmigan's Brandeis HQ. 'You said you were followed from here to your hotel on the way to Finland, but gave them the slip. How did they know to follow you from the airport when you came back? How did they know where you'd gone – or when or if you were even *coming* back?'

'A flag must have been put on my passport.'

'Who the hell by? The government?'

'I'm not sure,' answered Straker.

'Oh my God,' said McMahon.'

'Maybe if I tell you what I learned in Finland, you might get to understand what we're really up against here ...'

Straker relayed the format of his meeting with San Marino to McMahon and Backhouse.

'Avel Obrenovich?' exclaimed Backhouse. 'What the fuck was *he* doing there?'

'Exactly what I thought, at first. I was so pissed off with San Marino – thinking he'd betrayed my confidence – not least as we had Obrenovich down as our principal suspect behind the crash.'

'But?' asked McMahon.

'I don't believe he *was* the cause of it ... at least not directly.'

Backhouse looked unconvinced.

'Indirectly, then?' asked McMahon. 'How could he be *indirectly* involved?'

Straker explained the relationship between Obrenovich and the president and the switch of the Grand Prix to Moscow.

'So Obrenovich thinks all this was instigated by Vadim Kondratiev?' asked McMahon.

Straker nodded.

Backhouse looked at McMahon. 'Is that serious?'

'Kondratiev is the disease that blights Russia,' McMahon said. 'Corruption infects every dimension of this country. He is our route to another Stalin.'

'He's that bad?'

'He's worse. He's wrapped himself in respectability and altruism – in the clothes of civic government. He has a reputation for being ruthless – vicious, a man verging on the perverted tastes of a … Joseph Mobutu. People are arrested without charge. There are rumours of torture, administered by him – personally – late at night beneath the cells of Butyrka Prison. People have been known to disappear without trace.'

'Jesus,' exhaled Backhouse. '*This* is what we're up against? This is completely *hopeless*?' Backhouse looked seriously agitated. 'We're up against a bent government – and caught up in the middle of its actions to destroy one of its political opponents. *And* we're facing a bent show trial.'

At this point, to Backhouse's dismay, Straker was smiling.

'*Fuck* it, Straker,' barked the race engineer, 'what the hell is there to smile about now?'

Straker declared: 'Every opponent has a weakness.'

'Yeah, right – and *we* don't?'

'Of course we do, but we haven't even tried looking for the weaknesses in our opponent yet – because we've only just worked out who he is. I agree with you, though: if we try and fight this head on, we will be crushed.'

'From everything you've said,' Backhouse replied, 'we'll be crushed any which way.'

'My approach to tackle this,' said Straker, gently ignoring the race engineer, 'will come from my favourite adage of Sun Tzu's.'

Backhouse's eyes widened. 'Son who?'

'The ancient Chinese military strategist,' replied Straker. 'Sun Tzu established one of the greatest military doctrines of all time. A bit of it includes: "If your enemy is in superior strength, evade him. Attack him where he is unprepared … appear where you are not expected."'

'How is … *that* … of any relevance to us when we are trying to take on the whole of the Russian State?'

'Let me show you my thought processes here,' Straker answered. 'Having the impending trial, particularly one elevated up to the Supreme Court, is a good thing – as it will give us a very public platform on which to fight our case.'

'Even if it's to be conducted in a corrupted state of "legal nihilism"?'

Straker nodded. 'Public opinion can be drawn to it – and turned by it. Let's start, then, with thinking about where our opponent *might* be weak. Public opinion can still be influenced, particularly if the trial process is visibly distorted. How about I put it this way: let's imagine that the State were to lose *one* part of its case or argument. Which one would weaken it the most?'

'The thirty-four deaths?' said Backhouse flippantly.

'Without question,' Straker agreed. 'Without them, there would clearly be no case to answer at all. But if they can't be removed, we *could* still change one significant thing in relation to them, couldn't we?'

Backhouse looked completely incredulous. 'What's that, then?'

'The *blame* for them,' said Straker.

'But you're forgetting we have *no* access to the evidence needed to prove those deaths were caused by someone else.'

'Okay, so what is the prosecution relying on to make *its* case, then?'

'The nature of the crash – the fact that it was a Ptarmigan car that caused the deaths,' offered McMahon. 'Mechanical failure or driver error, implicating Ptarmigan in corporate manslaughter.'

'Quite,' answered Straker. 'So if we could prove our cars and systems did not fail, the blame *would* shift, would it not?'

'How do we have any hope of doing that without access to the wreckage?'

'A fair point,' nodded Straker.

'And, making it worse,' Backhouse went on, 'is that *any* conclusion we come up with will be flat-out contradicted by Baryshnikov. *He* is now the Russian expert – *he* is the trump card that the authorities will use to stomp on any explanation we come up with.'

'*Precisely!*' breathed Straker. 'Andy, you've hit the bullseye.'

Backhouse gave him an I-don't-get-it look: 'We're going to get slaughtered. Every which way we turn we will hit that impregnable legal wall or, worse, we will get contradicted.'

'Exactly,' said Straker, 'so, let's see whether we can't pick away at that contradiction, shall we? Let's see if there isn't a way to weaken some of the bricks in that impregnable wall?'

FIFTY-SIX

Backhouse and McMahon found Straker's findings from Helsinki utterly demoralizing, while they found his strategy for dealing with the threat they now faced far too nebulous to feel any kind of reassurance.

Straker was aware the others were not onside. Even so, he was ready to explore the lines of defence he had mentioned. Once he'd been left alone in the inner HQ, he made straight for his earlier spreadsheet of the telephone data from Baryshnikov's Quartech phone. He wanted to juggle the Sort Data facility a couple more times. His mind kept going back to Baryshnikov's diffidence during both of his press conferences. This was the first of the "surprises" that Straker wanted to investigate.

Half an hour later, Straker called McMahon. She joined him shortly afterwards in the inner HQ.

He said: 'Right, this is what I want to do.'

McMahon listened.

'Except under no circumstances, though, can we be followed out of the building.'

McMahon's face showed concern.

'After the break-in at your flat, Sandy, this sort of activity goes far further than your legal brief. You do *not* have to come – if you don't want to.'

Ten minutes later, McMahon – having said she would participate – made ready to exit the building through the basement garage.

She was on edge.

For this sortie, they weren't going to use their usual Brandeis car. Instead, Straker and McMahon were climbing into the back of a van

– one of the small fleet used by the firm's messengers to transport legal documents around the city. Its sides and doors were opaque; Straker was pleased. The moment the doors were shut on them, he knew they could not be seen from the outside. Concealment, though, had its price; they had to suffer the discomfort of squatting on a couple of filing cartons in the back of the van's enclosed dark compartment.

Straker and McMahon were heading for a destination two miles away, in the north of Moscow.

When they got there, the van pulled in through a gated entrance into an office compound.

Instructing the driver to park the van out of sight from the road behind, Straker and McMahon climbed out and transferred into a pre-booked taxi already waiting for them. Straker remained vigilant, looking out for any sign that their escape might have been spotted.

It seemed to have worked. He was sure he had got them away without being seen.

McMahon remained uncomfortable that such evasive action was even needed.

It took just under an hour to make their way through Moscow towards the Odintsovsky District. Their taxi entered a less built-up area of low-rise buildings with larger spaces between them, typically occupied out here by stretches of mature pine trees. Their line of approach took them along the modest Rublyovo-Uspenskoye Road, which straightened up as it reached the village.

Straker's first indication of their arrival came from the rows of unexpected shop fronts boasting some of the world's most luxurious brand names: 'Blimey,' he said, 'Gucci, Dolce & Gabbana, Ralph Lauren, Ferrari, Bentley, Harley-Davidson? What *is* this place?'

'It's the smartest – and richest – place to live in Moscow.'

'In the middle of a pine forest?'

'Barvikha was where the Soviet leaders built their dachas – their weekend homes … retreats. The cachet this place had in the USSR survived into the new regime. Anyone who's anyone, now, has a place out here.'

Straker stared out of the window as their taxi turned off the main road and headed down what looked like a ride cut through a forest. Mature pine trees edged the lane on either side. The density of their trunks limited the distance they could see into the woods from the road to fewer than fifty yards. Imposing entrances with Keep Out gates appeared every quarter of a mile or so.

McMahon chatted to the driver. 'He says it's just down here, along this lane.'

Straker said: 'Okay, ask him to slow down as we get close.'

Presently they were approaching their target destination. It was very quickly clear that they had got the right place. Two large black vans protruded out into the road. Straker and McMahon saw that beside them several men, dressed in black, were standing guard.

'Oh my God,' said McMahon, 'they're all armed.'

Their taxi drew level with the gate. They had a clear sight of the entrance. A semicircular expanse of asphalt was flanked by two large pillars. Edging the semicircle was an imposing eight-feet-high wall, curving back to two more pillars flanking a vast set of double wrought-iron gates. Flowers of different colours and shapes filled the borders to either side; these were set off against the smooth brilliant-white painted walls. The gates were locked. The black vans were parked directly in front of them. Clearly, no one was going to be going in or out through there.

'*Look* at Mrs Baryshnikov's security,' said McMahon.

Straker studied the security detail closely. The men were armed with the stumpy 9A-91 carbine, with what looked like holographic sights. 'They're equipped with highly specialist weaponry,' he said, 'but is that to keep people out – or to keep her in?'

As they drove on past, the density of the trees on that side of the road reduced slightly. Visibility – further into the woods – was soon possible. There were even intermittent gaps in the pine trees. Both

Straker and McMahon craned over to the right of the taxi as they were offered fleeting glimpses of the property inside.

Straker saw that the house was set some way back in the middle of its grounds, in its own clearing among the pine trees. A mature garden showed further investment in horticulture, with a profusion of ornamental trees and shrubs right across it. Straker's stroboscopic glimpses between the tree trunks allowed him to snatch an impression of the house itself – which, at that moment, was bathed in sunshine.

Architecturally, Straker would have likened it to a Bauhaus take on a traditional design. It had neo-classical references: a triangular pediment, columns that stood over two storeys in height and a magnificent set of stone steps leading down to the circular sweep of the drive. But instead of decorative baroque-style flourishes, it had a cold line in plain function. To either side of the main facade, stretching off left and right, were two wings whose frontage was in the same style as the central section, again in classical proportions, but these hosted numerous windows. Glass even seemed to take up more space than the white-painted walls in between. Upstairs, each window had its own balcony. And that was when Straker's interest in real estate ended.

Almost like silhouettes, two black figures stood out on the central left-hand balcony.

'Look at that,' he said pointing through the window. 'There are "security" people all over this place.'

They lost sight of the house as the density of the trees increased again. Straker's taxi reached a junction in the forest road. He instructed the driver to turn right, and so the car was soon running down a second side of the Baryshnikov property. Some distance along there, they came across something else.

'That's interesting,' said Straker. 'Would that be some sort of service entrance?'

McMahon asked the taxi to pull over on the opposite side of the road. Straker was able to study what looked like a back gate. This was much smaller than the main entrance, even though it, too, had its pillars and walls. But instead of wrought iron, this entrance had solid wooden gates – and looked much more workaday. To one side, set in the wall, was a narrow pedestrian doorway with an accompanying grille, camera and intercom.

Straker turned to McMahon: 'I have an idea, which you may not like. After that conversation you had when you rang this house, I'd like to see whether any of our suspicions are justified.'

McMahon looked apprehensive.

'The moment you feel uncomfortable, though,' said Straker, 'just turn and walk away, yes?'

The Brandeis lawyer nodded with hesitant determination.

'I would do it,' offered Straker, 'but I can't speak Russian. Behave as you did when you stopped those policemen impounding the Ptarmigan motor home – and you'll be fine!'

Managing a forced smile, McMahon climbed from the taxi and, checking the road for traffic, crossed the forest lane.

Straker watched McMahon as she approached the pedestrian gate. He could see her press the intercom.

He then saw her leaning in towards the grille.

A conversation seemed to take place.

After less than a minute McMahon was hurrying back across the road; she grabbed open the door.

'Drive,' she snapped in Russian to the driver.

With no delay the driver fired up the engine and pulled sharply away.

'I was threatened.'

'Shit, for doing what?'

'Trespassing on police property.'

'*Police* property? How is this police property?'

McMahon opened the window and breathed deeply.

'I said I was a friend and was worried because I usually popped in to pick up Tatiana's prescriptions from the doctor.'

'That's good,' offered Straker.

'I asked whether she was all right. The thug on the intercom said it was none of my business.'

'Shit.'

'I then asked: "Can you at least reassure me that Tatiana is okay."'

'What did he say to that?'

'Otvyazhis!'

'Eh?' he asked.

'"Fuck off", in Russian.'

Straker placed a hand gently on hers. 'Sandy, I'm so sorry.'

She smiled apologetically and shook her head. 'Don't be. At least we do know something.'

'What's that?'

'Mrs Baryshnikov's definitely in there.'

'How can you be so sure?'

'Because, through a gap in the gates, I just caught sight of an ambulance ... being unloaded.'

Straker didn't look convinced.

'It's more conclusive than you fear,' she said. 'Written down the side of it was the word нефрология.'

'That sounds far too much like "nephrology" for it not to be,' he said.

Despite her apprehension and her uncomfortable experience, McMahon managed an easier smile. 'There is very clearly someone – in there – right now ... with something of a kidney problem.'

FIFTY-SEVEN

On their way back to rendezvous with the Brandeis messenger's van, Straker's phone rang.

Dominic Quartano.

'Sorry for the delay in returning your call from Finland,' said the tycoon. 'I'm in conference with the Foreign Office all day. What more do you have?'

'A fair amount,' replied Straker.

He ran through everything from the unexpected appearance of Obrenovich at the San Marino breakfast, the judgement call he had had to make before deciding to discuss the case in front of the oligarch, the political consequences of hosting the Grand Prix in Moscow, and a potted version of the dire *krysha* and corrupt legal situations in Russia.

'And the cause of all this – Obrenovich – offered no help in trying to sort it out?'

'None at all, sir.'

'I expect your brain to be fired with anger, frustration – and, if I'm lucky, a desire to get even,' said Quartano. 'Okay, Matt, that's it – I've had enough of this. I'll leave you to think about how you want to handle it, but just remember two things: I control a business worth £50 billion ... and I want my people home.'

Straker smiled at the simplicity and scope of the brief. 'I have several ideas,' he said. 'One involves Yegor Baryshnikov, which I'm working on with Sandy McMahon right now. There's another I'd like to come back to you on very soon.'

'Good.'

'In the meantime, we could try and get *something* out of Obrenovich. He can at least get me a meeting with the mayor of Moscow.'

'No problem. I'll get straight on to San Marino and make sure he arranges it. Anything else?'

'I'm going to need some specialized Quartech equipment.'

'Whatever you need.'

'Good, I'll be in touch the moment I've finalized my plan. But I'm definitely going to need Bernie Callom.'

'I'll get him to Moscow straight away.'

'Now that we know what we're up against here, Mr Q, I suggest that we all speak to each other only by encrypted sat phone from now on.'

'Good idea. Okay, Matt – I'll let you go to work. Just make sure you come up with a way to get the Ptarmigan guys out. If, in the process, your plan happens to teach any of these political arseholes a painful lesson about involving innocent civilians, you'll have my backing to the hilt. Let me know the moment you come up with something.'

PART THREE

Правда

"Pravda"

THE TRUTH

FIFTY-EIGHT

Echoes and hollowness. Darkness and isolated specks of light here and there. Damp. A feeling of metal all around and concrete. Coldness, subterranean coldness.

A voice could be heard along the corridor, muffled by the walls and heavy doors of the prison.

Silence. For a moment.

And then:

A scream that came from the pit of a man's soul.

Light poured down the corridor in the direction of this hellish noise. A door admitted a figure. There were sounds of striding footsteps before the light was swept away as the door swung shut behind him. The figure reached the end of the corridor.

A deep gong-like boom resonated from the thick metal of the door. A sharp metallic clang came in reply. Swinging slowly towards him, the massive door opened outward, ready to admit the visitor.

'You've started,' barked the new arrival as he stepped straight inside.

The guard looked on edge. 'Only just, sir.'

'I told you to wait. Who's here?'

'Soskov, sir. He *is* waiting for you.'

The door was slammed behind him as the visitor went deeper into the underground complex. Opening the inner door, the new arrival entered the interrogation suite. Right then he felt energized. This was him entering *his* space, his night-time escape. He felt the skin tighten around his scrotum – and the joyous, anticipation that came with an erection.

Lit with a naked bulb hanging from the centre of the ceiling, the inner room had the presence of an abattoir. White tiles lined every inch of the walls. They also covered the floor, forming gentle slopes down from each wall to a central dark drain – an open grate. There was a rack against one wall with a series of hooks and magnetic strips supporting oversized instruments that looked like a cross between those of a surgeon and the tools of a farrier. A steel joist spanned the room above head height, along which ran a bogey; down from this hung chains via a block and tackle – which, in turn, supported further chains and hooks hanging from them.

Two men were already in the room.

One nervously saluted as the visitor appeared. Dressed in uniform, but without his jacket, he wore a clear plastic apron covering the whole of his front and arms. In his hand, he held what looked like a set of bolt cutters.

The other man in the room was naked.

And hanging upside down.

His ankles were shackled to chains hanging from the joists. His arms were hanging, too – straight down from his shoulders below his head. Around his wrists were leather manacles below which hung further chains, each supporting a sizeable weight. These weights had the effect of stretching the man's entire body, tightening the musculature of his legs, thighs, abdomen, chest and upper arms. It gave the body a sleekness, despite the man carrying an excess of several stone.

In such a stark, contrasting environment – the whiteness of the tiles and then the blackness of the grout, machinery, tools and grate – one colour did stand out.

A brilliant red.

Blood was flowing from one of the suspended man's fingers. This stream of colour was hitting the white of the tiles below him, where the low surface tension of the glaze splayed the blood outwards. Rivulets then carried the blood on down to the central drain.

The visitor surveyed the room. A smile crossed his lips as he savoured the smell and aroma of the room. He seemed to be inhaling exaggeratingly through his nostrils. Walking over, he grabbed the bolt cutters from the man in the apron.

What the man was smelling, though, wasn't physical or chemical.

Vadim Kondratiev was getting aroused by the smell of fear.

Léon Gazdanov entered the office of the prosecutor general, head-quartered in 15A Bolshaya Dmitrovka Ulitsa, at six o'clock that morning. He had not slept at all well. Last thing the night before, he had been briefed on the Grand Prix case, as they were now refer-ring to it; Gazdanov had been given some unwelcome news. He was anxious to understand its implications and plan any necessary actions. Gazdanov had ordered the police officer he, personally, had appointed to run the operation to be in the prosecutor general's rooms at 0600 hours. Moving up through the art deco office build-ing, Gazdanov had no time to take in the architecture or decor. The stakes were growing far too high for that kind of indulgence.

Gazdanov, wearing the blue uniform and gold flashes of his office, carried a slim briefcase. He strode through his anteroom. His elegant PA stood as he appeared; she, too, wore the uniform of the department. Gazdanov handed her his peaked cap. In return, he was told the police colonel was already waiting. The prosecutor general walked towards the tall double doors and barged through the doors of his office.

Police Colonel Arseny Pudovkin turned as Gazdanov appeared and saluted smartly.

'At ease, colonel,' said Gazdanov as he heard the heavy walnut doors close behind him.

Gazdanov walked round behind his desk, placed the briefcase on the leather surface and lowered his bulky frame into the upholstered chair. Above him, the large emblem of the double-headed eagle seemed to confer on Gazdanov an air of imperious authority. Being only five feet one, overweight, with a round fleshy face and thinning orange hair, the prosecutor general needed to draw on that branding for all it was worth.

'What's the latest, colonel?' he asked.

Pudovkin, physically the near opposite of Gazdanov – tall, slim, with a full head of blond hair, a craggy outdoorsy face and pierc-ing blue eyes – retained his own authority and presence despite the senior man's home-court advantage.

Gazdanov finally offered Pudovkin a seat.

'We have several things, Mr Prosecutor General. There has been some proactivity from the other side. Your recent decision to put a number of their people under surveillance has produced some results.'

'Sandy McMahon,' said Gazdanov, struggling with the pronunciation. 'The Russo-Irish lawyer at Brandeis Gartner.'

'Indeed.'

'The Ptarmigan officer – Andrew Backhouse?' which the prosecutor found easier to pronounce. 'The English.'

'Correct.'

'Are they aware they are under surveillance?'

'I think they are, but I doubt whether they would have become aware of it by themselves.'

'But you *do* think they are aware now?'

'Yes, sir.'

'How?'

'Because of the other British man – Colonel Straker, sir.'

'Army or police?'

'Royal Marines, Mr Prosecutor. My military contacts tell me the British Marines are a "special" unit, and are more than regular infantry.'

Gazdanov looked deliberately unimpressed.

'Marines are not to be underrated,' responded Pudovkin. 'We've all heard of the British SAS. The Marines have a close association with the SBS, the Royal Navy's equivalent of the Special Air Service. I am told – on good authority, Mr Prosecutor – that Colonel Straker passed what they call "Selection" and served two tours with this Special Forces unit.'

'We don't suspect him of anything more, though, do we? Intelligence services?'

'Why do you ask that, Mr Prosecutor?'

'How does a man with a normal military background have the tradecraft to spot our surveillance?'

'It seems Straker served with other agencies connected with Special Forces, sir – most notably the British Army's 14 Int Company.'

The prosecutor general nodded but in a way that was meant to show he still wasn't impressed. 'Okay, so he may have alerted the civilians to our surveillance. What, though, have we learned from them so far?'

Pudovkin looked down at some of his notes. 'Straker has been accompanying the lawyer – this McMahon woman – to various places over the last few days: the press conference at the Ministry of Justice, and a meeting with the arrested Ptarmigan director in the cells at the Moscow Police HQ.'

'Mr Nazar?'

'Yes, sir. In addition, he has made two visits to Ms Sabatino, the racing driver who caused the deaths.'

Pudovkin, at this point, seemed a little less confident. 'McMahon was also the one who blocked my attempt to impound the Ptarmigan motor home, which is still parked at the Autodrom.'

'But you have it now?'

Pudovkin nodded but did not elaborate, not feeling compelled to volunteer that the Ptarmigan people had locked all the computers on board, putting their data behind impenetrable passwords.

'I am told something happened with the racing driver at the hospital,' said Gazdanov.

'It did, Mr Prosecutor. On your instructions, two of my men were authorized to interrogate the racing driver.'

'And?'

'They were interrupted, sir.'

'How? They were given a direct order.'

'The doctor, Pyotr Uglov at the Yeltsin Medical Centre, accepted that Ms Sabatino *was* fit enough to be interviewed. Somehow, the Brandeis woman got to hear the interview was taking place. She and Straker turned up unexpectedly and pressurized the doctor. After that, Uglov stormed into the interrogation and halted it. He then signed a certificate – contradicting himself – stating that Sabatino *wasn't* fit to be interviewed.'

'What? Who the hell does this doctor think he is? Have him struck off – investigated for something. What have we got from the driver?'

'Nothing as yet, Mr Prosecutor. But we still have time.'

'I hope so, for your sake.'

Pudovkin was intimidated by the law man's tone.

'What else?'

'The Brandeis woman, accompanied by Straker and Backhouse, attended the press conference we held at the Autodrom to reveal the causes of the crash.'

'There were *Ptarmigan* people there?' asked Gazdanov incredulously.

'Yes, sir. The question about the black boxes – and whether they'd been read by the FIA – came from the Backhouse man.'

Gazdanov was annoyed. 'That was a *Ptarmigan* question?'

Pudovkin nodded.

'Why the fuck wasn't that pointed out? Why the fuck didn't *Baryshnikov* point that out? What the hell was Baryshnikov playing at?' Gazdanov shifted in his large chair. 'Baryshnikov was crap during that press conference,' he stated. 'You need to sort him out before the trial, colonel.'

'Yes, sir.'

Gazdanov asked: 'What else have these people been up to?'

'They tracked down Vladimir Kosygin.'

'The former Moscow deputy?'

'Sir.'

'And?'

'My men were in the Komsomolskaya Metro Station where they met him.'

'Did they hear what Kosygin was talking about? Did they find out what the Ptarmigan people were asking him?'

Pudovkin shook his head. 'No, sir.'

'Do you know where Kosygin is now?'

Pudovkin shook his head.

'He's in Butyrka Prison,' replied Gazdanov.

The police colonel looked surprised.

'He's had a personal visit from Mr Kondratiev,' reported the prosecutor general.

Pudovkin blanched for a moment.

'During one of his "question and answer sessions", Kosygin "revealed" that Straker had been asking him about the money behind the Autodrom.'

'Did he mention Avel Obrenovich, then?'

'Must have. Do you know where Straker was the night before last and yesterday morning, colonel?'

'In his hotel – the Baltschug Kempinski,' replied the policeman.

Gazdanov shook his head. 'Helsinki.'

'That's impossible, sir,' said Pudovkin with strained assertion. 'My people had him under surveillance all evening – at the hotel.'

'Straker ordered a taxi to pick him up from an entrance in a side street, which was very clearly not being watched by your surveillance team. And,' said Gazdanov, pulling a set of papers and photographs out of his briefcase before handing them over, 'Straker was tagged at Sheremetyevo International Airport yesterday afternoon, arriving back on the direct flight from Finland. I want to know how your men managed to lose him for eighteen hours, colonel.'

Gazdanov went on: 'You were thwarted in interviewing Sabatino, colonel. We had our statements about the black boxes challenged at a press conference, by someone not exposed as a Ptarmigan plant. Deputy Kosygin has been questioned by the opposition and has divulged key facts about this case. And one of the other side's main protagonists managed to slip out from under your surveillance – even leaving the country.'

Pudovkin suddenly realized he was on dangerous ground. And felt he had to put up a stand: 'Mr Prosecutor, these are minor glitches.'

Gazdanov held up a hand.

'None of these incidents, Mr Prosecutor General, has damaged our case.'

'Not as individual items, perhaps,' said Gazdanov. 'But when they are all put together, they add up to more. We have no idea why this man Straker travelled to Helsinki. It *had* to have had something to do with this case. Do not drop the ball again.'

Trying to regain some esteem, Pudovkin declared confidently: 'I will be able to find out exactly what he was doing.'

Gazdanov looked momentarily thrown. 'How?'

'I have a mole, sir.'

'Where?'

Pudovkin replied: 'Inside the Brandeis Gertner law firm, sir.'

FIFTY-NINE

Police Colonel Pudovkin was glad to leave his meeting with the prosecutor general. He felt he had managed to salvage something with his announcement of having a source inside the opposition camp. A valuable asset of that kind ought to safeguard Pudovkin's position, at least for the time being.

Returning to his office on the sixth floor of the Moscow Police HQ, the police colonel was anxious to re-establish his credibility as soon as possible.

He wanted to show he could still make a contribution.

To preserve the mole's concealment, Pudovkin had set up a handling procedure. First, a supposedly mundane text would be sent from an untraceable phone, which would reference a number, the context of which would be varied: a temperature reading, a football score, a number preceding some groceries. That would be a time, preferably outside office hours. Then, depending on the urgency of the contact, a colour would be mentioned, using the colours of the rainbow. Red was the most urgent, while violet was the least. Pudovkin immediately sent a message to his mole: *Don't forget the red peppers, need 6!*

Now, the police colonel had to wait until six o'clock when his mole would ring him via a neutral landline – a public payphone, a telephone in a third-party office, or from the mole's own phone at home.

In the meantime, Pudovkin had to make sure of his other responsibilities in this case.

An hour later Police Colonel Pudovkin's car pulled off the forest lane, turning in to face the entrance of the Baryshnikov estate in Barvikha. Radioed in advance, the black-clad guards had opened the main gates to admit their commanding officer as he was driven in.

Pudovkin's car made its way through the grounds of the mansion. Shrubs and blooms lined the drive as it followed the asphalt through the pine trees. As it emerged into open space, Pudovkin saw the large garden extend away to his left, and the imposing facade of the mansion to his right. Swinging round on the drive, he pulled up at the foot of the wide flight of steps in front of the house. One of Pudovkin's unit commanders, Police Major Ustinov, was there to meet him. Ustinov was a short and stocky but fit-looking thirty-something officer with a broad face, starey eyes and jet-black hair. Pudovkin had put him in charge of managing the police operation at the mansion. He saluted Police Colonel Pudovkin before accompanying his commanding officer up the steps and into the house.

Inside, it was decorated in a style Pudovkin could only imagine was consistent with the lifestyle of a millionaire. A large white-painted hallway stretched up two floors. A grand staircase rose from the centre of the hall and split at a mezzanine level into two flights of stairs, one to either side – rising on up to reach the upper floor. A massive chandelier hung in the centre, which certainly wasn't needed today – daylight poured in through the windows and the entire space was bathed in sunlight. Furniture around the room was modern but sparse. Numerous vases held sizeable displays of flowers, but each of these had wilted or died and turned grey, offering a strangely macabre feel to the place.

The only source of colour in the hall was a collection of Malevich paintings, easily more than thirty in total. Bold geometric shapes and colours were loud against the expanse of white walls. Whoever designed their display had a curatorial understanding of how to show off such masterpieces; they were as well presented as if they had been in any specialist art nouveau gallery.

'We've got Mrs Baryshnikov confined to her suite in the west wing,' explained the police major.

Pudovkin nodded.

'Would you like to see her?'

'Is she as bad as they say?'

The major led the way up the stairs, turning left at the first floor. A collection of smaller works of art were carefully presented along this landing, each lit with its own picture light above it.

Pudovkin then heard music – a piano – emerging from inside the house. He was led into a room through a heavy set of doors. Sunlight poured in here too, through the three floor-to-ceiling windows along the outer wall. A large Persian rug covered the floor, and a nest of armchairs was arranged around a large fireplace. At the other end of the room was a concert grand – a Steinway – at which an elderly woman was playing a movement from *Pictures at an Exhibition*.

Pudovkin saw that although Mrs Baryshnikov looked a little pale, she was immaculately dressed with her hair tidily set.

While continuing to play, she declared in a loud voice: 'You have the impertinence to kidnap me in my own home. That does *not* entitle you to enter my private rooms without invitation.'

'This is Police Colonel Pudovkin,' said Major Ustinov. 'This, sir, is Mrs Baryshnikov.'

'I don't care,' said the woman. 'I assume this to be another lackey of the dictator Tarkovsky. I do not welcome him, nor any of you police thugs, into my home – violating my privacy.'

'Mrs Baryshnikov,' said Pudovkin. 'I would like to speak to you.'

Tatiana Baryshnikov kept playing, ignoring the request.

Pudovkin walked towards the lady of the house; he made to lower the lid of the piano, not quite making contact with her fingers. 'Mrs Baryshnikov, it is important you understand all of our responsibilities,' he said. 'Your son has a duty to Russia – to defend the memory of its citizens during the trial of the foreigners who killed our people at the Grand Prix.'

Tatiana Baryshnikov rose from her piano stool and faced Police Colonel Pudovkin. She was a good twelve inches shorter than the policeman. 'What you choose to do to intimidate my son is of no consequence to me,' she said. 'Your tactics are despicable.'

Pudovkin was about to reply when an unexpected noise could be heard from outside.

'What the hell is that?' he asked.

There were raised voices in other parts of the house.

'What's going on?' asked Pudovkin.

'I don't know, sir.'

'Find out!' yelled the colonel.

'Yes sir,' answered the major who dashed out of the room.

A high-pitched whine could be heard, which seemed to be getting louder.

Pudovkin strode across the sitting room to one of the tall windows. A light breeze billowed the white net curtains to either side. Pudovkin swept them apart and stepped out onto the balcony. Below him, the wilderness garden fell away across a hundred yards of lawn, leading down to a lake edged by the pine forest beyond.

Pudovkin, though, found himself looking up.

Fifty feet off the ground, a wasp-like sound continued to whine. Pudovkin squinted against the brightness of the sky to make out what it was.

An eight-prop drone was hovering overhead, flying level with the roof of the house. It then moved in towards him.

'What the fuck?' he shouted. Hastily, he worked to unfasten the strap over his pistol. The drone gained height rapidly, maintaining its attitude – still pointing at the balcony.

Explosive noises suddenly rang out. Pudovkin fired his Makarov semi-automatic repeatedly at the drone, its reports reverberating off the mature pine trees all around.

Inside the sitting room, Mrs Baryshnikov flinched at the commotion. Walking to another of the large windows, she tentatively pulled back one of its net curtains and peered out. She heard a further volley of shots, this time from somewhere below in the grounds. She managed to catch a fleeting glimpse of the strange object as it flew along in front of the house – to the right as she watched – before it disappeared over the tops of the trees.

Pudovkin came back inside. 'Stay here,' he barked over his shoulder.

He stormed out and down the stairs.

Major Ustinov was just re-entering the hall.

'Did you hit it?'

'I'm afraid not, sir,' came the reply. 'It looked like a camera was underslung beneath it; whatever they were filming would surely have been uploaded. Do you think that was from a news channel, sir?'

'I don't know,' he said. 'All you and I can hope for, major, is that it was.'

Half an hour later, while Pudovkin was still at the mansion checking through all the security arrangements, his phone rang. It was Pudovkin's other unit commander, Police Major Kuprin.

'Colonel, I thought you should know. We've had a development.'

'What?'

'It's Colonel Straker, sir – him and that female lawyer.'

'Yes, yes. What?'

'Neither of them had been out of the office all day, which I thought was strange.'

'So?'

'I got one of my guys to walk past the Brandeis building.'

'And?'

Pudovkin sensed there was something going on.

'In the basement garage of the Imperatorskaya Tower, my guy happened to spot Straker and McMahon climbing into the back of one of the delivery vans. They left the Brandeis building ten minutes ago. We're now in pursuit.'

'Shit, how often have they been doing that? Where are they heading?'

'Going north.'

'And?'

'They've just pulled in through a set of gates off Tverskaya Ulitsa.'

'Which number?'

'The only one that would prompt this call, sir.'

'Christ,' said Pudovkin, 'what the hell's Straker up to now?'

SIXTY

Two minutes later, Police Colonel Pudovkin was back in his car and heading for the centre of Moscow. All the car's sirens and blue lights were on.

By the time they had travelled a few hundred yards along the lane through the trees, Pudovkin's car was already doing over a hundred miles an hour.

Grabbing his phone, the police officer rang a number. The call was answered: 'The prosecutor general's office.'

'I need to speak to Prosecutor General Gazdanov, urgently. Colonel Pudovkin here.'

'One moment, sir.'

Their car swerved to overtake a large gardener's van parked on the side of the road as a team of ground staff worked on the outside of another mansion in Barvikha.

'Colonel Pudovkin, what's so urgent?' came the nasal voice of the prosecutor general.

'Straker and the lawyer, McMahon, sir – they've just turned up at City Hall.'

There was silence for a moment on the line.

'Who are they there to see?' the prosecutor asked.

'We don't know yet, sir. I'm on my way there, now, to debrief my officers who've followed them there.'

'Do you have any contacts in City Hall?'

'I'm afraid not, sir.'

Surprisingly, Gazdanov did not explode; all he said was: 'I do. Get yourself there as soon as possible and report in. This is an unwanted development.'

Pudovkin's car, with lights flashing and sirens blaring, charged on into the centre of Moscow, still at breakneck speed. Little consideration or allowance was made for anyone in their way, even on the other side of the road. Pudovkin's police car frequently crossed over into the oncoming lane, dived across pavements, ignored traffic lights and, on two occasions, went the wrong way down a one-way street.

Remarkably quickly, the police car was closing in. Pudovkin cut the sirens and lights a few blocks away. He instructed his driver to pull up close to Tverskaya Ulitsa 13.

Moscow City Hall, also the official residence of the mayor, came into view. It was an imposing building over six floors. Its top half looked like a self-contained neoclassical building with a central triangular pediment, eight Corinthian columns and symmetrical wings to either side. This well-proportioned facade, though, looked like it had been plonked down on top of another building, almost serving the role of plinth to the top half. It had the same symmetrical wings, but a much more blocky, out-of-proportion central section. Where the building was painted, it was coloured a deep maroon – a striking contrast against which to set off the gold-leaf-covered crest of Moscow at the very apex of the building.

Pudovkin radioed Major Kuprin and was directed to the watchers' mobile HQ. Leaving his car, Pudovkin strode into a side street; there, he climbed into the back of the unmarked police van. Kuprin and two other officers were inside the command vehicle, watching screens and wearing headsets as they monitored the visual and radio reports being sent in by the men out around City Hall. Pudovkin was told Straker and McMahon were still inside the building. He was briefed on the extensive net of police officers that Major Kuprin had deployed to watch all the exits. Pudovkin was about to ask some questions when his phone went. He saw it was the prosecutor general.

'Sir?' answered the police colonel.

'Straker and McMahon are there to meet the mayor.'

'Hell. Did your contact have any idea of their agenda?'

'None. It's scheduled as a private audience – no officials.'

'What do you think this means, sir? Do you think Straker's made the connection between the Grand Prix circuit and Mayor Pavlova?'

'We don't sodding well know what he knows,' barked Gazdanov.

At the Baryshnikov mansion, Major Ustinov had been unable to think of much else since the incident with the drone that afternoon. Pudovkin had since rung him, leaving a clear impression that things were not right. Several actions seemed to have been initiated by the other side: Pudovkin declared that the drone they had frightened off was unlikely to have been a news-gathering organization, and that they should consider it to be connected with their task of containing Mrs Baryshnikov.

Ustinov set about shoring up his operation.

He cancelled all leave, extended all periods of duty, doubled the size of each security detail and instigated a series of foot patrols around the grounds. No fewer than three teams were now to be out in the gardens, trawling through the trees around the property, twenty-four hours a day. In addition, Mrs Baryshnikov was not to set foot outside her designated living space: her bedroom, sitting room and bathroom.

All around the mansion and grounds there was a heightened sense of alertness.

Six o'clock came and went. Police Colonel Pudovkin was getting anxious.

There was no call from his Brandeis mole.

By a quarter past six, Pudovkin was worried that their arrangement might have been compromised.

After what seemed like an age, his mole inside Brandeis Gertner finally did ring through – at ten to seven. The voice at the other end sounded breathless. Nevertheless, Pudovkin pushed on: 'Why did Straker go to Finland?' he asked.

'To see the FIA president,' came the reply.

In part, Pudovkin was relieved. Straker seeing a neutral third party – particularly one that he and the prosecutor general had taken pains to shut out from the case – would be of little consequence to him.

'He also saw someone else,' said the mole.

'Who was that?'

'Avel Obrenovich … I … I have to go.'

The call was ended.

Pudovkin was left listening to dead air.

Pudovkin realized that Straker had now managed to make a number of key connections. Ringing the prosecutor general, he passed on the news.

'My mole at Brandeis has just told me that Straker went to Finland to see the president of the FIA.'

Gazdanov merely grunted.

'He also saw Avel Obrenovich.'

'Holy shit.'

'It means, Mr Prosecutor General, that his meeting with the mayor of Moscow was no courtesy visit. Not when we know for certain that Straker can now connect Mayor Pavlova to the oligarch Obrenovich.'

SIXTY-ONE

Dusk fell over Barvikha. A clear afternoon gave way to some cloud as the sun went down, causing twilight to come a little earlier than it had done for the last few days. Major Ustinov sat in the police's make-shift control room, keeping watch on every aspect of the mansion via the bank of CCTV cameras. He had increased their coverage even further that afternoon, including the precaution of installing a number of cameras in Mrs Baryshnikov's own apartment.

With daylight fading, Ustinov decided to turn on all the outside lamps and arc lights around the grounds. The residence and gardens were immediately bathed in halogen floodlight. Ustinov scanned each one of his TV screens to make sure that all was well around the house. Reassuringly, he could spot his three foot patrols in very different parts of the estate, illuminated by the glare.

Having seen for himself that all his deployments were as they should be, Ustinov went to make a coffee – getting ready to settle in for the night.

Before he even got to the kitchen, the whole house shook.

There was a massive explosion.

Everyone felt the blast.

'Where the hell was that?' Major Ustinov shouted as he ran back into the control room to stare at all the TV monitors. He couldn't see anything of an explosion on any of his screens.

Grabbing the radio he yelled: 'All stations, all stations. Report on that explosion – *NOW!*'

Two radios responded at once, completely blanking each other out.

'One at a time!' Ustinov yelled. 'One at a time.'

'Control, this is Charlie,' came one of the call signs.

'Charlie, come in.'

'We're in the woods. Behind the house. It sounded like it came from down by the road – down by the main gates.'

'Okay,' replied Ustinov, 'go and investigate – right now. Out to you. Hello Alpha – this is Control.'

'Alpha here, over.'

'What can you see of the explosion?'

'Nothing.'

'What do you mean, nothing? The explosion was down by you.'

'No, sir,' replied the main gate. 'We can't see anything.'

'Wait out.'

Major Ustinov hurriedly flicked through the pre-set "F" keys on his computer keyboard, trying to get a view of the explosion through one of the CCTV cameras.

Nothing.

Ustinov tried swivelling and zooming in with the one mounted on the end of the house, to get any kind of visual on the explosion. It didn't take long to realize the blast was in a blind spot. Homing in with one of his cameras, though, he could just about pick up a glow through the trees; there was no direct light – the density of the forest was too great.

Ustinov then saw movement down by the lake at the bottom of the lawn.

'Hello Delta,' he radioed.

'Delta, send over.'

'Get your patrol from the lake to the area behind the main gate, right now. Report in on the explosion.'

'Right, sir.'

The moment Ustinov had given that instruction, he heard something quite unexpected.

An agitated voice said: 'Control, this is Charlie.'

'Charlie, send over.'

'Call off the dogs! *Call off the dogs!*'

'Dogs? What dogs? We don't have any dogs.'

'We're being attacked by guard dogs – Rottweilers. Vicious.

We've had to take cover – we've shut ourselves in the swimming pool building.'

Major Ustinov stood incredulous for a moment.

Another radio message was heard: 'Control,' shrieked the voice, breathing heavily – panting, even. 'Call off the fucking dogs!'

Major Ustinov looked down at the TV monitors. In a number of them he saw scenes he could not believe. How many of them were there? Ten, fifteen, twenty?

'Where the fuck have all those animals come from?' he yelled at the room.

'Control, this is Bravo – we've had to evade the dogs.'

'Where are *you*?'

'In the garages, sir.'

'Get back out there,' he barked into the radio. 'Get out and patrol the grounds.'

There was no reply from either Charlie or Bravo call sign. Flicking his eyes between TV monitors, Major Ustinov saw that the doors to the indoor pool were firmly shut ... as were those of the garages.

'Hello Control.'

'Control, send over.'

'Delta here,' came a breathless voice. 'We've had to escape your dogs, too.'

'Where are you?'

'Out on the road. We've jumped the perimeter fence. We're down by the main entrance.'

Major Ustinov suddenly realized the significance of this. The release of the dogs had driven all his patrols into cover. Grabbing the radio he transmitted: 'All stations in the house. All stations. We are under attack. We are under attack! Be on your guard. Look out for intruders. Make sure all windows are battened down. Secure all doors!'

Before he could issue any further instructions, there was a loud popping sound – in the control room – and throughout the house.

In an instant they were plunged into total blackness.

'What the fuck?'

The house remained completely dark.

It wasn't a flash fault.

'Where the fuck is the emergency generator?' asked Ustinov into the darkness.

Ustinov suddenly realized that this was obviously their intention.

'Shit!' he screamed.

Everything remained completely black.

Pulling out his phone, Ustinov tried to use the light from it as a kind of torch. Holding it in front of him, he opened the door of the control room and bolted along the ground floor corridor. With the ghostly light from the phone's display as his only form of illumination, Ustinov sprinted towards the main hall.

Climbing the stairs, the police officer bounded up two, three steps at a time – to reach the first floor. Turning onto Mrs Baryshnikov's landing, he barged into her apartment.

'Mrs Baryshnikov?' he yelled into the dark of the sitting room.

There was no sound.

'Shit!'

Striding over to the bedroom door, Major Ustinov grabbed the handle and strode in.

Before he had managed to raise his improvised torch to scan Mrs Baryshnikov's bedroom, he was regaled with a bellowed: 'Get out! Get out of my room.'

Almost flinching at the woman's command, Ustinov lowered the torch.

He was at least relieved she was still there. Breathing deeply after his exertion up the stairs, he backed out of the bedroom.

It was then that he noticed something.

There was a break in the total blackness – over by the window.

Had the curtains been partially drawn?

Ambient light from outside was seeping in. It didn't produce enough for him to see clearly, but it created the faintest hint of an outline of things on that side of the bedroom – a dressing table, a lampshade, a chair.

'Didn't you hear me?' barked Mrs Baryshnikov.

'I wanted to make sure you were … okay,' he said, as he resumed backing out towards the door.

'Like you could give a *damn* for my well-being,' she bellowed. 'Now get the hell out of my room.'

Major Ustinov walked back towards the main entrance hall, his mind racing. Suddenly, he had to squint badly. Lights glared from every direction. The power seemed to have been instantly restored; lights were burning again all over the house.

Ustinov rang Police Colonel Pudovkin.

'Sir, I think you should get down here. You won't believe what's been going on.'

Police Colonel Pudovkin strode into the mansion thirty minutes later. Although he had been reassured that Mrs Baryshnikov was still secure, he was anything but calm. 'What the hell happened?' he asked.

Major Ustinov led him to the control room. 'I trebled the patrols in the garden and grounds, as we discussed, sir; I had doubled the number of officers in the house.'

'So?'

'At nine o'clock there was an explosion in the woods – over near the main gate.'

'Did your men see anything?'

'No, sir. They never got there. They were attacked by the dogs. They had to take cover.'

'What dogs? You haven't got any dogs.'

'Precisely.'

'Christ, so you had the surprise of the explosion – and the confusion it created – followed by an invasion of dogs, prompting all three of your foot patrols to go into hiding.'

'Yes, sir.'

'Leaving the grounds completely unguarded?'

'Yes, sir.'

'Then what?'

'The power went out in the entire mansion. But there was no power from the emergency generator.'

'Why not?'

'We've since found it's been damaged, sir. The fuel line had been severed and the leads to the batteries have been cut.'

'Cut! Christ, and what about Mrs Baryshnikov?'

'Still in her room, sir. I went straight up there, of course. I found her in her bedroom. She was as uncivil as usual.'

Shaking his head rapidly, Pudovkin looked concerned. 'You have been on the receiving end of a highly organized attack, major.'

'What did they want, though, sir?' asked Ustinov. 'Mrs Baryshnikov's still here.'

'When you went up to her room, was there *anything* in there that struck you as odd?'

'I couldn't see anything, because it was pitch dark – what with the power cut.'

'So there wasn't anything out of the ordinary?'

'Well,' replied Ustinov hesitantly, 'there was something.'

'What?'

'One of the curtains was slightly open.'

'Oh Christ,' roared the police colonel forcefully. 'Search the place – right now. Immediately. Get the Baryshnikov woman out of her room. Take her place to pieces. Strip it down! Strip it! Strip it right down – top to bottom.'

Pudovkin was summoned to 15A Bolshaya Dmitrovka Ulitsa for a meeting at six thirty the following morning. Léon Gazdanov, the prosecutor general, was in an agitated state. The trial of the year – and for him the trial that could define his career – was imminent; he was clearly unnerved by recent events.

'What the hell's been going on at the Baryshnikov mansion?' he asked with barely any preamble.

'It's been strange,' replied Pudovkin.

'I don't want strange, colonel,' he snapped. 'I warned you to take care of this man Straker.'

'We don't know it was him, sir.'

'After all we know of what he's been up to, how can it not be his handiwork at the Baryshnikov house?'

Pudovkin fought to hold his presence together. 'We cannot be certain, Mr Prosecutor, but there was this,' he said producing a photograph from his briefcase. 'This was taken from some CCTV footage recorded at the house.'

Gazdanov looked down at the grainy, dark grey photograph. In the extreme top-right corner was the blurry shape of a figure dressed in black. 'This is no use. You can't make out anything from this. How close was this even taken to the Baryshnikov woman's apartment?'

Pudovkin looked sheepish.

'This man seems far too clever to be that obvious. If there was a figure captured on film, you can bet your life it wasn't him. This man deals in diversions – decoys – and misdirection. When we get to the trial, colonel, you are going to have to fucking well get your act together.'

'I will remind you, Mr Prosecutor General, that you instructed me *not* to interfere directly with this man – when I could so easily have had him in custody and out of the way by now. What do you want me to do? What will you *authorize* me to do?'

Gazdanov looked down at the dark figure in the CCTV photograph again.

He paused.

Under his breath, he sighed: 'We've got to stop this man Straker.'

SIXTY-TWO

The trial loomed.

Media coverage beforehand was excessive. Not just in State-controlled Russian outlets, but around the world. Speculation was rife. Pictures of the aftermath of the crash at the Grand Prix were again being shown in never-ending loops on the television news, while the faces of the thirty-four who had been killed had been composited into a mosaic. That visual representation of the human losses had become a form of logo – and a constant reminder of the accident.

Then a carefully timed announcement caused a further media blowout.

It was made on the Friday afternoon, before the trial was due to start on the following Monday; it contained two major developments in the format of the hearing.

It announced that not only was Léon Gazdanov, the prosecutor general, responsible for having compiled the case against Ptarmigan and the two accused, but that for the trial he would also act as the state's *advokatura*, the prosecuting barrister.

The second element of the announcement implied that this case was almost completely cut and dried: the prosecutor general had decided to have the trial heard by a panel of three judges, rather than by a jury – an option within the prerogative of the Supreme Court.

The media went into a feeding frenzy.

Editorial after op-ed discussed the prosecutor general's decision to dispense with a jury, particularly when a jury was considered far more likely to side with the prosecution – wanting to see an avenging of the deaths at the Grand Prix. Opinion had it that if Gazdanov was prepared to forego such an advantage, as well as put his name to the advocacy in the trial, the prosecution's case had to be utterly watertight.

An opposing view, only expressed in the international media, was that dispensing with the jury left the entire outcome in the hands of two or three judges, who would be far more susceptible to the influence of "telephone justice".

At nine o'clock on the Monday morning, Léon Gazdanov, accompanied by Police Colonel Pudovkin, arrived at the Supreme Court of the Russian Federation in Povarskaya Ulitsa. On the pavement outside they were received by the clerk of the building. Huge crowds had gathered, standing behind a funnel of crash barriers.

Gazdanov, wearing his bright blue uniform with gold flashes and brass buttons, spotted the bank of television cameras and couldn't resist walking over to make a statement.

'The Russian legal system will, today, start the process of setting out the truth about the deaths of our beloved citizens. I will have the people responsible for this tragedy behind bars – and starting their periods of hard labour, within a week. Thank you.'

The clerk then escorted him and Pudovkin into the building.

As they entered the courtroom, Gazdanov realized, instantly, that he had taken quite the right decision. This setting was definitely the place to hold a high-profile trial. It had all the attributes of a magnificent stage upon which this drama should be played out. Red oak panelling covered the walls. A row of seats – thrones – formed an imposing line at the front of the room where the presiding Supreme Court justices would sit. In front of them an open floor space extended forward to the first row of concentric hemispherical seats which radiated outwards and slightly upwards to the back of the room. As in his own office, Gazdanov gloried in the double-headed eagle emblem on the wall above the judges' heads. That crest gave this space a feeling of unchallengeable authority.

Gazdanov had ordered specific alterations to this room for the trial. One was that most cases before the Supreme Court were for review only, rather than their being heard in the first instance; there was, therefore, no need for permanent boxes for the jury or for witnesses. For the sake of this trial, Gazdanov had arranged a temporary witness box to be brought in.

The second departure stemmed from the absence of dedicated seats for the accused and their police escort. For today, this had been rectified with an addition that Gazdanov relished: a ten by six foot grille had been installed to the left of the judge's row. He had ordered that the accused would sit inside this cage. Seeing the accused already behind bars would project an impression that Gazdanov savoured, knowing it could only help his cause.

The third departure for the Supreme Court was the presence he had granted to the media and press to cover the trial, never normally allowed anywhere near this rarefied judicial body. Gazdanov's permission had resulted in an unbroken row of television cameras lined up along the right-hand wall of the courtroom. His locating them there was going to offer – all within the same camera shot – a clear line of sight across the room to the judges, the accused in their cage and of him at his table. When broadcast around Russia, it would project a powerful message of law and order, showing him centre stage as the law-enforcer-in-chief.

An hour later, the Supreme Court was packed.

Standing room only.

Pudovkin, sitting one row back from the prosecutor general, couldn't help but feel a tingle of excitement.

Gazdanov gave the signal to begin.

An announcement was called out. Everyone in the courtroom was ordered to stand and be silent. Through a set of doors at the front of the courtroom, three justices of the Supreme Court appeared in simple black gowns, along with several men and women in attendance.

Pudovkin watched the three elderly men take the middle three seats in the row of thrones at the front of the room. As they lowered themselves into their chairs, the other people in the room were invited to sit.

Léon Gazdanov remained on his feet.

Pudovkin watched the room focus its attention on the prosecutor general. Adding to his stage presence, Gazdanov was – today – sporting a pair of reading glasses, which, worn while he was about to address the bench, were clearly for show.

'Justices of the Supreme Court,' he announced in his nasal voice, 'I, as prosecutor general of the Russian Federation, bring before you a case the country is anxious to see punished. I am here – as I would say we all are – to represent thirty-four of our citizens who can no longer speak for themselves. We are here to do justice for them. It is my job to present to you, sirs, with incontrovertible evidence, that one company and two individuals are responsible for these deaths. With your justices' permission, I will start by summoning the accused.'

In response, the middle judge nodded.

Another announcement echoed around the courtroom, calling for the prisoners.

'Mr Tahm Nazar. Ms Remy Sabatino.'

A few moments later the Ptarmigan officials were escorted into the room. Nazar, shuffling in, was chained at the wrist and ankles. Behind him, Sabatino was being pushed in a wheelchair; she was still wearing the halo brace, while her left arm and leg remained in plaster. Nazar was manhandled into the steel cage. Then one of the police officers manoeuvred Sabatino's chair within its small space. A clang was heard as the metal door was shut and locked.

'Mr Justices, the accused are represented in this trial by the solicitors Brandeis Gertner, and their appointed *advokat*, Mr Oscar Brogan QC, from the United Kingdom.'

Pudovkin didn't know anything about the British barrister.

He looked across and studied the tall bewigged and begowned figure.

Brogan, he saw, had long silver hair under the wig, but he thought any suggestion of age was instantly dispelled by the force in his eyes. They seemed to take everything in, even though his facial expression conveyed an attitude of being noticeably unimpressed. Beside Brogan was the harridan woman who had humiliated Pudovkin in front of his own men when he tried to impound the Ptarmigan motor home. Sandy McMahon was dressed in a dark trouser suit with a white shirt. Her pale red hair was wound into a neat swirl behind her head. Pudovkin could not deny that the woman had a striking and authoritative presence.

As he looked at her, the police colonel suddenly thought of her accomplice. Where was Straker?

What the hell was he up to now?

Looking back at the justices while the defence team was introduced, Pudovkin saw them offer perfunctory courtesy to Brogan and McMahon before turning back to face the prosecutor general.

'I, as the prosecution,' declared Gazdanov, 'will prove to this court and the Russian people that Ms Sabatino's crash – at the Russian Grand Prix on the twenty-third of July this year – was completely avoidable. I will prove, with the help of a member of the very same team that caused the crash, that the manoeuvre she was attempting was reckless, if not dangerous. Moreover, this was a manoeuvre she had been reprimanded for by the sport's governing body only last month. I will therefore prove to your justices' satisfaction that the blame for the thirty-four deaths rests entirely with Ptarmigan, with Mr Nazar as the controlling mind of this organization and with Ms Sabatino, whose own recklessness directly caused the crash.'

Pudovkin, as the police officer responsible for compiling the evidence for the trial, allowed himself a moment's satisfaction as the robustness of the case was outlined. But Oscar Brogan, Ptarmigan's defence counsel, was soon on his feet.

'My Lords,' he said in fluent Russian – commandingly but with respect, 'I raise an objection to the timing of this trial, in particular to the uncommon haste in which it has been called. My principal objection centres on the treatment of Ms Sabatino. She is hardly in a fit physical state to undertake the gruelling ordeal of a trial. Not only that, she is still mentally in no fit state to have produced a

witness statement, let alone to account for herself before your Lordships under the stressful ordeal of trial conditions. She was declared
psychologically *un*fit to be questioned by the police – a certificate
signed by the senior trauma consultant, Mr Pyotr Uglov of the Yeltsin
Meditsinskiy Tsentr, where she was being treated. Not only was she
interviewed before she was medically sound, but she was interviewed
by the police – without being allowed any legal representation. As a
consequence, the prosecution is affording Ms Sabatino no right to
defend herself equitably.

'Moreover,' Brogan went on, 'it is not solely Ms Sabatino's fate
that is in the balance, here. Much of what your Lordships will decide
in relation to Ptarmigan and Mr Nazar will depend directly on Ms
Sabatino's evidence. As her testimony can only be *un*reliable, how
can your Lordships possibly be confident in their judgment of the
other two accused?'

Gazdanov jumped up and interrupted: 'Mr Justices, we cannot
rely on the evidence of this doctor, Mr Uglov.' With disdain he said:
'This man gave his clear approval for Ms Sabatino to be questioned
before the interview was started. And then, no more than an hour
later, the same man declared her to be unfit. If we are to take Uglov
at his word, I suggest we take the doctor's *first* opinion – offered
freely – before he was intimidated and threatened by the lawyer for
the accused.'

'You will notice, my Lords, that my learned friend did not respond
to the lack of legal representation afforded to my client.'

'This was merely a preliminary interview,' replied Gazdanov dismissively. 'A simple process of fact-finding, only.'

Pudovkin and the rest of the courtroom watched and listened to a
consequential series of tit-for-tat arguments over the viability of the
trial, all predicated on the uncertainty of Sabatino's state of health.

Despite the delay to proceedings, Pudovkin was relieved that
Gazdanov was not conceding any ground. But the balance of argument shifted when the defence lawyer did make one particularly
resonant point: he invited the court to look at Ms Sabatino, who,

in her neck brace and plaster casts, appeared anything *but* a picture of health.

Gazdanov kept rebutting Brogan's points, but eventually the defence managed to trigger a private conference between the judges and the two advocates.

At the decision of the senior Supreme Court justice, the court official announced that the court was temporarily adjourned. The judges filed out, followed by the two advocates – to thrash out the legal issues in private chambers.

Pudovkin moved out of the courtroom. Finding himself some privacy, he telephoned his watch commander, Major Kuprin.

'Where is Straker? What the hell is that man up to now?'

Twenty minutes later a court officer appeared back through a door at the front of the room. Calling for attention, he announced that the court would be adjourned for the rest of the day. It would resume at nine thirty the following morning.

Pudovkin hung around the Supreme Court until Gazdanov finally reappeared. He rode with the prosecutor general back to his offices. The police colonel found the prosecutor to be in an upbeat mood. 'I take it things went well with the justices over Sabatino's fitness to stand trial?'

'That man Brogan never stopped jumping up and down. My points about public opinion, though – quoting the president's comments at the memorial service after the crash – were powerful arguments with the judges.'

'Have you won the right to continue with the trial, then, Mr Prosecutor?'

Gazdanov manifested an expression of cautious optimism. 'There is an urgent matter, though, colonel. Get onto your mole in the Brandeis office, immediately. I want an insight into the opposition's response and mood after today. I want to see if there are any developments from the other side we ought to know about.'

'It takes a few hours to set up a call or a meeting, so that I don't compromise the contact.'

'We don't have that sort of time,' replied Gazdanov. 'Do it now. That mole is only useful to us for a few more hours, anyway.'

Pudovkin was not pleased. Having expended considerable effort in cultivating that source, all his work – and potentially valuable future intelligence – could be blown. What could he do? Gazdanov had issued him with a direct order.

Pudovkin sent his mole a text with the agreed signal for instant communication – a reference to FC Dynamo.

Once inside the office of the prosecutor general, the police colonel sat quietly, while Gazdanov went through some of the witness statements again.

Pudovkin's phone rang shortly after.

As the policeman looked down, he knew instantly that something was up. His Brandeis mole was calling him straight back – on an identifiable mobile phone, clearly not following their normal procedure.

Pudovkin answered the call. 'Can you tell us anything about today?' he asked, looking at Gazdanov as he spoke.

It didn't take long for Gazdanov to realize that something wasn't going to plan.

Pudovkin ended the call.

'What is it?' the prosecutor general asked. 'What's wrong?'

'Anatoly Pokrovsky, my mole inside Brandeis Gertner, has been fired.'

'What? Why? For God's sake.'

'Colonel Straker suspected him of being a mole, sir.'

'Jesus – how the hell did he know that?'

'Straker is sharp, Mr Prosecutor. With all that's been going on, he must have anticipated that we would try and infiltrate his team.'

'This man Straker is a pain in the arse, Pudovkin,' said Gazdanov, his face noticeably flushed. 'What else is he capable of doing in this trial? He has to be stopped.'

SIXTY-THREE

Police Colonel Pudovkin left Gazdanov's office an hour later feeling troubled. How *had* Straker been able to identify his mole? Had Pokrovsky been careless? Highly unlikely: the man was fastidious to a fault – to an irritating degree. This sacking, though, showed just how much Straker understood of their modus operandi; the British colonel had clearly managed to get one step ahead of them.

More concerning to Pudovkin, personally, was that Straker had cost him his valuable inside source – the one element of leverage Pudovkin was banking on to keep him indispensable to the operation. The policeman suddenly felt he needed to do more to protect his position and standing.

Pudovkin decided to take direct charge of the police's surveillance.

Radioing his team, he wanted to find out where Straker was now. Apparently, the British man was back in the Brandeis office in the Presnensky District.

'Right, I'll be with you shortly.'

Pudovkin had his car pull up two streets away, from where he walked in to rendezvous with the watch commander just round the corner from the lawyer's office. Climbing into the back of the unmarked command vehicle, the police colonel was briefed on the extensive net of watchers Major Kuprin had deployed to surround the building. Five detachments of police were secreted in the streets and alleys around the different exits of the Brandeis building.

Pudovkin looked at his watch.

Seven o'clock in the evening.

With Straker still inside, it looked like it was going to be a long night. Even so, the police chief was not prepared to leave anything to chance.

At ten past midnight the police watchers were suddenly on alert.

Kuprin declared: 'We've just spotted the Brandeis Mercedes, sir. It's pulling out of the underground car park, right now. There are two people in the back; their descriptions tally with Straker and McMahon, the female lawyer.'

Pudovkin quickly called in one of the unmarked cars, parked in a staging area a few streets away. It soon pulled up. Pudovkin climbed in and gave an instruction to the driver to move off. Edging forward, the car reached a junction with the main drag beside the Brandeis office, the same road that Straker and McMahon had just turned into. There was virtually no traffic; further down to his left, Pudovkin could easily see the back of the Brandeis limousine driving away. Responding to a hand signal, Pudovkin's driver pulled out – over to the far side of the road – crossing several lanes to follow Straker, from some distance behind.

A light rain was falling from a moonless sky with low cloud. Pudovkin watched the Brandeis car closely through the swipe of the windscreen wipers. It turned right into Shmitovskiy Proezd, and then ran east for over a mile before indicating right into Krasnaya Presnya Ulitsa. Pudovkin sensed where they were heading: straight for the centre of Moscow.

Over the radio to his team, he said: 'All stations, it looks like they're making for Straker's hotel.'

Several other radios on the net acknowledged the call. One call sign said it would go on ahead and be ready to spot them, from the far side of the bridge as they crossed the river.

Pudovkin told his own driver not to get too close.

Seven minutes later the target car reached the edge of Red Square. Here, too, there was no traffic. Moscow seemed deserted. The rain – the hour – appeared to have driven everyone from the streets.

Pudovkin continued to watch the car in front as it turned left at the end of Ilyinka Ulitsa. Surprisingly, despite the low levels of traffic, it wasn't travelling that quickly.

The Brandeis car ran down the side of the square, heading towards Saint Basil's. The cathedral's floodlit bauble-like domes loomed above it to the right.

Pudovkin watched the car disappear from view as the street descended gently round the back of the cathedral. He issued an instruction to the driver. In response, his own car accelerated slightly, and, as he rounded the corner, visual contact was quickly restored. He was able to watch the target car head down the slight ramp and then out onto the Bolshoy Moskvoretsky Bridge.

There was no traffic here, either. The six lanes across the top of the bridge were completely deserted. The two cars drove out into the middle of the river.

Pudovkin happened to be looking down at his radio when it happened.

There was a flash of light.

His driver stabbed at the brakes; Pudovkin was hurled forwards against his seat belt. He quickly tried to look up.

Pudovkin suddenly felt that everything was happening around him in slow motion.

Another blinding flash came an instant later, whiting out his vision.

Pudovkin blinked, trying to focus on the car in front.

There was a ground-shaking boom.

The rear of the Brandeis Mercedes was being heaved off the surface of the road.

His view of the car disappeared in the explosion.

A second charge had gone off somewhere in the Brandeis car.

Pudovkin's own windshield shattered. His ears screamed with a stabbing pain, overwhelmed by a terrifying noise. Pudovkin was soon fighting to breathe, the air having been sucked out of his lungs.

A hail of debris rained down on the bridge, some of which banged onto the roof of his car.

Then nothing seemed to happen.

Had he not been deafened, Pudovkin would have become aware of an eerie silence.

He couldn't concentrate, though. He was shaking.

Uncontrollably.

He tried to open the car door.

Managing to stand – in the middle of the bridge – Pudovkin staggered forward. He looked out over the devastation.

Moscow was dark, lit only by the floodlights bathing the occasional landmark up and down the river.

Hardly anything remained of the Brandeis car.

There was nothing left of Straker or of McMahon, or of whoever had been unfortunate enough to have been driving them. Everything inside had been incinerated in an instant.

The blast had all but obliterated or scattered its components; what was left of the car was little more than a buckled, bare frame slumped in a thirty-foot bowl in the road where the asphalt surface had ruptured in the force of the explosion. To one side of the car, Pudovkin noticed a pool of blood. To the other, he saw a six-foot-wide hole, blasted right through the solid structure of the bridge – giving a clear view of the river below.

With his hand – his whole body – still shaking, Pudovkin pulled out his phone.

He had to keep blinking – bright swirling worms were distorting his vision. It took several attempts to hit the right contact.

Pudovkin spoke with the duty officer in the Moscow police headquarters and reported the explosion. The incident was now in someone else's hands.

Ending that call, he rang another number.

After numerous rings, Léon Gazdanov picked up. Sounding sleepy.

'How could you do it?' Pudovkin asked judderingly.

'Do what?' the other croaked.

'Straker and McMahon are dead. You've just blown them up – on the Moskvoretsky Bridge.'

'What the *fuck* are you talking about?'

'I followed them out of the Brandeis office.'

Gazdanov groaned. 'Going where?'

'I don't know – to his hotel? Their car exploded right in front of me. On the bridge. There's nothing left. How could you do it?'

Gazdanov sounded like he was being shocked awake. 'What do you mean: How could *I* do it?'

'You were the one talking about *stopping* Straker,' said Pudovkin. 'Well … all I can tell you, Mr Prosecutor … is you've stopped him all right. There's absolutely nothing left of him now …'

SIXTY-FOUR

Pudovkin hardly slept. His reaction to the explosion tormented him. He woke at five o'clock and got up, leaving Ivan asleep in their bed; Pudovkin didn't want to disturb him – he, too, had had to work late, at the club. In the kitchen, Pudovkin thought to console himself with a fresh cafetière of coffee. He clicked the television on with the remote and turned away to make himself some toast.

Russia-1 was in the middle of a bulletin.

The news channel was announcing the explosion of a car in the middle of the Bolshoi Moskvoretsky Bridge.

Pudovkin spun round and then just stood there. In his kitchen. In his boxer shorts.

The news bulletin ran a video clip – in black and white – that looked like CCTV footage. It showed the empty bridge, running top right to bottom left across the screen. Framed in the very top right-hand corner were the floodlit domes of Saint Basil's Cathedral. To either side of the bridge, left and right of the screen, were the untroubled waters of the Moskva River.

As the car reached the dead centre of the picture, there was an initial flash – temporarily whiting out the camera. Then came the second blast.

After the smoke and debris had cleared, all that was left was what Pudovkin remembered: the denuded frame of the car in the middle of the bowl gouged into the surface of the bridge.

He then had a secondary shock.

As the clip ran on, it showed the first person to appear on the scene after the explosion. Pudovkin could see all too clearly.

It was himself.

Then came another element to the broadcast.

The news programme's director switched back to the studio. An announcer was speaking straight to camera; she spoke in a solemn tone. Two photographs – formal portraits – appeared on the screen, one to either side of the newsreader.

On the left was a picture of a soldier – Colonel Straker – wearing a grey/blue uniform, Sam Browne, dark green beret, and a chest full of medals.

On the right came a picture showing the striking face of Alexandra "Sandy" McMahon – her pale blue eyes, strawberry blonde hair and freckled complexion – looking determinedly out from the photograph. Captions were placed under each picture, but all Pudovkin managed to catch was "decorated war hero" and "defence lawyer".

He couldn't believe it. The newsreader then declared: *'Two members of the Ptarmigan Formula One Team's legal team – in the trial of the thirty-four deaths at the Grand Prix – were killed earlier this morning in Moscow. It is not yet clear who was responsible for this act of violence, or how it will impact on the legal proceedings of the case.'*

'No shit,' said Pudovkin.

The police colonel hit a number on his phone. The prosecutor general answered immediately.

'Are you near a television?'

There was a reticent grunt from the other end.

'Well, Mr Gazdanov,' he said, not using the law officer's title for the first time. 'What do you want to do now?'

Pudovkin's attention was suddenly drawn to the TV picture. It had just switched to a new shot – tagged live – with "City Hall" encaptioned in the top right-hand corner of the screen. The remainder of the picture showed a table with a bank of microphones set up in the middle, ready for an announcement of some kind.

Pudovkin said: 'It looks like the mayor is about to make a statement.'

'What about?' asked Gazdanov huskily, still not sounding fully together.

'One can only guess.'

Into the shot, walking behind the table and its forest of microphones, came a striking middle-aged woman with short black hair, large brown eyes and a narrow mouth. She wore a dark suit with a black pashmina swirled around her shoulders and across her neck. Oksana Pavlova stood motionless for a moment – her eyes lowered as if in contemplation – before looking up, straight down the lens of the TV camera.

'*Last night, an event of seismic political significance occurred, right here – in Russia's capital. A lawyer handling the defence of the people charged with the deaths at the Russian Grand Prix was killed. What possible threat could she have posed? Unless, of course, someone feared she was in danger of proving that the people charged in the case were* not *responsible for the accident at the race track.*

'*What had this lawyer discovered? What threat did she pose? And to whom? The key question, therefore, is: Who had her killed? Was it, perhaps, the real culprits behind the accident at the Grand Prix? It's not hard to see that this young lawyer was not killed – but assassinated.*'

'Get that off the air,' barked Gazdanov. 'Now!'

'Good God,' exclaimed Pudovkin. 'What the hell is *this* going to do to our trial?'

'Nothing,' barked Gazdanov nasally. 'The mayor of Moscow is irrelevant to our case. We have Baryshnikov – who will validate the technical aspects of the car, the race and the crash. Once that testimony is in the minds of the judges and the media, the case will be over. No one will need to look any further than Ptarmigan for responsibility and blame. Be in my office for seven.'

Pudovkin could not believe the other man's attitude, either towards the deaths of Straker and McMahon or his single-minded pursuit of this case.

Pudovkin reported to the prosecutor general's office at the appointed time. He found Gazdanov energized for the day ahead.

'I've just been told the judges *will* allow Sabatino to stand trial,' the prosecutor said. 'We can *proceed*.'

Pudovkin demonstrated as much enthusiasm as he felt he ought to show, almost having to force himself to pay Gazdanov adequate attention until they left for the Supreme Court.

SIXTY-FIVE

The three Supreme Court judges filed in at nine thirty that morning. Shortly afterwards, the accused – in their chains and wheelchair – were paraded in and locked in the cage. Pudovkin looked at the faces, particularly of Sabatino. She must have been told of the deaths overnight, he thought. She looked desiccated. Her eyes were damp; her cheeks were red, while her head was slumped forward as low as the halo brace would allow.

Pudovkin sensed a very different mood around the Supreme Court that morning. Evocatively, the defence barrister had left an empty chair at the table where Sandy McMahon had sat the day before.

Oscar Brogan was the first to his feet after the judges had sat down. 'My Lords, I stand before you in mourning following the tragic death last night of my learned colleague, Ms Sandy McMahon. I would ask your Lordships one question: Does the murder of a leading and indispensable member of the defence team not concern your Lordships as to the troubling influences on this case?'

There was a murmur around the courtroom.

The three judges could be seen conferring with each other. After a few minutes the central judge turned towards Brogan: 'We have had no application or evidence laid before us that links Alexandra McMahon's death with this trial.'

Brogan, at this point, made a show of scoffing.

'Until any link is proven,' continued the judge, 'we can only try what is before us.'

Brogan did not rise to his feet to acknowledge the last point from the senior judge. As a result, it earned him a change in tone from the bench: 'Furthermore, Mr Brogan, we have reached a ruling on your application in respect of Ms Sabatino's readiness to stand trial. We find in favour of the prosecution. We cite the first assurance offered by the consultant at the hospital – Mr Pyotr Uglov – on the grounds that this came before the accused's lawyer, Ms McMahon, had exerted undue pressure on the trauma consultant. We are led to understand that she threatened to accuse him of professional misconduct.'

Pudovkin looked at the back of the prosecutor general's head; even from behind he could see that Gazdanov was reacting triumphantly to this ruling.

'Mr Gazdanov,' continued the senior judge switching his attention to the prosecution barrister, 'please call your first witness.'

Pudovkin was suddenly distracted. His phone was vibrating in his pocket. Looking down, it didn't take long for the police colonel to realize the urgency. Discreetly as he could, he rose from the concentric bench and let himself out through the main doors at the back of the courtroom.

Pudovkin rang Police Major Ustinov immediately at the Baryshnikov mansion. The news from there was alarming, to say the least.

Three-quarters of an hour before, at precisely nine o'clock, Major Ustinov had arrived for duty at the Baryshnikov residence. His first port of call – as every day since this operation started – was the police's makeshift command centre. Two of his officers were on duty inside. He asked for an update on the night's events; Major Ustinov was encouraged that all had been quiet. Assuming command, he stood the two officers down and, helping himself to some coffee, settled himself into the control room for the day.

Ten minutes later everything changed.

Ustinov heard something in the distance, a muffled sound – through the trees.

What was that? A blast of some kind – some sort of air horn?

He listened out.

It went off again a few seconds later – and then again … for a third time.

Then it was gone. That was it.

After the incidents from a few nights before, everyone around the Baryshnikov house had become decidedly jumpy. Mrs Baryshnikov was now confined to her apartment. But with her state of health, the police had taken the extra precaution of installing a panic button, which linked her directly to the control room.

So far, she had not had need of it.

At nine fifteen, Ustinov was startled by an ear-piercing screech. Hurriedly, he checked the feed from the security cameras in each room of Mrs Baryshnikov's apartment. When he saw the picture from her bathroom, he leapt to his feet.

There was a figure.

Lying on the floor.

Motionless.

'Christ,' he shouted aloud. Grabbing a radio and running for the door as he spoke, he transmitted: 'Principal down! *Principal down!* Mrs Baryshnikov's bathroom.'

Police Major Ustinov ran down the corridor to the main hall, swung round the end of the staircase banisters, hurtled up the steps – three at a time – and sprinted down the landing to Mrs Baryshnikov's private rooms.

Fumbling with the key in the lock, he burst in through the door and on towards the bathroom. The moment he was inside, he grimaced at the smell. A powerful waft of urine hit him hard.

Two other policemen, answering the call, charged into the room shortly afterwards. They, too, recoiled at the smell before looking down at the shape of the elderly woman lying on her side on the bathroom floor.

As Ustinov stooped down to look at her face, he saw she was beyond sallow; almost as a reflex he yelped: 'Oh my God – she's *yellow.*'

'What does that mean?' asked one of the policemen.

'Well it can't be good – must be something to do with her piss, given the smell in here.'

'Her kidneys?'

Major Ustinov climbed to his feet; barking into the radio, he ordered: 'Someone call an ambulance. Now!'

Ustinov and his men struggled to lift the lifeless form of Mrs Baryshnikov out of the bathroom and into the bedroom. Repeated attempts were made to speak to the old woman, but she wasn't responding.

'Is she going to be okay?' asked one of the men.

'We'd better fucking hope so,' replied Ustinov.

A few minutes later a distant siren could be heard.

'Thank fuck,' said Major Ustinov as he proceeded to shout new orders into the radio: 'Hello Alpha – Hello Alpha. Ambulance inbound. Ambulance inbound. Open the gates. Let it in – immediately!'

Ustinov's command was acknowledged.

He looked down at the still inanimate Mrs Baryshnikov. His only relief came from hearing the siren grow louder. It then became deafening, as it closed in on the house. Ustinov ran to one of the floor-to-ceiling windows and stepped out onto the balcony. He could see the ambulance coming to a stop at the foot of the main steps. Two paramedics climbed out.

'Up here,' he shouted, 'quickly – you'll need a stretcher.'

He was pleased to see an urgent reaction from the two medics. In a matter of seconds they were climbing the front steps and charging towards the main entrance into the mansion.

Inside, Major Ustinov had run to the top of the staircase. He shouted: 'Up here,' his commands echoing around the spacious hall.

The paramedics ran on up the stairs. Major Ustinov turned to lead the arrivals along the landing, and showed them into the private apartment.

Wasting no time, the paramedics – carrying the stretcher between them – made directly for the bed. One of them pulled out a stethoscope and listened to Mrs Baryshnikov's heart. The other looked at her face, lifting the woman's eyelids.

'Christ,' he said, 'how long has she been like this?'

'About ten minutes.'

The first paramedic looked up, as if to say any such estimate was wildly out.

'She looks uraemic,' said the second medic. 'She's clearly gone into shock. Does this woman have a kidney problem?'

'Yes,' said Major Ustinov.

'We've got to get her to dialysis – and fast.'

'She's got a dialysis machine – in there. Next door.'

'Show me!'

The police major led him into the bathroom. As the medic entered, he said: 'Urgh, it should *not* be smelling like that in here. Where's the machine?'

'Over there.' Ustinov pointed to the trolley-borne artificial kidney against the wall.

Bending down to check it over, the medic said: 'How long's it been smelling like this?'

Ustinov couldn't admit they didn't know; that they didn't check it.

'This thing must have sprung a leak,' said the paramedic from almost underneath the machine. 'Yes, look,' he said, sticking his finger under one of the pipes. 'This has come loose. That poor woman must have been recycling her own urine.'

'How bad is that?' asked the major.

'Well it's not good. We've got to get her to the hospital.'

The medic dived out of the bathroom, back to the patient's bedside. The other had set up an oxygen line and placed a mask over Mrs Baryshnikov's mouth. Without a word of command, the paramedics manoeuvred the stretcher in beside the woman and lifted her onto its canvas. Her oxygen supply was also loaded and secured. Grabbing each end of the stretcher, the medics lifted her clear. One of them barked to the policemen: 'Get the door!' as they headed across the bedroom.

'Where are you taking her?' asked Ustinov.

'It's obviously her kidneys, so the Moscow Nephrology Unit.'

Fewer than three minutes later the doors of the ambulance were being closed. One of the medics remained in the back with the patient, while the other climbed into the cab. As he fired the engine, he hit the siren and lights. Dropping the clutch, he accelerated the ambulance away down the drive, and out through the gate. Turning left, towards the centre of Barvikha, the ambulance sped away heading in the direction of the main road to Moscow.

SIXTY-SIX

Pudovkin listened to the report from Major Ustinov at the mansion.

'Christ, that's all we need – another death,' said the police colonel. 'Is she going to be all right?'

'The medics said she was in a bad way. But never said she was critical.'

'Where have they taken her?' he asked.

'The Moscow Nephrology Unit.'

'Find out which ward she's in, will you – and how she is. Gazdanov will have our balls if we don't know.'

Discreetly, Pudovkin retook his seat behind the prosecutor general in the courtroom.

Léon Gazdanov declared: 'The prosecution calls its next witness: Yegor Baryshnikov.'

Pudovkin turned to watch the Russian Formula One driver's entrance, and then glanced across to see the reaction from the two accused sitting in the cage to the left of the judges. Pudovkin suddenly felt conflicted. For the prosecution, he was buoyed by the impact Baryshnikov's testimony would have on the State's case. For the other side, Pudovkin could not fail to notice the hate-filled expressions on the faces of the accused. Baryshnikov's switch of loyalties was having a clear effect on his erstwhile teammates.

There was a moment's pause while the accused were set up with earphones for simultaneous translation. In Russian, Léon Gazdanov asked the witness: 'Will you give the court your name, please?'

'Yegor Valentinovich Baryshnikov.'

'And your profession?'

'Formula One driver.'

'And your employer?'

'Formerly ...' said Baryshnikov quietly, '... the Ptarmigan Formula One team.'

'And how long have you been a Formula One driver.'

'A test driver for two years. A race driver for this season.'

'Because of that, would you say that your knowledge of Formula One, its safety procedures and the drivers' code – or whatever you might call it – is well established?'

'I'd like to think so.'

'And your knowledge of Ptarmigan – the culture of the team, and its management practices? Would you say that you have an understanding of those, too?'

Baryshnikov nodded.

'I'm sorry, Mr Baryshnikov,' boomed Gazdanov, 'would you please answer the question loud enough for the justices to hear.'

'Yes,' stated the driver, looking up at the row of judges.

'Now, I'd like to give us your professional driver's opinion of the Zhar-ptitsa Autodrom circuit.'

'It's a modern complex.'

Gazdanov sounded like he was trying again: 'So, does that mean it fulfilled all the safety requirements of a modern Grand Prix circuit?'

'My Lords,' came an intervention from across the room. 'I would be grateful if the prosecution did not lead the witness.'

Gazdanov smiled at Oscar Brogan.

The senior judge looked from Brogan to Gazdanov and seemed to nod.

Brogan sat back down.

Gazdanov turned to face Baryshnikov: 'In your opinion, was ... is ... the Zhar-ptitsa Autodrom a safe circuit?'

Baryshnikov said: 'Yes.'

'Please tell us, Mr Baryshnikov, about the circuit from a racing point of view. For instance, how many of its corners were designed so that you could safely overtake each other?'

'There were considered to be five corners where overtaking was expected.'

'And was Turn Eleven – where the accident took place – one of those expected overtaking places?'

Baryshnikov did not respond straight away. He even turned and looked round to face the cage, looking directly at the figure sitting in the halo brace. 'No,' he said.

'I'm sorry, Mr Baryshnikov,' said Gazdanov, 'could you speak up, please. Was Turn Eleven one of the expected overtaking places on this circuit?'

'No,' repeated Baryshnikov loudly enough to be heard this time.

'So what did – what *do* – you think of Ms Sabatino's attempt to overtake you at that point?'

'I wouldn't have done it,' he said, lowering his head again, his voice trailing off.

Pudovkin saw that Gazdanov's cockiness seemed to have tempered slightly. The words Baryshnikov was using were completely in line with the prosecution's "script", but the delivery was flat; as a witness, he wasn't selling their points with any conviction.

'Mr Baryshnikov, *your* Ptarmigan car was working well in the build-up to – and during – the Grand Prix?'

Brogan was back on his feet: 'Once again, my Lords, I object – the prosecutor is clearly leading the witness.'

'I am merely reciting back to the witness the thrust of his own witness statement, but…' said Gazdanov with an exaggerated gesture '…to indulge the defence counsel, I will instead ask: Mr Baryshnikov, could you tell us how you thought your car was performing before – and during – the race?'

'It was okay.'

'Did you, in fact, say in your witness statement that it was performing superbly?'

'Yes.'

'Thank you, Mr Baryshnikov. Now, each Formula One car has on it a form of data recorder – a sort of black box – does it not?'

Baryshnikov nodded.

'Answer verbally, if you would, *please*, Mr Baryshnikov.'

'Yes.'

'Does that go for the Ptarmigan cars, too, Mr Baryshnikov?'

'Yes.'

'And have you had a chance to examine the data recorder recovered from the wreckage of Ms Sabatino's car?'

Pudovkin watched Baryshnikov's expression intently. He saw the driver swivel his head and look across at the cage again. A whole gamut of emotions seemed to cross his face.

Baryshnikov turned back towards Gazdanov.

Pudovkin could see the prosecutor general was now leaning forward slightly, as if in anticipation – as if going in for the kill.

Gazdanov prompted: 'Mr Baryshnikov … '

Pudovkin did not know what occurred next.

Or how.

But he knew instantly that something had happened.

SIXTY-SEVEN

There was an instantaneous change in Baryshnikov's demeanour.

Baryshnikov boomed: 'Data recorders – or "black boxes" as you call them – can only be read by the FIA, the governing body of Formula One. You, Mr Gazdanov, have denied the FIA access to the "black boxes". So, no, I don't know what's in them – and neither can you.'

Gazdanov jolted upright.

Pudovkin looked up at Baryshnikov.

What on earth was going on?

Pudovkin scanned the faces of the Supreme Court justices. Each judge looked as if he had just been slapped.

Looking across at Brogan, Pudovkin saw that he was equally surprised.

'More to the point,' said Baryshnikov – now projecting powerfully across the room – 'when I said I would not have attempted an overtake at Turn Eleven, what I meant was that *I* would not have attempted an overtake there – because I am not brave enough. What Remy – Ms Sabatino – did on that corner was quite outstanding: the mark of an intuitive driver. Ms Sabatino is in a completely different league to me.'

The courtroom burst into chatter.

Pudovkin stared into the face of the witness, trying to understand his astonishing volte-face. What was he doing? Then Pudovkin turned to look round.

He scanned the rest of the room.

Suddenly it came to him.

He realized what had happened. In an instant.

All the pieces fell into place.

There, standing at the back of the courtroom – just inside the main door – was a man wearing the bright turquoise of a Ptarmigan Formula One team jacket. Pudovkin didn't recognize him. This man, though, had his arm round the shoulders of an elderly lady, a lady with short dark hair and striking dark eyes. Another man, also dressed in the same turquoise livery, stood on the other side of this woman, also with his arm across her shoulders.

Tatiana Baryshnikov, the Formula One driver's mother, was standing there, quite clearly, under the protective wing of the Ptarmigan Formula One team. It was an unequivocal signal to Yegor Baryshnikov that the police no longer had possession of his mother.

A gavel banging down hard rang out across the grand courtroom. The senior judge also called for quiet.

'Silence, silence!' he called.

'Yegor Valentinovich,' said the middle judge severely when the noise finally abated, 'I do not understand. What you have just said is in direct contradiction – not only of your witness statements, but of everything you have told this court this morning. Kindly explain yourself.'

Pudovkin looked over at the prosecutor general; Gazdanov looked like he had been winded, kicked in the stomach – perhaps even somewhere more painful.

Yegor Baryshnikov said firmly: 'I am able to speak the truth now, Mr Justices – because I am no longer being held to ransom.'

The senior judge said: 'I beg your pardon?'

'Mr Justice, on the twenty-first of July the police kidnapped and have since held my mother hostage at her house in Barvikha.'

No one heard the end of Baryshnikov's sentence as the reactions to this shock announcement flowed back from the front of the courtroom.

Further smacks of the gavel thundered out, but they had minimal effect.

'Yes,' affirmed Baryshnikov barely loud enough to be heard. 'My mother, Mr Justice, has just joined us at the back of the room.'

At this, everyone turned to look.

Even the judges.

Mrs Baryshnikov's handsomeness radiated out.

'Are you the witness's mother?' asked the senior judge.

The woman nodded.

'And is your son's claim true, madam?'

'Yes,' Mrs Baryshnikov replied, her voice sounding slightly strained. 'I have only just been rescued from police captivity – by Yegor's colleagues at Ptarmigan.'

Once more the room dissolved into noise and chatter.

After several attempts at calling for order with the gavel, the middle judge chose to rise to his feet. A court officer bellowed for quiet.

'Mr Baryshnikov,' said the senior judge with a noticeably more sympathetic tone. 'We would clearly need more of an explanation, if not a specific hearing to consider your extraordinary claims. As it happens, we are in the middle of a very serious trial – in the highest court in the country. You have made a series of highly contradictory statements. And you have just offered us an explanation as to why you have been so inconsistent – which, if true, would be quite extraordinary. In any event, given your inconsistencies, I am beginning to question your reliability as a witness in this trial.'

At this point, Oscar Brogan QC moved quickly to his feet. 'My Lords, this court heard yesterday about one witness – a doctor – who had said one thing to the authorities and then quite another to the former defence counsel about the state of health of one of the accused, but we don't know why. Today, your Lordships, we have just heard from Mr Baryshnikov – incidentally, the only expert on Formula One being put forward by the prosecution – who said one thing in his witness statement, some of which he has repeated from the witness box today, but who has, within the space of an hour, gone on to contradict himself, almost completely. One of the reasons given would even suggest that some form of coercion has been exerted over members of this witness's family by the police.'

Brogan, keenly reading the mood of the courtroom, chose to

leave his unofficial summation there, and sat down. His implicit challenge to the reliability of the prosecution witnesses had done enough. It seemed to throw the entire procedure of the previous day and a half into question.

Noise from the room was even louder after this torpedo fired at the prosecution's case, and the potential damage it might be doing to the credibility of the entire trial.

With a repeat of the senior judge rising to his feet, and the court official bellowing for quiet, the room finally settled.

The middle judge retook his chair. He seemed to be weighing up the situation and how he should proceed. 'We will have to rise to deliberate on this extraordinary development,' he said solemnly. 'Before we do, I would ask Mr Baryshnikov one question, though – in order that he might help us.'

The Formula One driver raised his eyes to meet the judge's.

'What, in your professional opinion, was the cause of this crash?'

Gazdanov leapt to his feet: 'Mr Justices, Mr Baryshnikov has answered this in his witness statement. It's all too clear,' he said lifting up a document. 'It was recklessness on the part of Ms Sabatino, showing an exact repeat of her conduct in Canada – which was criticized only last week by the international governing body of Formula One.'

The senior judge glared at Gazdanov. 'I think we have found that Mr Baryshnikov's circumstances, particularly in relation to his mother, have vitiated that statement – rendered it unreliable, Mr Gazdanov. Would the witness please answer my question about the causes of the crash, as you see them.'

Baryshnikov said: 'The cause of the crash cannot be known until the wreckage of the car has been fully examined by professionals. To date, that has not been permitted – because the police chose to impound it.

'Mr Justices,' Yegor Baryshnikov continued, 'Grand Prix races are conducted at extraordinary speeds. There is always risk. On any race track, there are always racing incidents. I have not had the chance to discuss things with my team since the kidnapping of my mother; however, both my car and Ms Sabatino's were perfectly set up for this circuit. Both cars were highly competitive for the first six laps. I do not believe that Ms Sabatino coming off the track at that point was driver error or a mechanical failure, nor was it a straightforward racing incident. Because of my own experiences of the background to this Grand Prix, I believe something happened to Ms Sabatino's car. Someone *wanted* something to happen to it.'

The judge's expression showed some element of surprise. He asked: 'Are you saying that you think someone *intended* Ms Sabatino's car to crash?'

Baryshnikov paused. 'I am, Mr Justice.'

Pudovkin's heart was racing. He looked at the prosecutor general; Gazdanov's body language indicated he was seething with anger.

'Mr Baryshnikov, if you think the crash might have been intentional, you must have had thoughts, then, about who you think was behind it?'

There was a murmur from the room. But it quickly settled, perhaps in anticipation of what might come next. Baryshnikov, now relieved at not being coerced while answering such questions, seemed calmer and, speaking in Russian, found a far more confident voice.

'I was involved from the very outset in trying to bring the Russian Grand Prix to Moscow. I was asked to join the board of Moscow 100, the bidding company for the race, funded by the patriot Avel Obrenovich. The moment we had the go-ahead from the FIA and Motor Racing Promotions, everyone involved in the bidding company – Mr Obrenovich himself, my fellow directors and I – found ourselves systematically harassed, attacked and undermined. Two of my colleagues even died under suspicious circumstances. The disruption suffered by the Moscow Grand Prix went far beyond any normal commercial practices. Someone, it seemed, had been going to extraordinary lengths to prevent the Zhar-ptitsa Autodrom from succeeding, not to mention hosting a successful Grand Prix.'

'Mr Baryshnikov, you have not answered my question,' said the senior judge. 'Let us try again: You must have a view as to who you believe was behind the crash?'

Baryshnikov nodded.

'Well, then, who do you think it was?'

This time the racing driver chose not to address his answer to the judges, but instead turned directly to face the TV cameras on the far side of the room: 'Vadim Kondratiev,' he said.

The crowd gasped.

Léon Gazdanov jumped straight to his feet. 'Mr Justices, this is an outrageous slur on a senior man's reputation and character. I implore your Justices to reprimand Mr Baryshnikov, to find him in contempt of court, and to instruct him to make a full retraction and apology.'

For the first time the presiding judge allowed his human side to show through his austere professional facade. His reaction to Gazdanov's defence of Kondratiev indicated a very knowing expression. But before the judge could respond, Oscar Brogan had also leapt to his feet.

'My Lordships, if I may? It might be worth reminding the court that Mr Baryshnikov is currently appearing as a witness for the prosecution.'

Pudovkin saw the judges nod in hesitant acknowledgement of that fact and one of them even smile.

'It may therefore come as a comfort to your Lordships to know that there is common ground – agreement – between us. Indeed, the defence agrees with Mr Baryshnikov. It may also interest your Lordships to know that, if this trial continues, it is now the defence's intention to call as a witness Ms Oksana Ivanovna Pavlova, the mayor of Moscow. The mayor, as political sponsor of the Moscow Grand Prix, has specific views on this race and the influence which Mr Kondratiev has brought to bear on the Zhar-ptitsa Autodrom – from its inception, through its development, right up to and including the cause of the crash.'

Pudovkin saw a flurry of movement among the bank of media over by the right-hand wall. Many journalists were already running from the court, clutching mobile phones. This was news that would go around the world in a matter of minutes. And it couldn't wait.

Finally, the judges regained control of the courtroom.

'We will rise now and adjourn until nine o'clock tomorrow morning. We command counsel from both sides to attend us in our rooms one hour before.'

So ended the second day of the Grand Prix trial held in the Russian Supreme Court.

SIXTY-EIGHT

Pudovkin stood up and walked round the end of the bench to speak to the prosecutor general. Léon Gazdanov was shaking with anger. Grabbing at his papers, he was stuffing them unceremoniously into his briefcase.

'We are going back to my room,' he instructed without looking up at the police colonel. 'I want to know what the fuck went wrong with Baryshnikov.' Then adding: 'You have just presided over your career-ending catastrophe. You are to *sack* the man in charge of the security operation at that woman's house.'

Pudovkin said nothing. He trailed along behind Gazdanov as the prosecutor general strode out of the courtroom, through the entrance area and out onto the street. The prosecutor's car was waiting for him there and the man climbed straight in. Pudovkin did the same from the other side. The law officer was still seething.

'How the fuck has this happened?' he bawled.

Before they reached the office of the prosecutor general in Bolshaya Dmitrovka Ulitsa, Gazdanov's phone was ringing.

As he answered it, Pudovkin witnessed something quite unexpected.

Gazdanov was soon smiling into the middle distance as he said: 'Mr President.'

Pudovkin couldn't believe the transformation.

'Right, sir. Yes, sir. I have Police Colonel Pudovkin with me. Right, sir. Yes, sir.'

Gazdanov ended the call.

Speaking immediately with his driver, the prosecutor gave instructions for them to head for an alternative destination.

'We've been summoned to see the president,' Gazdanov announced.

Pudovkin had never set foot inside the Kremlin, nor had he met any Russian president. The prosecutor general hadn't explained why they were going, but it had to be about the trial, didn't it? How high did the interest in this case actually go?

Suddenly Pudovkin had concerns.

Would he be asked about this case?

With the upsets of the afternoon, Pudovkin realized that he no longer knew the official line on the status of the trial. He would want to sound knowledgeable and on top of things in front of the president. Trying to gain perspective on the current situation, he asked: 'What are your plans for the trial going forward, Mr Prosecutor General?'

Gazdanov now looked shaken. 'You undermined this case by letting Ptarmigan snatch that Baryshnikov woman,' he barked. 'You've destroyed the technical element of our prosecution.'

'Baryshnikov's testimony was hardly convincing, even before the appearance of his mother.'

'Baryshnikov was laying the foundations of the technical causes of the crash,' insisted Gazdanov. 'Faults or even doubts, there, would have readily placed responsibility for the deaths at Ptarmigan's feet. If a culprit could be put in the mind of the court, why would it go looking anywhere else?'

Pudovkin had a new feeling of unease. What kind of irrational case was Gazdanov pursuing here? Foisting blame was a clear distortion of what Pudovkin believed even Russian justice should be about. Evidence, leading to truth was what he expected; he may have known that, on occasion, cases had to be made without the State having everything it might wish for. But what *was* this man playing at?

Except Pudovkin suddenly realized it could be far worse than that.

If foisting blame was Gazdanov's thing, Pudovkin suddenly came to a fearful realization. Why was he – a middle-ranking police officer – being taken to meet the president of Russia at all? He didn't need to be there; he could easily be stood down. Such a summons certainly wasn't out of courtesy. If Ptarmigan was intended to be Gazdanov's sacrificial offering to appease public opinion over the Grand Prix deaths, was Pudovkin about to be the equivalent sacrifice to appease the president's opinion of the trial?

Pudovkin's pulse was now racing.

He was suddenly sure that he was being set up for his own kangaroo court.

After being waved through, Gazdanov's official car swept up the ramp and through the gate under the Borovitskaya Tower set in the wall of the Kremlin. Inside the red-brick citadel, the car ran along the frontage of the Grand Kremlin Palace and below the cluster of gold onion-shaped domes of the imperial churches. Pudovkin could soon see they were heading for the ominous Senate building, looming at the far end of the complex; above this was flying a flag bearing the Russian coat of arms.

They were met formally by several members of the presidential guard.

Without delay, Gazdanov and Pudovkin were escorted from their car and up towards the president's office.

There was no waiting – they were marched straight in.

Despite Pudovkin's rising apprehension, his attention was momentarily distracted by the grandiosity of this inner sanctum: oak-panelled walls, the intricately patterned silk carpet and the spectacular crystal chandelier burning with twenty or more bulbs. For all its stylish decoration, the room was dark. Windows that should have afforded a view out over Red Square were obscured by heavy gauze – bombproof? – curtains. Whatever their purpose, they reduced the natural light getting through to a dim suggestion of the day outside, hence the room needing to rely on its artificial lighting.

Pudovkin was surprised the moment they were in the president's presence. Gazdanov's entire demeanour seemed to change in an instant; gone was the strutting egotist. The man now appeared decidedly unsure of himself.

The president of Russia was sitting behind his desk and made no sign of getting up. Pudovkin recoiled. The man's Easter Island features appeared all the more uncompromising in the flesh. Gazdanov moved to stand directly in front of him. Pudovkin felt he should do the same.

The president's first words were: 'What the fuck is going on with this trial, Gazdanov? The death of that defence lawyer is a catastrophe! The international press are saying it's Sergei Magnitsky all over again.'

Gazdanov answered: 'McMahon's death was nothing to do with the State.'

'That's a fatuous answer, and it does nothing to reduce the shock of her death – or the world's perception of it. Who did kill her, then?'

There was silence.

'You don't have any idea?' asked the president.

He turned to Pudovkin. 'You don't have an idea, either, colonel?'

Pudovkin decided to hold his peace … for the time being. He shook his head and simply uttered: 'Sir.'

'The death of the defence lawyer,' the president went on, 'casts huge suspicion on this trial. Russia is already being lambasted for the integrity of its judicial system. I now hear that the defence *advokat* is applying to call the mayor of Moscow as a witness.'

Gazdanov offered no opinion.

'Maybe – just *maybe*,' the president continued, 'all this could be weathered if your case was cut and dried. But everything's being bungled. What happened with our Formula One driver's testimony? And what the hell was all this business with Baryshnikov's mother?'

'She was allowed to escape,' Gazdanov said. 'If the police operation had been effective, she would never have been allowed to undermine our key prosecution witness.'

Pudovkin swallowed.

The president turned to face him. 'What do you have to say for yourself, colonel?'

Pudovkin knew this was it.

He wondered whether he should gamble, gamble on getting his retaliation in first. Pudovkin was no stranger to taking risks. Every day of his career had been a gamble. Joining the police force as a gay man during the Putin era had been a huge risk. Pudovkin had lived with the constant threat of being outed – and ousted from his job – every day since.

He suddenly realized he was ready.

This was going to be it. Make or break.

'What moral authority does a state prosecution have, Mr President,' he said, 'if it can only rely on testimony that's been extorted from witnesses?'

Pudovkin forced himself to look the president of Russia in the eye.

The police colonel waited … for an outburst … fully expecting to be reprimanded for such insubordination.

Through his peripheral vision, Pudovkin could see that Gazdanov was now severely agitating. 'It would have worked,' came the nasal voice, 'if the police operation hadn't been such a cock-up.'

Pudovkin was still on edge. He desperately tried to gauge how the president was taking this.

'What other witnesses do you have, Gazdanov?' asked Tarkovsky.

Silently, Pudovkin heaved a huge sigh of relief.

'Er, plenty,' said Gazdanov.

'Name them,' demanded the president.

'The Ptarmigan people. The Sabatino woman … er, a number of spectators on that grassy bank. The doctors at the scene of the crash, and … Police Colonel Pudovkin, here.'

'You expect Police Colonel … Pudovkin, is it? … to testify for you after you've just shat on his bogus operation?'

'I have no doubt that Colonel Pudovkin will do his duty,' said Gazdanov, 'to make up for all that's gone wrong so far.'

The president shook his head. 'Just out of interest, colonel,' he said looking directly at Pudovkin, 'how *did* an elderly woman escape from your custody?'

The police officer replied promptly: 'Colonel Straker, sir.'

After a moment's pause, the president asked: 'The man who was killed in the car bomb – the Ptarmigan man?'

Again, Pudovkin was relieved. 'Yes, sir.'

'He outwitted you.'

'Yes, sir.'

'That's pretty candid,' said the president.

'Thank you, sir.'

There was another pause.

'Is *that* why you had Straker killed, then?' the president asked him.

'I didn't kill him, sir.'

'Who the fuck did, then? Was it you, Gazdanov?'

'*No* … Mr President.'

'If neither of you two clowns bumped Straker and this lawyer off, then who the hell did?'

The silence in the office was broken only by the tick from the movement of a Fabergé clock egg on the mantelpiece.

Gazdanov finally said: 'What about our friend?'

The president's expression changed in a heartbeat. He rose straight to his feet. 'The death of this lawyer changes everything,' he snapped. 'CNN is likening her death to those of Sergei Magnitsky, Anna Politkovskaya, Alexandro Litvinenko and Boris Nemtsov. And, *now*, we have the defence lawyer – in your trial – saying he'll call Mayor Pavlova as a witness. This is a total fuck-up. Leave me,' he said, and gave them a dismissive wave of his hand.

The two men turned to go.

Just as Pudovkin neared the door, though, he was to be hit with another surprise.

The president said: 'Oh, Colonel Pudovkin, I want an *immediate* investigation into the deaths of this lawyer and Colonel Straker. You are to find out who was responsible. Liaise directly with my chief of staff. Have something to tell me within twenty-four hours.'

SIXTY-NINE

The prosecutor general had clearly tried to shaft him during the meeting with the president – nevertheless Pudovkin fully expected Gazdanov to savage him for having challenged the integrity of the trial. As they left, Pudovkin braced himself, ready for Gazdanov to throw a fit, even to fire him on the spot.

Disconcertingly, the prosecutor general said nothing as they were escorted back down through the Senate building to their car.

Gazdanov strode on ahead.

Climbed straight in.

And drove off.

He ended up saying nothing to Pudovkin.

The bemused policeman was left standing in the Kremlin car park. He might have been worried by Gazdanov's silence, were it not for his new assignment – delegated by the president himself, no less – to investigate the deaths of Straker and McMahon. Maybe the magnitude of that commission had been enough to spare Pudovkin the prosecutor's wrath.

The trial wasn't due to resume until nine o'clock the following morning, so Pudovkin set about heading back to Police HQ in Petrovka 38 – to make an immediate start on his new and unexpected task. He walked out of the Kremlin – through the gate under the Spasskaya Tower – into Red Square, emerging directly opposite St Basil's Cathedral.

As he thought about it, Pudovkin realized the irony of the situation. He was now being asked to avenge the deaths of Matt Straker and Sandy McMahon – the very people who had recently caused him so much embarrassment. Except that, now, he felt he might be pursuing their killers for reasons more to do with politics than justice.

Back in his offices, Pudovkin primed himself with a triple espresso, shut the door of his room, and settled in behind his desk.

Where the hell did he begin?

He considered what he might have to go on. He quickly concluded it wasn't promising. He kept reminding himself, though, that even a thousand-mile journey started with a single step.

So what could possibly *be* his first step?

Pudovkin began jotting down anything he could think of: the nature of the bomb blast, how it might have been orchestrated, what happened to the car and the people in it. He was aware that forensics worked with the smallest traces these days; maybe there was something in the wreckage that could be examined? Pudovkin then thought about the footage he had seen on television in the various news bulletins before the State had censored them.

He quickly realized he was going to need help; he put out a call to the two detachment commanders he had deployed during the earlier elements of the Grand Prix case.

Police Majors Ustinov and Kuprin joined him within ten minutes.

Pudovkin asked for his office door to be shut. 'There's a shit storm brewing over the Grand Prix trial,' he told them.

Ustinov looked sheepish, particularly after the breach of Mrs Baryshnikov's house arrest.

'The president has put me in charge of finding out who killed Colonel Straker and the Brandeis lawyer, Sandy McMahon.'

Their expressions changed in an instant.

'We don't have much to go on,' Pudovkin stated. 'Major Ustinov, I want you to liaise with the scene of crime officer at the bomb site – the duty officer's desk here in Police HQ should be able to tell you who was involved. Those at the scene must have retrieved whatever was left of the car and its occupants. Requisition it all. We need to have everything analyzed.'

'Right, sir. Where do you want it brought?'

'I'll let you know. Major Kuprin? The footage of the bomb blast: there were clips shown in the early news bulletins that looked like CCTV footage. I want that tracked down, and any other coverage. Bring it all in.'

'Yes sir.'

'Right, then. Let's get on with it. We have an opportunity here to rectify our standing, which has been damaged by the problems with this mission so far. Don't let's waste it.'

As his energized lieutenants walked out with their latest assignments, Pudovkin reached into his desk drawer and rooted for a small address book. He turned to "F" for Forensics. Leaning over to his desk phone, he punched out the number for Professor Igor Sorokin at the Russian Federal Centre of Forensic Science of the Ministry of Justice.

The call was answered.

Pudovkin re-introduced himself and explained the case he was working on, specifically stating on whose authority he was now acting. He got the director's attention. 'I saw the footage of that explosion on the TV news,' said Sorokin.

'Professor, can you help me with something? How much explosive would be needed to kill the three people in that car – if there was one in the front and two in the back?'

'Nothing like the amount used in that blast.'

'That's what I had kind of thought. Can you give me a sense of scale, though? How much *should* have been needed?'

'It depends entirely, I'm afraid, on the materials used,' said the professor. 'It would, almost invariably, have been RDX-based, otherwise known as hexogen – dubbed "plastic" explosive in everyday speak. That sort of material can be used with a large number of variables: it can be mixed with other explosives, such as PETN. There are further variables involved in the composition, such as which oils are used, et cetera. All of these can have a bearing on the power of the bomb. But, to answer your question: in practice, half a kilo of explosive, at most, would easily kill the occupants.'

'And what would that do to the car?'

'Make a mess of it. There'd be no windows, no soft remains, it would certainly catch fire.'

'But what *would* be left of it?'

'A fair amount: there'd be a frame and chassis – wheels, probably – everything, though, would be damaged.'

'But there *would* still be a shell – a carcass?'

'Oh, without question.'

'So how much would you say was used in the explosion on that bridge, then?'

'With what little was left of the car after that blast, not forgetting the hole it punched through the structure of the bridge? Fifty to seventy-five kilograms?'

'Christ, as much as that? Why would someone use so much more than necessary?'

'Because they didn't know what they were doing, and just over-egged it…'

'Oh I think we are dealing with people who knew *exactly* what they were doing. What if the size of the blast was for effect? I assume you've seen hits overdone simply to make a point?'

'Anything's possible. Except a small blast would still produce a sensational outcome, producing enough of a statement by the per-petrator – particularly where it happened – on that bridge; it was highly theatrical. I think it's much more likely your perpetrators made it as large as that for an entirely different reason.'

'Which was?'

'To remove all evidence of the bomb. The less that's left, the lower the chance of forensic identification. From what's left behind after a blast we can normally trace the type, source and consignment of the material. Then, by determining the proportions used in the mix, we can even read the signature of the bomb maker.'

'So how much residue would you need to glean any of this infor-mation? What sort of quantity?'

'Something the size of a golf ball would be enough.'

'I'm not sure how much residue would have been left after that blast,' he said. 'If I could get you a trace, would you be able analyze it?'

'Sure.'

'Thanks, professor. I'll get whatever we can sent over to you straight away.'

Pudovkin rang Police Major Ustinov. 'When you get hold of the SOCO for the bomb blast, I need to know how much residue from the bomb itself was recovered.'

'Right.'

'Then, send whatever you collect immediately to the Russian Federal Centre of Forensic Science in Khokhlovskiy Pereulok, marked for the attention of the director, Professor Igor Sorokin. I'll send you a text with the details.'

'Okay, boss.'

Pudovkin was feeling slightly less daunted by his task now that he had taken what he hoped might be his first tentative step in trying to source some evidence. Forensics were only one possible line to ID the perpetrators, of course. Pudovkin then thought: what about investigating this from the other end? What about looking for the motive? Who could have wanted the lawyer McMahon and Colonel Straker taken out?

Pudovkin quickly felt this line of approach could become far too nebulous; he would much prefer to deal in hard fact. Much better to work *back* from the evidence, once he had found the smoking gun – to find the motive.

Even so, the question was: Who could have wanted Straker and McMahon killed?

Pudovkin didn't know where to start.

Very unexpectedly a word popped into his head: he remembered Gazdanov repeating the need to have Straker "stopped" – during the times they had been discussing the man's unwanted actions in the case. But had that word been meant in that way? The prosecutor general was showing a fanatical approach to this trial, indicating a readiness to distort normal procedures. Could Gazdanov be too heavily invested in the case? Despite these musings, Pudovkin struggled to see the country's top law enforcer as a suspect; not least as his suspicions seemed based entirely on interpreting Gazdanov's use of the word "stopped".

Who else could be a suspect?

Pudovkin thought about the deaths at the Grand Prix. A grieving relative of a dead spectator? They might kill Straker and McMahon to ensure the accused were prosecuted with as little interruption as possible. But that was a pretty indirect way of ensuring a conviction.

What if the theatrics of the hit were meant to be seen as a signal – to the judges, perhaps? *This is what awaits you if the wrong judgment is made.* Somehow, Pudovkin didn't feel that was convincing, either.

Then he had another thought.

One that soon filled him with dread.

It came from the oblique reference Gazdanov had made during their meeting with the president – when they'd been questioned about who they thought was the perpetrator.

The prosecutor general had made that veiled reference to "our friend".

Did Gazdanov mean what Pudovkin now feared he meant?

Everyone in government service had heard the stories, about the malignant, corrupting presence. Gazdanov had even mentioned the man's name when they were discussing Deputy Vladimir Kosygin and what that wretched politician had revealed while in the Butyrka Prison.

The man in question was Vadim Kondratiev.

Could it possibly be that *he* was "our friend"?

Furthermore, hadn't Baryshnikov even mentioned the man's name in the witness box as a disruptive influence during the development of the Zhar-ptitsa Autodrom?

What, then, would have been Kondratiev's motive?

Straker and McMahon had been crawling all over the Grand Prix case, popping up here and there, getting in the way. Would any of that interference have been enough to provoke Vadim Kondratiev?

It wasn't impossible. Pudovkin couldn't rule it out.

Particularly when he linked everything back to the method of dispatch – to that spectacular bomb blast. Urban legend would easily have Kondratiev behind a hit like that: a vast vanity statement. A car bomb on the Moskvoretsky Bridge, smack in the middle of iconic Moscow? It all seemed right up Kondratiev's alley.

Pudovkin uttered 'Oh shit' aloud to his empty office.

Even *thinking* about Vadim Kondratiev as a suspect made Pudovkin nervous – let alone the prospect of actually having to investigate him. To the police colonel's knowledge, no one had ever got close to investigating the man before – not successfully, at any rate. The last two to try had each paid a heavy price: Messrs Magnitsky and Nemtsov.

Christ, thought Pudovkin.

Do I really want to start bandying around any sort of accusation?

The rumours alone were troubling. Most of them had Kondratiev down as exceptionally dangerous – a brutal, vicious thug. Who knew what reprisals could be possible if word got out that he had even considered him as a suspect?

Pudovkin was desperate to draw a conclusion that Kondratiev *couldn't* have had anything to do with the bombing.

In an effort to be methodical, he set about stress-testing his suspicions. First, the police colonel needed to challenge whether Kondratiev would have known about the court case.

How could he not?

Why else would Kondratiev have picked up Kosygin, taken him to Butyrka Prison – and paid him one of his late-night visits. Straker's interest in tracing the money behind the Autodrom would have clearly indicated the Britisher's danger to the prosecution. How, then, could Kondratiev have known about Straker's movements? Would the crime boss have had Straker watched? Certainly not impossible, but how could Pudovkin ever know for sure? His own surveillance teams had not mentioned being aware of other watchers during their surveillance. But then Pudovkin grimaced: who knew what secretive or specialist units Kondratiev or the FSB operated or could call upon? Would his own policemen and their techniques have been good enough to spot the sort of men from the shadows that Kondratiev could deploy? The idea that Kondratiev had arranged to have Straker watched and followed was, clearly, not impossible.

Could Kondratiev have bugged Straker's room, car, office or phone to keep tabs on him? Perfectly easily. Except Pudovkin could have no way of knowing whether he had done that, either.

A related thought then struck him.

What had Gazdanov said about Straker giving his police watchers the slip on his way to Helsinki? Hadn't Gazdanov told him that Straker had ordered a taxi to pick him up from a side entrance of his hotel? How the hell had Gazdanov known *that*? Didn't that mean someone *had* bugged Straker's room or phone? Again, instigating that kind of surveillance would represent little challenge to Kondratiev. But if it was Kondratiev, how did *Gazdanov* come to know what Straker was up to? Didn't that tie Gazdanov to Kondratiev in some way?

Oh crap, thought Pudovkin. How murky *is* this?

Even if Kondratiev hadn't tailed Straker, Pudovkin considered the likelihood of the man having informers within any of the organizations that Straker had visited. Would Kondratiev have a big enough network of sources to build up a picture of Straker and McMahon's movements that way? Of course he could; after all, Pudovkin had used the exact same technique himself to run a mole inside one of those organizations. Pudovkin went through what he knew of Straker's contacts and whereabouts: Ptarmigan, the firm of solicitors, the hotel he was staying at, the hospital where Sabatino was being treated and the meeting with Kosygin. Finally, there was Straker's meeting at City Hall.

Pudovkin rang his former mole inside Brandeis, Anatoly

Pokrovsky. 'Come and see me next week,' said the police colonel to the sacked middle-aged lawyer. 'I'm sorry for the trouble I've got you into. I'll set up a meeting with our legal department here in the police force: see if we can't put matters right?'

'Thank you, Mr Pudovkin.'

'Least I can do. Tell me something else, though, would you? Was there any sense at Brandeis of an influence from Vadim Kondratiev?'

The phone suddenly went silent.

Not an uncommon reaction when the man's name was mentioned.

After a pause, the legal analyst said: 'I heard some talk of protection money, *krysha*, several times. But nothing specific.'

'And that was generally thought to be connected to Kondratiev?'

'Yes.'

'But there was no other involvement that you heard about between Kondratiev and Brandeis Gertner?'

'Not that I know of.'

Pudovkin groaned. That was hardly conclusive.

Pudovkin moved on to the next – and possibly last – of Straker's interactions: Straker's and McMahon's private audience with the mayor of Moscow. If that hadn't alerted Kondratiev to Straker's rate of progress, Pudovkin wondered, what would have?

The police colonel soon realized that even this flimsy line of thinking had left him both blessed and cursed. His attempts to stress-test his hunch that Vadim Kondratiev might have been involved in the car bomb was a long way from being scientific, but these "deductions" made Pudovkin curse for an entirely different reason. Nothing in his flimsy challenges had come remotely close to *dispelling* the basis of that hunch, either.

Oh fuck, thought Pudovkin.

I can't rule out Vadim Kondratiev as a suspect for the car bomb, after all.

SEVENTY

Pudovkin needed another cup of coffee and some fresh air to calm himself. He took a troubled leg stretch along Petrovka Ulitsa. How the hell could he make any sort of enquiries into Kondratiev, when the man's presence was ubiquitous? Any indication of Pudovkin's enquiry taking that direction could easily land him in deeply unpleasant trouble.

Before Pudovkin had even thought of a way forward, he received a call from Police Major Kuprin.

'Colonel, I've just sent you the CCTV footage of the car bomb you wanted.'

Pudovkin picked up his pace, walking straight back to Police HQ. 'Good work, Mikael – well done for tracking that down.'

'After its first airing on the morning of the blast, it was then blacked out. I had to get it from abroad, from a friend of mine in the diplomatic service with uncensored access to the web. The footage had something like 35 million hits. I've managed to source a copy of the original. *Fox News* had it.'

'You're kidding?' replied Pudovkin. 'How the hell did *they* have the original?'

'You'd have thought it would have been one of the local TV stations or news outlets, wouldn't you? I've also found some clips of the initial news bulletin on *Russia-1* – before they too were censored, just in case they might be of help?'

'Thank you.'

'By the way,' added Police Major Kuprin, 'I still have all the pictures we snapped of Straker and McMahon on their travels round Moscow.'

Pudovkin asked: 'Are they likely to be of any use? You haven't mentioned anything significant in them before?'

'I guess that depends on what you're looking for, now.'

'Good point. I'd better take a look. Send them over too, would you?'

Pudovkin arrived back at his desk and set about rewatching the CCTV clip of the car bomb.

Its footage of the explosion was no less sensational than the first time he'd seen it on the television news.

A slightly grainy shot, in black and white. Shown in a CCTV-like format.

An empty bridge.

The car emerging from the top right.

And then – *kaboom* – the explosion going off smack bang in the middle of the screen.

Pudovkin ran it again and again, trying to see if there was anything about it that could tell him anything new.

Nothing.

He switched to the international bulletin within which it had been first broadcast. An attractive newsreader was projecting directly into the camera, announcing the bomb – and the names of the people killed – almost as if they were nominees for a set of film awards. Soon came the portraits Pudovkin remembered of Colonel Straker, in military uniform, and the elegant face of Sandy McMahon.

Pudovkin suddenly noticed something.

Something he ought to have thought about before, except that the eye too readily accepts what it sees in a moving image for whatever it appears to be. Pudovkin's attention drifted to the bottom left-hand corner of the screen – to the digital clock above the channel's logo. It was showing: 9:15 p.m. – where, though: presumably somewhere in America?

That suddenly triggered a series of thoughts about timings. And then about logistics.

He checked the time code and date on the original CCTV footage of the blast. It *did* tally with what he remembered. It had been that early in the morning. The explosion on the bridge was clocked at 00:21 a.m. Moscow time.

Just to be sure, Pudovkin ran through the clip of the subsequently censored press conference given by the mayor. He remembered it being very early in the day, having drawn Gazdanov's attention to it while they'd been on the telephone with each other. Pudovkin found not only the date but, more significantly, the time of the mayor's press conference – 6:00 a.m. – that same morning.

Pudovkin hadn't been wrong.

It all tallied.

What the hell was he to make of this? What was his conclusion? It was this, wasn't it: the news dissemination of the blast had been *fantastically* quick…

How had that happened?

The bomb had gone off in the middle of the night. And yet, fewer than five hours later – during the dog hours of the night – *Fox News* had managed to secure the CCTV footage, as well as source a formal portrait of the two occupants killed in the blast *and* they had procured more than headline biographies of both Straker and McMahon.

Then Pudovkin realized that this was not the only indication of extraordinarily fast news dissemination.

What about the mayor of Moscow? How quickly had *she* been informed? In the same limited timeframe, *she* had managed to call a press conference – with enough advance warning to ensure that all the press and TV were there – *and* she'd managed to have enough material to present her own statement, live, at six o'clock that same morning.

How could all of this news have been gathered – and all the journalists been present – *that* quickly?

Pudovkin's pulse was now racing.

Questions were bouncing round his head. How had the mayor of Moscow been so prepared? Didn't that indicate that she must have known in advance?

Couldn't that mean, then, that the mayor was connected in some way to the perpetrators?

SEVENTY-ONE

Pudovkin was so engrossed that he flinched when one of his phones rang. It was the one on his desk.

'Colonel Pudovkin? Igor Sorokin at the Forensic Service,' said the director of the RFCFS. 'Just to let you know, we've received the samples of residue from the site of the explosion. I gather you were concerned about the quantity available. I'm pleased to say we should have enough for our programme of testing: we've got about a tennis-ball's worth. It's ready to be examined.'

'That's good news, professor.'

'You might like to know that we've also been sent a reasonable sample of blood recovered from the road beside the car. There's not much point in running a DNA test, though, unless we have data records to match it against.'

'We do know who was on board,' said Pudovkin. 'But I guess it wouldn't hurt to confirm it.'

'What about comparative DNA records or samples – do you have any of those?'

Pudovkin thought. 'I might just have. If I do, I'll send them over. By the way, professor, how long will it take you to run all your tests?'

'A day or two.'

'That's too long. I need to speed this up.'

'I could do it in a matter of hours, but I'd have to deprioritize other work already in hand. Without being difficult, that's only possible with some meaty authorization.'

'Consider it given,' said the police colonel busking his response. 'I'll let you have whatever permission you need to accelerate these tests. Expect to hear confirmation from me within the hour. If you haven't within that time, please feel free to put everything on hold.'

Professor Sorokin seemed impressed. 'I'll hear from you shortly, then.'

Having been so liberal with his authority, Pudovkin now wondered how on earth he could deliver on his undertaking. He realized he had to take a long shot. Telephoning the Kremlin, he didn't really know who to ask for. He asked for the office of the president's chief of staff, feeling ridiculous even as he said it. To his amazement his call was patched straight through.

And answered.

Pudovkin explained that he needed to authorize the analysis of the explosive residue recovered from the site of the blast. To Pudovkin's further amazement he was told his request would be granted within the hour. He replaced the receiver of his phone barely able to comprehend the access he was being granted.

Expectations on him were clearly extraordinarily high.

Police Colonel Pudovkin needed to pick up on a loose end. Telephoning Major Ustinov, he updated his subordinate on progress at the forensics laboratory. 'I gather the SOCO had a blood sample from the blast site? We need a match, though, for confirmation. Can you do something on that? Get over to Hotel Baltschug Kempinski. Get into Straker's room and try and lift a DNA sample from his bathroom – hairbrush, or whatever.'

'Right, boss.'

'If you manage to find something, get whatever it is over to the RFCFS forensic lab as quickly as you can.'

Ustinov sounded as if he was already on his way.

Police Colonel Pudovkin saw that his other Police Major – Kuprin – had sent through the batch of photographs his watchers had taken while trailing Straker and McMahon round Moscow.

There were in excess of three hundred shots.

For two hours Pudovkin clicked through all of the pictures. He was desperate to find a way of prioritizing them. Which of these photographs, he wondered, could have any significance? As he rethought this, he cursed his brain once again – for not picking up on things sooner.

Pudovkin found himself looking at the snatched shots of the mysterious visit Straker and McMahon had made to City Hall. For that visit, they had switched from their earlier Brandeis car – and hidden in the back of an unmarked van. If Straker's behaviour meant anything, it had to mean he *knew* he was being watched, didn't it? Meaning that Straker did not want their meeting at City Hall to be noticed.

Why?

Pudovkin dived back into the pictures, carving out those of Straker's visit to City Hall. There were thirty-odd shots of it, apparently snatched by a long focal-length lens from a fair way down the side street. It all looked pretty clandestine ... and strange. Straker and the Brandeis lawyer were being smuggled in through a delivery entrance *... to visit the mayor of Moscow ...*

Why would Straker have gone to such extraordinary lengths?

With the camera's distance from the subject, the length of the lens it required caused most of the images to be grainy, more frequently out of focus and occasionally even blurred. Even so, he was readily able to recognize the subjects via the overall sequence.

Pudovkin studied each shot, trying to glean anything – willing them to reveal something.

Then something clicked.

Pudovkin was looking, again, at the second half of the City Hall batch.

These photographs showed Straker and McMahon at the time of leaving, surreptitiously via the same delivery entrance. It looked as if they were being escorted to the door by someone from inside the building. A woman. Who was that, then? Firing off an email, he attached one of the photographs and asked Major Kuprin to follow it up – to see if this unknown woman could be identified.

Then something else, which he felt he should have seen much earlier, also finally popped. It happened at the point when the sequence skipped from the last picture of them arriving at City Hall to the first shot of them leaving.

How had he *not* spotted this before?

When Straker and McMahon were leaving, it was just the two of them – accompanied by this unknown woman from inside. Hurriedly, Pudovkin scrolled back to the sequence which showed them arriving. He suddenly spotted the anomaly, realizing that there had been *three* of them going in. How had he missed the third person? Had he confused that individual with the driver of the van or with a passer-by, perhaps? No, that third person was *definitely* part of the Brandeis party. The individual had got out of the back of the van with Straker and McMahon. Pudovkin shuffled quickly through the other pictures of their arrival, to try and find the clearest shot of this third person. Enlarging a segment of one photograph, Pudovkin could see a shortish man, with a closely shaven head, wearing a preponderance of pastel-coloured clothes. Who the hell was that? Much more importantly, why hadn't this man left at the same time as Straker and McMahon?

Why had this man stayed *behind* in City Hall?

Pudovkin could only force his concentration for so long. He realized he was already missing things. He decided he had to sleep and, so finally, went home.

Rising early the next morning, the first thing he did was check the television news. There was absolutely nothing being broadcast about the Grand Prix trial – on any of the channels or even on the radio.

Pudovkin put a call through to Gazdanov's office to see if there were any last-minute instructions before they left for court. Instead, he was told by the office that the prosecutor general was not there.

He tried Gazdanov's mobile.

Voicemail only.

Where was the prosecutor general?

SEVENTY-TWO

Police Colonel Pudovkin entered the Supreme Court building shortly after seven thirty that morning and made his way to his usual place. He was in his seat on the concentric bench by a quarter to eight. He looked around the courtroom. Everyone there seemed to be waiting with obvious anticipation, except the space felt different. Then Pudovkin realized why. There were no media present that morning – no cameras down the far-side wall.

At five minutes to nine, a door opened at the front of the courtroom and Oscar Brogan QC, the British defence counsel, appeared wearing his wig and gown. This, thought Pudovkin, must be the man returning from the eight o'clock conference of the barristers called by the judges. Brogan was accompanied by another man wearing the pale blue uniform of the Prosecution Service, whom Pudovkin did not recognize. This man walked on into the courtroom and sat down directly in front of Pudovkin, where Gazdanov had been sitting earlier in the trial.

Where was the prosecutor general?

At one minute to nine a court official appeared through the same door and, taking up station, announced the opening of the session, instructing the room to stand.

Pudovkin watched the three judges take their seats in the row of thrones. As they lowered themselves into the grand chairs, a nod was given by the middle judge. Another call echoed around the red oak panels of the courtroom summoning the accused.

The two Ptarmigan officials were shuffled into court. And, once again, the slamming of the steel door reverberated around the room as they were locked into the cage.

The court fell silent.

Pudovkin could still see no sign of the prosecutor general.

The senior judge announced: 'Mr Brogan.'

The British barrister rose to his feet. 'My Lords,' he said.

'Mr Brogan, I declare to you and your clients – by which I mean Ptarmigan, as a corporation, Mr Nazar and Ms Sabatino – that the prosecution in this case has filed with us this morning a Notice of Discontinuance.'

Pudovkin exhaled.

Not everyone in the room, and certainly not the accused, was familiar with the full meaning of the phrase. Pudovkin looked around to see *how* this news was being taken. If it were taken badly, he feared a backlash of public opinion against the Russian State. The public might suddenly realize that *no one* was being held to account for the thirty-four deaths at the Moscow Grand Prix.

Finally, the meaning was explained to the Ptarmigan prisoners. A yelp was heard from Nazar, while Pudovkin also saw Sabatino break down, weeping uncontrollably.

The noise continued in the room, intensifying as everyone caught up with the meaning of the announcement.

The State's prosecution had been dropped.

The trial was over.

Oscar Brogan was still on his feet. He had attended the eight o'clock conference with the judges where this must have been discussed; the discontinuance could not have been news to him. There was, though, a concerned look on the barrister's face.

'My Lords,' he called, but was completely drowned out.

A gavel bang sounded out repeatedly around the room. The court official called for order. Eventually, the room heeded the instructions.

'My Lords,' repeated the defence barrister in a tone that again surprised Pudovkin, 'my clients and I are mindful that the people of Moscow are still mourning the loss of their comrades in the accident at the Grand Prix. It is hard for us, therefore, to applaud Russian justice for acknowledging that my clients were not to blame for the tragedy. I am nevertheless anxious, my Lords, to secure for my clients an unequivocal and full release from any ongoing legal responsibility in this matter, enabling that they may not only be released immediately but that they also be free to leave the country.'

Pudovkin saw Mr Brogan sit down.

The senior judge, without conferring with his colleagues, answered without hesitation: 'Yes, Mr Brogan. Your clients are fully discharged from the Russian legal process and are free to leave Russia.'

A wall of police officers quickly formed around the cage, as protection against any kind of vigilantism from anyone who might take exception – either to the prosecution's capitulation or to the judges' ruling.

The prisoners were then released from their cage.

Once the chains had been removed, Nazar and Sabatino hugged each other at length – as much as the halo brace would allow.

Pudovkin watched as, in no time at all, the two Ptarmigan officials were spirited out through a side door of the courtroom and into the back of the building.

SEVENTY-THREE

Police Colonel Pudovkin left the Supreme Court shortly afterwards. Had a wrong outcome been avoided? If not, why did he feel a sense of relief?

His relief, though, didn't last long.

Pudovkin started mulling over everything to do with the case, especially the extraordinary experience of meeting the president. He now realized the significance to him of the car bomb. If the explosion and deaths hadn't unnerved the president, Gazdanov would never have been summoned to the Kremlin. Without that meeting, Gazdanov would never have taken Pudovkin along as his prospective scapegoat. Without the consequences of the car bomb, therefore, Pudovkin realized he would not have had been brought to the president's attention. But that, now, might yet come at a price: with the Grand Prix trial having collapsed, expectations in avenging the thirty-four deaths could only turn on him. All that was left of the State's response to the tragedy was his own investigation into the perpetrators of the car bomb. There were no other distractions. Pudovkin had every expectation of the president chasing him imminently for news of his progress.

While walking back to his office, along "Embassy Row" in Povarskaya Ulitsa, Pudovkin heard a call to his mobile. He looked down at his phone. It showed no caller ID. When he answered it, though, he somehow knew instantly who it was.

'Mr President,' he said.

Pudovkin was anxious. He had no concrete news to give him on the investigation. Hoping to pre-empt, he blurted out: 'Why did you halt the trial, Mr President?'

Pudovkin then held his breath, fully expecting to be shouted down.

To his surprise and relief, the president replied in a measured tone: 'We have separation of powers in Russia, this was a judicial decision.'

Pudovkin raised his eyebrows. 'Of course, sir.'

There was a pause.

'The *judiciary's* view,' said the president, 'was that the trial had lost its way. You'd lost your pivotal witness. Then, the deaths of the defence lawyer – McMahon, was it? – and this Colonel Straker were attracting damaging publicity internationally.'

'It wasn't anything to do with the Ptarmigan lawyer calling the mayor of Moscow to testify in the trial, then?'

'The defence calling her as a witness,' the president scoffed, 'would have been completely unnecessary for the trial. It would have added nothing to the evidence. Pavlova, though, would have been given a platform, enabling her to play on the international outrage at the death of *another* Russian professional asking questions about the State. She would have made up a load of crap about the State's opposition to critics – and perhaps, justifiably, ridiculed the prosecution's attempt to extort a witness by taking his mother hostage. The stage would have been perfect for Pavlova – all the more prominent being in the Supreme Court – to sound off about the failures of Russia's legal system. The world's media would have lapped up every salacious word and accusation. American politicians and the self-styled geopolitical experts on CNN were already bullshitting on about Russia reverting to its Cold War attributes, reverting to a communist-style oppression of civil liberties – and insisting that the US should increase its sanctions against us. *Fox News* were going even further in their coverage of this case and trial. No, Colonel Pudovkin, Oksana Pavlova being called as a witness would have been a catastrophe ... At least,' added the president hurriedly, '... that's what I'm told the judiciary thought.'

Pudovkin was staggered: Why was the president opening up to him like this? Not wanting to push it any further, and anxious to prevent the president from feeling he might already have divulged too much, Pudovkin again decided to pre-empt: 'I am making some progress in investigating the car bomb, sir,' he said with as much confidence as he could manage. 'I'm chasing several leads.'

But the president didn't ask any questions about that.

Instead, he replied: 'Keep me posted. In the meantime, I want you to do something for me. Something controversial.'

Pudovkin's heart missed a beat. *Here we go*, he thought. *You get in close to the centre of power, and before long the price they exact from you is control of your soul.* Despite the pressures of this conversation, Pudovkin found the presence of mind to think clearly. He was not prepared to play under all conditions. Almost to his own surprise, he found himself saying: 'That depends, Mr President.'

The president went on to explain the task.

Pudovkin listened with growing astonishment.

How should he respond to that?

Despite the momentousness of this conversation, Pudovkin did manage to voice one response:

'I'd like written authorization, please, Mr President.'

Within an hour, Police Colonel Pudovkin had gathered his men together. Present with him were his two lieutenants: Police Majors Kuprin and Ustinov. This time they were on the pavement of Bolshaya Dmitrovka Ulitsa, right in the heart of institutional Moscow. After confirming the orders he had already issued inside Moscow Police HQ, Pudovkin led his men into their next task.

His posse strode as a group towards the main entrance of the building. Without impediment, they made their way up through the office block. Within two minutes the police colonel was entering the same room he had visited numerous times during the preparation for the trial.

'Léon Andreiovich Gazdanov,' he declared, 'I am arresting you on the orders of the president of Russia. I have here the necessary papers and warrant for your arrest.'

After such a high-profile act of service in the name of the president, Pudovkin felt slightly deflated returning to his investigation into finding those responsible for the Brandeis car bomb. But his fear of antagonizing Kondratiev prompted him to concentrate. Once back at his desk, he fired up his iPad.

There were several emails from both his Police Majors. Major Ustinov had visited Straker's hotel, barged his way into the dead man's suite and managed to recover items that he hoped would hold some of his DNA.

I found a comb, a wet-shave razor and a toothbrush. All three items have been sent to the RFCFS forensic laboratories, hopefully to be matched with the blood found at the blast site on the bridge.

Pudovkin was pleased.

Next, there were a couple of emails from his other police major, Major Kuprin; he, too, seemed to have delivered. He was sending through information he had discovered about the City Hall employee who had been photographed clandestinely escorting Sandy McMahon and Colonel Straker out of the building after their meeting with the mayor.

The person in the pictures has been identified. I have had this con-firmed by another source. She is Natalia Brassova, the mayor's PR director. Hope that helps?

Pudovkin shook his head and shrugged. 'What the hell use is that?' he asked his empty office.

Then there were two emails from Professor Sorokin. The first reported that the Federal Forensic Science laboratories had managed to recover good DNA samples from Straker's wet-shave razor and that, yes, there was a perfect match with the blood recovered from the road at the bomb site. It was Colonel Matt Straker's, all right. There were two other blood samples found on the bridge, but they had no match for those. One of them, though, was definitely a female.

The second – much longer – email from the professor laid out his findings on the explosive residue found at the bomb site. Pudovkin opened the attachment and eagerly read the forensic report. Right up front it stated that the RFCFS had been easily able to identify the types of explosive that had been used. They didn't mean anything to Pudovkin. As further detail was given, Sorokin had gone to considerable lengths to remark on the unusual inclusion of polyisobutylene and di(2-ethylhexyl)sebacate, identified in turn as the binding agent and plasticizer – whatever the hell that meant. Given the obvious sophistication involved, though, Pudovkin began to get a feeling.

Finally, the professor had got round to naming the manufacturer.

The answer was completely unexpected.

How could that *be*? It didn't make any sense …

Except Professor Sorokin seemed unequivocal – emphatic in his findings.

Pudovkin tried to think past the shock. How *could* that be right? After thinking about it for ten minutes, though, he thought he saw how it could just be.

Before too long, it was all Pudovkin could do to remain calm.

Maybe it was a reaction to the tension of the trial, the stress of dealing with Gazdanov, and the adrenalin rush of the last few days. But after trying to cope with his reaction to Sorokin's report for a quarter of an hour, Pudovkin finally capitulated.

He had no choice.

He had to let go.

Staff on the open-plan floor all around him – those who could see the police colonel clearly through the glass panels of his office – were astonished to see the normally upright and stern police officer appearing to crack up.

He was howling out loud.

Uncontrollably.

With laughter.

SEVENTY-FOUR

Andy Backhouse had had no prior warning of the Notice of Discontinuance when he turned up to attend the trial in the Supreme Court that morning. The moment he realized which way it was all going, though, he went straight into action – immediately calling a car to Malaya Molchanovka Ulitsa, the smaller road running down the back of the Supreme Court building.

Backhouse was anxious on two levels. Sabatino and Nazar may have been released by the court, but they could still be mobbed – even attacked – when leaving the trial if the public disagreed with the judges. His other concern was a change of mind somewhere in this twisted government, which on past behaviour seemed disturbingly possible. What if the Russians revoked their freedom to leave – putting out an order to re-arrest them?

Backhouse was notified by phone the moment the car had pulled up in the side street. He shepherded the two Ptarmigan personnel as far as the outer doors of the building. Sticking his head out to check up and down both ways, Backhouse opened the door. Nazar and Backhouse – wheeling Sabatino – made a dash across the narrow pavement to the open door of the people carrier.

Raised voices could be heard from the mob crowding around the entrance to the rear courtyard, over to their left.

Terrified of being spotted and set upon, Backhouse and Nazar hurried. They lifted Sabatino from the wheelchair and into the car. Backhouse closed the door on her. At the run, he wheeled the chair back through the doors and pushed it into the Supreme Court building.

Backhouse had stipulated that the car was to have blacked-out windows; the moment the doors were closed, he heaved a sigh of relief. The Ptarmigan "Two" could not now be spotted from the outside.

Pulling straight off, with Backhouse looking over his shoulder and then into the passenger door mirror, the vehicle headed on down the narrow street to reach the T-junction with Bolshoy Rzhevskiy Pereulok. Turning right, they made their way up the second side street edging the Supreme Court complex to reach "Embassy Row".

Backhouse's anxiety rose again as they waited to cross over.

A short distance to their right they could see and hear another crowd agitating outside the front of the building.

Not a moment too soon – for Backhouse – they pulled forwards through a gap in the traffic, turning left before turning immediately right into Malyy Rzhevskiy Pereulok.

Finally, they were out of sight of the mob.

The people carrier accelerated down this one-way street. Several hundred yards later they reached the more arterial road of Bolshaya Nikitskaya Ulitsa. There, turning left, they made to go north-west – away from the centre of Moscow.

Backhouse remained concerned.

What kind of backlash would there be from the public when they realized that nothing was being done to avenge the deaths at the Grand Prix?

He couldn't get out of his mind the threat to the two Ptarmigan accused of being re-arrested.

Backhouse was relieved that they had a covert exit all lined up, even though it was going to be a slog.

Against every expectation in the build-up to the trial, Nazar and Sabatino were free. Having been kept apart for the last four weeks, they seemed too shocked to say anything now that they found themselves back together again.

Finally, Sabatino asked Backhouse: 'Andy, is it true about Matt – and the Russian lawyer?'

Backhouse's face fell slowly.

Sabatino couldn't hold back. Tears ran again, but this time with much greater intensity. Everyone in the car was affected with sadness, made all the more intense as it conflicted with their sense of relief. After everything they had been subjected to during the last few weeks, their emotions were utterly raw.

It took eight hours for the people carrier to reach the outskirts of Saint Petersburg. Instead of heading for the golden domes and spires of the ancient capital, the escapees entered an area of old and seedy-looking docks. Backhouse was soon on edge, as if he was looking for something. Rounding a warehouse, they drove beneath a vast rail-borne crane. He sighed with relief. Up ahead, berthed alongside the dilapidated quayside, was a black motor yacht that appeared to blend effortlessly with the tired, industrial, grey-field backdrop of the docklands.

Backhouse paid off the cab. He and Nazar lifted Sabatino out of the car and carried her aboard the Hunton XRS43. As the powerboat's lines were slipped, there was a growl from the bow thruster as the vessel was nudged laterally away from the harbour wall. White water burbled to her stern, the helm pushing forward on the throttles – engaging the two 662 horsepower Mercury diesels. At the frustrating speed limit of 6 knots, the Hunton made her way impatiently to the entrance of the harbour.

Once out in open water, the helm pushed fully forward on the throttles. Both engines spooled up to full revs. One hundred yards from the mouth of the harbour, the Hunton was already up on the plane. Across the calm waters of Saint Petersburg harbour, the 43-foot motor yacht was soon doing over 35 knots. Savouring the breeze, the Ptarmigan escapees looked back at the receding baroque skyline of Saint Petersburg, just catching the late afternoon sun.

Still the Hunton powered on.

The smooth, still surface enabled the helm to maintain both engines at full throttle. In a short while they passed Kotlin Island, and shot the bridge through the Saint Petersburg Dam – letting them out into the Gulf of Finland. The helm nudged forward on the throttles again, to make sure they were fully open as they headed on out to sea.

Thirty minutes passed. The skipper turned and gave Backhouse a confirmatory nod. The race engineer reached down, pulled out a bottle of champagne and made the announcement with a pop from the cork. 'We've just this minute passed the Estonian border – and are, now, safely in international waters. Friends,' he declared loudly, 'we are *out* of fucking Russia.'

At this distance from the shore, the surface of the water was showing a little more energy. While only modest, there was the beginning of a small swell. Easing back their speed to 20 knots, the Hunton settled into a soothing rhythmic motion as she continued to make her way out to sea.

Not long later, they felt the power being significantly reduced. Backhouse stood up and looked out through the long scoping for'ard windscreen of the yacht. Proudly, he announced: '*The Melita*!'

The others got to their feet, too, to take in the sight of the mother ship as they made their approach. Dominic Quartano's 1930s three-hundred-foot-long superyacht was clearly visible. Low sunlight was catching her majestic superstructure and, against the cobalt blue sky and dark waters of the Baltic, she was an eye-catching sight.

Bringing the Hunton down to a walking pace, the helm man-oeuvred the powerboat in alongside. Lines were thrown fore and aft. Moments later a gangplank was lowered. With help from two of her colleagues, one in front and one behind, Sabatino – hesitantly, as her left leg was in plaster and she was still wearing the halo brace – teetered across the gangplank to board *The Melita*. The lines were thrown back to the Hunton. Another growl came from the bow thruster as the pow-erboat traversed away from the yacht. The helm applied power from the engines, as he made his way back to her home port in Finland.

The moment Sabatino was on board, the captain escorted her to the sickbay. Dominic Quartano had arranged for a spinal consultant to be on hand. He was waiting to cross-reference her condition with her scans and to take additional X-rays, using *The Melita's* state-of-the-art medical equipment, if necessary.

Surprisingly her examination took just over an hour.

Following her medical check-up, Sabatino limped into the yacht's art deco saloon; Andy Backhouse and Tahm Nazar were already sitting there in a set of armchairs, each with a flute of champagne in their hands.

Backhouse observed enthusiastically: 'Fantastic, Rems, you've lost the halo brace! Does that mean everything's better than expected?'

Sabatino nodded. 'Dr Uglov, at the hospital in Moscow, was good enough to email through the scans and X-rays he'd taken. Mr Q's spinal guy was convinced Uglov had played it ultra safe. So, thankfully, the brace is no longer required.'

'Wonderful news,' said Backhouse offering to help her sit.

'It's a testament to the robustness of your car, I suppose,' she said as, still sore, she lowered herself down into an armchair, 'that I can go through a crash of that magnitude, survive and come away with only relatively minor injuries. I'm expected to mend physically. But I'll never get over the deaths of thirty-four Russians ... or the loss of Matt.'

It was as if the realization from saying this out loud for the first time finally hit her.

Sabatino's face crumpled.

Tears were soon pouring down her cheeks.

Backhouse offered her a glass of champagne, but she declined with a polite wave of a shaking hand. 'I really don't feel like celebrating.'

'I'm afraid we did all know how bold Matt's strategies could be.'

Sabatino sniffed in response.

Backhouse turned away from her, casting an eye to the end of the room.

At this, the double doors of the saloon opened.

Two figures appeared, silhouetted by the bright evening sunlight behind them. Sabatino was surprised by any new arrivals. Looking up, she was unexpectedly faced with two strangers. And because of the backlighting, she couldn't see them clearly. She squinted hard, her expression soon verging on alarm.

A man with a completely shaven head and large black sunglasses walked forwards, wearing clothes styled somewhere between gothic and grunge. Beside him was a woman with very short, jet-black hair, dramatic raccoon eye make-up, black lipstick and wearing ill-fitting black clothes. Sabatino's brain was screaming. *People don't dress like that around F1 – around Ptarmigan – in a room like this – on a yacht like this.*

The two figures continued into the room.

Sabatino's attention was trained on the man. Bald head … Dark glasses … Gothic clothes. Who the hell was this?

She didn't know where it started.

In a recess of her mind there was the tiniest flash of familiarity. Not with the bald head, she had never seen that before. There was something in the shape of the man's mouth.

Suddenly there was an ear-piercing shriek.

Sabatino, struggling awkwardly, fought to heave herself up and out of the chair. Then, with her leg still in plaster, she shuffled – limping hurriedly – across the silk carpet of the saloon.

Sabatino flung her arms around the man's neck.

The bald man's face broke into a radiant smile as he reached up and removed his dark glasses.

He hugged her close, squeezing her gently, for well over a minute.

Tears were streaming again down Sabatino's cheeks.

Finally, she opened her eyes.

Looking across, she addressed the gothic woman standing next to them who was also smiling broadly. 'You must be the lawyer,' said Sabatino with a catch in her voice as she released Straker and limped across to give Sandy McMahon a long hug too.

'What … the? … What the *fuck*?' was all that Sabatino could say.

SEVENTY-FIVE

Matt Straker finally held out both arms and took a step forwards, encouraging the women to take a seat with the others. Nazar and Backhouse shuffled along to make room for them. Straker was about to sit when a white-tunicked steward appeared in the saloon.

'Please forgive me, everyone, but there's a call for Colonel Straker in the command centre. It's Mr Quartano, sir.'

Straker smiled his apologies to the others: 'I'd better report in,' he said, and followed the steward out of the room.

Another steward approached them with a silver tray. This time, Sabatino did accept a glass of champagne. 'What the *hell's* been going on?' she asked.

Backhouse, sitting across the corner within the nest of chairs, was beaming. 'We've probably witnessed a Straker stratagem at its most audacious,' he declared in broad Brummie.

'Is this a two- or a three-glass story?' asked Sabatino looking at her drink.

'It's a *case* of Moët & Chandon, is what it is.'

Backhouse looked like he couldn't wait to retell their horrific experiences. First off, he described the challenges they'd faced as the Russian institutions denied the access of Ptarmigan's legal representatives.

'So it wasn't just getting access to me that was a problem,' said Nazar.

'No, it wasn't,' replied McMahon. 'Our challenges were compounded, though, by the case being escalated to the Supreme Court, your being prosecuted by the highest law officer in the land and the trial being called within four weeks. Of more concern was the police impounding the wreckage of Ms Sabatino's car and the crash site.'

Backhouse chipped in: 'You were both adamant there had been

nothing wrong with the car. So how had you crashed? We were being denied the chance to examine the wreckage for ourselves, and the telemetry was taking time to gather in and be analyzed. We did look at the video records, though; and something had clearly happened to your car, Rems. So, Matt, being Matt, he felt he had to go and recce the crash site for himself – to see what that could tell him. A lot was the answer. It produced the first proper evidence of sabotage. Matt was even shot at as he made his escape. His discovery, that the circuit had clearly been tampered with, led to questions about the Autodrom – which led us to none other than … Avel Obrenovich.'

'No!' said Sabatino. 'That's not possible.'

Backhouse nodded. 'I'm afraid it was. *He* was the money behind the circuit.'

Nazar took a gulp of champagne. 'So did it mean that that arsehole was also behind the sabotage?'

'No, but unwittingly he probably triggered it. He'd initiated the transfer of the Russian Grand Prix from Sochi to Moscow … for entirely political reasons: to promote Mayor Pavlova as a presidential contender. Doing so upset some pretty powerful figures – the president and his ruthless puppetmaster, Vadim Kondratiev. We found out that, between them, they have direct control of every aspect of government. From that moment on, we knew we were in serious trouble – the trial was going to be nothing less than a sham.

'And then, of course, we had Yegor doing the dirty, turning himself over to the prosecution. From that point on, Baryshnikov would have been able to contradict anything we said. Who, then, would a jury believe? A bunch of foreigners with blood on their hands, or a loyal Russian who had sacrificed his place in a Championship-winning car to reveal the truth? All of this *guaranteed* that the trial was going to be a foregone conclusion … against us.'

'Your hands were completely tied,' offered Nazar to McMahon.

'They were. Early on,' she added sheepishly, 'I was all for respecting the system, and fighting our cause within the legal opportunities of the trial. But, completely against my protests, Matt was adamant that if we did that – and relied solely on that – we were only ever going to lose.'

'How *did* he fight it, then?'

Backhouse smiled. 'This was where we saw Matt's mind go to work. He wanted to chip away at any weakness in the prosecution's assertions – and, most spectacularly, he wanted to destabilize the *politics* behind the case and trial.'

'How the fuck did he think he could do that?' asked Nazar swaying slightly. 'Where the hell would you even *start* with doing that?'

'Straker was convinced – but we didn't see it – that Baryshnikov had been got at.'

'Meaning what?'

'That Baryshnikov was not being himself.'

'You mean smug, egotistical, selfish and a right bastard?' suggested Sabatino.

'Almost precisely,' said Backhouse. 'Matt kept banging on about Yegor's body language during the press conferences, and crap like that. When we looked at the video coverage, of course, Matt had been right: Baryshnikov wasn't being *anything* like his normal self.'

'So?'

'We found out that he was being manipulated. Baryshnikov's mother had effectively been taken hostage – by the police – in order to hold Yegor to ransom.'

'Good God. What did you do then?'

'Matt took on the police at the Baryshnikov house,' said Backhouse. 'Step one, he flew a Quartech drone around the mansion and grounds, building up an intelligence picture of what security arrangements were there, as well as the lie of the land. During that operation, he managed to spot Mrs Baryshnikov at an upstairs window, which did at least confirm that she was inside. He then mounted an attack on the house.'

Backhouse said with a smile: 'You should have seen it, Rems. He kicked it off with a huge explosion – as a shock and diversion.

Matt then released twenty Rottweilers – which he'd sourced from a local security firm – to clear the gardens of any police patrolling the grounds. After they'd been called off, he broke in and made straight for the house's standby generator, which he knocked out. Then he blew the mains power into the property, causing a total power outage.'

'Fantastic,' applauded Sabatino, 'so that's how he got Yegor's mother out?'

Backhouse shook his head. 'No, no, he left her there – which was actually the clever bit. During the attack, he broke in through her bedroom window, and managed to convince her that he was on her side. Matt then briefed her on what she could do to help.'

'Why didn't he get her out, there and then?'

'Because doing that would have told the police immediately how much we knew, and Matt reckoned that it would have made us more of a target. Besides, from a timing point of view, he wanted to get the most out of Yegor being a witness for the prosecution while he was still being manipulated.'

'So what did Matt tell the mother when he broke into her bedroom?'

'He made the most of the situation there, too,' answered McMahon. 'We discovered a key fact about Mrs Baryshnikov: the poor woman suffers from serious kidney trouble. She needs regular dialysis.'

'How did *that* help?'

'On its own, probably wouldn't have done,' replied Backhouse, 'but it was a useful factor for what came later. Matt wanted a coup for the second day of your trial, when we expected Yegor to be called to give evidence. Matt's aim, therefore, had been to release Baryshnikov from being an enforced prosecution witness. The sweetness was that this happened *while* he was still in the witness box. As he was then free to come clean, of course, he completely undermined the evidence he had already given and, with it, a large part of the prosecution's case.'

Sabatino gently shook her head before saying: 'How did you manage to release Yegor from the police's grip – so that he wasn't being manipulated any more?'

Backhouse took a hurried sip of champagne. 'Matt planned the springing of his mother from captivity for a specific time, predicting the procedure in court. During the evening of the break-in, he showed Mrs Baryshnikov how to sabotage her dialysis machine. He also gave her a morphine tablet. She was to take the pill when she heard three blasts of an air horn near her house. That would be the signal. The morphine was meant to put her into a stupor. Pretty quickly after taking it, she would be harmlessly sedated. Matt reckoned if we could induce her into a state of apparent distress, the police in the house would panic and call an ambulance. Which is precisely what they did. Our ambulance was parked just up the road, and was easily first on the scene. We had some of our guys dressed as medics who attended Mrs Baryshnikov. They were briefed to throw in words like "uraemic" and told the police that the patient needed to be taken away for immediate hospital treatment. Luckily, the police were so panicked by her collapse that they didn't ask any questions. The moment we got her away she was to be given a dose of Naloxone, which was expected to counteract the effects of the morphine. Mrs Baryshnikov responded almost at once, meaning we could bring her straight to the trial. Yegor was still in the witness box when we walked her in. The moment we presented her, from the back of the courtroom, Yegor could see she was no longer a police hostage – and he understood that his emotional shackles were off. He started telling the truth straight away, even accusing the police of kidnapping his mother. That, of course, completely undermined all the testimony he had given on behalf of the prosecution so far.'

'That was the first major undermining of the prosecution's case,' said Backhouse.

Nazar pulled a face in admiring disbelief. 'What were the others, then?'

'Matt convinced me,' answered McMahon, 'that we could not get you two out of Russia if we only fought the trial in court, even if we won the case. He was determined to undermine the politics behind it as well.'

'I don't even know *why* you would think about doing that, let alone *how*?'

'We've come to learn about Sun Tzu,' replied McMahon.

'What?'

'Some ancient Chinese strategist,' she replied. 'Colonel Straker became fascinated with the political situation in Russia, having gained some important insights during his meeting with Mr Obrenovich. Matt was convinced that the key lay in the uneasy relations between the president and the mayor of Moscow, as well as the fear of this Kondratiev mobster. Matt wanted to find a way of getting each of these parties to be even more suspicious of each other. He also wanted to stage something big – something so massive that the political stakes would be raised so high they would be too nervous to continue with the trial.'

'*How* ...?' muttered Nazar.

'Matt didn't know much about Russia when he arrived,' explained McMahon, 'but hearing more about the recent political deaths fascinated him: those of Sergei Magnitsky, Alexander Litvinenko, Boris Nemtsov. What struck him was the damage these "assassinations" did to Russia's standing in the world, as well as the damage done by the subsequent international sanctions. Matt reckoned that another example of that kind of barbarism could get the Russian political system really jumpy.'

'So,' said Backhouse, 'he set about staging his own and Sandy's death.'

Sabatino's face fell.

'You should take a look at this.'

A laptop, sitting on a low ornate table in front of them, was swivelled round. A file was booted up and a clip of video was set running.

'This stroke was as bold as it was technologically ingenious,' explained Backhouse as the CCTV footage appeared on the screen.

'That, there, is the Brandeis car – which Matt and Sandy had been using since Matt's arrival in Moscow.'

Backhouse hit Pause.

'Matt had rigged it up so this car could be driven remotely by radio control; it was to be aided by a drone flying overhead – which relayed back these pictures. All that was arranged to stage *this*,' said Backhouse as he re-pressed Play.

Sabatino and Nazar watched the screen as the car was shown making its way onto the bridge. They actually flinched at the sequence of blasts – and the explosion that obliterated the vehicle.

'Holy cow,' said Sabatino.

Backhouse stopped the clip. 'Matt had *packed* that car – to the roof – with highly specialized Quartech explosive. He didn't want anyone on board, obviously, so he put three dummies inside. He also didn't want anyone else to get hurt, which was crucial given the size of the explosion. His hotel room overlooked the bridge and he'd spotted that it was typically empty in the middle of the night.'

'Did it need to be that big?' asked Sabatino.

'Matt had to obliterate all the remotely operated equipment inside, as well as conceal the absence of human remains in and around the car,' replied Backhouse, 'because of course there weren't any. However, Matt had arranged for Sandy, the Brandeis chauffeur and himself to give a pint of blood each, bags of which were then strapped to the underside of the car. These were expected to burst onto the road during the explosion, meaning there would be some – verifiable and even identifiable – human remains at the scene.'

Nazar smiled and shook his head at the thinking behind all this.

'Matt had arranged for the scene to be filmed by the accompanying drone. He then asked Bernie Callom to doctor the footage – to make it look like CCTV taken from a lamppost camera – and made sure it was sent to *Fox News*, to give them the scoop. Matt and Bernie reckoned that *Fox* were likely to go nuts for this story, giving them the chance to slag off a bad regime.'

'No wonder it made such good copy,' said Nazar. 'Sensational footage like that would send any news channel into a masturbatory frenzy. A monumental car explosion, right in front of the floodlit Saint Basil's Cathedral and Kremlin – creating a spectacular visual. What more could you want for over-sensationalized drama?'

'To give it even more,' added McMahon, 'Matt, Mr Callom and I went to see the mayor of Moscow, whom we knew from Mr Obrenovich was incensed by the actions of the Kremlin and Kondratiev, not to mention the corruption in the legal process. When Matt explained to the mayor the intended political impact from his plan, she bought into it straight away. Straker impressed upon Mayor Pavlova the need to liken the deaths of Sandy McMahon and Colonel Matt Straker to those of Magnitsky, Litvinenko and Nemtsov – so as to fuel the right media reaction.

'To make sure the mayor was ready to make a statement to the press first thing the morning after, Matt got Mr Callom to prepare relevant pictures and biog details of the supposed victims.

'Those images went all round the world. It was then followed by the mayor's press conference, in which she deliberately used the word "assassination". The media readily declared the deaths of Matt and Sandy to be another indictment of Russia's attitude to justice, and condemned the State for having rubbed out yet more of its opponents.

'And it worked,' declared McMahon. 'In a matter of hours, the United States Congress was even talking about introducing a new round of sanctions against Russia.

'The next coup came from using the apparent assassinations of Matt and me to escalate the political risk of continuing with the trial. Matt's masterstroke was to get Oscar Brogan to say – in court – that, as a result of the death of the leading lawyer for the accused, he would call the mayor of Moscow as a witness. She was the *last* person the president would want to appear. Our trial, in the Russian Supreme Court, would have given Mayor Pavlova a platform to speak to the world and criticize the corruption in the Russian regime and State institutions – as well as the chance to condemn the "assassinations". Matt's reckoning was that giving so much profile to his chief political rival would be too much for the president to bear.

'Within twelve hours of the car bomb, the case was dropped by the prosecution.'

Sabatino could only sigh in admiration.

'Holy fucking cow,' said Nazar. 'What a game of chess you've all been playing ... Wow ... However far-fetched this seems, though, it's sodding well worked. Somehow, Matt's managed to get us out of yet another inescapable hole.'

SEVENTY-SIX

Matt Straker did not reappear for another half an hour. By the time he did, the escapees had moved out into the Baltic's warm balmy air to take supper out on the quarterdeck. When Sabatino saw him, she climbed to her feet again, and made to give him another hug.

Out of the corner of his eye Straker saw McMahon cast a glance at them and then look away. He was intrigued by McMahon's reaction, but was uneasy about causing her any discomfort.

'What you did was amazing,' said Sabatino. 'What you both did,' she added turning to face the lawyer.

Straker merely shook his head in response as he disengaged from Sabatino. A steward offered him a glass of Moët before he sat at the table on the white leather bench next to McMahon.

'The Big Man sends his regards to all,' said Straker, 'offering his congratulations on your "escape" from Russia.'

'Any congratulations are entirely yours,' replied Sabatino.

As they looked out on the blue sky and the evening sun catching the haze, Straker added: 'You should know that DQ has re-instated Yegor – on the understanding that he was being blackmailed into testifying against us.'

The reaction from the Ptarmigan members was neutral. 'I guess that's fair,' offered Sabatino. 'Extortion of that kind would test anyone's loyalties.'

'You might also be interested to know what DQ's heard through the Foreign Office: Léon Gazdanov, the prosecutor general, has been arrested.'

Around the table champagne glasses were raised in celebration.

'And, the weasel that he is, Gazdanov's already tried to do a deal to save himself – turning "State's" witness – to spill the beans on Kondratiev.'

'Poetic justice, as well as actual justice,' said Nazar.

Straker gently shook his head again. 'No doubt Kondratiev will get to Gazdanov long before he ever gets to testify. Kondratiev's far too powerful to let that scumbag do him any harm. Domestically, though, Kondratiev's position has taken a serious knock; maybe his network of corruption can now be challenged, particularly as Mayor Pavlova has just appointed that police colonel to head up a full-blown anti-corruption task force. Internationally, it doesn't look good for Vadim Kondratiev. The US Congress is working itself up to pass the Kondratiev Act, much as they did after the death of Sergei Magnitsky. That would freeze all Kondratiev's assets, bank accounts and business interests in the US. DQ says the UK are minded to follow suit, as is the EU. There's even talk that Interpol are about to issue a Red Notice arrest warrant. Kondratiev is so powerful, though – he'll probably be able to look after himself. Even so, all of these measures together could help to colour the man, even back home, so maybe ... just maybe? Anyway, those are no longer our problems,' stated Straker with a smile.

With that, all their glasses were raised, clinked and drained – before they were quickly refilled.

The Melita sailed into Copenhagen the day after they left Saint Petersburg. From there, the Ptarmigan team split up. Nazar and Backhouse flew on to Spain for the next Grand Prix. Remy Sabatino left for the UK to rehabilitate and to spend time on the simulator at the team's factory in Shenington. She was expected to sit Valencia out, but hoped to be back for Monza, after the August break.

Dominic Quartano offered Matt Straker something of a thank you. Having interrupted his leave – recalling him from the North Pole for the assignment in Moscow – he offered him time off in lieu. *The Melita* was scheduled to travel from the Baltic to Valencia, in time for the reinstated European Grand Prix. Quartano suggested that he might like to make himself at home during her passage to the Mediterranean and for the race. She was at his disposal – fully crewed, with her resident masseuse and Michelin Star chef both on board – if he was interested.

Straker readily accepted, but then asked for an additional favour: Could Sandy McMahon join him? After all, she had agreed to be "killed" in the contrived Moscow car bomb. Her legal career in Russia was over; she could never go back. She was meant to be dead. Quartano agreed immediately, also stating that he would organize a meeting for her with Stacey Krall to discuss McMahon joining Quartech International's Legal Department, whenever she wished.

Matt Straker was now looking forward to the next seven days – of having the chance to be alone with Sandy McMahon.

After everything they had been through together, he relished the escape this would offer, particularly in the unabridged luxury of the superyacht, which they could now enjoy entirely by themselves.

Above all, Straker was looking forward to losing himself in the mischief that he was convinced lay behind her impish smile.

The End

Acknowledgements

I am keen to highlight the support, effort and patience a number of outstanding people invest in my writing:

Maggie Hanbury is unbeatable as a literary agent; her understanding, experience and judgement are invaluable as well as hugely reassuring. Also at the Hanbury Agency, I am indebted to Harriet Poland for her ceaseless efficiency, help and enthusiasm.

It was always my aim to establish a series of thrillers set in the world of Formula One. But being a subject matter that was unprecedented as a mainstream genre, the risk aversion across the publishing industry made the idea a particularly hard sell. As publisher of *Driven* and now *Crash*, Piers Russell-Cobb at Arcadia Books is exactly the type of entrepreneurial publisher I had always had in mind to give this franchise a go. I am grateful to him for taking the risk. In the same vein, I am keen to thank Joe Harper at Arcadia Books for his unstinting guidance, patience and support throughout the publishing and marketing process.

I am lucky to work with some other true masters of their craft: Martin Fletcher, an outstanding editor with an exceptional clarity of vision, Angeline Rothermundt, whose precision and patience as a copy-editor has fine-tuned the text, and James Nunn, the team's graphic designer. I am grateful to them all for the polish they have given the finished publication.

I would also like to pay tribute to my 'reading committee' and to thank them for their invaluable help, professional feedback and suggestions: Dr Jane Charles-Nash, Heather Jervis, Richard Freeman, Joe Ellis, Dr Clare Johnson, Katie Bertie, my father John Vintcent and my wife Anne-Marie Taylor.

First and last, though, I say thank you to Henry de Rougemont.